Corpies

by Drew Hayes

Edited by Erin Cooley (cooley.edit@gmail.com)
Cover by Barry Behannon (barrybartist.com)

Acknowledgements

This book is for my dad, Lee Hayes. While he might not have a lot in common with Owen Daniels, to me he will always be as strong as Titan.

Special thanks as well to my beta readers, who made this novel better than it could have possibly been without their help. Thanks Priscilla Yuen, E Ramos E, and TheSFReader.

Wait!!!

Hang on a second, you awesome reader, you. I know you're excited to get in to the book that you just purchased (or are inquisitively sampling), but there's a bit of context you need to know before moving forward.

First and foremost, you need to be aware that this book, *Corpies*, is a spin-off of my *Super Powereds* series. Now, while you will still be able to enjoy the tale even if you haven't read those other stories, you should be aware that there will be references to people and places that seem random but are in fact pointing back to the *Super Powereds* series. Just something to take the burden off your mind, assuming you panic that you missed chapters when you see stuff like that (like I do).

Secondly (and this part is really only relevant if you do read the *Super Powereds* series), this story occurs during the events of *Super Powereds: Year 3*, starting after the Lander HCP semester has begun and wrapping up a while before Intramurals. That's why there might be some allusions to impending things that you, as a caught-up reader, know have already occurred.

Lastly, though this has no bearing on the spin-off stuff, I just want to say thanks for picking up *Corpies*. Despite starting as a tentative Web serial side-project, this book has grown in to one of my favorites to work on over the years. I appreciate you taking a chance on it, and I sincerely hope you enjoy.

Prologue

Owen sat in one of the waiting room's many reinforced chairs and flipped through an old *Capes & Cowls* magazine. It detailed the rise of one of the latest crops of Heroes, fresh off their internships and making quite a splash in the world. Their costumes were crisp, their dialogue concise, their images squeaky clean. These were the kind of wholesome, homespun, moral warriors that would take the lead in creating a new world, free of immorality. These were the kind of Heroes the world needed more of: or at least that's the idea the reporter espoused.

It would have been vastly more impressive if Owen didn't know that two of the featured four were already dead. He'd heard one was in rehab upstate, and though the final member was still active, she wasn't quite so eager or wholesome anymore. She certainly didn't schedule in time for op-ed pieces with interviewers. Now she just focused on getting the job done. That was the trouble with old magazines. Media darlings rarely lived up to their initial hype, and for the ones who did, the eventual fall just became all the more catastrophic.

Owen had just set the magazine down when the door a few feet away flew open. A muscular man younger than Owen stepped out. He wore a bright red costume with yellow trim, a matching mask, and a cape that fell to just above his calves. Owen hoped this kid was a flier or a strongman, otherwise someone was going to make him regret that fluttering fashion choice. A couple of steps behind the costumed kid was another man, this one older, shorter, and sporting a significant paunch instead of a body rippling with muscle.

"Don't worry about a thing; you just go on home and relax," the smaller man assured the larger. "We'll get this whole mess cleaned up and fixed before you can say Bam Piff Zow."

The costumed Hero nodded his head and set off through the waiting room. His gaze lingered on Owen for a moment, the spark of recognition flickering through his eyes almost immediately dismissed. No way. Couldn't be Him. Must be a new guy who was a fan, paying homage with the outfit. He walked through the door without another glance; this man had more worrisome things on the brain.

"Good to see you, Lenny." Owen rose from the chair and towered over the smaller man. From here he could see Lenny's prominent bald spot. A different person might have gone for a toupee or a comb-over, or tried some radical drug to fix such vain failings. Not Lenny. He spent every day around people who were physically superior to him; if his ego were wrapped up in his looks, it would have hanged itself long ago.

"My stars, look at you," Lenny muttered, taking in the massive form looming over him. He'd have almost sworn it was a few decades ago and this was the same fresh-faced newbie who was hot out of the HCP. Same chiseled frame, same red shirt and jeans, same dark wavy hair, same bright mask. The most notable differences were under the mask, though: a crooked smile that wasn't as carefree, the stubble of a working man who didn't have time to shave, tired green eyes that lacked the luster and hope of a new Hero. That might have worried others in Lenny's field, but personally, he preferred his clients with the shine wiped off. They'd learned they weren't invincible, and they made smarter choices because of that.

"Genetics is bullshit," Lenny said at last. "I bet you don't even have to watch what you eat."

2

"Not really, no."

"Hell, my doctor has me eating whole wheat and cheese curd every day for breakfast. Do you know what it takes to make that crap taste good?"

"No, what?"

"Damned if I have a clue, I was genuinely asking. Enough jawing in the waiting room; let's go to the office."

It was strangely comforting how little Lenny's office had changed since Owen left the Hero world. The tacky décor, the oversized filing cabinets, the weathered globe that turned into a bar when you swiveled it, all of it was still there. What *had* changed were the posters on the walls. Lenny always kept his brightest stars up, the hot tickets constantly on display so that everyone who came in knew the kind of clientele this man catered to. A few of the posters were even framed. These were the ones that weren't coming down, the Heroes Lenny considered "legendary". Owen only knew of one framed poster Lenny had taken off the wall, and he didn't hold it against the smaller man one bit.

"So," Lenny said once he was situated behind his desk. "You want to come back to The Life."

Owen smiled; he'd forgotten the way Lenny referred to working the Hero scene. The Life. It was actually a pretty apt phrasing. Being a Hero wasn't a nine-to-five; it dominated every aspect of who someone was. Even the parts they might wish it didn't.

"Yeah. I do."

Lenny ran a hand through his ever-thinning hair. "Listen, Titan, you know I never held the whole fiasco against you. Shit happens. If it didn't, I'd likely be out of a job. That said, time does not heal all wounds as far as public perception is concerned."

Owen appreciated Lenny trying to be diplomatic, skirting the details and not outright referring to what had happened as The Titan Scandal, as it had gone down in history. Still, it was an unnecessary nicety. They both knew what had happened, as did a vast majority of the nation, if not the world. Titan, the world-famous Hero with a family man image, had been caught by a hidden camera having sex with another Hero. Bad as that might have been on its own, what had compounded the issue was the fact that Titan's partner in the scandal, Tower, wasn't female. Infidelity was one thing, but closeted homosexuality, especially in those days. . . it had led to a fall from grace that was more akin to a plummet. What little of the Titan reputation that remained was almost entirely due to the effort of Lenny.

Heroes didn't need agents, technically speaking, any more than a cook needs butter to create a nutritionally-sound meal. However, most quickly found out that having a job in the public eye led to a lot of pressure, and people like Lenny made everything flow a lot more smoothly. He was a confidant, a fixer, a PR virtuoso, and a damage control specialist all heaped into a single roly-poly package. Still, even Lenny had his limits, as Owen had learned firsthand.

"That's okay. I know I'm not going to be walking back to a warm reception."

"You always did have a knack for understatement," Lenny said. "They'll come after you hard. A lot of people took what happened really personally, and there is nothing they'd love more than a chance to tear you apart."

"I know. Believe me, Lenny, no one knows better than me how hated I am."

"If only you were just hated. Hated I can work with. We play you as a gruff counterpart to some guy whose image can tolerate it, do a turnaround over time, and presto, you're golden again. No, you're hated *and* held up as an icon by different groups. That gets people fighting—bickering, really—about some deeply-held beliefs. When you've got one man with two different images you can't shift one without impacting the other."

"I can deal with that."

"Of course you can, you're fucking Titan. But not so long ago this was enough to make you hang up the mask. Thankfully, your certification never expires, but getting you relicensed for Hero work will be a bear after so long, not to mention the headaches I'll get once the media gets a hold of it. Now, we go way back, and I like you, so that's shit I'm willing to wade through. But only if you can convince me that I won't do it only to see you walk off again three months later. What's changed?"

Owen sat silently for a few moments, his giant frame hunched in on itself. "My sons came to see me a few months ago."

"Oh yeah?"

"Yeah. This stays quiet, Lenny, dead quiet, because if you think I'm a PR shitstorm you have no idea what kind of hellhole they would open. Roy and Hershel are in the HCP themselves now and doing pretty good, from what I hear. "

"I didn't think the HCP took Powereds."

"They don't."

"Ho-lee-shit." Lenny turned and popped open his bar, poured himself a healthy measure of vodka over ice, and motioned for his prospective client to continue.

"Anyway, Roy was having trouble getting his ability to the next step, so Hershel hunted me down. I took a week, got them on the right path, then asked them to keep in touch. I'll spare you the finer points of the conversation, but they essentially told me to go fuck myself."

"Look, hurt feelings can run deep, especially at that age."

"See, that's the thing, Lenny. I don't think they were just hurt. I think they were right. Why should either one want to talk to me? Why should they care? I walked out on their mother and them; reasons be damned, I still did it. I could have made more of an effort. I could have tried to stay in some part of their life. I fucked up. I let my own shit get in the way of people who needed me. That's a hard truth to accept, but I faced it. Unfortunately, that was when it occurred to me I had only scratched the surface on people I abandoned."

Lenny could already see where this was going. "Titan, come on; you're strong, but there're other Heroes on the job."

"It isn't about that, Lenny. It's about the fact that I could be out there, I could be helping people and making a difference, and instead I holed up in Colorado to lick my wounds. I missed out on the opportunity to be a real father, and I know I'm never going to be an A-list Hero from a popularity point of view, but I think it's time I stopped running away. I'm a strongman. We hit and we get hit. It's time for me to finally shake off that last one and start moving again."

Lenny sighed. "Shit, Titan. Why couldn't you give those kinds of speeches back in the day? I could have made you freaking king of the Heroes if you tugged the heart strings on command."

"What can you do now?"

"I can make a few calls," Lenny said slowly. "No promises, just a few calls. For an old friend. A favor, if you want it."

Owen gave him a smile, and for an instant Lenny was staring through time at the enthusiastic kid he'd first signed so very long ago.

"I'll take it."

1.

Two Months Later

"You're sure about this?" Lenny asked for somewhere around the ninth time, if Owen's count was correct. "That's the beauty of living behind a mask and a costume. Change those elements up and Poof! New Hero. It takes a little wiggling here and there, especially with guys of your proportions, but it's nothing I can't pull off."

Owen shook his head solemnly. They were in Lenny's office, cheesy decor surrounding the two very different men. Owen was suited up in his Titan costume, red shirt, red mask, and blue jeans all wrapped around nearly seven feet of solid muscle. As strong as he looked, he was actually far more powerful. Lenny, on the other hand, was still round and balding with a nose that looked like he'd tried to win a few boxing bouts by attacking his opponent's fists with his face. Still, there was more than a touch of smarts and charisma in that foul-mouthed cherub's eyes. Both were masters of their respective trades, though one had been out of the game for a long while.

"I'm not changing identities," Owen said. "I'm coming back as Titan. If I don't, then I feel like I'm still running. It might not make sense to you, but this is how I have to do it."

Lenny ran his hand across the top of his head, touching more skin than hair by a large margin. Habits didn't die easily, though, even if follicles did. "I was afraid you were going to say that. You know that makes things harder, right? The other way would open up a lot more options."

"The options for going at it the right way are the ones I want," Owen insisted.

"Don't say I didn't warn you." Lenny slid a manila envelope across the desk to his client. "Even with your license reinstated, there weren't a lot of people clamoring to have you on their team. You come with more heat than most folks are willing to take."

"Solo Heroes exist," Owen said.

"Not for you they don't," Lenny countered. "We let you go solo and that's how you'll be until the end. You'll look like an outcast, the guy that no one wanted after his scandal. People like me will use your story as a cautionary tale to keep younger Heroes in line."

"But no one *does* want me," Owen pointed out.

"Why would you bring that up? My ulcer isn't bad enough this week without you reminding me what we're trying to pull off here? You're a hurtful man and you should be ashamed," Lenny chastised. "Besides which, you're wrong. The team in that folder agreed to take you, so at least some people want you."

Owen took the clue to flip open the folder. As soon as he began reading, a frown formed at the corner of his mouth, visible just below the bottom of his skintight mask. The frown deepened the longer he read, until finally his gaze rose from the pages and across the desk to his agent.

"Corpies? Are you shitting me?"

"Oh, I'm sorry, did my months of trying to impress upon you how few your options were not provide a slight clue that you were getting the bottom of the shit-bucket? And don't call them that. The technical term is Privately Employed Emergency Response Supers, or PEERS if you don't have all day."

9

"Come on, Lenny, these people aren't even Heroes." Owen dropped the file onto the desk. "Why would I be on a team of corpies?"

Try as he might, Owen couldn't imagine what sort of justification Lenny would use for this proposal. Corpies were Supers who hadn't gone through the screening or training to get their Hero Certifications and therefore were not allowed to confront criminal Supers. However, through some loophole maneuvering and fancy legal footwork, it had been established that a Super did not need a Hero Certification to assist in any emergency response operation that didn't involve combat. This charge was led by corporations that yearned to get their logos emblazoned on the capes of champions doing good, saving innocents, and spreading the word about how this particular laundry soap got your whites the whitest. Rarely did a corpie attain any real popularity; however, the few times they had gotten a following had been so profitable that companies eagerly rolled the dice and kept right on paying to keep their names on Supers. Though many Heroes considered them worthless hacks who couldn't cut it in the Hero game, the fact remained that having them on hand usually did more good than harm, so their continued existence was tolerated with minor grumbling. But that didn't mean Owen wanted to babysit a damn group of them.

"Why? Because in order for them to function as an independent team, working in their own fancy headquarters, responding to various disasters and calls, they have to have a Hero Liaison on staff. Someone to bat cleanup if things get messy or trouble shows up. This team, as luck would have it, just lost their Hero to retirement. No others are stepping forward, so they either had to take you on or go back to working in the basement of a police station where the lights don't work and it smells like piss. Those were their options: piss smell or you."

"But-"

"AND," Lenny said, raising his voice and rising slightly off his chair, "I had to wheel and deal to make it happen. It was you and a luxury high-rise loft, or no you and a dank piss-scented basement, and I had to *convince* them to take you. Are you getting the picture here?"

"Then forget it," Owen replied. "If no team wants me then I'll go solo after all. Let me be a story. Let everyone call me an outcast and a failure. Better that than chaperoning a bunch of corpies."

"That is your prerogative," Lenny said, his temper cooling as he lowered himself back into his seat. "You have the right to go at this alone. But if you do, then you're doing it completely alone."

A pang of uncertainty smacked Owen in the gut. "What are you saying?"

"I'm saying that if you go solo, I'm out. I'll finish the paperwork to make you official again, and that's it."

"What the hell, Lenny? Suddenly it's my way or the highway? What ever happened to finding what works best for the Hero?" Owen resisted the urge to jump out of his own seat, only because he was afraid he might crack the floor.

Lenny didn't yell back this time. Instead, he took an antacid from his desk drawer and dropped it into a glass of water with a fizzy plop.

"I am thinking about what's best for you. We worked together for a long time, back in the day. I know you, and that's why I'm telling you that you need a team. The family man image we sold you as worked because you *are* a family man. You need people around who depend on you. They give you strength. They are what push you past your hardest moments. Last time you went off on your own, your funk lasted over a decade and didn't break until your sons called you a fucker. You need a team, Titan. Without one, it's just a matter of time until it all becomes too much and you fall apart again. And I'm not hanging around for it this time."

Owen felt his indignation morph in to shame. He'd been calling Lenny a quitter when he was the one who'd walked away. Lenny was doing what he did for all his clients: just trying to make sure they were put in the best position to stay happy and employed. He was watching out for Owen, even after Owen had nearly cost Lenny his reputation all that time ago.

Owen reached across and picked back up the folder. "Are they expecting me?"

"You report for duty at nine tomorrow morning," Lenny informed him.

"Seems late."

"They have a photo shoot at seven."

Owen resisted the urge to groan, but only barely.

2.

Owen stared up at the building, admiring the way it jutted into the sky as though it were trying to spear clouds. On days with the right weather, it probably succeeded. He adjusted the duffel bag on his shoulder more out of nerves than necessity. Even as fully as it was packed, the bag was nowhere near heavy enough to actually cause him discomfort. Most of his possessions had been stored back at his place in Colorado, though some had been sent ahead to this building via courier. The things in the bag he never trusted to anyone else. They were too important to be risked.

"Titan?"

The voice snapped Owen out of his marveling and brought him back to reality. He wasn't dressed as Titan currently; instead he wore simple clothes and a generic gray mask. Wearing such masks was standard practice for Heroes who didn't want to be "in character" but still needed to go places without showing their face. It was inconvenient; however, it beat the hell out of having one's identity blown. Since he wasn't wearing his Titan costume, though, it meant this was the man who had known he was coming. Or someone who was a really good guesser.

The fellow who had spoken was tall and lean, wearing a suit that was conservative enough to say corporate but expensive enough to show he was high on the food chain. His glasses and watch were designer, and his hair had been expertly styled. Owen suspected he was not going to like this person.

"You're Harold?"

"Mr. Greene, if you don't mind," the man replied.

"Whatever you say." Owen hefted his bag again. "We going inside?"

"Of course," Mr. Greene said. "If you'd be so kind as to follow me."

Mr. Greene and Owen walked through the front doors, large glass ones that opened into a sprawling lobby that seemed to be made of marble. All around them other people in suits and business appropriate outfits scuttled about, doing things that they no doubt believed were of the utmost importance. In the center of the lobby, just ahead of a long row of elevators, was a circular station where a pair of guards sat. Mr. Greene stopped at this station and handed them a card extracted from his breast pocket.

"We'll get your keycard and I.D. done this afternoon," Mr. Greene informed him. "You'll need them at all times while on premises, otherwise you won't be permitted access."

"That so?" Owen said the words casually, but as he spoke his eyes swept the room, years of experience alerting him to the bits and bobbles of security a casual observer wasn't supposed to see. "Have to say, the tazing system built into the floor wouldn't really slow me down, and the knockout gas dispensers you've got disguised as fire alarms would only tickle my throat. Now, the pulse cannon you've made to look like a potted plant, that might set me back a few steps."

"Impressive," Mr. Greene commented. "I suppose there is more to you than size and reputation."

"I aim to please."

Once they passed the security guards, Mr. Greene flashed his card in front of an elevator near the end of the line. Its doors whooshed open and the two men stepped inside.

"All this for one team?" Owen asked as the elevator began to rise.

"Don't be silly. This building houses offices for multiple companies, all owned, at least partially, by Mordent Holdings. Each member of the team is sponsored by at least one of our companies, so we made a few floors into facilities for them. We find it best if our representatives stay on site."

"You mean where you can keep an eye on them," Owen said.

"We provide housing, food, facilities, and entertainment, all at no deduction from their salaries. I'd say that's quite a generous situation for them," Mr. Greene shot back.

"Because we all know corporations love doing things from the goodness of their hearts." Owen fiddled with his duffle bag once more. "Look, I'm not telling you how to run your company or your team, just calling it like I see it."

"I'd suggest you call it more quietly." Mr. Greene's eyes never wavered from the climbing numbers on the elevator's display. "We approved taking you on as the Hero Liaison because it was deemed to be an overall net gain. Should that equation change, we may need to revisit your position's feasibility."

"Yeah yeah, toe the line like a good boy or I'm out on my ass. If you don't mind me asking, what made you decide to take me on, anyway? I'm not exactly the best PR magnet these days."

"Mordent Holdings has recently received negative publicity at the hands of discrimination lawsuits alleging we create a hostile working environment for women and homosexuals. Some of the recordings played in court and leaked online were particularly damning. As part of our efforts to assure the public such culture will not be tolerated, we're making strides to earn back the trust of the female and LGBTQ communities. Hiring you was one of many examples of our new corporate culture."

The elevator dinged and the doors slid open, revealing a carpeted hallway leading to a single door at the end. Owen peered down its depths, counting at least four more security measures designed to take down anything from humans to rhinos to Supers with enhanced durability. These people didn't skimp on security, at least.

"So you give me a second chance and hope the public will give you one. Not bad. What about the rest of the team? They picked to smooth out scandals too?"

"No, they were chosen for their abilities, appeal, marketability, and talents. There are four, aside from yourself: Galvanize, Hexcellent, Bubble Bubble, and Zone. Galvanize is their leader, since he has the most training and experience." As he spoke, Mr. Greene stepped out of the elevator and began walking down the hall. "Don't worry; the system recognizes biometrics, and anyone accompanied by me is considered friendly. We'll get you programmed in when we do your keycard."

Owen contemplated telling this man that he hadn't hesitated out of worry for himself, he had been more afraid of breaking something if the system went after him. He decided to stay quiet, however. No need to rock the boat too much on the first day. Besides, there was zero doubt Mr. Greene was the kind of man who'd read up on Titan. He knew it would take more than standard safeguards to bring down this near-giant of a man.

"Anything else I should know before we go in?" Owen followed his escort off the elevator, noting that it closed swiftly as soon as he exited.

"Only this: even though you are not sponsored by any of our companies, by aligning with people who are, you become a de facto representative of us. We expect you to take that seriously and behave appropriately."

"Me? I'm always appropriate," Owen said, making an expression as innocent as he could behind the gray mask.

"Glad to hear it."

"Glad to say it. Now let's go on in, fuckwad."

The look on Mr. Greene's face was worth the earful Owen knew he'd be getting later. With a slight chuckle and a genuine smile, he took the last several steps and opened the door.

3.

Owen's first headquarters hadn't been much. Whether it was a Hero, a doctor, an MBA, or a bartender, a recent college grad is a recent college grad. True, Owen had made a little money during his internship under Citadel, his Hero mentor; however, he'd likely have made better cash waiting tables during that time. The end result was that when his first team formed, their financial resources were limited. Their headquarters/living area had been a near-condemned old mattress store that they'd erected half-assed partitions in. It had been derelict, dirty, and largely unsafe. Still, he carried fond memories of that time in his life, if only because both he and the people he worked with were still young and idealistic enough that the future looked like a bright and wonderful thing.

His first thought upon walking into this new team's headquarters was that if his first team had been able to get a place like this, they would have taken a lot fewer calls in favor of staying home and being comfortable. The front doors opened in to an expansive living room. Next to it was a large kitchen, gleaming with stainless steel appliances. Windows lined the far wall, looking out toward the city and providing a breathtaking view. The floor was carpeted with lush, soft material. In the living room, a gigantic television stood in the center of an entertainment unit, surrounded by various videogame systems and flanked by a wraparound leather couch. A young woman with ink-black hair and makeup- pale skin mashed on a controller and a small male figure on said giant screen plummeted down a spiked pit to his doom.

"Fucking bullshit horsecock dickgarglers," the woman swore, spitting it all out as nearly one word. She jammed a button on the controller and the screen reloaded, the digital man immediately resurrected.

"Keep it down," said another woman, this one sitting on an end of the couch so far away it faced the door rather than the television. Her skin was pale too, though it was also dotted with freckles at irregular intervals. Her carefully-styled copper hair was swept to the side, purposely not obscuring her line of vision as she flipped the page on her magazine.

"Why don't you go try to suck a gig out of a producer's cock?" the other woman shot back.

"Why don't both you notice we have a guest and show a little a class?" said a new voice, this one from a young man emerging out of the kitchen with peeled orange slices in hand. He turned to greet Owen and Mr. Greene with a wide, practiced, and dazzling smile. His wavy brown hair and boy-next-door features only completed the effect, making him appear affable, friendly, and immediately accessible. "I'm sorry about that. I'm Galvanize, the team leader."

"Titan," Owen replied, taking the young man's hand in a firm shake. It had been a lot of work learning to shake hands without shattering bones, but he'd perfected it ages ago.

"The one playing video games is Hexcellent, and the woman reading is Bubble Bubble," Galvanize said, pointing to each as he spoke.

Hexcellent paused the game to give Owen a half-hearted wave, turning in her seat rather than standing up. She was lean, slender all over, but with the type of tight muscle one saw in athletes and Heroes. Her face was probably pretty, but since it was obscured by several piercings, dark lipstick, and so much eye makeup that it even coated her cheekbones, it was hard to tell. She wore all black and had a tattoo of some bat-like creature on her left shoulder.

Bubble Bubble, on the other hand, was especially put together. She wore clothes that had the kind of simple elegance that looked ordinary but Owen

19

knew actually cost a dump truck of money. She had a more classic beauty, the kind one might find in the Marilyn Monroe era. This one, at least, gave a smile and said "Hello" before turning back to the magazine in her lap.

"Where's Zone?" Mr. Greene asked, interrupting the already awkward introductions.

"In the gym," Galvanize replied. "His exercise quota is higher than ours, after all."

"Of course. That is acceptable then, just be sure he is introduced to Titan when he finishes," Mr. Greene instructed. He turned his attention to Titan. "I'll send someone to help you get set up in an hour or two. In the meantime, settle in and meet your new team."

With not so much a "good luck," Mr. Greene turned around and walked through the doors, which closed with a whooshing sound afterward.

"Isn't he just a ray of sunshine," Owen muttered.

"You get used to him," Galvanize said. "Why don't you get comfortable, take off your mask and shoes? Can I get you something to drink?"

At the mention of his mask, Owen's eyes immediately went to the glass, which was so clear it barely registered as present. Galvanize saw where he was looking.

"Don't worry; it only looks that way from our side. It's custom. Durable beyond durable and impossible to see through from the outside."

Owen trusted Galvanize's words; however, unmasking in an unfamiliar place was something every bit of his life's experiences told him not to do.

Besides, he was going to have to leave soon to go get his access card and whatnot. Better to be masked in case the person coming to get him had access.

"I'm fine for now. As for the drink, what kind of beers do you have?"

"Oh, I'm so sorry, none of us are allowed to have alcohol," Galvanize told him. "Part of our contracts and health requirements. I can offer you fresh squeezed guava juice, mango juice, specially made vitamin-infused water-"

"Water is fine," Owen said, reeling at how kids this young could be okay with being banned from beer. Afterward, he chastised himself; these were accomplished professionals in their own right, he didn't need to start thinking of them as kids just because he was old.

"Coming right up." Galvanize walked to the kitchen and returned with a colorful bottle mere moments later. "So, since you're new here, what would you like to know?"

"Let's just start with the basics." Owen grabbed a chair in a part of the living room not dominated by the giant couch where the two women were still largely ignoring him. "What are everyone's powers?"

"A perfectly great place to start," Galvanize agreed enthusiastically. "To go around the room, Hexcellent has the ability to summon creatures out of thin air."

"Demons," Hexcellent corrected, not looking away from her game.

"They are somewhat scary looking, and given the goth image her advertisers pay for, we would like it if you referred to them as demons," said Galvanize, soothing his teammate while shooting Owen an apologetic look.

Summoners weren't too common. Owen had only met a few in his Hero career. Of course, the term was a bit of a misnomer. What they actually did wasn't summoning, it was creating an animate energy construct. It worked the same as people who could duplicate themselves, only instead of a personal copy, they formed something else. Most only had a few things they could create: the complexity to form one was so intense that having more than a couple of options made it too muddled to keep straight.

"How many can she summon?"

"I got three," Hexcellent answered from the couch.

Three wasn't bad. It was definitely HCP grade. Owen made a mental note to find out more about her power later, then motioned for Galvanize to continue.

"Bubble Bubble can create energy spheres that are pretty durable, and she can even move them with her mind. Not terribly fast, so we can't use them for rapid transport, but they are quite helpful in getting people out of high places and the like."

Evidently Bubble Bubble saw no need to correct Galvanize's assessment, as she continued to read quietly.

"Zone is in the gym, but his ability is basically enhanced agility, strength, and reactions. He's not at the level of really powerful Supers, but from the human perspective he's the best athlete alive. That's why he picked that name, because it's like he's always in the zone," Galvanize said. "Which leaves me. Aside from a nearly negligible side-effect of minor enhanced durability and strength, my main power is to give people a little extra push. I can amp them up and bring them to their peak."

"You're an *enhancer*?" Owen's eyes went wide. Enhancers were rare, damned near mythical Supers who could increase the strength of a person's power.

"Not a true one, no. I just bring people to their own physical best, and I have absolutely no effect on people's abilities. Again, it's all physical. I can't make them better than they normally would be, just take them to the maximum of their own level. It's like if you were a car, and the absolute best you could get up to, with ideal handling, was one hundred and ninety miles per hour, I would jump you to that speed. A real enhancer would bump you to, like, three hundred."

"I see. So when you use this ability of yours, anyone you target is suddenly going at maximum strength, speed, et cetera, within the limits of what their body can physically do?"

"You got it," Galvanize said. "It doesn't last long, but it's made the difference a few times in helping get people to safety."

"I want you to listen to me very, very carefully," Owen said, leaning in slightly so that he was towering over Galvanize, even while they both sat. "Never use that power on me. Never. No matter what. Are we clear?"

"I. . . okay," Galvanize mumbled, clearly taken aback. "There's no shame in needing a push on occasion, though."

"My worry is not that I will need a push. It is that I am incredibly strong and have worked for years to make sure I am in total control of that strength. If you suddenly jack me to maximum power then I don't know how much destruction I'll cause, but it will be a lot. Now, are we clear?" Owen repeated.

"We're clear," Galvanize replied.

4.

Owen surveyed his new room. It was large: not that he was surprised by this, but aside from the few boxes that had been shipped from Colorado, its size made the space seem surprisingly sparse. A bed in the corner, dresser by the far wall with a small television perched on top, and a desk across from the door dominated by a monitor and keyboard. Upon further inspection, it only seemed under-furnished compared to the opulence that had been present everywhere else.

After basic introductions, Galvanize had shown him around. The area set aside for their residence consisted of three floors. Below the elevator entrance was the gym, a sprawling, state-of-the-art facility with enough equipment to accommodate a team of Olympic hopefuls. Unfortunately, since none of his new team had supremely advanced strength, there were no ultra-dense weights that Owen could use. He didn't mind that too much, though. Part of his ability kept his muscles from atrophying, so it wasn't as though he'd get weaker without training. If the need arose, he could always have someone ship his old weight set from Colorado over. He'd just have to pick a company that didn't charge by the pound.

The gym level also housed a large room outfitted with various sandbags, movable platforms, and mock-building fronts. Galvanize had explained to Owen that this was the room where they honed their rescue skills, doing drills through constantly-changing scenarios to make sure they were on top of their game. Here Owen had met Zone, a tan young man with frosted tips, a dazzling smile, and a body-fat percentage so low it had to be unhealthy. They'd exchanged pleasantries then Zone had hustled off to shower before an appearance promoting a skateboard company he represented. From the speed at which the younger Super moved, Owen suspected he was less than thrilled to have this new addition to their team. Owen didn't really mind; he wasn't exactly dancing at the idea of being here himself, after all.

The middle floor was the one where he'd entered. Aside from the living room and kitchen there was a large dining room, a conference room, and an office with several professional-grade computers, printers, and the like. Galvanize explained that this was so anyone who needed to print out headshots or other such paraphernalia before an appearance could do so in the comfort of their own home. Evidently they had formerly outsourced such tasks, but it had turned out that doing them in-house was far more cost and time efficient.

The last floor was their living quarters: five large bedrooms, private bathrooms, a small nook with a coffee bar, and a sealed door. Owen had asked about the sealed door, which according to Galvanize was a high-tech area that only upper-management was allowed to access. Evidently, inside was a variety of gadgets and technology they were only permitted to use during training and missions. For a brief moment Owen contemplated snapping the metal door down with a minor exertion of effort, then thought better of it. It was only his first day, and he'd promised Lenny he'd try and be on good behavior. Given the abundant wealth of the team Owen was now on, he suspected his manager had pulled more than a few strings to make this happen. He needed to play nice, at least until he knew if he could handle this place or not.

Once the tour was done, they headed back to the main floor, where a pretty woman with a notepad was waiting for Owen. She took him back through the building, down to a normal business floor, and set about the task of registering him in the system. Stacks upon stacks of forms were signed, so many that Owen nearly spaced out and used his real name several times. Heroes' code names were, for purposes of legal contracts, considered acceptable alternatives to their own names. This had come about as more Heroes sought to enter private industry based on their Hero credentials but were not willing to compromise their secret identities. The only exception to this rule was for Heroes who inherited a legacy name, a name used already by a previous Super. They had to add a number after their signatures, distinguishing their identities, so that they were not bound by contracts or agreements their predecessors had signed.

After the seemingly endless forms, he'd been taken to a different area where he was forced to step into a strange machine that catalogued his biometrics, which would in turn allow him access to his new home. Then he was given a badge and card for entry into the building. Owen could not, for the life of him, understand why they insisted on taking a picture for his badge even though he was wearing a mask. He'd pointed this out, even offered to go back and change into his Titan mask so that it would be consistent, but his guide had merely shushed him down and assured him this was all part of standard procedure and had to be done in a precise way. Owen tried once more, pointing out it made no sense. The woman agreed, then told him to sit in front of the camera and not to smile, because that would make the picture harder to recognize. Owen gave up and complied.

Now, at last, he was done for the day. Officially registered, he was a part of this team in every legal way. He might have made an effort to connect with them more, but by the time he finished, everyone was out doing various appearances. Owen wondered if they spent every day like this, and if so, how they were ever around to respond in time to emergencies. He needed to see what these kids could do, and soon, otherwise when they finally did go on a call he'd have no idea how to treat them if something went wrong. It was an issue he'd try and remedy tomorrow.

Owen carefully unpacked his duffel bag containing the possessions too important to trust to a courier service. First were his Titan costumes. He kept six of them so that if one was dirty or in need of repair he had spares on hand. They were made from hardy material, but Supers like him were often put in situations that not even technology-enhanced cloth could stand up to. Next came a large metal box with a strange, orb-shaped lock on it. Inside were a variety of trinkets and trophies from his first round of Hero days. Some were too dangerous to let out of his sight, but most just held too much sentimental value.

The final item extracted from his bag was a picture frame. Inside it were two photos set side by side. The first showed a younger Owen and a small boy in a junkyard, the boy proudly holding a washing machine over his head. The second was Owen and another boy, this one noticeably heavier, clutching a spelling bee trophy in his hands. In both photos, one could easily make out traces of Owen's strong face in the children's features.

Owen carefully set this frame on his desk, next to the monitor. Now, he was home.

5.

"This is stupid," Hexcellent complained loudly, hands incessantly tugging on her sweatshirt as she tried to get comfortable in the unfamiliar garb. "You're not our fucking leader; you're just here as a token Hero so we can do our job. We don't need to prove shit to you."

"Hexcellent, that's enough," said Galvanize, his tone gentle but firm.

"No, it's okay, I don't blame her for calling bullshit," Owen replied, his own chest bare as none of the sweatshirts he found in the gym were large enough to fit him. As it was, the sweatpants he'd found only came halfway down his calves, looking as though they'd been meant as capris.

The first thing that morning, Owen had found Galvanize to request a full team meeting. Galvanize had complied and gathered everyone in the gym less than an hour later. Unfortunately, since it was an official meeting, the rules demanded they wear their official team sweats, rather than whatever was comfortable and fit them best. Currently they were all standing around in the part of the gym designed for rescue simulations, eyes set on the now unmasked newcomer in their midst.

Walking in maskless had been a tough decision for Owen, one he'd ultimately realized was inevitable. Teamwork hinged on trust. They had it with each other; he could see that in their body language. As the new guy, he would have to earn it. Showing them his face was a small but necessary step in that process.

"I took the time to read up on all of you last night before bed. You have good response rates, excellent percentages of civilians saved, and zero unauthorized encounters with criminal Supers. The first two are good, but the last one struck me as odd. Given that nearly half of the incidents you responded to last year were caused by criminal Supers, it seems like you'd at least have needed to retreat or work around one at some point."

"We don't take unnecessary risks," Zone said. Even wearing dumpy gray sweats, the man still looked as though he'd walked in from fashion shoot. "If Mirror Fog suspected any criminal Super involvement, we kept our distance until it was clear." Mirror Fog had been their last Hero on staff, now retired to somewhere tropical and pretty.

"That's because Mirror Fog's ability allowed him to discover if one was at the scene of the emergencies," Owen pointed out. "I don't have that power, which means when we go on calls, there will be a very real chance of running into a criminal Super."

"Sounds like your problem," Hexcellent said.

"It is my problem. But getting civilians out of the danger zone is yours. That's why I need to see what you each can do. It will tell me whether to call for a full retreat or have you keep helping people while I handle the situation."

"Technically, that would be my call," Galvanize said.

"With all due respect, no, it wouldn't." Owen phrased his reply as carefully as he could. He liked Galvanize. The kid seemed earnest in his efforts to help, but it was important to make things clear from the get go. "Most of the time, yes, you're the leader and I respect that. But the minute we have to deal with some Super causing trouble, I'm in command. I've got the training and experience to make those kinds of calls."

"Mirror Fog never tried to pull rank on us like that," Zone snapped.

"Mirror Fog kept you away from other Supers, so it never came up," Owen countered. "Our goal here is the same; we don't want anyone to get hurt. The difference is that when things go wrong, you have to worry about civilians and I have to worry about you."

The debate might have gone on longer, but at that moment, Bubble Bubble stepped forward and made a gesture at one of the dummies. A blue-tingled sphere appeared around the false person and began moving upward slowly.

"They're slow, and they only get slower the more bubbles I try to move at once," she said, her tone as even as it had been when reading her magazine. "At best, I could move one across a football field in two minutes. At worse, it would be around ten. The largest sphere I can create is big enough to hold around five people or one sedan-sized car. I can partially engulf large objects without destroying them, but that leaves the bubble's integrity extremely compromised. "

"How many can you conjure at once?" Owen asked.

"Up to five, but any more than three and the durability begins to degrade," Bubble Bubble answered.

"I see, and how durable are they before that happens?"

"They've stopped bullets, repelled flames, and taken large chunks of debris falling on them without giving way. But if you would like to test for yourself, feel free." Another gesture and a sphere roughly five feet wide materialized in front of Owen.

"You read my mind," Owen said, looking the bubble up and down. The thing about energy barriers people often failed to realize was that in order to stop something physical, force had to be exerted on it. Force flowing one way meant it could flow back the other, so while energy barriers were resistant to physical attacks, enough strength behind a blow could still shatter them.

Owen went slow, first doing nothing more than giving it a one-fingered thump. The sphere rippled, but held firm. Next he made a loose fist with his hand and struck it with a knocking motion, as though he were rapping on someone's door. The rippling was far more evident this time, yet still the bubble held. The fingers in his hand grew closer as his fist tightened. When he struck this time it was like he was pounding on a door, a hammer of flesh trying to pierce the obstacle before it.

The bubble shattered in a bright burst of energy, whooshing sounds and a surge of heat accompanying the event.

"What the hell, B.B.? I thought your bubbles were supposed to be tough. Gramps there barely even touched it," Zone chided.

"No, it was surprisingly strong," Owen corrected. "The force I used on that last blow was roughly equivalent to it being hit by a speeding car."

"Sounds about right for the reaction it generated." Bubble Bubble made a quick motion with her hands to drop the suspended dummy everyone had forgotten about.

"Horseshit it does; that was barely a punch, even for an old man," Hexcellent said.

"Then I say it's time we tested your power next," Owen replied. "I think this old man may just surprise you. Unless you're afraid to put your power where your mouth is."

"Bring it on, Gramps." Hexcellent evidently had no qualms about stealing the nickname Zone had used. "I've always wanted to show up one of you fancy-ass Heroes."

6.

"You should walk more to the center of the room," Galvanize advised. "So there's space to move about."

"If you say so." Owen wasn't too worried about needing to dodge, but stranger things had happened in his life. A few large steps brought him to the center of the unobstructed area with ample space around him. Hexcellent made no such motions.

"Aren't you coming?" Owen called to the dark-haired woman.

"I don't get my hands dirty, I've got people for that," Hexcellent replied. "Let me demonstrate."

"No." Galvanize held up a hand and Hexcellent, to her credit, froze in place instantly. "I know what you're about to do, and no. Show him the other two first. This is supposed to be a full assessment, not you trying to prove a point."

"Fiiiiiiiiiiine," Hexcellent agreed, drawing out the word into a whine. "I'll start from the bottom. My smallest demon is Impers. We use him for recon and message relaying." She stuck out her hand and exerted a minor bit of focus. Next to Owen, a small creature appeared in a puff of red smoke.

It was about a foot tall, human-shaped with red skin and diminutive horns on its head. Large, bat-like wings nearly as long as it was tall extended from its back, and a three-inch tail swept from side to side out of its rear. The creature made a chittering noise then leapt into the air. Owen was surprised with the grace it had in flight; it moved through the air with precision and speed.

Impers circled the room four times then landed on Hexcellent's shoulder and made the chittering noise again.

"How is that thing used for messages?" Owen asked. "It can't talk."

"'It' is a he, and we worked out a system," Hexcellent explained. "Impers can understand the questions we ask him, plus he can control the clicks he makes. One click means yes, two means no, three means follow me, and four means run like hell. As long as you ask the right questions, it's pretty effective."

"Useful," Owen said, trying his best to hide the surprise at this creature being any gender, let alone male. Still, since it sprang from the summoner's mind, no one was more familiar with it than she. "Anything else I should know?"

"Impers is the smartest of my summons, so he can take the most complex directions. The others make noise, but they have to be ordered more directly. Impers excels in situations where we're trying to locate people who are trapped, since he can remember where he sees them and point to it on a map. He's frailer than the other two, but fireproof. All of them are fireproof, actually."

The fireproof part didn't shock Owen at all. "Okay, what's next?"

Impers vanished in the same smoke he'd appeared in. Another motion from Hexcellent and a much larger cloud of red smoke appeared near Owen. Out of this came a creature roughly five feet tall with the head of a vulture atop a hunched body. Its feet were taloned and in place of arms or wings were two long, translucent white blades in the shape of scythes.

"Her name is Huggles," Hexcellent informed Owen.

"Huggles?"

"I was feeling a bit feisty and sarcastic when I created her," she admitted. "Anyway, those blades on her arm are sharp enough to cut through most metals, and she's got the strength to wield them. She's most useful for getting people out of cars, sawing through debris, that sort of thing."

"I see. Mind having her strike me?"

"I can, but it won't prove anything," Hexcellent said. "Huggles can't cut through anything stronger than steel, and even that gives her trouble. I'd assume a veteran Hero like you is at least that tough."

"None the less, I'd prefer if you did." Owen stuck out his left arm and left it there, freely exposed.

"Have it your way. Huggles, cut his arm!" Hexcellent yelled. The words had no sooner left her mouth than the bird-thing whirled into action, again moving with more grace than its form should allow. She swung both arm-blades down in a smooth slice, striking two places on Owen's forearms. As soon as the blades met his skin, the motion ceased completely. He'd never expected Huggles to be powerful enough to move him, but he was surprised by the amount of strength the demon could muster. It was good to know this thing had some power behind it.

"Not bad," Owen complimented. "I take it there's one left?"

"Yup, and I saved the best for last." This time Hexcellent's motions were slower, and there was a noticeable delay between Huggles' disappearance and the next demon's cloud of smoke. Once it appeared, though, it was impossible to miss. The cloud was huge, and Owen caught the faint scent of brimstone in his nostrils. Once the smoke cleared, he found himself in the rare position of looking up.

This monster stood over seven and a half feet tall, likely eight if one included the large, black horns jutting upward from its forehead. Thick, chitinous black plates covered much of its body, concentrated on the disproportionately large arms, the broad chest, and the thick legs ending in large hooves. Its face was dog-like, black sharp teeth in its muzzle and a pair of glowing red eyes above the snout. Any monster movie company would have paid top dollar for this creature to appear in one of their films, assuming they could keep the rest of the cast from pissing themselves.

"His name is Big Henry," Hexcellent supplied helpfully. "His job is heavy lifting. Clearing rubble, moving cars, holding up support beams, that sort of thing. More or less the only things you'd be good at, except he doesn't need a room and pay."

Owen examined the creature closely. He knew enough about summoners to know that their creatures were often born of a problem or a need. Creating another being from nothing was intensely difficult; the only way to succeed was to pour an aspect of one's self into it. The summons were supposed to do something that summoner couldn't. They represented a strength to fill in a perceived weakness.

This summon was not built for heavy lifting. It was built for fighting. Maybe for killing.

"Guess we should give the people what they want," Owen said, pointing to the other three Supers. "Why not have him give me a little tap?"

"I thought you'd never ask," Hexcellent replied. "Big Henry, punch him with everything you've got." This time she didn't yell, she barely even raised her voice. Owen had just enough time to wonder if her summons even needed to be close enough to hear for her orders to work when Big Henry sprang at him.

This one didn't have as much grace as the other two, but he made up for it with a shocking amount of speed. He whirled forward, hooves nearly cracking the floor with each step, closing the gap between him and Owen in mere moments. The punch came at the end of the movement, part of the motion's flow that utilized the extra momentum. It was impressive, especially for a being that Owen suspected had never been trained. The black armored fist drove directly into his torso, right between his sternum and stomach. It had so much power that, even braced in an appropriate stance, Owen was still moved back several inches as the concrete under his feet crumbled against the indirect force.

"Better than I expected," Owen said, clearly unharmed or inconvenienced by the attack. He glanced up at Hexcellent, whose face had morphed from its usual antisocial glower into an expression of genuine shock. Given how strong this summon was, she'd likely thought it would at least do some damage to him. Owen didn't fault her for that belief. She hadn't been inside the Hero world; her sense of scale for what constituted strong didn't even have a ranking for someone like Titan.

"How durable is this one?" Owen asked, his question shaking her out of her surprised reverie.

"Damn near indestructible." Her jaw was setting, her eyes growing narrow. She was gearing up for round two, when she'd show that her summon was at least no less durable than he. If it could take his blow with the same lack of effect, it would prove they were on even footing. Owen, fortunately, knew better.

"Good to know," Owen said, taking a step back from the summon, which remained half-crouched to attack. "Luckily, since you don't have to use him to fight, we don't need to test that. Let's move on. Zone, how about you show me what you can do?"

Hexcellent stared at him for a few moments longer before dismissing Big Henry back to smoke. Owen was sure she wasn't happy with him at the moment, but that would have to wait. He needed to finish seeing everyone's skill set for now.

After that, he could work on making them better.

7.

Before either Zone or Owen could step forward, a bright red light flashed through the room, followed by a brief siren. That abated in moments, replaced by the calm voice of Mr. Greene.

"There is a fire two point five miles away from here. It's an older building, and structural integrity is a concern. Firefighters are currently spread thin, so they've requested our help."

"We'll do it," Galvanize yelled into the air. Owen presumed Greene could hear them, a suspicion confirmed moments later when the voice came back into the air.

"Understood. They'll be expecting your arrival. Transport is in the basement when you're ready."

"You heard the man. Everyone, into your costumes and downstairs. If you take longer than five minutes, you're getting left behind," Galvanize commanded. His tone had seamlessly shifted from controlled but friendly to authoritative. Owen had no doubt he'd be abandoned if he dared go over the five-minute mark. Evidently the others believed Galvanize too, as they immediately dashed off toward the door, Zone peeling off part of his sweats before he'd even gotten clear of the room.

"Feeling nervous?" Galvanize asked, breaking into a light jog so as not to violate his own edict.

"Lil bit," Owen admitted. "Been a long time."

"You'll be fine. Fires are where B.B. and Hexcellent really shine. Just follow orders and everyone will get home safe."

"That would be a pleasant outcome," Owen agreed. How nice these kids had it: when if they did their job right, no one died. In the Hero world, even if you did everything perfectly, sometimes success still meant blood on your hands.

* * *

Titan nearly missed his debut that day, due to the mirror in Owen's room. He'd tried on his old costume before leaving Colorado, of course, but that had been a piecemeal ordeal, donning and checking each section separately so problems could be identified in turn. It wasn't until he was fully suited up, walking toward his door, that the figure in the mirror caught his attention and stopped him cold.

It had been over a decade since he'd seen this person looking back in a reflection. This was different than going to see Lenny; this was a man about to walk out into a world of danger. He wasn't just Owen Daniels wearing a costume. He was Titan, and the full of weight of that realization nearly sent him to the ground. So many memories, so many ordeals. So much loss. Part of him wanted to shrink back, to let Titan fall away in costumed pieces and turn back into Owen.

Instead, he reached up to the side of his mask and pressed a device in his ear, hidden by the red material covering his face. None of the others would have this accessory; it was only for Heroes. They'd made improvements to the ear pieces since he last suited up. This one was light and nestled in the crevice of his ear with total security, giving a sense that no sideways blow would knock it loose. The things had always been damned tough, but a good rocking could send them flying. Titan was unsurprised to find this flaw had been addressed.

"Titan, reporting in." His words echoed through the empty room.

"Dispatch recognizes Titan," said a soft voice in his ear. Somewhere in his stomach, a knot of worry loosened. Part of him worried Dispatch would have changed as well, but her voice was the same as always: strong, well-enunciated, and with a vaguely European accent. No one, at least no one Titan had ever talked to, knew Dispatch's real name, location, or even powers. She was just always there, no matter what time anyone plugged in. Always there, always the same.

"Titan, please respond," she repeated.

Owen realized he'd zoned out, listening to her voice but not her words. "Sorry, repeat the question."

"You are cleared for active Hero assignments and for monitoring of a Privately Employed Emergency Response Supers team. Which of these tasks are you signing in for?"

"I'm babysitting the corpies tonight," Owen replied, working very hard to keep the annoyance out of his voice. If he signed in for active Hero duty, it would mean she'd direct him to any calls for help that fit the bill. Being on oversight duty meant he could use her if a situation arose, but she wouldn't try to assign any new tasks to him.

"Confirmed," Dispatch said. "Is your team responding to the fire on Forty-Third Street?" Since corpies and Heroes overlapped on rescue duties, Dispatch always knew who was going where.

"If that's about two miles from my current location, then yes." Owen broke his eyes away from the mirror and headed out his door. The earpiece wouldn't be bothered by anything like walking. He'd seen people easily hold conversations with Dispatch while flying at supersonic speeds.

"Confirmed. You are on note." Owen winced, involuntarily. "On note" meant he was officially working the incident, and any other Hero who wanted to check and see if it was handled could find out he was there. Being a working Hero made it pretty much impossible to keep a low profile.

"Thank you. Anything I should know going in?" Owen rounded the corner and stepped into the elevator at the end of the hall. The team had already informed him that the space below the lobby button would take him to a transport basement if pressed by someone with the right biometrics. A small push from his thumb and spot of clear metal suddenly lit up, sending him on a rapid journey downward.

"No documented Supers or Powereds in residence at the building. Cause of fire is undetermined, though given degree of neglect and decay in the neighborhood, natural causes are highly possible. Nothing in the reports so far suggests any variant-human activity."

"So if it is a Super, I'm going in blind," Owen muttered. He preferred to get at least a forewarning on these sorts of things.

"Again, nothing suggests-"

"I know, I know, sorry Dispatch. I'm just a little on edge," Owen told her.

"Ah yes, this is your first active assignment since renewing your license." Dispatch paused, an occurrence so rare it stood out like a curse in

43

Owen's ear. "In that case, let me be the first to say welcome back. The world has missed you, Titan."

The elevator opened with a pneumatic whoosh, revealing a large black vehicle with a single open door. Owen moved toward it.

"Tell the world I'm on my way."

8.

Their vehicle had a siren, which Owen found surprisingly delightful. In his Hero days, they'd had people with flight, teleportation, and other various means of covering distance, so the only time he'd heard sirens was from the police and emergency responders showing up in the aftermath. Sitting in the vehicle making the sound reminded him of his childhood, before his abilities manifested, when he would feel a thrill every time the firefighters or police officers would drive by.

Certainly, this team's transportation had far more advanced accoutrements than the siren. It was constructed out of an SUV; however, the whole thing had been heavily fortified, from the wheels to the antenna. Even with five people inside, one of whom was far from slender, the car had only dropped a few inches. Bright lights buzzed along the dashboard. Zone was fiddling with something where the passenger glove box should have been while Galvanize drove them quickly, but safely, through traffic. There was likely an electronics' store worth of useful gadgets and pricey doodads, all at their fingertips, but Owen was really only fond of the siren.

Everyone could see the telltale smoke billowing up from the fire a few blocks before they reached it. Had it been darker, Owen knew there would have been an orange glow cast against the clouds, visible for miles. Daytime stole much of the scenic drama away.

They came to a stop just outside a police barrier, Galvanize dashing out the door before the rest of them could even unbuckle their seatbelts.

"He has to go talk to the cops and firemen," Hexcellent said, answering a question that Owen would have been tactful enough not to ask. "Unlike

Heroes, we can't just gallivant in wherever we want. We have to respect the chain of authority." She'd changed into her costume, a black number with lots of zippers, buckles, and torn fishnets. Several logos, apparently for makeup companies, dotted her outfit; one for a clothing store named Fiery Discussion was featured no fewer than four times.

"To be fair, it's also a good practice because they can tell us where our help is needed most," Zone added. His costume was comprised of a skintight material across his torso that was see-through everywhere a logo wasn't present. It seemed he was heavily sponsored by skateboard companies, a few football franchises, and one very enthusiastic energy drink. The latter logo, for a brand called Punch Juice, took up almost the entirety of his back.

"He's right," Owen agreed. "When we can, Heroes talk to uniforms, too. It's smart to get all the information you can."

Zone gave a nod, but pointedly avoided making eye contact with Owen, despite the older man's agreement. This, it seemed, was going to be the least cordial of his working relationships. He idly wondered if Zone was a fundamentalist, a bigot, or just didn't care for having a washed-up Hero on his team. It didn't really matter; as long as the young man could stay polite, he was free to dislike Owen all he wanted.

"We should catch up," Bubble Bubble advised them. Her costume was barely a costume at all, more like an experimental outfit from a high-end designer. It was white and green, which went well with the emerald contacts she'd slipped over her naturally brown eyes, and hugged her body in a way that spoke to the figure beneath without going so far as to divulge secrets. Even the logos she wore seemed a bit more tasteful than the others', colors downplayed so they didn't clash with her ensemble. Bubble Bubble was sponsored by makeup companies, as well as skin management creams, and a name Owen fleetingly recognized as someone who made designer handbags.

Corpies didn't need costumes or masks, of course, since they didn't undertake activities that earned them enemies. Heroes wore the capes and cowls by tradition as well as necessity: when one's job required capturing or killing powerful people who often have powerful friends, it's essential for them not to know where one hung their hat. Corpies were effectively specialized rescue services, like EMT or firefighters. They weren't making anyone mad, so it was assumed by most, Owen included, that they wore the costumes in a vain attempt to seem more like the Heroes they weren't. He kept those thoughts to himself as they exited the car and headed toward Galvanize. It was a free country, and they had as much right to wear costumes as they did to wear t-shirts or jeans.

Their leader met them a few feet from the building, his outfit's cape flapping slightly in the breeze. Galvanize wore a costume closest to the style of real Heroes: a navy and white ensemble with cuffed gloves, calf-high boots, and even an emblazoned cape. He was sponsored by Punch Juice as well, along with several protein and nutritional supplement companies. The enthusiastic young man wore a serious expression, exactly what one should look like when dealing with a dangerous situation. Owen knew the pictures of him would look great, which he took to be the point.

"All right, team. I just spoke with the firemen, and this place is very unstable. They believe they've gotten everyone out from the bottom floors, but the top ones have proven treacherous to explore. We need to search for any survivors. Hexcellent, get Impers up to the top floor immediately and have him let us know if he finds anyone. Zone, I want you to start on the floor below. Bubble Bubble, that means he needs a way up. Titan, you and I will make our way from the ground. Hexcellent and B.B. will stay out here to evacuate anyone from the higher floors with Big Henry and energy spheres. Be quick, be adaptable, and make sure you don't get in the any of the firemen's way. Any questions?"

"Do they know what started the fire?" Zone asked.

"Nothing conclusive. It's an old building, lots of smokers and ancient wiring," Galvanize replied. "If that's it, let's go!"

Galvanize had no sooner yelled the last part than everyone sprang into action. Hexcellent summoned Impers in a cloud of smoke and had him leap into the air, heading for the top floor. Galvanize took off toward the entrance, pausing only to throw a small black mask on over his mouth and nose. Owen was a few steps behind, lagging a bit out of curiosity. Bubble Bubble had been told to give Zone a way up to the second highest floor. Given what Owen knew of their powers, he was wondering how they were going to pull that off.

The spectacle did not disappoint. Zone took off running, aiming himself at the side of the building. In a smooth, fluid motion he leapt from the ground, foot catching a brick window sill that he used for a second leap. Another jump off the top of the window's outcropping brought him a few feet higher, but with it he was out of usable footholds until the next window. When Zone's sneakers met the flat, brick wall, he pushed backward instead of up, executing a perfect backflip that sent him twirling through the air. Instead of plummeting to the ground, as one would have expected, he momentarily landed on the energy sphere Bubble Bubble had placed directly under him. Launching himself off of it, Zone's nimble feet made it to the next window sill and the dance began all over again. It was difficult, dangerous, and stupidly risky.

But it was impressive. Owen had to give them that.

9.

The wave of heat that washed over Owen was oppressive, stifling, and strangely familiar. It had been well past a decade since he plunged into a wild inferno; he found the experience a touch nostalgic.

The bottom floor of the building was almost entirely engulfed in flames to some degree, thick, dark smoke pouring out and limiting visibility. From what he could see, the situation looked grim. Despite the brick exteriors, almost the entire inside was made of wood, wood that was rapidly turning to ash. At the rate the fire was spreading, it was a matter of when, not if, the entire structure was going to come crashing down. By his estimates, they had maybe twenty minutes left, and that was only thanks to the incredible efforts of the firefighters to control the flames.

"Come on," Galvanize urged, his voice coming through the communicator in Owen's left ear. Right ear was always reserved for Dispatch, but he needed to be able to talk with his team as well. Their earbuds weren't quite as good as the Hero-issued ones; however, they weren't as far behind the curve as he might have guessed they'd be.

Owen followed his leader, taking careful steps. The floor appeared solid enough, but the stairs were a source of concern for him. They weren't blazing in earnest yet, so thankfully their structural integrity was enough to hold his weight as he ascended to the second floor. Still, Owen continued being watchful of his movements. Him falling through a few burning floors wouldn't injure him in the slightest, but it would definitely hasten this building's destruction.

The first and second floors were clear of everyone save for emergency responders, and it was obvious they were going to have to pull out soon. The building was eight stories tall, so that meant they likely had at least two more levels to go before they met up with Zone and Impers, assuming neither team had to stop and facilitate any rescues. He hoped they would find the whole place properly evacuated. Getting someone out of the middle floors might be tricky.

"Does the heat bother you?" The question came so suddenly that Owen nearly twitched in surprise, a move that easily could have crushed the smoldering wood beneath his feet. Luckily, his entire career of experience hadn't quite deserted him, so he managed to keep control.

"No, not really," he replied. "I'm a little surprised at how well you're taking it, though."

"I did mention I was a bit hardier than normal," Galvanize replied. "Besides, the costume does a lot of the work. It's specially built for extreme temperatures in either direction, along with a fair bit of armoring in the more vulnerable spots, just in case I get hit by debris or something. Pair it with the breather mask, which keeps me from getting carbon monoxide poisoning, and it's a handy ensemble."

"Pretty snazzy," Owen said, dating himself unapologetically with his word choice.

"One of the perks of working for the big guys. When I started out all I got was a t-shirt with a logo on it. This is much safer."

Galvanize's word choice struck Owen as intriguing. He'd have expected the glorified model to use words like "nicer," "cleaner," "more appealing," or even "sexier." "Safer" implied that his first concern was for the job the uniform denoted, not how it made him look. Owen had known Heroes who wouldn't have said safer. Again he felt his respect for the wavy-haired young man raise a few degrees. Even if he was only playing a part, he played it exceptionally well.

It was on the third floor that their streak of finding everyone safely removed came to a halt. They'd just come off the stairs when Owen heard muffled screaming coming from a few apartments away. His hearing was good—above human grade but not so impressive that it would count as an ability on its own—so he could also make out sounds of someone scuffling about.

"We've got people," he declared, alerting Galvanize while taking two careful, but sizable, steps toward the apartment that the noise was coming from. A single attempt on the doorknob told him it was locked, and he could see keyholes for three deadbolts. He reared back his hefty fist and prepared to turn the door into splinters.

"Titan, hold!" Galvanize's order was curt and quick, spoken with the sort of veteran authority that reminded Owen of his intern days. "Time is short, but we don't know where they are behind that door. You punching it could seriously injure someone."

"Got a better idea?"

"Yes, actually. You're incredibly strong, so just stick a finger through the door and run it down past where the knob and deadbolts are. That should let us in without sending chunks flying through the home."

Owen bit back a terse remark and did as he was told. It was easy, like sticking a finger into pudding. The deadbolts put up a valiant effort to stop his index finger, but they may as well have tried to reason with a thunderstorm. In less than half a minute the locks were removed. Galvanize moved forward, pushing the door open and stepping into the apartment's living room.

The two men had both been in rescue situations before, and this was not the first fire for either, so they'd had certain expectations of what to find behind the door. A huddled, scared group of people awaiting rescue, a panicked cluster that would race forward and possibly knock their rescuers down, or even the worst case scenario: one or more bodies that had already been claimed by smoke inhalation. This was none of those situations. Not even close.

A group of four adults were racing about, filling buckets from the sink and, judging by sound, the tub, emptying them on to a person in the center of the room, then repeating the process. This person in the center was young, roughly seven to nine if Owen had to guess, and sitting in a metal washtub that was glowing from the heat. This heat wasn't from the fire that was engulfing the building; it came directly from the source.

This young person, a girl, Owen realized as he noticed her hair and facial features, was the one who had released the muffled screams. They didn't seem to be ones of pain; that would have been impossible to bite back. No, these screams were likely of fear, or guilt, some mixture containing elements of the two. She was clearly terrified, and Owen didn't blame her one bit.

Because, in addition to sitting, crying, and screaming softly, the young girl was also engulfed in fire. Her whole body rippled with flame, cascading off and flowing to the world around her.

"Shit," Galvanize said, taking a step back. "We've got a Super."

10.

Owen didn't fault Galvanize for assuming they were dealing with a
Super. He was in a dangerous situation, and a Super willfully causing fires
would be his worst case scenario. It meant he had to run like hell and leave these
people behind, because he wasn't cleared to stop a fire-coated arsonist. It was a
reasonable leap to make, but it was wrong.

There were things he recognized, as a former Hero, and as a father, that
told him something was off. The blackened spots on the metal tub showed it had
been used for similar purposes before. The people, probably her family, were
scared and frantic but not lost in terror, and that meant this was something
they'd come to terms with. The way the girl was sobbing and trying to bite back
her fear spoke volumes of how much she hated what was happening to her.
Above all was the efficiency of the system they were using to douse her. This
had been planned, worked on, and drilled. They knew she might start burning,
and they had a method in place to deal with it.

"She's not a Super," Owen said, correcting his team leader. "She's a
Powered. She can't control it."

"You can't. . ." Galvanize's words trailed off as his brain finally
snapped to the context clues Owen had already seen. Fear had made him
momentarily slow, not stupid. "Crud, I think you might be right."

"I am right," Owen stepped forward, his large body's movement finally
seeming to snap the people in the apartment to awareness of the costumed men's
presence. One of the older men lowered his bucket and raced over to Owen.

"No. . . go. . . Go away!" His voice was heavy with a Hispanic accent,
and his stilted way of speaking made it clear he was still learning English. Once

upon a time Owen could have faked his way through some basic phrases, but Spanish was a skill he'd long ago let rust to oblivion on his mental shelf.

Galvanize, thankfully, had not been so lax in his language exercises. He hurried over immediately, snapping into a quick, fluent conversation with the older man. Owen was impressed; the kid even rolled his *r's*, a trick Owen had never managed to get down.

"I'm hitting a wall," Galvanize told him after a few moments of conversation. "They understand that the building is on fire, but they're refusing to leave. They seem to think we're here to take the girl away." He shot Owen a confused expression, visible even through the mask and breather apparatus on his face. "Any insight you want to offer?"

"Mirror Fog really did keep you kids away from other Supers, didn't he?" Titan gave a small shake of his head. "Powereds with abilities that are a severe danger to others, ones like hers, are often put in 'protective custody' until they find a way to let them safely interact with society. Usually some tech-genius can slap a suit or something on them, but there's always rumors of people never being heard from again." Owen pointedly refrained from commenting on his own suspicions of the validity regarding those rumors. There were more important things at the moment.

"I can see how he'd be worried about that," Galvanize said, sparing a moment to glance at the growing amount of fire filling the building. "But we need to get them out. I'm going to have to ask you to pick them up and remove them forcefully."

"You open to a suggestion?"

"I'll hear it out," Galvanize assured him.

"They're here to protect the girl. If I take her out, they'll follow on their own. Faster and safer," Owen pointed out.

"True but. . . well, I guess you're allowed to deal with her. But be gentle: Powered or not, she's still a person."

In that moment, Owen's grudging respect for the young man leading this team of corporate shills metamorphosed into genuine affection. Job be damned, he liked this kid.

"Don't worry," Owen assured him, stepping past the older man still jabbering in a language he couldn't understand. Dimly, he felt a pair of hands grip his bicep, some poorly thought out attempt at stopping him. His assailant, like countless others who'd tried such things before, was in for disappointment.

Owen continued forward, kneeling down next the metal tub and staring at the girl in the face. He smiled at her, his big, wide, corny grin that had endeared him to the hearts of the public so many years ago. It seemed he still had a bit of his old charming magic left, because the girl stopped crying long enough to turn and look at him.

"Are you okay?" His voice was calm and gentle, ignoring the urgency of the situation around him.

"No," she said, her words high-pitched, hoarse, and heartbreaking. "I can't stop this time. I keep trying and it won't stop."

"Don't worry," Owen assured her. "I'll get you out of here. We'll go out to your apartment's pool and help you cool down. Does that sound okay?"

She shook her head fiercely. "I can't leave. I can't get up. I'll burn people. I've burned Papa and Mama and my sister and our house. . . I burn everything."

With great care, Owen reached out his hand and brought it down on top of her head, momentarily smothering out the flames before they regrouped and dashed across his skin. The girl tried to pull away, but he held fast, holding his hand there long enough to send the message. Then, he pulled it away and held his fingers in front of her face.

"You can't burn me. I'm special, like you. No matter how scared you get, no matter how hot you get, you can't hurt me. I promise."

Her eyes grew wide (an unsettling sight since they were still coated in flames) as she stared at his unmarred skin. Not even the hair from the back of his knuckles had been singed. She reached out and grasped his fingers with hers, ever so carefully, and watched in amazement as the fire coating her failed to scorch him in the slightest.

"Who are you?"

"My name is Titan. What's yours?"

"Alexandria."

"Well, Alexandria, how about that swim?"

She nodded, and he reached over, delicately scooping her out of her metal washtub and pulling her against his chest. His uniform crackled and wrinkled as she came into the contact with it, but his words held true as the fire proved unable to burn him.

"Ready when you are," Titan told Galvanize, who gave a quick nod and hurriedly escorted the rest of the apartment's occupants to the stairs. Titan followed, even more careful with his steps than before.

11.

It took a good ten minutes of submersion in the apartment complex's pool, now partially filled with ash, before Alexandria's cloak of flames started to dissipate. Titan spent that time talking with her, asking her about life and school, pretending he wasn't gently holding her face above water while the rest of her body sent steam billowing into the late-morning air. Before taking her out of the building, he'd wrapped her in his fire-resistant over-shirt, illustrating one of the many reasons that Heroes always dressed in layers. It had held up well, which was a stroke of good fortune because he was relatively certain she'd have torched through anything else he could have used.

Having fathered Powereds, Titan was more familiar with their condition than most. Their abilities were triggered involuntarily. Sometimes this response was purely physical, like a nervous tic. Sometimes it happened from other stimuli, like sneezing. And for many, their ability was tied to their emotions. So while the water was keeping Alexandria from burning anything else, Titan had a firm suspicion that it was the act of calming her down that finally banished the flames.

The rest of the team had finished checking the building and reported there were no more people left inside. Only Alexandria's family had stayed behind, too scared to move her and perhaps set something else aflame. With the coast clear, the firefighters had pulled out and focused on getting the blaze under control. Galvanize, Hexcellent, Bubble Bubble, and Zone had all gathered out in front of the smoking building to catch the eye of various reporters and news crews that were gathering on the scene. Technically, Titan should be with them, but he felt he was doing better work standing waist deep in dirty water, getting a little girl down from her emotional rollercoaster.

"Titan, the Powered girl's transport is en route. Estimate arrival in five point two minutes." Dispatch's voice hummed in his ear, nearly startling him. He'd forgotten about the earpiece already. It would take some time for the Hero habits to kick back in. At least he'd remembered to call the incident in. A person with her ability and no control needed some serious help.

"Understood." Titan tapped the side of his mask covering his ear as Alexandria looked on curiously. He stuck out his thumb and pinky, making an "I'm on the phone" gesture to explain his apparent discussion with no one. "The secondary transport as well?"

"Yes, another car for the girl's family is paired with the one for her. They will not be able to ride in the same vehicle."

Titan smiled down at the girl, but inwardly winced. If he threw her into a mysterious van without so much as a friendly face, it was highly likely she would flare up again. The team getting her would have things to control her fire, but it wouldn't be a great first impression.

"I can accompany. There shouldn't be any danger for me."

"It was never an issue of danger. We have equipment to completely neutralize a fire-conjurer of the level you described; however, that equipment occupies a large amount of space. We cannot fit anyone in the van aside from the driver and the Powered."

Damn, there went that idea. If a normal person couldn't fit, then Titan had no chance of squeezing in. He was still trying to think of another way to help when Dispatch's voice grabbed his attention again.

"Titan, another Hero has flagged your location as a destination. Gale is currently en route."

"Make that 'arrived.'"

The new voice came from a source high above the pool: a woman floating forty feet in the air. She wore a green and black outfit: standard pants and top paired with a matching ankle-length coat. It fluttered out behind her, billowing in the breeze as she began to descend.

She was halfway down when Titan realized there was no breeze. That probably meant air-elementalist, and if she had enough oomph to fly herself without riding on something as ostentatious as a hurricane, then she must be a pretty good one. Her brunette hair flitted about as she descended, coming to rest a few inches below her shoulders when she finally landed.

"Gale, I presume?"

The woman, Gale, nodded, and then flashed a warm smile at Alexandria. She turned her attention back to the man in the soot-covered outfit a moment later. "And you're Titan, or so I'm told."

"That I am."

"From what I heard, Titan left the business years ago. So that leaves me with a question: original or legacy?" Her tone was cheerful, and the smile she'd shown Alexandria had only faded a bit, yet Titan could still sense the tension in her body as she quizzed him. He didn't blame her; the return of someone as legendarily infamous as himself was bound to stir up a lot of something. Maybe it would be bad, maybe it would be good, but it would be something.

"Original," Titan replied. "Just reinstated, actually. You caught me on my first job."

"A burning building? Interesting choice for a strongman."

"Long story," Titan said with a sigh.

"Are you really Gale?" This question came from neither of the registered Heroes, but rather from the small girl who had finally stopped burning a few minutes prior. Both adults looked at her, realizing they had something more important on their hands than a pissing contest.

"I really am," Gale told her. She took a step off the edge of the concrete and began to hover over the water, making small ripples below her feet as she glided across the water's surface. "See? I can fly and everything."

Seeing her interact kindly with Alexandria, it struck Titan that Gale was quite pretty, a fact that was evident even through the mask that concealed all save for her eyes, a bit of nose, and from the mouth downward. Dark skin, full lips, and likely a fit body beneath all the armored clothing she wore. If his inclinations had lain in that direction, he'd have been a bit tempted to ask for her number.

"You came to speak at our school last year," Alexandria said. "You talked about how being a Hero meant making good choices, even for young people like us."

"And I meant every word," Gale assured her.

Alexandria nodded, even though nothing had been asked of her. The girl was clearly star-struck. Titan would have bet dollars to donuts that somewhere in the cinders of her now-charred room were the remains of a Gale poster. That thought, sad as it was, gave him an idea.

"Gale, maybe you can help me—us—out," he said carefully. "I've got friends who are coming to take Alexandria and her family somewhere secure, where she won't have to worry about setting things on fire. Unfortunately, her car will be too small for anyone else to ride with her, but I want her to know she's still got people watching over her. Are you free to fly alongside her car and make sure she arrives safely?"

"Of course I can," Gale said, giving the young girl another comforting smile. "That works out well, actually. I wanted to see if you had some free time later on to chat, so now we can meet up after and I can assure you everything went fine."

Titan had known he was handing out a favor by asking her to do escort duty, but he hadn't expected her to cash it in immediately. Clearly she wanted to know about his return as soon as possible. From the way Alexandria had recognized her and her skill at diplomacy, it seemed a fair guess that she was one of the better known Heroes in the city, which meant she likely also belonged to one of the top teams. He'd hoped to avoid getting too mixed up in the Hero world before he settled in here, but it looked like that wasn't going to happen.

Oh well. At least he was going to get something out of it.

"Sounds like a great idea," Titan agreed.

12.

"Nice job."

Mr. Greene was the first thing the team saw when they stepped through the door of their base; he stood between the living room and the kitchen, wearing an almost aggressively neutral expression.

"Thank you, sir," Galvanize responded immediately. "We were thankful to get everyone out with no injuries or deaths. It was a good day."

"Very good," Mr. Greene amended. "The firefighters actually went on record thanking you for your help, the footage of Zone leaping into the building is being picked up by a station running the story, and the post-rescue photos came out looking quite striking."

Owen wondered how this man knew so much about pictures he hadn't taken and stations he didn't run, then let the curiosity slide away. This place had a lot of money, and Owen had been around more than long enough to know that with the right amount of cash, there was almost nothing one couldn't access.

"Unfortunately, our newest team member wasn't present in any of the group photos." Mr. Greene's face was still neutral, his tone still even, yet one could feel the disapproval radiating off of him. "Titan, you understand that as Hero Liaison to this team you're expected to appear alongside them, don't you?"

"I know what I signed up for, and I've got no issue with that, when time permits. My priority was taking care of a little girl who couldn't stop herself from radiating fire. Once she was safe, I went to join in the photo-shoot, but it had already wrapped up."

"A girl radiating fire? Galvanize, please explain," Mr. Greene said.

"There was a Powered in the building. She seemed to be cloaked in flames and was unable to extinguish herself. Titan secured her, calmed her down, and arranged for her to be transported somewhere safe where she wouldn't present a danger to herself or others. He prioritized it as higher importance than dealing with the media, and I agreed. Left unattended, she could have injured someone or started a new blaze."

Owen felt a spark of surprise at Galvanize's words. That was only somewhat how it had happened; in truth, he'd just taken the girl down and Galvanize hadn't stopped him, but this made it sound like the actions of Titan had been done at Galvanize's orders. The kid was putting himself on the chopping block instead of Owen.

Mr. Greene stared at the two men for a long moment. "And why couldn't Hexcellent have had one of her demons restrain the child? They are also fireproof, as well as less necessary to be seen on camera."

"The fire was coming from fear," Owen said, not about to let Galvanize try and absorb anymore blame. "Powereds' abilities often tie to their emotions. She was scared because she lost control and that fear fed her ability, causing a chain reaction that almost torched a whole building. Hexcellent's demons aren't what anyone would call child-friendly, so I seemed like a smarter pick for calming her down."

Mr. Greene remained silent for a few seconds then seemed to relax.

"Very well. Our first job is to provide emergency services, and it appears your choices were made with the public's safety in mind, so missing a photo-op is an acceptable loss. Just make sure everyone, Titan included, writes up their standard post-response report. Every detail, every action, every name of every person encountered. There were no injuries today, but we all know that doesn't preclude reports surfacing later. Good day."

Mr. Greene strolled out of the room, eyes staring straight ahead as he headed down the hall.

"What's this about reports now?" Owen looked around, finding that the rest of the team didn't seem to share his confusion.

"Post-response reports," Galvanize told him. "PEERS are big targets for the occasional lawsuit. We'll have people we pull out of cars claim we caused exacerbations to their injuries, or that our presence made things worse, stuff like that. The company can usually beat them with telepaths, but those can get muddy, legally speaking, so one of the ways they combat it is to have us document everything we did. A lot of lawsuits have fallen apart when the person's story didn't match up at all to what we recorded."

"Sounds like a massive pain in the ass," Owen said. "No one mentioned paperwork."

"Why don't you blow it off then, like you did doing camera work?" Zone had been silent for most of the trip back, but it was immediately clear that it hadn't been because he had nothing to say. "Just let Galvanize stand in for you again. God forbid the legendary Hero cop up to his own fuck-ups."

"Zone, that's enough," Galvanize snapped.

"No, let him go." Owen patted Galvanize's shoulder then turned to face Zone. Looking the younger man in eye required Owen to tilt his head at a noticeable incline. "He's been biting back his tongue since I got here; that shit isn't healthy. Come on, kid, if you've got something to say then say it."

"Gladly! I think it was a mistake to bring you on. Mirror Fog was a Hero, but he wasn't like you. He was a decent guy, humble, never looking down on us. But you? From the minute you stepped in here you've acted like Babe Ruth sitting at a tee-ball game. Missing the photo-op is just one more example of the real problem: you think you're better than us. You didn't want to be seen with us. And while I'm used to that from Heroes, to see it from you just chaps my ass, because you are in no *fucking* way better than us. "

Zone's face was red, a vein bulging near the top of his forehead. He looked half-ready to swing; likely the only thing holding him back was the knowledge that it would injure his hand if he struck Titan's legendarily tough body. Owen leaned closer, until he was less than a foot from the fuming man's face.

"And what, pray tell, makes me so much worse than the other Heroes?"

"Because you're a goddamned coward." Zone spun around and stormed out of the living room, off toward the gym.

Owen stood there, frozen in place. He'd expected any number of things to come out of Zone's mouth: bigotry, arrogance, outright hate, but he hadn't been braced for that little bastard to cut to the quick of him.

Coward. That was what he'd called himself countless times over his years in exile. He'd tormented himself with that word for so long, but it had been a private pain. It had genuinely never occurred to him that others would see his failings all on their own.

"Ignore Zone; he's got a short fuse and an ego bigger than he needs," Galvanize said. "He'll calm down once I explain that you skipping the photos wasn't a personal slight."

"It's fine," Owen said at last. He looked over; it hadn't escaped his notice that while Galvanize was keeping the peace, Hexcellent and Bubble Bubble had both remained silent after Zone's rant. One look at their faces told him why: they agreed with their teammate. Maybe not about him being worse than other Heroes, but certainly about him thinking he was too good for them.

And they weren't really wrong, were they? He had been thinking that way, ever since Lenny handed him their folder.

"I promise, we'll get things smoothed out-"

"Just show me where to get one of those report things," Owen said, and Galvanize went quiet. "Please. I want to get it done with." As much as he would have liked to sink into a funk over his lifetime of failings, Owen needed to knock the paperwork out as soon as possible.

Little as he felt like going, he still had to meet with Gale.

13.

There were all sorts of Hero-themed bars and restaurants: Supper with Supers, Capes & Cocktails, and Planet Hero were only some of the more nationally franchised ones. For the most part they were horrendously tacky affairs, with staff wearing costumes and walls decorated in art featuring Heroes or sometimes vintage Hero memorabilia.

In larger cities, Heroes would frequent these establishments in costume, stopping in to have a quick beer or bite then sign autographs for the adoring fans. Such appearances were, of course, purchased by the respective establishment and carefully scheduled. They wanted patrons to think that any trip could lead to meeting a real-life Hero in the flesh.

Off-duty Heroes, or ones not contractually obligated to show up, avoided those places like they'd seen the kitchen. A real Hero bar was one that catered to them when the capes were off. This type of bar masqueraded as unassuming watering holes, a place akin to a dive without the rustic charm. There was, of course, no way to turn away non-Heroes without advertising what clientele they actually catered to. Instead, the staff made sure regular people didn't want to stay. Horrid service, flat beer at room temperature, and food that would turn a garbage disposal's stomach ensured that if you weren't supposed to be at a Hero bar, it wasn't a place you felt inclined to linger.

Owen felt the assessing stares as he stepped through the door of Brin's Gate, a small bar twenty minutes' jog from base. He was dressed in street clothes, as was everyone else here. Stepping into a place like this wearing a costume would have defeated the whole point. The staff, sizing him up from afar, could clearly see he was big. But "big" might only mean he was a Super, not a Hero, and even that required some assumptions. He'd probably be stuck getting treated like a mundane until Gale arrived and vouched for him.

"Hey, over here!" A breeze hit his left ear and Owen turned to find Gale standing up at a booth and waving him over. He noticed the staff relax, accepting him as a proper client. It usually took more than a wave to do that. Either this place had lax standards or Gale had more clout than Owen realized.

He lumbered across the room and slid onto the bench that awaited him. Instead of the usual groans and creaks he was accustomed to from furniture, the seat held firm. That was one thing about Hero bars: they either started out with reinforced furniture or very quickly learned to get some.

Gale was dressed in slacks and a blouse, the sort of outfit that said she might have just gotten off work or might be heading out for a proper dinner after her drink. In front of her was a cocktail, halfway watered down by the melted ice.

"Been waiting long?"

"I had another meeting here earlier, so I just hung around for this one," Gale replied. "I appreciate you being prompt."

"Course. We all have our schedules to keep."

The waitress came by, and Owen ordered a local beer. Once she left, he turned the conversation toward the most important subject, so far as he was concerned. "Everything go okay with Alexandria?"

"No issues. She made it to the facility without so much as a flare-up. I think it helped that she was a little star-struck." Gale was keeping a neutral face

69

while she examined Owen with attentive eyes. "I'm surprised you care so much about one Powered girl."

"First job back. Haven't had time to get jaded again. . . yet." Owen's beer arrived and he took a long draw from it. Dark, yeasty, and potent; he'd have to find out the name of the brewery so he could try more of their wares.

"About that. I was wondering what made you decide to leave retirement. And why you picked Brewster, Illinois, to reappear in, of all places. We're a decent-sized city, but we're no New York or Los Angeles."

"I left retirement because I wanted to start doing some good again," Owen said. "As for why I came here. . . my agent had set up shop locally, and this is where I got a job."

"You're on a team?"

"I'm. . ." The urge to lie, or at least tell half-truths, was almost overpowering. But Zone's words were still ringing in Owen's ears. He thought he was better than them, and what right did he have? Those kids didn't have his power or training, yet they were still doing the best they could to help people. Meanwhile, he'd taken all his abilities and holed up in Colorado. Like a coward.

"I'm working as a Hero Liaison for a team of Privately Employed Emergency Response Supers. I'm also going to do a little Hero work when time permits, but they're my main job."

Gale stared at him then let out a short, sharp, laugh. "You expect me to believe that Titan, *the* Titan, finally came out of hiding just to lead a bunch of corpies? I'm not an idiot."

"No, you're the leader of Elemental Fury, one of the most well-known teams in Brewster. It's been in existence for over two decades and you're the fourth leader they've had, presiding for the last three years. Your team is efficient, skilled, and great at minimizing collateral damage, which is probably part of why you're so liked by the citizens. It also means you're on top, which makes you a target for criminals and Heroes more concerned with image than the job. You think I'm the latter." Owen had done more than just paperwork in his time before the meeting; he'd also pulled up some background information on Gale. Knowledge was usually more useful than muscle, in his experience.

"Titan was quite a media juggernaut in his day. I find it hard to believe you plan on lying low. Seems like you might want to be the new big dog in town, and the only way someone with your rep could do that would be to make us look bad."

"I'm not here for the media, and I'm sure as shit not a gunner who is going to sabotage your PR. Those guys don't last as long as I did before I quit, and you know that."

"I'm not sure what I know when it comes to you," Gale said. "Nearly every piece of information I have on you is from hearsay and propaganda. The one thing I do know is that you're powerful and experienced, which makes you dangerous."

"Only if I come with ill intentions, which I don't."

"Why should I believe that? You come here and feed me a story about baby-sitting corpies, giving me nothing to go on. I'm not trying to be a bitch, Titan, but this is my city. I was born here, I grew up here, and I lay my life on the line every day to keep it safe. Glory-seekers are a real danger; they take

71

stupid risks that get people killed. For someone on your scale of power, that could be a whole lot of people."

"Gale, you can either trust me or not. What you can't do is stop me." Owen meant it in a general sense, but he saw her tense. She probably had a hurricane ready to go the moment he made a sudden move. "I mean that in a technical way. I've got my certification and my license. Until I do something worthy of bringing before the DVA, I'm free to fulfill my Hero duties as I see fit."

"I can make it hard on you."

"That just gets us into a stupid feud, and I don't need that kind of headache," Owen replied. "Here's what I'd suggest instead: watch me. Let my actions tell you if I'm here to hunt glory or here to help. If I fuck up, then you've got something to bring before the DVA. If not, well, maybe along the way you'll realize I'm telling the truth."

"You know damned well I was going to put surveillance on you anyway." Gale gulped down the last of her drink, half-melted ice cubes and all.

"It might have occurred to me." Owen gave a lopsided grin and finished his own drink.

"All right. I'll back off for now, on one condition."

"Let's hear it."

"I want you to come by my base for an ability assessment," Gale replied. "I'll feel more comfortable once I know what you can do, and it'll be interesting to see how my team stacks up against a legend."

"I'd have to schedule it around my own team. I wasn't kidding about them being my main priority."

"Understood. We'll shake our schedules and make something work. Bring them along if you like. Might be a thrill for them to see what a real Hero team looks like."

For a reason Owen couldn't yet define, that comment rankled him.

"I'll find a time. Hate to tell you this, though, but you were wrong about one thing."

"What's that?" Gale asked.

"Once you've seen what I can do, comfortable is the last thing you'll be feeling."

14.

The powerful knocking on his door roused Lenny from a pleasant dream. In it, he'd been just about to sign three coordinated Hero teams under a group contract, with a percentage that was so high he'd have never allowed himself to indulge it in real life. The caped leader had been putting his signature on the contract when he jerked, slamming his knee into the desk. Then he did it again, and again, over and over until Lenny tore free of his dream world and realized someone very strong was knocking on his door.

It took him exactly one guess to figure out who'd come a-calling. Truthfully, he'd expected this visit to come earlier.

"Gimme a damn minute!" Lenny rolled out of bed and put on his orthopedic slippers. Other men might have been embarrassed to greet a visitor comparable to the gods while wearing gray house-shoes. Other men lacked the brass-balled confidence of Lenny.

He trudged through his home, a one-bedroom apartment next door to his office, heading toward the door. Lenny could certainly afford better. One didn't get to be as renowned as he was without squirreling away a good nest egg, after all. But that was for when he retired. Lenny lived and breathed the job; you had to if you wanted to be good at it. The closest thing he'd had to a vacation in the last decade was when he went to the coast to bail one of his clients out of a drunken indecent exposure charge.

The knocking ceased as Lenny pulled open the door, revealing the mountainous form of Owen holding a twelve-pack.

"Can I come in?"

"Wipe your feet." Lenny trudged back in, heading for the kitchen. He heard the door close behind him as he reached into the fridge and pulled out one of the frozen coffee drinks his doctor said was bad for his stomach lining. "Tough shit, Doc," he muttered as he downed the frosty concoction. That done, Lenny walked back into the living room.

"So, I take it things are bad." He'd known Owen long enough to skip the preamble. The big lug was bothered about something, and Lenny was the only person he felt he could talk to. That in itself pretty much spoke to the problem: he wasn't getting on well with his new team, else he'd have been talking to them.

"They're not great." Owen cracked open a beer and took a lengthy sip. His body had long ago lost the ability to be affected by alcohol; that didn't mean he didn't find enjoyment in the flavor, though. "Looks like I've alienated my team by acting like I'm better than them, one member seems to have hated me before I walked in the door, and I managed to catch the eye of Elemental Fury's leader, Gale. She seems to think I'm here to cause waves and might just make it her goal to be a pain in my ass."

"That is pretty damned not great," Lenny agreed. He reached over and pulled a beer free from the case. If the man was going to barge into his home at almost midnight, the least he could do was share his drinks. "Not great, but not unmanageable either. Gale is a righteous bitch if she suspects someone of making trouble; however, she's one of the best people to have in your corner if she trusts you."

"One of your clients?"

"No, though I manage Birdsman and Granite, two people on her team. I'm involved enough to get a sense of her. Lady's got a lot of pressure on her to perform, and Brewster has been growing more active with criminal Supers over the last few years. Once she sees you're genuinely trying to help, she'll back off. Until then, just keep your temper in check and try to keep the dick-measuring to a minimum."

"Might be tough; she invited me over to do an ability assessment."

Lenny held in the exasperated sigh that might have escaped from an individual less tenured in his role. Ability assessments were officially used by Heroes when they were looking to work with someone and needed to know exactly what that person was capable of. Unofficially, they were a great way to put rookies in their place or settle grudges of which Super was more powerful. Heroes were good folk, but that much power and training definitely resulted in equally superhuman egos.

"Did you agree?"

"Sort of. I said I would do it when schedules aligned, so I bought some time at least." Owen gave a wide-shouldered shrug.

"It'll have to be enough. Let me try and finagle a few things. Until you hear from me, focus on your real problem: the team."

"That's the one I'm most clueless about," Owen admitted. "I know I'm pissing them off by acting like I'm better than them, but the thing is, that I *am* better. I've got more power, more training, and more experience, even with my time away from the life. They're good kids, and I respect Galvanize's attitude, but at the end of the day we exist on totally different levels. I have no idea how to make that gap disappear, and if I try to fake it, I'm pretty certain they'll hate me even more."

"No, don't fake it," Lenny advised. "These folks already get shit on by Heroes who see them as sell-out wannabes. If you start acting fake they'll think it means you've decided to placate them like children."

"Then what's my other option?"

"Tell them the truth," Lenny replied. "Meet it head-on like you would any other challenge. Let them know you're having trouble fitting in like you told me, except maybe don't be quite such a dick about it. Then, and this is key, realize what a fucking schmuck you're being."

"Schmuck?"

"Titan, you're a great Hero and an all-around unstoppable guy. No one could do your job like you," Lenny said. He ran his hand through the wisps of hair that remained on his bald head; this part would require careful wording.

"Thank-"

"But do you think you could do my job?"

"Be an agent?"

"Yes, be an agent. Handle PR disasters, coach rookies how to deal with the spotlight, wake up to console grown men who show up with beer in the middle of the night. Do you think you could do my job better than I do?" Lenny was wide awake now, locking eyes with the man who could kill him in a single motion and refusing to blink.

"Of course not. I mean, you're Lenny."

"Good, there is a bit of humility left in that skull of yours." Lenny let the staring contest lapse and leaned back into his chair. "Titan, you're a fucking beast of a Hero; never let anyone tell you different. Thing is, your job is not to be a Hero: not with this team. Your job is to be their liaison. And you kind of suck at that job. Being a good Hero is a wonderful achievement, but it doesn't automatically make you the best at everything. It just means when a Super needs putting down, you're the guy we call. If you need an agent, you call me, and if your toilet won't flush, you call a plumber. None of us is inherently better; some jobs are just more prestigious."

"I get it: just because I'm good at my job doesn't mean I'm better at theirs." Owen had the sense to look at least somewhat ashamed.

"You're damn right. So, my advice to you is to get to know these people, find out all the areas where they can smoke your ass. Learn to respect them, because they deserve it, and the rest of your problems will solve themselves."

"Thanks, Lenny. I don't know what I'd do without you." Owen stood up to go, reaching for his beer.

"Leave the case," Lenny instructed. "That's quality stuff and I have some new clients coming by tomorrow that I'd like to woo."

"Your midnight consultation rates have gone up," Owen said.

"Economy's a bitch," Lenny replied. "Now go home and sleep. You're going to need your rest, because you've got a lot of crow to eat in the morning."

15.

When Hexcellent walked into the living room the next morning, she was struck with a smell that was foreign and familiar all at once. She'd been with Mordent Holdings as a PEERS for over two years, subject to their rules, restrictions, and endless examinations. One aspect of that included a carefully controlled and monitored diet to ensure that everyone on the team looked camera-ready at all times. This meant that in her time doing the job she'd somehow managed to forget this heavenly aroma's source as a result of scarcity. This morning, though, the memory came flooding back as she witnessed Titan add his latest batch of flapjacks to an already sizable stack.

"Morning," he greeted. "I made pancakes." He was dressed in sweats again, though this time they were topped with a cream-colored apron what was far too small for him. This was no surprise; Hexcellent recognized it from their linen closet. It was a communal apron they used when cooking, and no one else on the team had the same proportions as Titan.

"Galvanize is going to fucking shit when he sees those," Hexcellent said, walking over to examine Titan's culinary efforts. She was clad in a black tanktop and silk pajama pants with silver spiderwebs stitched across the legs, attire demonstrating her intention of lazing about for as long as she was able.

"Why am I going to shit?" Galvanize stepped in from the hallway. Unlike the other two, he was fully dressed for the day. "And what's that smell?"

"Pancakes," Zone told him. He and Bubble Bubble were directly behind Galvanize; evidently the trio had just finished something and were coming toward the kitchen together.

Galvanize frowned, the expression strange on his perpetually positive face. "Titan, we can't have pancakes. They aren't on the approved dietary restriction list."

"These are. They're some sort of hippie-whole-grain-low-gluten-low-taste-clusterfuck, but they pass the bar for acceptable breakfast. I even checked it out with Greene first."

"That was. . . quite kind of you." Galvanize headed over, with Bubble Bubble trailing close behind. Zone took his own time in crossing the room.

"It wouldn't have been much of an apology if I made you something you couldn't eat. And that's what these are: apology pancakes. Last night I went for a walk and did a lot of thinking. What I ended up with was the realization that Zone was right: I have been thinking that I'm better than you four, which is stupid. You kids, sorry, you four do a damn respectable job and I've got no right putting myself above you just because we have different career histories."

"Nice words," Zone said. "But they don't mean shit without action."

"Zone, control yourself," Galvanize chided. "Our teammate just gave an honest apology and is trying to make amends. That is not the sort of thing we stomp down, regardless of our personal feelings."

"Let it go. I think Zone and I are going to have to square on some different issues sooner or later." The last of the pancakes were pulled from the griddle and slid onto a waiting plate already piled high. "But he's dead-right about words meaning nothing without action. Which is why I'd like you all to know something: my real name is Owen Daniels."

Zone's mouth had already been open, ready to snap something at him, but the words rotted on his tongue. Revealing one's name was far more personal than a face. Faces were changeable and concealable; names were dangerous. Names opened the door to research, to history, to learning everything there was to know about a person. It was widely regarded as fact that the only people Heroes shared their real names with were their families and their teams.

"Tit- Owen, that gesture means the world to us," Galvanize said. "Truly, it does."

"It's just a name," Owen replied. "The pancakes are the good gesture, or as good as this healthy stuff can be. I already stuck some of those juices you stock and chunks of fruit on the table. I thought we could all have a team breakfast, then move on to the next part of my efforts to stop acting like a prick."

"More than healthy pancakes and name-dropping? Sir, you do us too much honor," Hexcellent said. Despite her words, she did come over and help him with two of the pancakes-bearing plates.

"What can I say? I'm a giver by nature." Foul-mouthed and strange way of dress aside, Owen enjoyed his gothy teammate. She had the sort of spitfire nature he'd always been fond of. Hell, he'd liked one woman with it so much he'd managed to convince himself he loved her enough to marry.

"So what's the plan then?" Bubble Bubble took her seat at the table, piling her plate with mostly fruits and veggies alongside a single pancake.

"That's up to you four," Owen said, putting far more than one pancake on his plate. Health-assurances aside, he suspected the bulk of the eating would fall on his ample shoulders. "I want to learn about each of you, understand how everyone works on their own as well as on our team. I don't even know what your jobs entail outside of actual response work, and that's something that needs rectifying."

"Sounds like setting you up for a shadow day is the best option," Galvanize said. "Unfortunately, today I've got a debrief meeting about yesterday's fire. Even if I thought it would be educating, only the team's leader is allowed to attend. Bubble Bubble, how about you?"

"Photoshoot. He's welcome to tag along, but it's just going to be posing for five or six hours."

"Let's call that our last resort," Galvanize said. He looked over at Zone, who was silently stuffing food into his mouth while purposely avoiding any eye contact with Owen. Had he been only a tenth of the leader he was, Galvanize would still have seen that situation for the train wreck it represented. Instead, he turned his gaze to the girl with ink-bottle black hair. "Hexcellent, what have you got today?"

"Decent assortment," she replied, mouth half-full of berries and pancake. "Doing a store promo, then a mini-photo-shoot with Spyda, plus a small branding meeting. All that paired with the usual shit, of course."

"Of course. Well, Titan, if you really want to learn more about what we do when not saving people, I think Hexcellent is your best shot today. That work for you?"

"If she doesn't mind, I'd love to tag along," Owen said.

"Fine by me," Hexcellent replied. "It'll be nice to have someone to carry my bags other than Big Henry. He scratches up damn near everything he touches."

16.

Owen was surprised to find a car waiting for him and Hexcellent. They'd finished breakfast and gotten into their respective costumes, then headed down to the street level. Hexcellent walked without pause to a dark sedan idling at the curb.

"You don't drive?"

"Company policy," Hexcellent sighed. "Two years ago one of their former PEERS got into a fender-bender with some old lady. She developed back problems, went after him and Mordent in court, and generally drummed up a lot of bad press, not to mention drained some cash out of their pockets. Now we're only allowed to use a car service, unless we're driving to an actual response in the approved vehicle. Keeps us from being liable."

"Also keeps you from going anywhere they don't know about," Owen added.

"For a guy whose whole career is built on having Armageddon-level muscles, you're pretty quick on the uptake." Hexcellent climbed into the back seat, followed by her massive coworker, and the car maneuvered back into traffic.

"I'm actually not Armageddon," Owen told her once they were buckled up. Laws were laws, even if he was effectively invulnerable. The minute a Hero began to think he was above them was the same moment his downfall began.

"Really? I thought you were this legendary dude with impossible strength."

"I am, but that doesn't change the fact that it's pretty much impossible for a strongman to be considered an Armageddon Class threat. We just don't have the damage capacity."

Hexcellent cocked her head to the side; today's blasting of makeup made her look like a somewhat befuddled bat. "Damage? Isn't the rating system like a power-level thing?"

"No, but a lot of people mistake it for that, even some Heroes." Owen tried to cross his legs in an effort to find a more comfortable position, but this only resulted in him slightly bending the window lever. "People have tried putting a level system in place plenty of times, actually, it just never holds up. First off, we're always learning about new people and powers that make us rethink things in terms of scale. Plus, it always goes to shit in that lots of powers negate or overwhelm each other. For example, a good telekinetic can knock most strongmen out of a battle by lifting them off the ground, even if the strongman would be rated higher in terms of raw power."

"You're explaining to me how there's no level system to help me understand the level system," Hexcellent pointed out. "I've got some old Algebra teachers you'd fit in just great with."

"Sorry, I just wanted to show why measuring Supers by level doesn't work. What you can measure, regardless of their power, is their capacity for destruction. As I recall, the default rule is it's how much damage a Super could do if left unchecked for an hour."

"Sounds sort of morbid, and that's coming from a girl wearing zombie-themed lipstick."

Owen nodded. "You won't hear me disagreeing. It serves a purpose, though: knowing someone's class tells you how dangerous they are. It informs on how we prioritize protecting civilians, minimizing property damage, and escalating force. There's minimal need to try to cripple or kill a Standard Class threat if subduing is an option."

"What if they're higher up the chain?"

"Then we do what has to be done. No Hero, at least none that lasts, enjoys that part of the job. But if we don't stop them, innocent people will die. Personally, I always try to subdue or de-escalate first for anything below Armageddon Class. Bear in mind, my power gives me that as an option. Others aren't so lucky."

"Jesus, and here I thought all you people did was pick kittens out of trees and foil bank heists." Hexcellent's eyes were wide, creating a strange contrast between the whites of her sclera and the ink-black of her makeup.

"PR departments try to de-emphasize that aspect of the job, same as with cops. It might be necessary, but that doesn't mean people like to think about it."

"No shit." Hexcellent turned to look out the window for a bit, watching the buildings roll by. "So what are these classes, then? Like, where would I fit in?"

"You'd be a Standard Class," Owen replied. "Most Supers are. It means you can do some significant damage and are a danger to life; however, you're not a threat to a large-scale area."

"Great, I'm lowest rung."

"Actually, that would be the NTC Class. It stands for Non-Threatening Combatant, though we just call them 'knocks' for short. That nickname comes from the fact that one little tap to the head can usually bring them down. They're Supers whose abilities are in no way dangerous, meaning they have the same propensity for damage as a regular human. Healers, people with low-caliber display abilities, that sort of thing."

"But Healers become Heroes, they can't be that weak," Hexcellent said.

"It's not about weak or strong, just about immediate destructive potential," Owen reminded her.

"All right: so it goes NTC, Standard, then I'm guessing there's something between that and Armageddon."

"Two steps: Demolition Class and Manhattan Class. Demo, which is my actual classification by the way, means a Super could level several city blocks if left unchecked. Manhattan means the level of destruction they can wreak would be roughly on par with a nuclear bomb. That's why Supers like me never hit too high on the scale; we just can't cover enough ground to be considered a massive threat."

"Well damn. Here I thought we were at least getting a hot-shit Hero and you're not even in the second to best class? Maybe we should see if Galvanize thinks you're really cut out for the penthouse." Hexcellent smiled at him, showing more warmth than she seemed to share with some of her other team members.

"You can try to throw me out, but I should warn you: I've kicked the dogshit out of countless Manhattans and even a few Armageddons. They might be better at large-scale destruction, but I'm in the top when it comes to one-on-one."

"Unless a telekinetic lifts you in the air," Hexcellent reminded him.

"I said that works on most strongmen. I'm not among that number."

"That so? Please enlighten me, great Hero, what secret technique do you use for getting out of such a precarious situation?"

Owen reached into the belt of his uniform and pulled out a few steel balls roughly the size of marbles. "I throw these at whoever lifts me. They'll at least break the person's concentration, and if I hit them, the problem pretty much takes care of itself."

"No way that works. I've seen a bunch of telekinetic Heroes hold shields while doing other stuff. They could just block them."

Owen slipped the balls back into his belt pouch and gave Hexcellent a smile of his own. "Shields, like everything else in this world, can only take so much. Put enough force behind it and the right blow can shatter them."

"You'd have to be throwing pretty damned hard."

"Unlike keeping my mouth shut, that's one of the few things I do well," Owen said.

17.

The store promo, as Galvanize had called it, turned out to be little more than thankless glad-handing at the opening of the latest Fiery Discussion, Hexcellent's most prominent sponsor. There was a small crowd there, no doubt drawn by the advertised sales and giveaways meant to promote the new store's presence in the South Brewster mall. A small black tent was partially obscuring the mall's walkway; it housed the store's staff, along with several corporate representatives gathered to greet the eager shoppers. As a representative of Mordent Holdings, the conglomerate that ultimately owned this "rebellious" company, Hexcellent was tasked with circulating through the meager audience.

More people recognized her than Owen had expected. This mystery resolved itself when he glanced through the glass storefront and realized she was heavily featured in posters on the walls. Even those who didn't seem to recognize her greeted Hexcellent with some warmth: that is, the males among them did. Hexcellent was pretty in a way that appealed to the store's particular clientele; at the same time, the way she used the store's products still showcased her natural gifts. True, she wouldn't be winning any classic beauty pageants even if she did scrub the makeup and tattoos away, but that was what they liked about her. She didn't look like a model grabbing a paycheck; she appeared to be the genuine article. Since Owen had seen her dress in similar fashions while on her off-time, he had no reason to suspect that wasn't the case.

"Nice costume."

Owen glanced down, noticing a gangly male somewhere in his teens staring up at him. Despite all the reasons he had to don his nondescript mask, Owen had shown up in full Titan uniform. He sat away from the corporate folks.

As a Hero he needed to take care not to accidentally endorse their products, but he still drew attention as he towered over the rest of the crowd.

"Thanks. Do I look like the real deal?"

"I mean, it's close, but the real Titan used bolder reds and had different stitching along the seams. Plus, he was taller, not that you can really help that. Still, all in all it's a commendable job. I bet you could win a few prizes at conventions if you attended."

Owen suppressed the urge to frown as the teen wandered off to find a new novelty to occupy his time until the doors opened. On one hand, he was glad not to have been recognized. It helped that almost no one knew Titan was back. But. . . taller? It was those damn television cameras, always choosing the perfect angles, making him look like he was even bigger than he was.

"Anyone pieced together that you're the genuine article yet?" Hexcellent asked, walking over with a water bottle in hand. It surprised him how few swears she'd used since they arrived, but he supposed even among this crowd certain personality aspects required corporate sanitization.

"Not so far," Owen replied. "Though that last kid said my costume was 'close.' So, that's progress."

Hexcellent snorted, trying not to spray water from her nose then quickly turning away lest any of the audience should see her near-mishap. "It's your own fault," she said as she delicately wiped her face, careful not to smudge any makeup. "You've got that gray mask, you could have come semi-incognito."

"Forget it; I'm here with you. We're part of a team. Sooner or later people will realize that Hexcellent and Titan are working together. Think of how thrilled these folks will be when they can say they were at the first public appearance."

"You severely overestimate how many fucks are given about our team." Hexcellent caught the curse only after it had exited her mouth and glanced around frantically to make sure no one else had heard. "What I mean is, yes, they'll shake my hand and all, but at the end of the day, that has way more to do with my face and body than with my professional exploits. Same is true for everyone on the team."

"I disagree," Owen replied. "You all save lives for a living. Just because this group doesn't understand and respect that doesn't mean there aren't others who do. I bet at least one kid you've pulled out of a wrecked car or burning building has a poster of you over his bed."

"Trust me; I've seen the sales numbers, and statistically your statement is probably true. Personally, I try not to think about all the other posters of me that get sold. You know, to people who don't know my name. Gives me the creepy-shivers."

One of the men wearing a collared shirt with the Fiery Discussion emblem on it was waving Hexcellent back over. It seemed they were nearly ready to open the doors, meaning Hexcellent had to stand by to do another round of greetings and handshakes that lingered a bit too long. Owen watched her leave when his ears suddenly pricked up.

"Titan, are you able to take assignments?"

He didn't jump in surprise at Dispatch's voice humming in his ear this time; maybe he would get the hang of this again sooner than he thought. By plugging his earpiece in that morning, he'd put himself on the grid of Heroes without going officially active. While he didn't anticipate a need so great they had to rally coverage, it was still his obligation to be prepared for such things.

Owen pulled a cell phone from his pocket and stuck it to his ear before he spoke. No need to make people worry that the enormous, muscle-bound man was also having a psychotic break. "I'm working as a Hero Liaison right now, so I'm not taking assignments unless there's a severe shortage or tremendous threat. Then I'll do my part."

A slight pause came before Dispatch's reply. "Status recorded. There is a disturbance some distance from you. It is escalating, but the responding Heroes are establishing control. Should you be needed, teleportation will be arranged. If you hear nothing from me in the next fifteen minutes, consider the issue resolved."

"Gotcha. What is this situation, anyway?"

"Mechanical constructs with capable weaponry and high levels of adaptability. Appeared and began wreaking property damage roughly ten minutes ago in the south-western area of the city. Elemental Fury has now arrived on the scene and diminished their numbers by forty percent. Likelihood of your needed intervention is dropping, but stay ready."

"Of course."

Owen put the phone away since their conversation had momentarily ended. Dispatch wasn't really gone; she never stopped being right there. She was simply not talking, at least to him. If Elemental Fury, Gale's team, was as good as their reputation then he probably wouldn't be needed. Even knowing that, Owen looked around to find the most likely route of entrance for a teleporter to take. In a real battle, nothing was ever certain, no matter how good the Heroes were.

Hexcellent looked up from her crowd and flashed him a pained oh-god-how-much-longer-do-I have-to-do-this grin. He responded with a small wave, doing all he could to tamp down the sudden spike of pre-battle anxiety rising in his gut.

18.

When Dispatch's voice crackled in Owen's ear, they were outside the mall, only a few yards from the town car that would whisk them away to their next location.

"Titan, you have hostile constructs closing on your location. Elemental Fury led the counterattack to wipe out the first wave, but a second appeared and scattered in various directions. One cluster is on a path that will intersect with your location in less than five minutes. Can you respond?"

Owen had stopped walking when he heard Dispatch speak, causing Hexcellent to shoot him a look of confusion. He held up one finger, gave a small shrug of apology, then replied to Dispatch.

"I can. One the Supers from my PEERS team is with me; do we have time to get her clear?"

"Negative. The constructs caused several accidents, leading to traffic congestion on every applicable route to safety. We have responders working on clearing roads, but until they're done, getting in a car will put her at higher risk."

"Excuse me, did you just ask if I could 'get clear'?" Hexcellent said, narrowing her eyes and sticking a hand on her hip. "If something's going down, I'm one of the people helping, remember, dipshit?"

"We've got robots or something like it less than five minutes away. If they come, it's possible they'll go after you, and I don't want to get you in trouble for engaging in combat," Owen explained. "Unfortunately the roads are jammed, so you're stuck here."

"Well, that sucks. But they're coming to us, right?"

"That's what I'm told."

"Then if I get attacked I can respond in self-defense. Just because we can't start shit doesn't mean we can't end it when some other douchenozzle does." A wry, daring smile lit up her face at the prospect of sanctioned battle. Owen again found himself wondering why a woman like this hadn't found her way into the HCP. It was a curiosity that would have to be sated another time.

"All right, I'm ready to respond and I've got a PEERS with me to help with the civilians. What can you tell me about these things?" He turned away from Hexcellent, not because he thought his words would in any way be muffled, but rather as a polite way of indicating that he wasn't speaking to her. Dispatch didn't require any such indicators; she always knew what was external conversation and what was meant for her. It was one of the many strange, yet useful, aspects of the mysterious voice.

"You have four heading toward your location. They have strength and resilience on par with a Standard Class strongman, laser weaponry on par with a Standard Class blaster, and reaction speed at elevated-human levels."

"If that's all there is then I don't see why they caused such trouble," Owen prodded.

"They also show adaptability to tactics, learning from the mistakes of others. Given your skillset, I do not foresee it being an issue. The other unique capability of these constructs is that they show minor regeneration. Disabled units would reenter combat after being left alone for some time. They cannot heal beyond complete dismemberment or destruction, however."

Owen stretched out his arms, tensing every muscle from his shoulder to his fingers. After a moment, he rose up on his toes, adding his legs to the procedure. He felt the mild strain in his tendons, and for an instant he was intimately aware of every fiber of muscle in his massive body. Ever-so-slowly, he released the stretch, pulling his arms back in and lowering down on his feet. It should only be a minute or so now.

"Hit them hard, hit them fast, and don't stop until they are scrap. That it?"

"That will neutralize the threat. We have others trying to gain information out of their wreckage and systems, but I'm aware your talents lie in other directions. They have continued on their current course and will be breaking into your line of sight momentarily."

With a squint of his eyes, Owen could make out the shimmering shapes of four sizable humanoids running toward him. They were big, probably a little taller than he was. Not that it would help them. He pulled back his left leg and judged the distance. It had been a while since he'd pulled this trick; Owen hoped he hadn't lost the touch.

"Am I finally going to see the legendary Titan let loose on some motherfuckers?" Hexcellent's tone was light but she'd positioned herself several feet behind him. Her attention was split, eyes darting between her teammate and the mall entrance where shoppers were already beginning to line up and point.

"I'll do my best to put on a good show, but to be honest, this is probably going to be a pretty boring fight. Stay ready, though; if any of them get past me, you'll have to draw attention from the humans."

"Big Henry ain't exactly a subtle sumnabitch, if you hadn't noticed," Hexcellent replied. She hadn't summoned any of her demons yet, but Owen had seen how quickly she could pull them. It was the right call; bringing them out might panic the civilians. Best to let him settle things quickly.

With a nod to Hexcellent and a minor grunt born more out of habit than effort, Owen pushed against the concrete with enough power that it cracked under his boots. The force of the jump sent him sailing forward in an arc more long than high, carrying him across the parking lot to where four metal behemoths were just arriving on the asphalt.

Whether by luck or skill, Owen hit his mark dead-on, landing only a few feet away from the cluster of constructs. The concrete sprayed them as he effortlessly tore through it upon landing. Before any of them had a chance to register him as a threat, Owen sprang. He darted up to the two on the left and slammed a hand into the torso of each. Flexing his fingers, he easily shredded their armored facades and gripped the firm inner workings that kept them moving.

His guess had been close on their size; each was nearly half a foot taller than he was. Despite this, he showed no apparent effort as he lifted the two constructs off the ground, spread his arms, and then clapped them together like two high-tech tambourines. Sparks and shards of metal rained down on Owen, who ignored it all just as he'd been ignoring the flailing blows that the two bots had been pelting him with since he arrived. He pulled them apart and banged them together again, and again, and again. After the fourth strike there was barely enough left to hold, let alone smash, so he dropped the remains of his first victims and turned to the other two.

This was the first time Owen got a good look at them, as he'd deformed the ones he held too quickly to get a mental picture. Each one possessed a small, dome-like head, as though someone had spray-painted a bowl and turned it upside down. They had awkward, triangular torsos and forearms that were vastly oversized and out of proportion. That anomaly explained itself quickly, as the one on his right raised its hands and fired red beams at Owen's chest.

He'd forgotten Dispatch's warning about the lasers. Owen dashed forward to the one attacking him, ignoring the slightly-singed smell of roasting costume, and grabbed it by one of its triangular shoulders. If the robot had the capability of feeling surprise, it certainly didn't get an opportunity to do so. With his other hand snaring its waist, Owen ripped the metal warrior in half as easily as one would tear serrated paper. Just for good measure, he quickly tore it into a few more pieces before scattering the remains about with a whip of his arm.

Spinning on his heel, he found the last one shuffling on its feet. Dispatch had said these things learned and were adaptable. It was probably trying to compute a strategy to overcome him.

"Good luck with that," Owen chuckled. The robot stopped shuffling for the barest of instants, and Owen pounced.

It was too bad, really. He had wanted to put on a better first exhibition for his new teammate.

19.

"Are you completely invulnerable or some shit?"

Hexcellent had been largely silent after they had calmed the civilians and let a DVA cleanup team grab the robot scrap. She'd mostly just been skimming her phone and throwing occasional, furtive glances his way until they had hopped into the town car waiting to take them to their next destination.

"No one is truly invulnerable," Owen told her. How many times had he used those words? Not only to fans or interviewers, but to upcoming Supers who hadn't yet learned how important a lesson that was.

"Yeah, you say that, but those robo-douches were whaling on you the whole time you had them, and one hit you full-force with lasers that could tear through concrete and steel. That seems pretty invulnerable to me."

"I never said I wasn't tough; that's part of my power. Invulnerable implies beyond all means of injury, and no one has that ability. No matter who you are, no matter how strong your power, we all have a weakness." Owen paused for a moment and considered her words. "Wait, how do you know what their lasers could do?"

Hexcellent waved her phone, which was really no more than a big screen, in his face. "It's all over the web. Those things did a shitload of damage before Heroes got there, and even then managed to put a few out of the fight. You went through them like Thai food through Zone."

Owen scrunched his brow in response.

"Oh, right, you haven't been here for Pan-Asian cuisine night. Just be glad we all have our own bathrooms. Also, the point was that you fucking wrecked them."

"I had the benefit of knowledge on my side. The others went in blind, but I got to know what they could and couldn't do. That let me tackle them efficiently, without having to worry about them secretly being explosive or having enough firepower to bring me down. First response is always the hardest, most dangerous work," Owen explained.

"Yeah, I get it, humility, politeness, and blah blah blah. Did they at least get all of those things?"

"They did." When Owen had told Dispatch about bringing his down, she'd updated him on the rest of the threat. The second wave had been smaller and less organized than the first; by the time a crew was picking up the remains of his fight, the rest had already been terminated.

"What do you think they wanted, anyway? To rob the food court?"

"Honestly, I think they were a test run," Owen replied.

"Wait, that was a fucking beta trial?"

"It's my theory." Owen glanced out the window, marveling at how quickly they'd gotten the messes cleaned up and traffic flowing. "Those things were strong, but they had some serious design flaws. Add in the lack of a clear objective, and it points to someone seeing how his first batch of bots stacked up against the town's Heroes. You'd be surprised how many tech-genius Supers use the exact same opening gambit."

"Oooh, or what if the robots sprang to life and got away from him? They surged out of the laboratory, hell-bent on destruction of the human world. Titan, you may have just helped stop the robot-apocalypse." Hexcellent reached over and patted him on the head, stretching her long arms to their limit. "Good boy."

"You just pretty much drift along in your own world, don't you?"

"I'm a quasi-celebrity. I think we can both agree that's my right." Hexcellent stopped patting as the town car whispered up to a curb. Before she could reach the handle, the door swung open and a hand literally covered in tattoos reached in. It delicately took Hexcellent's hand and helped pull her out of the vehicle as Owen emerged on his own side.

He surfaced to see Hexcellent lip-locked with a man whose bald head and face were nearly as tattooed as his hands. After a kiss long enough to register as uncomfortable for all bystanders, the two finally parted.

"What kept you?" The tattooed man had a slightly southern twang to his voice, the sort of lingering accent that belonged to people who tried to remove it from their voice. Owen might not have noticed it, but his time with his ex-wife, Sally, and her south Texas family had trained him to pick up on the vibrations.

"Robots causing traffic," she replied. Hexcellent turned around and pointed at Owen. "This big bastard is Titan, our team's new Hero Liaison. Titan, this is Spyda, my boyfriend."

"Pleasure to meet you." Spyda walked around the car and grabbed Owen's vast hand in an enthusiastic shake. The Hero was a bit taken back at how friendly this man who looked like an advertisement for biker gangs was being.

Hexcellent seemed to read the expression on his face, even through the mask. She explained, "Spyda is a guitarist for a hardcore metal band. Don't let the look fool you, he's actually a fucking softy."

"But let's keep that between us. Image and all to consider, I'm sure you understand." Spyda released Owen's hand and turned back to Hexcellent. "Darling, I hate to rush you, but the photographer doesn't have much time left and we'll both catch heat if the shoot isn't done."

"Lucky for you, my hot ass is always camera ready," Hexcellent replied. "Titan, you can hang out in the prep room if you want. We shouldn't be more than an hour."

"You two go on ahead, I'm going to take a walk," he said. "I'll be here when you get out."

"See you then," Hexcellent called as they head toward the front door of the large office building.

"It was wonderful meeting you," Spyda added before they vanished behind the frosted glass door.

As soon as they were gone, Owen turned and headed up the street. He'd seen an internet café on their way over, and Hexcellent had piqued his interest to see whatever footage was already online. Back in his day they had to rely on the scrap footage put together from cameras sewn into the team member's costumes. Now, with a whole world watching, it would be interesting to look at an attack from so many different angles.

Besides, his experience told him that this wouldn't be the last rampage of robots from whatever low-rent techie had cobbled them together. Best to see as much as he could and be ready for next time. If these things had really brought other Heroes down, Owen had a feeling he would be called in a lot sooner when they resurfaced.

20.

When Hexcellent emerged from her photo shoot, Owen was already waiting by the town car. Despite his best efforts at the internet café, he hadn't been able to pull up much more than he'd learned from Dispatch. The civilian videos and pictures seemed to capture a few interesting moments of the robots fighting Heroes, but nothing that gave him information on their abilities beyond what he'd experienced personally. Of course, that didn't mean such video didn't exist, only that it wasn't easily discoverable. Despite the advances in technology since he left the life, he suspected the DVA's attitude on showing the public confidential information hadn't changed.

"Sorry we ran over," Hexcellent said, sliding into her seat. "That photographer was a shitshow. Had me changing outfits every five minutes and getting into impossible positions. If she weren't so damn good I'd have told her to fuck off like twenty times."

"Don't worry about it, I found a way to kill time."

"Let me take a shot in the dark: you spent it trying to learn more about those bots you fought." Hexcellent flashed him a cocky grin as the town car began the drive back to the Mordent Holdings office.

"Am I that obvious?"

"Obvious seems like a mean way to put it. How about we say dedicated?" Hexcellent pulled her phone out and began checking mail and messages. "You've been with us for a few days now, and I've only seen you really light up two times: when you were pulling that fire-girl from the building, and when you were tearing those scrapheaps new metal assholes. After you darted off as soon as we left the car, it didn't take a lot to figure out what was up."

"You're pretty observant," Owen replied, glancing at her out of the side of his eye. Smart, determined, not shy about confrontation, and with an ability that showed strong potential. The more time he spent with Hexcellent, the more she seemed like a candidate for the HCP. It was certainly possible she'd rejected that sort of life, preferring the more pacifistic work of being on a PEERS team, but he had trouble buying such an idea. The girl had a streak of grit and violence running through her; a trait like that usually led to a job where it could be expressed.

"Let's not get heavy on the compliments; like I said, you didn't really make it hard." Hexcellent's eyes widened a touch as she stared into the depths of her phone's screen. "Say, when you were researching, did you notice anything interesting about the fight at the mall?"

"I didn't look it up," Owen said. "Since I was there for all of it, there wasn't anything I needed to know. I figured the time was better spent reading up on the first wave of attacks."

"Ahhh. That explains it." Hexcellent put her phone away and tried to keep a straight face, though a defiant smirk keep worming its way across her mouth.

"Going to tell me what's so funny?"

"Hell fucking no. You can wait until we get back to the penthouse. This is too good to spoil."

Owen considered pressing the subject, but thought better of it. Hexcellent was willful and stubborn; she'd demonstrated that since he first arrived. If she thought it was more fun to wait, then that is exactly what she would do. Besides, the day had gone pretty well. May as well let it end on whatever positive note she had in mind.

Hours later, he would look back on that naivety with the clarity of hindsight and wonder when in his absence he'd allowed himself to get so stupid.

*   *   *

Lenny popped an antacid as he watched Gale walk over to him. Though her costume wasn't especially sexualized, the woman had a certain appeal that no amount of clothing could bury. In his younger years, when libido was able to fight with bottom-lines and ethics, Lenny had tried to woo a few female Heroes. He'd even pulled it off a couple of times, but it never ended well. He was as married to his job as any of them, and when that was the case, the pressure got to be too much for a romantic relationship to bear. Still, seeing Gale stride across the conference room in Elemental Fury's headquarters made him wish, just a little, that he was still young and dumb enough to swing for the fences.

"Gale, you look lovely, as always." Lenny rose from the serviceable chair he'd been sitting in, taking her hand and shaking it firmly. While some female Heroes liked a warm welcome and perhaps a kiss to the cheek, Gale was all business.

"Lenny, a pleasure to see you." Gale took her own seat, and Lenny followed suit. "I apologize for making you wait; the construct attack caused our whole team to be delayed."

Lenny waved a hand through the air like he was trying to smack an invisible fly. "Please, it's nothing. When you work with Heroes, you learn to write your appointments in pencil. There are far more important things out there than me; I'm just thankful you were willing to take this meeting at all."

"Birdsman and Granite hold you in high esteem," Gale said. The barest traces of a smile crested her lips. "Though I must admit, my own agent cursed you from here to the heavens when I told him I was taking a meeting with you."

"Mick's a solid guy, but he knows how to hold a grudge. Ever since a few of his A-listers decided to come over to my camp, he's been convinced I'm out to steal every client he's got."

"And is that what brings you here today?" Gale asked.

"If I thought I had a shot at pulling it off, you'd better believe I'd try and woo you," Lenny admitted. "But I do my research, and that means I know you're the loyal type. So long as Mick does right by you, you're going to stay with him. Of course, if he ever fails in that regard, expect to get some very nice wine with my card attached."

"At least you're honest about your intentions. Shall we get down to the business of why you've come here, then?"

"Gladly." Lenny shifted slightly in his seat. The chairs were made for tall, powerful people and didn't accommodate his small and round frame as adequately. "I'm here about you requesting to do an ability assessment with one of my clients."

"I haven't asked any. . . wait, you rep Titan?" The shock on her face was easily visible even through her mask.

"Always have, from the day he first stepped out of the Sizemore Tech HCP. Even sent him birthday cards during what I've chosen to think of as his 'hiatus.' I'd tell you he's a good man and is out here trying to make right by the world, but I doubt you'd really take my word for it."

"Agents aren't exactly renowned for their truthfulness," Gale said. "I take it you're here to try and talk me out of the assessment, to tell me that I should just leave Titan alone and forget about him."

"Talk you out of it? Why in the nine hells would I want to talk you out of it?" Lenny reached for the briefcase at his side, pulling it up and slapping it on the table. "Elemental Fury, the current top team in Brewster, testing out Titan, a living legend come forth from the past. People would sell their kids to see that kind of show. And not the black sheep, either, kids they really like."

Gale felt herself grow suddenly uncomfortable. Despite being bigger, stronger, and overall more powerful than the bald man sitting before her, Gale had the unmistakable sensation that he was trying to make a play for control of the situation.

"Hero assessments are generally held in private," she said.

"Oh sure, when they're real assessments that makes total sense. But this isn't a real assessment, is it? This is a pissing match you set up so that you could try and intimidate Titan into toeing the line."

"I wouldn't-"

"You don't need to deny it or defend yourself to me. Honestly, I love the idea. The only problem is that you didn't think big enough. If we're going to do this, we're going to make it profitable." Lenny pulled out a stack of papers and shoved them over to Gale. "Basic contracts regarding filming and distribution rights of the event. Show them to Mick, but even he'll admit I gave you a damn fair shake. Once you've signed we'll get the scheduling worked out."

Gale flipped through the pages, scanning paragraph after paragraph of small type and large words. Finally, she set it down and looked the short man dead in the eyes.

"Why are you doing this?"

"Because you created an unfair situation," Lenny replied, snapping his briefcase shut. "If the assessment is private and you make Titan look like shit, then you get what you wanted: the old dog will feel like he's not up to the life anymore. If it's private and he stomps you all, however, nothing really bad happens to you. A little wound licking and maybe some humbled egos, but nothing horrid. To me, that seems like bullshit. Putting pride on the line is only a good way to gamble when both go in at equal stakes. Now, with an audience, if Titan handles that assessment like a pro, you get to look like start-ups who can't hold a candle to the old guard. You can still call it off if you want, of course, but if you go forward with it then it will be under my terms."

"Don't you mean Titan's terms?" Gale asked.

"That big lug has no idea I'm doing this. He'll probably shit a chicken when he finds out. This is me, all me, doing my job and protecting my client's interests." Lenny hopped out of his chair, briefcase clutched firmly in hand. "Tell Mick to fax those over when they're ready. He knows the number."

"You may be the most ruthless agent I've ever spoken to, let alone dealt with," Gale said, still a bit dumbfounded by Lenny's surprise strategy.

"It's also why I'm the best." Lenny pulled out a business card and set it on the table. "Just in case you want to shop around for a new rep once this is over."

"I thought you said there'd be wine, too."

"Give me a little credit here," Lenny said. "It's already been delivered to your room."

21.

As soon as he stepped through the door from the elevator hallway to the living room, Owen realized something was up. Granted, Hexcellent's inability to stop smirking and snickering throughout the entire drive back had clued him in that he was in for some sort of surprise, but seeing Mr. Greene standing there, with Galvanize nearby, drove the point the rest of the way home.

"Oh shit, did I screw something up?" Owen held the door for Hexcellent, who scampered through and immediately made a beeline for the large television on the other side of the room. She snatched up the remote from Zone, who was sitting next to Bubble Bubble as she surfed the web on a slim tablet.

"Not at all," Galvanize quickly assured him. "This is something that we knew would happen eventually. "It was part of the package when we chose you to fill the role of our Hero Liaison."

"While that is true, we also had planned a nice, well-framed release of the information specially designed to cast you in a positive, crowd-tested, sentiment," Mr. Greene added. He wasn't angry; men like him were too proper to ever get angry. Instead, he was "putout" : a careful combination of annoyance, discontent, and resolve. Owen had known a lot of people like Greene in his life, and he'd prefer someone who called him a fucker and took a swing at him far above people who got put-out.

"Could someone at least tell me what I'm in trouble for?"

"You're not in trouble, dumbass. You're just not our little secret anymore." Hexcellent made this announcement just before she drilled her finger into the television's volume button, filling the room with crystal clear sound from expensive surround-sound speakers.

"-which were cleaned up less than an hour later. Neither Elemental Fury nor Shifter's Assembly were able to be reached for comment.

"If you're just joining us, today in downtown Brewster several automated robots attempted to carve a path of destruction before being thwarted by several of our local Hero teams. Later tonight our team will tell you what this most recent uptick in violence will mean for your weekend.

"In related news, the most surprising part of today's attack was not the robots themselves, but who appeared to help stop them."

The picture on the television switched from the anchor with perfectly-sprayed hair and unnervingly white teeth to shaky footage clearly taken by someone with a cell phone. It only took Owen a glance to recognize what was happening on the film. It wasn't hard to remember; after all, he'd been there only a couple of hours ago.

"Sources have confirmed that the man in the picture is in fact Titan, a Hero formerly associated with the Chicago area and known for both his strength and the scandal that drove him out of the public eye over a decade ago. Already people are having powerful reactions to his reappearance;, let's go to Janice-"

Hexcellent hit mute, then turned to Owen. "Seems you still look enough like yourself to get recognized."

Owen allowed himself a brief moment's chuckle. "I bet that kid from the store opening is pissed he didn't grab an autograph."

"I'm glad you two find this so amusing, because your little escapade has torched our entire plan for announcing your new position and controlling the spin of the story," Mr. Greene snapped. "Dozens of carefully planned, focus-group-tested events and promotions all rendered useless because you couldn't stop yourself from punching some robots."

"Hang on now, are you trying to give me shit for doing my job? Hero Liaisons are still Heroes, we have responsibilities to the public. I'll say I'm sorry that this made controlling your precious image harder, but if you're waiting for me to apologize for stopping threats to innocent people and property then you better have a toilet and a novel handy, cause it'll be a while."

"No one is upset with you for stopping those things," Galvanize said, hurriedly stepping in. "Mr. Greene just wishes you'd told us as soon as it happened so he could have gotten ahead of the story. It's my fault as much as anyone's. I should have briefed you on that policy before you and Hexcellent went out this morning. It just didn't occur to me that anything would happen."

"Are you kidding?" Zone said from the couch. "How could it not? Once he was away from us I bet Titan couldn't wait to get the cameras on him. He probably called in favors specifically to have them routed to him, all so he could play big bad Hero for the camer- OW!"

The last bit came as Hexcellent took the remote still clutched in her hand and brought it down on Zone's well-gelled head. It struck so hard that the back flew open and one of the batteries popped out.

"Cut the fucking temper tantrums, Zone. He didn't do shit. Titan came with me, stayed properly to the sidelines, and minded his manners the entire day. The only reason he took on those robots is because they were literally coming right for us. I've watched videos of what those things did to downtown, and if he hadn't hung around to tear them up, that mall would be in pieces and at least some people would be dead. Even at that, he still took the time to try and get me away to safety before fucking those things up. Be a pissy bitch all you want about real shit, but there was a situation that needed handling and Titan handled it. End of story."

For a moment, the air between the two teammates grew very tense. There was a second, a very long and dangerous second, when Owen thought Zone was legitimately going to take a swing at Hexcellent. Thankfully, the moment passed, and Zone leaned back into the couch, a sour expression on his face but otherwise silent.

"Right then. Since I've already spoken with the DVA and they confirmed that you were pulled in out of necessity, you didn't violate any protocol with your actions." Mr. Greene didn't need to add the "this time" to his statement; his tone already implied it perfectly. "Please do a better job of keeping us in the loop in the future, though. I'd like to remind you that it isn't just our 'precious image' that I'm here to manage, it's yours as well."

"Appreciate the concern, but I already pay someone for that."

"And I'm sure he's just as good as an entire staff of trained and experienced public relations professionals," Mr. Greene scoffed. "Regardless, you need to tell us when these incidents happen, *especially* when one of our people is on the scene with you."

Owen bit back his planned retort, a very graphic description of what Greene could do to his "public relations professionals," and made himself calm down. While Owen was the new guy and couldn't be held too accountable for not calling things in, Hexcellent didn't have his excuse or his level of fame.

Making waves might end up with her head going below water, and he wouldn't be responsible for that.

"I'm sorry I didn't call it in," Owen said slowly. "In the future, I'll make sure to report these sorts of things as soon as they happen."

"That's all I wanted to hear," Mr. Greene said. "Now go fill out an incident report. I have damage control to do."

Owen just nodded. He didn't trust his tongue with the freedom to speak.

22.

Owen had barely finished filling out the incident report when he heard a soft knock on his bedroom door. After no one immediately came through, he realized the person on the other side was waiting for permission, not announcing their entry. These kids were a lot better about personal space than his first Hero team had been, though given the way some of them got along, that might have been out of necessity.

"Come in."

The door opened and Galvanize stepped through, already suited up in full costume. "Titan, we've got some work to do."

"No voice over the speaker this time?"

"Mr. Greene only uses the emergency alert system when we have assignments of a time-sensitive nature," Galvanize explained. "Today we're going downtown to help with the cleanup efforts. No one is in immediate danger."

"Why would we go help with cleanup? There's already people for that." Collateral damage from fights between Supers was a constant issue in any major city, even with Heroes doing their best to keep situations contained. Decades ago, some enterprising people with useful abilities had recognized that this situation had the potential for profit and founded companies specifically to handle the cleanup. With a few Supers whose talents lent themselves to quickly moving or fixing rubble and a teleporter who had decent range, anyone could land contracts with a city to fix what the Supers broke.

"They handle the large-scale issues: clearing streets and making sure no buildings come crashing down. There's still a lot left to do after a conflict like what we saw today. Streets to sweep, glass to clear, small repairs to be made, that sort of thing. The cleaners are there to make sure the city stays up and running, they're far less concerned with helping everyone impacted by a battle."

"Well, that seems a lot like bullshit to me," Owen said. "I thought the city paid them to take care of everyone."

"Some services do exactly that, but they also charge more for it. Brewster's mayor and city council decided to use companies that get the bulk of the work done and let the citizens handle the small stuff on their own."

Owen let out a sigh and got up from his chair. Once upon a time that sort of thing would have set him off on a tirade, but he was too old and too jaded to get worked up over it now. Government officials were always going to find ways to move money from essential services to things they thought were more worthwhile. . . usually their own pockets. Heroes might be able to lift buildings and defy gravity, but no one could keep greedy, self-serving shitheads out of government. Some things were simply too impossible.

"How long do I have to change?"

"Fifteen minutes. We're meeting in the garage again."

"Gotcha. I can be there in five." Owen grabbed the papers off his small desk and walked over to Galvanize, thrusting them toward the younger man. "Here's my report about the robots. I think it'll get Greene off my ass."

"Mr. Greene is just worried about the team," Galvanize assured him. He took the papers from Owen and gave them a quick scan. "But speaking of Mr. Greene, I feel it only appropriate to warn you that there will be a very large media presence when we get downtown. He wants you out in the limelight under the company's approved plan."

"Of course he does." Owen shook his head; it was becoming more and more apparent that Greene was going to be a problem. It wasn't an issue when he pulled this crap in regards to Owen's Hero Liaison duties, but if he got uppity every time Titan was seen doing Hero work then they were going to quickly come to an impasse. "Don't worry about me and the cameras; I used to deal with them all the time. Are you guys going to be okay, though? There's going to some people mighty pissed off that your Hero Liaison is me."

Galvanize smiled, showing two perfect rows of bleached-white teeth that were both impressive and unnatural. "Oh no, you mean people might not think that highly of us? We might become the butt of the Super community's jokes, or treated like a bunch of loser wannabes? How on earth would we ever handle something like that? Personally, I can't even get out of bed in the morning unless I'm roused by screaming fans outside my window."

"Okay, smartass, you made your point. I guess being associated with me won't be that bad."

"I'm sure we'll still catch a fair amount of crap," Galvanize said, tucking Owen's report under his arm. "We're just used to muddling through it. Being a corpie isn't a glamorous life, despite what the companies are hoping for. But at the end of the day we make the world a better place. No amount of people being jerks or looking down on us can take that away. I'm sure I don't have to explain that to a Hero."

"I've known a few who could have benefited from hearing that," Owen replied. "I'll be down in the garage in a few minutes, just need to change into a shirt that doesn't have robot laser scorch marks."

"And here I didn't take you for the vain type."

"Like I said, I used to do this a lot. What we have today is an unveiling, and you always go to those looking your best," Owen said. "As my agent told me back when I started: you want to look clean, put-together, and ready for anything. You want to make the regular people fall in love and the criminals shit their pants. Always be bigger than life."

"Sounds as though your agent and Mr. Greene would get along."

"Yeah, I sort of doubt that," Owen replied.

"Well, do what you need to do; just be ready to go soon. All media attention aside, there really is work to be done." Galvanize took Owen's report and headed out of the door, leaving the large man to change.

Owen walked over to his closet and pulled it open. He still had four unmarred Titan shirts left. The things were durable as all hell, but no one doing Hero work could keep an outfit clean for long. One of the first things a Hero learned to budget for was all the new costumes they would need. He'd thought six would be enough to last him a while, but between Alexandria's flames and the robot's lasers, his shirts were dropping fast. Tonight he'd call Lenny and see about getting hooked up with a new distributor.

In the meantime, he had rubble to clear and cameras to greet.

23.

Despite Galvanize's warnings, there wasn't an enormous media presence when the giant SUV pulled to a stop on a slightly-cracked downtown street. In fact, there were fewer reporters than people in costumes. Many of the latter had trash cans and brooms positioned near them. Owen recognized a couple of people from the recent research he'd done about Brewster's current lineup (being caught off guard by Gale had been quite the wake-up call) and was surprised to realize there were actual Heroes involved in the efforts and not just other corpies. He wondered if Chicago had been worked by cleaners who handled the little stuff, or if he'd just been too caught up in the action part of the job to realize there were people in need even after the fighting was done.

Though there were fewer reporters than Owen had been expecting, it seemed that those who were present really had been waiting for him. No sooner had his giant boots touched down on the broken pavement than a flurry of people with inhumanly perfect skin and professionally tailored outfits descended on him. It was like being attacked by department store mannequins. Owen held up a single hand and they halted their charge, though it didn't keep their voices from ringing out.

"Titan! Is it true you're really the original Titan and not a legacy?"

"What Hero team are you looking to work with?"

"Have you come here to be a solo Hero?"

"Is there any truth to rumors that you're still involved with Tower?"

Owen's fist tightened at that last one, a gesture he purposely hid by shifting his hand down to his side. Things hadn't gone well for Colby, or Tower as the world knew him, after they'd been caught. To hear his name come out of the mouths of one of the same sort of media vultures that had helped tear him down. . . it was a good thing Owen had learned a lot about self-control in his time away from the life.

"I'm the real Titan, the one and only, with all the good and bad that brings with it," he told them. "I've decided to come out of retirement, and Brewster seemed like a great town to work in. As for Hero teams, I won't be needing one of those, nor I am truly working solo. I'm proud to be working as the Hero Liaison for the fine PEERS group you see around me. Now, if that settled everyone's questions, we really should start helping clean up all this broken glass."

One of the reporters, the same one who'd asked about Tower, broke away from the group, getting in so close that Owen could smell the recently-chewed mints on the man's breath.

"Titan, what about the rumors that you and Tower have-"

"You're new to this job, right?" Owen stared down at him, doing his best to keep his face impassive.

"That's right! I'm Kip Sterling of the Brewster Evening Edition, the hardest hitting-"

"Uh huh. I guess either your production team doesn't like you, or they thought it would be a good initiation prank to keep you in the dark." Owen gently spun the man around and pointed to the other reporters, who were maintaining a safe distance from everyone in a costume. "See how none of them kept pressing things once I told them we were done, or even kept coming forward when I held up my hand? Why do you think you were the only one to rush over?"

"Because Brewster Evening-"

"Wrong. Because when a Hero is on any kind of duty, the press is only allowed to be as close as we say they can be. Just like cops don't let you in to active crime scenes or dangerous situations, Heroes have to be able to work without worrying about innocent people getting hurt."

"But that's only for when there's an actual fight going on," Kip Sterling said, finally losing some of the naïve luster in his piercing blue eyes.

"Or for when we're doing heavy lifting, or suspect a threat isn't entirely neutralized, or that an area is unsafe for those without proper training or abilities. I can keep going, but you get the point. Yes, this area doesn't have any robots terrorizing it that we know of. That doesn't negate the broken glass, uneven concrete, and various bits of debris, not to mention the Supers using their abilities. We all have skills and clearance that let us walk around in these sorts of places safely. You being here puts your safety at risk, and as a Hero I can't very well have that."

Owen patted the reporter very gently on the back; the last thing he needed was to accidentally bruise this little asshole and have that be a headline story. "Now, go back to the sidelines with the others. I'll overlook the mistake this time, since I believe that's what it was, but next time be more cautious. On scenes like this, unless a Hero specifically gives you permission, going where you aren't supposed to is a serious crime that will get your station heavily fined. I've seen it happen before, and they are never happy about it."

Kip Sterling seemed like he was about to voice another objection, but a glance to his fellow reporters quelled his resolve. They were all shuffling about, avoiding eye contact and refusing to come any closer. Kip Sterling wasn't secure enough in this job to risk bringing down a fine on his station. The truth of the matter was that Brewster Evening Edition was a relatively new show, which was why he was trying so hard to get a sound bite for it. This also meant that if the program caused the network too much trouble, they'd have no issue canning it. Kip slunk back to the sidelines with the others, leaving Owen alone with his team.

Galvanize approached as soon as the reporter was gone. "I thought you said you knew how to handle reporters. That one looks like someone stole his teeth-whitening trays."

"You're one to talk, Smiley. Besides, I think it went pretty well. I could have slapped that guy with enough fines that his stations wouldn't let him mop the floors, let alone hold a microphone. Instead, I let him off with a warning and explained the situation to him. Yeah, I took no bullshit, but I did one of their own a kindness. That sort of thing shows itself in the way they write up the stories."

"And you didn't think you needed to answer more than three questions? Even we usually do full five-minute interviews after big rescues," Galvanize said.

"Of which I'm guessing maybe three seconds end up being used, if that." Owen grabbed a trash can from the back of the vehicle, hyper-aware of photographers snapping dozens of photos of even that mundane an action. "Dealing with the press is like being a performer; you leave them wanting more. The less they know, the more they'll speculate, and the more they speculate the more coverage they'll devote to that speculation. Sometimes it's good, and sometimes it's bad, but either way it's coverage, so I think Greene will be happy."

Galvanize thought it over for a moment. "I don't know if Mr. Greene is ever actually happy. Hopefully he'll be ambivalent. I think that's his version of happy."

24.

With the media handled, or at least subjugated enough to where Owen no longer considered them an issue, the team turned their attention to tidying up the area ravaged by the robots. The cleaners had done an exceptional job of making sure all the roads were clear and the buildings stable. They'd even rebuilt several structures before calling the job done. Nevertheless, there was still a fair bit of debris strewn along the sidewalks and in the drainage gutters of the streets. Shattered glass was abundant, as well as small chunks of concrete. Some pieces were quite sizable, the sort that would have required more than one person and might have resulted in an injured back; Galvanize sent Owen and Bubble Bubble to deal with that particular obstacle.

Owen's method for handling them was to simply lift the bits of concrete effortlessly off the ground and set them into the trash can he'd been provided with. Initially, he'd worried that it would fall apart when it was filled and he tried to lift it, but that concern proved groundless as the repository held together flawlessly. These kids really did have the best of everything, even trash cans.

Bubble Bubble made slower but steady progress. She would summon one of her energy spheres, carefully encasing the bulk of the debris, then move it over to her own trash can and let the sphere dissipate. Her speed didn't bother Owen—she was using her abilities the best way they'd function—but he did notice she seemed to take a lot of time between each piece of debris, fixing her hair and repositioning herself several times. At first he thought she was trying to find the best angle of approach for her pieces. By the fifth time it happened, Owen had recognized the all-too-familiar behavior.

"Are you posing?" He set the sizable bit of broken building onto the top of his trash can, keeping his eyes on her the whole time.

"Of course I'm posing." If she was bothered by being called out on that fact, she didn't let it show. In fact, she kept the same poised, neutral expression that she'd been wearing pretty much since Owen met her. Even her smiles and reactions were subdued, as though she were constantly on a job interview.

"Let's back up. Why are you posing? This isn't a shoot, it's work."

"For some of us, those are one and the same," Bubble Bubble replied. "Many of my sponsors are clothing and makeup companies, which means I have to be camera-perfect at all times. It wouldn't be proper for someone to capture an unflattering photo of me." A sphere crackled into existence around several small but jagged pieces of concrete and floated on a slow path toward the trash can.

"I really hope you're joking. What's the worst that could happen if someone took one bad picture of you?"

"I'm not concerned with what could happen. I'm worried about what couldn't." Even as she manipulated the sphere through the air, Bubble Bubble was able to keep her tone and expression perfectly placid. "A proper presence at all times is what opens doors to other opportunities, like modeling jobs outside of the costume, and those are a stepping stone to roles in television or cinema. Constant composure and beauty are the hallmarks of a successful media icon. We can't all afford to brush off the press at our convenience."

She set her latest load into her trash can and looked down. "Pardon me. I'm going to take this over to the large dumpster." A new sphere appeared, this one encasing the whole trash can, and Bubble Bubble walked off toward the industrial-sized dumpster that had been set up to hold the accumulated debris.

"Don't let it bother you; she's a career girl." Hexcellent came over, broom and small bin in her hands. Useful as her demons were, none were suited for delicate work, and they already had enough lifting power without Big Henry. "B.B. climbed her way up from a bit role on a minor PEERS team in South Dakota. The girl has ambition like a mother fucker. She's probably the best person on the team at working crowds and cameras."

"So this job is just. . . what? A step on the path?"

"If you know of another career that gets a Super media exposure and access to professional PR teams *and* minimizes personal risk, then I'd love to hear it," Hexcellent said. "I give her shit at home, but honestly I sort of get it. The girl wants to go to the top, and as long she keeps her ass working hard at this job while she's here then I don't care where she goes next."

"You make it sound like you aren't even friends," Owen replied, lifting a few chunks of debris into his trash can.

"We're not. We're teammates. I trust her to do her job and she trusts me the same way. Before I came on to the team there was someone else she trusted with that duty, and when she leaves for greener pastures I'll get used to someone new. That's all work, though; our personal lives stay way the fuck separate. It's the same for basically everyone on the team, except for the monthly game nights that Galvanize always tries to organize."

That Galvanize would try and get his team to interact socially didn't surprise Owen at all; what shocked him was the idea that any team could work so well together yet be so separate. His Hero groups had been thicker than family. Then again, they'd also been facing the very real threat of death every day. That sort of pressure forced bonds between people, making small differences irrelevant.

The more he thought about it, the more he realized the truth in what Hexcellent was saying. Even today, during breakfast, Galvanize had gone over everyone's schedule and they'd all been doing different things. Helping clean downtown was the only team activity of the day, and it couldn't possibly have been planned. These four were living entirely separate lives that happened to brush against the others' on occasion.

He grabbed his trash can and began hauling it to the dumpster, lost in thought. Maybe this was good enough for most of them, but Owen deeply suspected Galvanize wanted more. As the Hero Liaison, it wasn't technically under Owen's purview to deal with that sort of thing.

Not that he gave a shit. Owen hadn't left retirement to sit on the sidelines when he saw a problem. If something needed doing, he was damn sure going to do it. The only hurdle to jump was figuring out how.

25.

"I saw it on the news, but I couldn't believe it until I confirmed it with my own eyes. Titan, *the* Titan, back in costume. And doing the work of the little people no less."

Owen felt his spine stiffen as soon as the voice reached him. He'd been bent over to grab a particularly large piece of rubble that required both hands to keep balanced when those words had washed over him like a wave from the distant seas of his past. Slowly he rose, turning his body until the speaker was in view. It was an older man, one who actually showed his years, unlike Owen. He wore a costume fashioned of red, gold, and white, with lots of burst and flare patterns woven throughout the fabric. A beaming smile was partly concealed by a bushy mustache as he stared across the slowly dissipating wreckage.

"Topsy?" Owen crossed the small gap between them. He towered over the mustached man, who generously could be measured at five-foot-three-inches tall. "Topsy, when the hell did you move to Brewster?"

"'Bout five years ago. After my wife passed—thank you for the flowers, by the way—the city was too full of old memories. Besides, I wanted to be nearer to my kids. That's a boring question, though. I'm much more interested in what brings *you* here."

"It's a long story, and not the sort you tell when there are reporters about," Owen said. "The short version is I'm here as a Hero Liaison."

"I already knew that part. Course, I checked up on you as soon as I heard you were back."

"Titan, we need your help hauling the dumpster. . ." Galvanize trailed off as he jogged over, realizing that his team member was engaged in conversation. "Sorry, I didn't mean to interrupt."

"Nuttin to apologize for. Job always comes first, no matter what that job might be."

"Topsy, this is Galvanize; he leads the PEERS team I'm a Hero Liaison for. Galvanize, this is Topsy. He was-"

"Titan, please. A Hero like Topsy needs no introduction." Galvanize stepped forward and took the older, shorter man's hand. "It's a real honor to meet you, sir. The Gentle Hammers were one of my favorite Hero teams growing up."

"Look at that, some of the young ones still know us old dogs," Topsy said, giving Galvanize's hand an enthusiastic shake. "And he even knows a Gentle Hammer other than Titan! Been a while since anyone bothered remembering that."

Owen winced inwardly at the remark, even though he knew Topsy hadn't meant it to be painful. The Gentle Hammers had been his first Hero team, founded mostly from Sizemore Tech graduates he'd kept in touch with through their intern years. In the beginning, they'd all been more or less unknowns. When their prestige grew, it grew as a team. Those were the golden days, back when everyone had been working together and happy. Unfortunately, Titan's reputation soon began to outpace—and eventually eclipse—the rest of the team's. The Gentle Hammers were still around when his scandal broke, but he, Topsy, and Shock Lock were the last founding members. The team had officially dissolved a few years after he went into exile.

"Topsy, I'm still not sure how I didn't know you were here. I just checked on all the active Heroes in Brewster last night," Owen said.

"Ah, but I'm not active anymore, am I? No, I'm working as an advisor and trainer for one of the local Hero teams. I can still jump in if the need demands, though these bones don't move as quick as they used to. Unlike you, some of us have to actually cope with getting older."

"If you try and tell me that a little thing like age has slowed you down then I'll grab you by your ankles and shake you until you admit you're a mimic," Owen threatened.

"Let's say it's half getting older and half getting less suicidal. I'd like to make it to see my grandkids one day. Plus, it's nice to pass on some of the lessons we earned through blood and broken bones to the next generation. The ones I'm coaching are plenty powerful, but heaven almighty, are they stubborn and impulsive."

It took all of his self-control for Owen to bite back the chuckle that wanted to escape his lips. Topsy had been the most easily provoked member of The Gentle Hammers, often barreling into fights without so much as basic recon. It was only an incredible ability, loads of skill, and a fair smattering of luck that had kept him alive.

"I'm sure you're teaching them a lot about control," Galvanize said. If there was even a hint of sarcasm in his words, he buried it under a mountain of sincerity. "May I ask which team you're an advisor to?"

"Please just don't say it's Elemental Fury," Owen mumbled under his breath.

The mumbling wasn't quite as soft as he'd intended, as Topsy replied, "No, they've got plenty of retired members of their own to do the advising. I'm helping a newer team, Wild Bucks: mostly offensive types with a couple of Supers for doing defense. They're getting better, but what I wouldn't give to snag a Subtlety Hero for them."

"I've heard of Wild Bucks," Galvanize said. "They came on the scene last year. Lots of physically-based abilities, not unlike The Gentle Hammers."

"Similar, to be sure. If you're ever up to stopping by and giving them some pointers, Titan, I'm sure they'd be grateful for the tutelage."

"Much as I'd love to, I'm already in over my head with the local Hero teams," Owen said. "I'm supposed to do an ability assessment with Elemental Fury soon, unless Lenny can somehow talk them out if it."

"Talk them out of it? That doesn't sound like the Lenny I used to know," Topsy replied. "If anything I'd expect him to turn the whole production into a circus and take a cut of everything from the clown makeup to the elephant shit."

"Damn it. . . that does sound a lot more like Lenny. Maybe I should call him."

"We'll be done here soon, Titan." Galvanize's tone was polite, like he was gently reminding someone of a schedule conflict rather than instructing his teammate to stay on task. "The rest of the evening is yours, barring any unforeseen crises, of course."

"Up for a drink, Topsy?" Owen asked.

"Another time. I've got my team scheduled for some training drills tonight. After how they performed against today's robot attack, they need to polish their skills." Topsy nodded to Galvanize, then headed off down the street.

"I didn't see Wild Bucks on the news reports," Galvanize said once he thought Topsy was out of earshot.

"They were some of the first to respond," Owen told him, hours of reading up on the incident finally paying off. "None got killed, but most were incapacitated within the first few minutes. The media leaving them out of the story was actually a pretty kind gesture, one I'm sure Topsy had a lot to do with."

"Sounds rough." Galvanize turned back to the street, where things were slowly beginning to look less chaotic. "Speaking of rough, we still need your help with the dumpster. It's a beast; none of our strongmen can get a grip on the whole thing, so we're coordinating a group effort."

"No problem," Owen said. "Just tell me where the team needs me. That's what I'm here for."

26.

"Yes, but. . ."

"That isn't how I wanted. . ."

"Of course I trust you. . ."

"Now you listen here. . ."

"Fine! Just do whatever you want."

Owen gripped the phone tightly as he jabbed the button to end the call. Only its hardy construction kept it from flying to pieces. As soon as he'd gotten back to the penthouse from the cleanup, he'd called Lenny, who had unapologetically confirmed his worst fears. Not only did he not get the assessment with Elemental Fury canceled, he managed to make the situation into a bigger shitshow than it already was.

Lenny could run his mouth all day about how Gale might back down now that odds weren't stacked in her favor; they both knew it was bullshit. Gale was young, powerful, and just successful enough to be insecure about her position. She wasn't going to back down from a damned volcano, let alone some washed up Hero and his bald agent.

With more care than he felt like using, Owen set the phone down. The last thing he needed to add to his frustration was the mountain of paperwork Greene would surely make him file to replace any of the room's furnishings. No, he needed to wind down a little, to take his mind off the growing mountain of crap he had to deal with.

For a fleeting moment, he considered hitting up Brin's Gate, the Hero bar Gale had shown him. It was tempting, but the risk of running into her was more than he was willing to undertake. If she'd been around Lenny today then she was likely to tear Owen apart the moment they laid eyes on one another.

Instead, Owen changed into sweats and headed off toward the gym. While they didn't have anything that would challenge his lifting abilities, it still calmed him to do basic aerobics and calisthenics. The focused monotony cleared his head, and if he kept at it for enough hours, he occasionally worked up enough of a sweat to release some endorphins.

No sooner had he opened the gym's door than Owen regretted his decision. Leaping around the rescue simulation part of the gym was Zone, normally spiky hair matted to his scalp thanks to the abundance of sweat pouring from his body. Briefly, Owen considered backing away from the door and hoping his teammate didn't notice. He decided against it, though, walking in with just enough noise to be sure Zone knew he was no longer alone. If the kid wanted to hate him, that was fine, but Owen would be damned if he let that affect his choices. Besides, if he really wanted to help Galvanize pull his team together, he would need to deal with this issue sooner or later.

"Evening," Owen said, keeping his greeting as neutral as possible.

Zone did a flip off a fake roof, landing lightly several feet away. When he came down, an incredibly short wince of pain shot across his face. Most people wouldn't have noticed it or recognized it for what it was, but Owen knew in an instant. He'd spent too many years around other Heroes, people whose jobs demanded a physicality that was impossible for most to manage for long. The kid had worn something in his body down and he was trying to keep it hidden.

"What are you doing here? None of the shit we have could train you."

"Maybe I came for the pleasant atmosphere," Owen shot back. He regretted it as soon as he'd spoken; he needed to try and mend this bridge, not torch it further.

"That got wrecked the minute you walked in." Zone grabbed a towel and started to head for the door.

"All right, kid, enough of this crap. You got something you want to say? We're right here, just you and me. No one to tell you to calm down, no one to hold you back. Either say your piece or quit all the sniping bullcrap."

Zone froze midway to the door and looked back over his shoulder. "Go eat shit. I don't have to do this your way. If I want to keep calling you out every chance I get and never tell you the reason why, I damn sure will."

"That would be a great point, except that you've been trying to lay into me since I got here. Only circumstance has stopped you. I'm not telling you to do it my way; I'm trying to give you the chance to do it yours." Owen crossed his arms and met Zone's withering glare. "But if you want to keep up the snide ridiculousness, go ahead. I somehow doubt you'll get any harder to ignore."

"You just think you know everything, don't you?"

"I know you're pissed off at me, sorry, at Titan, and clearly have been long before I was ever on your team. What's the deal? You think I'm a shithead for walking away? That's fair. Dislike that I lied to the public? Tough shit; I was lying to people that I cared about way more, myself included. Hell, maybe you just don't like gay people."

"Fuck you!" Zone yelled, all composure gone as he stormed back toward Owen. "You really want to do this? Fine! I hate you—not Titan, *you,* Owen—because of what you could have done. Look at you! You're tough, strong, and intimidating as all hell. If you'd come out of the gates as gay, you could have given an icon to all the Supers out there who wanted to be Heroes but were scared their orientation didn't fit the masculine ideal. You could have been the symbol they held up to show that being gay didn't mean they couldn't kick ass. You could have given people hope and encouragement and instead you did *the exact fucking opposite*! After your scandal, every openly gay Hero has had to live in the shadow of the bullshit you pulled."

"Yeah, that's a damn good reason to be pissed." Owen's voice was calm as he stared at the red-faced young man in front of him. Zone had gotten so worked up during his speech that a few flecks of spittle had struck Owen on the chest. Owen had expected to get pissed himself when this finally came to a head, but instead he felt oddly serene. Zone hadn't said anything Owen hadn't told himself countless times over the past decade. He already knew he'd fucked things up. Being called out on it didn't change things.

"Is that it? Is that your apology?"

"No, Zone. I was raised that we don't sincerely apologize with words; we do it with actions. Words are washed away by time and memory. They're easy to create and easier to forget. I owe an apology to a lot of folks, the ones I lied to and the ones I let down by leaving. I'm saying I'm sorry to everyone, you included, by going back out there and trying to do good. You may never accept my apology; I know plenty of people won't. That's damned sure your right, but I'll be out there making it regardless. That is literally all I can do."

"I don't think it will ever be enough," Zone said, the fire and energy gone slowing draining out of him.

"Probably not. Doesn't mean I don't have to try."

Zone turned to walk out of the gym, slowly now, not even bothering to storm away. Owen called to him.

"Who was it? Friend, family-"

"Big brother. Strongman, like you. His powers are worlds above mine. Easily could have been a Hero and helped a lot of people. Instead, he does construction in Ohio."

With that, Zone exited the gym, leaving Owen alone with his thoughts and his guilt.

27.

Owen walked in the living room the next morning to find two men he'd never seen before talking to Galvanize. The taller of the two had dark hair and the kind of wiry frame Owen associated with easily excitable computer guys. The shorter one had brown hair and a rounder build. They both were sporting crisp white lab coats, and the taller one held a clipboard in his hand. At first, Owen took in this sight with curiosity bordering on interest, but everything inside him turned to panic when he was struck by an overpowering realization.

He wasn't wearing any kind of mask.

Instincts kicked into gear. He spun around, ready to dart down the hallway and pray they hadn't noticed him. Before he could, Galvanize's voice rang through the room.

"Titan, good morning! Come over here and meet the docs. I doubt you'll need them, but you're going to see them around from time to time."

Owen tried to steady himself. These men were probably on staff, meaning they'd signed the kind of nondisclosure agreements only large corporations and sociopathic villains could conjure up. Galvanize wasn't an idiot; he'd already shown a lot of deference to Owen's need for privacy and hiding his identity. If he was calling Owen over, then there had to be some sort of safety system in place. Still. . . it wouldn't hurt to double check before he turned his face back toward them.

"Morning, all," Owen said, keeping his back facing the group. "Galvanize, I came down without my mask on. Is that going to be an issue?"

It wasn't Galvanize who replied, but one of the men in lab coats instead. "Titan, you have nothing to worry about. My assistant and I have been signed to so many contracts and clauses that if we leaked even a fraction of what we've dealt with here we'd bankrupt ourselves, our families, and at least six generations of children."

He was probably exaggerating, but the man had a kind tone and a bit of humor in his voice. Owen could see himself getting along with this fellow. Besides, if they were going to be around a lot he'd have to get used to it eventually.

"Six generations, huh? These bastards really don't mess around." Owen turned and walked over to the two men, the docs, as Galvanize had called them. He shook their hands, starting with the taller of the two. "Nice to meet you both. I'm Titan."

"Edgar Willoughby," said the tall man. Owen recognized his voice as the one that had spoken already. "But I absolutely insist you call me Edgar. This is my assistant, Thaddeus Kirkland."

"Please, just Kirk," said the shorter man. "Thaddeus is a family name."

"I understand how that goes, Kirk," Owen replied.

"The docs here work for Mordent," Galvanize explained. "They do a lot of stuff, but one of their responsibilities is taking care of us. We're all subjected to weekly physicals to make sure we're still in tip-top shape."

"Precisely," Edgar agreed. "We can't very well have one of Mordent's wonderful PEERS going out to help someone only to slip a disk or blow a joint. As folks entrusted with rescuing people in peril, their health is of the utmost concern."

"Plus we have to make sure they haven't slipped up on their body-fat percentages," Kirk added.

Edgar threw a quick disapproving look to his assistant.

"What? We check it. You and I know it, and the PEERS sure as heck know it since it's in their contracts. Titan is exempt, but I'm sure by now he's realized there's certain conditions put on the rest of his team."

"It's fine. I figured that out just from the fridge," Owen said. "No way four young people in this line of work would willingly refuse to stock any beer. Surely at least one them would want to enjoy unwinding with a drink if they had any say in it."

"Yes, well, while the superficial aspects are less intrinsic to the accomplishment of their duties, we are still required to monitor them," Edgar admitted. "And on that note, I believe we are due in Hexcellent's room. Galvanize, we'll see you in about half an hour. Titan, it was a pleasure to meet you."

"Quite an honor," Kirk added.

"Same here," Owen said.

The two men headed off down the hallway Owen had just emerged from, presumably on their way to Hexcellent's room.

"I know what you're thinking, but they really are nice guys," Galvanize said once the docs were gone. "Last year I seriously messed up my ankle while helping out with a multi-car pileup. The team was due to put on an exhibition at a sporting event two weeks later. Mordent had sunk a lot of money into it and the exposure was going to be huge, so they expected me there, fully-functional ankle or not. They wanted the docs to give me a clean bill of health so I could make the show. Edgar and Kirk told them to blow it out their ass, that if I tried to do anything too active I would cause serious, long-term damage. Mr. Greene finally got the company to spring for a healer so I could be properly patched up in time for the event."

"Damn. This doesn't seem like the kind of company that would take that shit lightly."

"I'm sure they wouldn't, but the docs are way too important to lose over something like that. They've both involved in all sorts of Mordent projects, the kind of stuff so classified I probably don't even know about the floor it's on."

"And they use these valuable assets checking on four Supers' fat levels?"

"Edgar and Kirk demanded the right to be our physicians," Galvanize told him. "Like most scientists, they're fascinated by Supers. We're the biggest mystery to come along in millennia, and people are dying for answers about us."

"I'm sure they're smart guys, but I'm not holding my breath on them cracking it," Owen said. "We had hundreds of guys in lab coats trying to figure us out back in my day too, and they never made much progress."

"Sooner or later, someone will. I'm pulling for the docs. At least they treat us like people instead of experiments."

"That is harder to find than it should be," Owen agreed. "Anyway, what's on the docket today besides getting you all checked out?"

"It was supposed to be another splintered day," Galvanize said. "However, after yesterday's unexpected reveal, Mr. Greene decided it was best if we had some more team exposure. We all need to be in costume and ready to go by nine."

"Not going to tell me what we're doing?"

"I'd rather wait until the whole team is here and deal with it once," Galvanize said.

"That kind of thing?"

"Unfortunately, yes."

28.

"As you all know, as of yesterday our team has been under increased media awareness," Galvanize said, eyes sweeping across his team as he spoke. Bubble Bubble was paying attention, though from the disinterested expression on her face it was clear this either wasn't news or wasn't news she cared about. Hexcellent seemed somewhat curious, despite her constant yawning. Zone was the least expressive of them all. Usually he was preoccupied with shooting dirty looks at Owen; today his anger seemed to have simmered down a few degrees to the point of general disinterest. How long that would last was anyone's guess.

"Consequently, Mr. Greene feels it's important that we appear as a team for the next few days. This might be an opportunity to catapult our brand awareness. As we've discussed, putting together a united front only increases our appeal." This was not mere speculation on Galvanize's part. Countless market research studies had proven that while the occasional lone Hero could gain renown, people by and large tended to prefer to see their Supers in teams. It only followed that this mindset would apply to PEERS as much as it did to Heroes.

"You're beating around the bush," Hexcellent accused. "What do we have to do?"

"There's a charity event coming up in several weeks. It's a joint venture of the Super Athletics Association, companies like Mordent, and individual Heroes. There are meet-and-greets, competitions, exhibition matches, and of course the SAA will have plenty of sports going on. Generally the only PEERS teams allowed to participate are those that have a substantial fan base of followers. Today, Mr. Greene informed me that we will be signing up for it with his blessings."

Both Zone and Hexcellent groaned loudly, and even Bubble Bubble lifted an eyebrow and pursed her lips in an expression Owen assumed was distaste.

"What's wrong with doing a charity event?" Owen asked.

"Nothing's wrong with helping charity," Hexcellent said. "But this means we have to be around Heroes. The nicest of them just ignore us, while some are outright dickholes. They even treat the players from the SAA better than us, because for some reason that's considered a more respectable job."

Owen reflexively felt himself about to stick up for those in his profession, but his brain stopped his tongue before it could wag. Only a week ago he'd thought of these people as pretenders, children playing dress-up and trying to grasp at a title they hadn't earned. How would he have treated them if he were on a Hero team working this event? Hexcellent was right; he probably would have just ignored them, at best. Instead of disagreeing with his team, he'd be better off finding out what they were in for.

"What exactly is our role at this thing?"

"That, we are allowed to determine individually," Galvanize said. "As I said, there will be plenty of events and activities we can participate in, though Mr. Greene has requested that you not sign up for meet-and-greets."

"Don't think anyone will want Titan's autograph?" Owen said, only half-joking.

"More that he feels Titan is better seen larger than life for right now. If you're on the ground, talking to people, inevitably someone will use it as a chance to protest or cause controversy. He thinks you should be doing things instead, reminding people about the power that made them adore you in the first place."

"That's a pretty fair plan and assessment," Owen said. It was exactly the sort of thing Lenny would have told him to do. Greene might be an anal-retentive overbearing jerk, but it was somehow slightly reassuring to know he was at least competent at his job. "Anything in particular he'd recommend?"

"No, only that showing up other Heroes would likely lead to bad blood, so perhaps something cooperative or with the SAA would be best."

If Greene didn't want him showing up other Heroes then he was going to be beyond pissed about Owen's assessment with Elemental Fury it. He briefly considered making a comment in this vein but thought better of it. He was still hoping that little fiasco-to-be would fall through and become a non-issue.

"Guess I'll do something with the SAA," Zone said. "Maybe join a baseball or basketball team. I've always been able to crush at sports; I should at least be able to hold my own there."

Owen nodded agreement, not wanting to stir up Zone so soon. It was unlikely that he'd really be able to play on the same level as SAA athletes, whose abilities had been specifically recruited and trained for use in sports, but now wasn't the time to bring that up. At least in basketball or baseball Zone was less likely to get injured. If he'd tried to play football, Owen would have had to step in.

"I'll see what they've got," Hexcellent remarked. "My summons are damned versatile, just a matter of seeing what suits them best."

"As Hexcellent said, I too will see what's available," Bubble Bubble said. "Though I doubt my abilities are suited to anything particularly spectacular. Perhaps there is an administrative or service role I can assist in."

"Mr. Greene assured me that we would all be able to find events we were suited to," Galvanize told them. "Remember, we're representing Mordent and there will be a lot of eyes on us thanks to Titan, so whatever you do, make sure you can do it well. This is a big break for all of us; we shouldn't waste it."

"Gotcha, kick ass and take names," Owen said. "Is there a website for this or something? How do we sign up?"

"They have a remote service for Heroes, but we'll be going down to the organization headquarters to volunteer in person," Galvanize said. "That's why I gathered everyone in full costume; the press will almost certainly be waiting when we do so."

"Let me guess: Greene told them we would be there."

"Of course *Mr.* Greene did," Galvanize said. "He wants us as much in the public eye as possible. Which means everyone needs to have their PR faces on as soon as we arrive. Anyone needs to do touch-up before we go?"

His question was met by a combination of silence and half-hearted head shakes.

"Right then: everyone head on down to the van. We have press waiting for us; we should at least try to be prompt."

29.

Unlike the night of the fire, Galvanize kept the SUV at a low speed as they wove their way through the streets of downtown. This was as much out of a concern for safety as it was for appearance. In truth, the address they were heading to was within walking distance from the Mordent Holdings building, but that would have meant several members of the team showing up sweaty and tussled. It was fine to look that way on the job, especially after particularly impressive rescues, but today they needed to arrive looking their best.

He pulled the SUV into a conspicuously open street spot outside several large brick buildings. From how close it was to the small cluster of reporters waiting nearby, Owen suspected it had been saved especially for them. It would provide a great shot, the team stepping out of their vehicle with skyscrapers jutting into the sky at their back. The media wanted a crack at him, and they were playing ball with his team to get it. Owen would have to be careful how he handled them; he might be used to getting savaged by the press, but he'd rather not see his people go through it.

"Out of curiosity, what charity does this benefit anyway?" Owen asked, staring out the window as cameras flashed and microphones emerged.

"Proceeds will be split up," Galvanize told him. "Some will go to Dream Granters, the company that organizes Hero visits to terminal children, and some will go to Shelby's House. They help Powereds whose abilities make it hard for them to find work or housing and provide services like counseling."

Bubble Bubble let out a small sigh. "Sick kids I can see helping, of course, but it seems like they could have found a better cause than Powereds."

Owen felt a familiar anger start to burn in his stomach, but before he could decide whether it was worth the blowback to speak, Hexcellent took her own action. From her position in the backseat, she leaned forward and flicked Bubble Bubble forcefully on the ear.

"Ow!"

"You deserved it. Don't be a bitch."

"I was not 'being a bitch.' I was just saying that there are other causes out there that might need the money more."

"Doesn't matter, we're not the ones doling it out," Galvanize told her, unbuckling his seatbelt. "Our job is just to participate and raise as much cash as we can. It also won't hurt us to look good doing it."

Everyone but Owen paused to a do a last-minute mirror check in the SUV's visors or carefully-stowed compacts. Only after each member was certain they looked their best did the team finally pop open the doors and emerge.

Immediately, the press members surged forward, the clacking sound of shutters filling the air. Owen noted the reporter from yesterday, Kip Sterling, stayed right in the center of the pack. Clearly he was determined not to slip up and make another rookie mistake. Good for him; Owen had given that same speech to a lot of other ambitious media hounds only to see them keep right on breaking rules. That strategy never ended well.

It was less intense than Owen had feared. No one peppered him with questions or shouted accusation like back in his Hero days. Of course, during those times they were trying to get information about wanted criminals or destroyed buildings. Now they were just getting some shots of him with his new

PEERS team going in to sign up for a charity event. The stakes weren't exactly the same.

The questions did still come, just without the aggression he was accustomed to. Owen smiled, made eye contact, and kept his damn mouth shut. If Greene wanted them to be good, then Owen wouldn't hand over any ammunition. A well-edited sound bite was a PR mortar shell when put into skilled hands. Until he caught up with Lenny and got a sense of where he wanted the story to go, it was best to give them nothing. Owen knew that if he wanted the right outcome then he needed to be the one to create the narrative of his story.

Galvanize was getting a few questions as well, mostly about which events Titan would be signing up for, though a few were about the team as a whole. He answered several, always polite and deferential, but kept the bulk of his attention on herding his team toward a large wooden door in one of the larger brick buildings. It took some doing, but eventually they made it and Owen easily pushed the barrier open. He expected the press to pour through it, like water through a funnel; however, they remained stationary as his team began to enter. Clearly whatever deal Greene had struck ended at the door.

Before Owen could make his way through, an unfortunately-familiar face popped up in front of him, microphone clutched in a sweaty hand. Kip Sterling had put himself ever-so-slightly between Owen and the door; he had just enough mass and was positioned just so that he was noticeable without seeming as though he intended to physically bar Owen's way. It was a ballsy move, and from the nervous fear he was trying to keep off his face, Kip clearly knew that. Still, he stood his ground as the larger man stared down at him, refusing to yield. Owen was tempted to brush him aside, but he had been

149

thinking about the importance of keeping on the media's good side. Besides, he respected this little guy's guts.

"Yes, Kip?"

"I was just wondering what you're hoping to accomplish at the charity event," Kip said. Beads of sweat stood out on his forehead and the microphone shook just a touch. He really was desperate for something to bring back to the station. He'd even lobbed a big softball of a question, open-ended and with a positive connotation.

"Obviously our biggest, most important goal is to help raise as much money as possible for these wonderful organizations," Owen replied. He knew he should cut it off there; it was a great line that couldn't possibly be misinterpreted. Owen knew that because he'd played this game so well for so long back in his original Hero days. It was why he'd distinguished himself from his first team, why his star had risen so high. He always had a good gut sense for the right things to say. Yet now, staring down at Kip's shaky microphone, Owen realized for the first time that he didn't want to be a media darling again.

He wanted to be Titan, on his own terms.

"But as a secondary goal, I hope for the chance to kick some serious ass."

Owen slid past Kip, whose eyes were lighting up like flickering fluorescents, and stepped into the building. Greene wasn't going to like that, and Lenny might not either, but Owen didn't really care. He'd only told the truth, after all.

30.

When Owen got to Lenny's office, he was braced for a tongue-lashing. After the event signup, which had been mercifully quick, Owen and the team had headed back to their home. No sooner had they walked in the door and turned on the television than they saw Titan's face staring back at them. His voice filled the room, answering Kip's question eloquently and tacking on the bit about ass-kicking at the end.

Owen barely had time to regret that outburst before Lenny called, calmly demanding Owen be at his office within the hour. Calm Lenny was usually a bad sign. Cursing, drinking, complaining, anxiety-ridden: these were all forms of Lenny that meant he had things well-under control. Calm Lenny meant business, and all too often that business involved a serious ass-chewing.

Owen walked through the door to the lobby, ducking slightly to avoid smacking his head against the frame. He would have suffered no damage, but he'd have been on the hook for repairs. Titan merchandise didn't exactly fly off the shelves anymore, so he wanted to keep his costs down.

It was a good thing he was already ducked, too, because what he saw in the lobby nearly made him jerk his head right back up.

Lenny's office door was open and the small man was sitting inside, talking to another Hero that was already seated. Owen might not have recognized her even a week ago, despite the amount of media saturation she'd achieved, but after meeting Gale up close there was no mistaking her. Owen stepped through the empty lobby, into the office, and shut the door behind him.

"Afternoon, Lenny. Gale." He took a seat in one of the sturdier chairs, doing his best to keep his face neutral. If she was here to call off the assessment, he didn't want to do anything to make her change her mind.

"Always a pleasure, Titan," Gale replied. Judging from the flat tone of her voice, if she considered this a pleasure then Owen would have hated to see how she reacted to an inconvenience.

"Gale here has come down to finalize the discussion of the ability assessment in person." Lenny was all business, not even bothering with any pleasantries. "Despite what I, and her own agent, have advised her, she is intent on going forward with this little spectacle."

"Up until this morning, I was seriously considering taking it off the table," Gale said, turning to face Owen. "That was until I saw his little interview. After that robot attack I thought maybe you really were trying to lie low and do some good. You managed to avoid charging into the spotlight like I expected. But no, the moment you get a few drops of media juice going, you hand them a sound bite that you know they'll play over and over. You're exactly what I feared you'd be: a showboat that puts his profile over the job. Well, I'm going to lower that profile, and thanks to your agent I'm going to do it with countless people watching."

"Gale, come on; it was one line. I was there to sign up for a charity event and I let my tongue get away from me. You really don't want to do this," Owen said.

"I'm telling you right now that I do. We're getting this done, and within the next week. Your agent has a list of my team's availabilities. Find one that works, or so help me I will personally use my connections to bury you in red tape and bullshit."

"What does this accomplish? Really, tell me that. If I do well, you've done the exact opposite of what you claim to want, and if I shit the bed all you've done is prove you can take a Hero two decades your senior."

"When we decimate you, it will prove that your legend is all fluff. There will be far less cause for the press to care about your antics, and without their attention I expect you'll soon shrivel up and vanish, just like you did before."

Gale stood to leave, but Owen was on his feet faster.

"So you want to drive another Hero out of town? Remind me: which of us is the one who cares more about the media than the job?"

"I want to rid my town of a man who has too much influence and power and not nearly enough integrity to know how to use it." Gale stared up at him, refusing to budge even an inch. "We both know it's just a matter of time before your fame-whoring causes you do something stupid and get innocents killed. I'm making sure that you never get the chance."

"And this has nothing at all to do with the prestige you think your team will get by embarrassing the legendary Titan?"

"I won't stand here and be insulted by such ludicrous insinuations," Gale snapped. "Unlike you, I have people to help." She wove her way around the large man and stormed out of the office, slamming the lobby door behind her.

With Gale gone, Owen slowly lowered himself back into his chair and looked at Lenny, who was placid as a monk on morphine.

"That woman is not fond of you," Lenny said at last.

"I think she hates me more than your ex-wife hates you," Owen added.

"Don't be silly. She didn't even take a swing at you, let alone reach for a knife. She's nowhere near that level of loathing. . . yet."

"Damn right 'yet.' What the hell am I supposed to do? If I go into that assessment and throw it, then the Titan name gets even more run through the mud than it already has been. I mean, for all the shit that gets hurled about, the one thing no one can ever say is that I wasn't a capable Hero. On the other hand, if I go in and tear her team apart, she really will hate me until the day one of us dies. I'd rather not have an archenemy that's also a Hero so soon into my comeback."

"It does complicate matters," Lenny agreed. "Just out of curiosity, you didn't mention the chance of legitimately getting shown up in either of your assessments. Did that not even strike you as a possibility?"

"I read up on Elemental Fury, including what they can do. So, honestly, no, it didn't occur to me."

"Me either," Lenny said. "You're in a real pickle here, no doubt, and it's even worse now that there's a giant audience contractually attached to the spectacle."

"Thanks again for that, by the way."

"My pleasure," Lenny leaned back in his chair, still exuding endless rays of calm. "And while we're on the subject of thanking each other for things, why don't we have a nice long chat about that little quote you gave the reporter."

Owen swallowed hard and looked down at his boots. This day was just getting worse by the hour.

31.

Owen was halfway back to the Mordent building, brisk evening air flowing around him as he jogged, when a noise suddenly crackled to life in his ear.

He tensed, waiting for Dispatch's voice to broadcast through. Since he wasn't registered as currently active, whatever she was tapping him for had to be serious. He was either the only one close enough to respond or others had already failed to contain the situation. Even if it was protocol, Owen had a feeling stepping one foot further into what Gale considered her turf would destroy whatever shreds of a chance there were for peaceful cohabitation. He'd have to deal with that later; in the moment doing his job was the only thing that mattered.

It was only when the voice spoke that Owen realized his mistake. He'd put the specialized earpiece for Dispatch in his right ear that morning, same as always, while the sound was clearly on his left, the spot where he'd stuck the lower-tech team transceiver.

"Titan, this is Galvanize. We're needed."

"What's up?"

"A Hero team, Wild Bucks, squared off against a small gang of Supers about an hour ago. They managed to get them subdued, but there was a significant amount of collateral damage. We just received clearance to enter the area and evacuate any remaining civilians from unstable buildings or rubble. The epicenter of the damage area is at Forty-Third and Quail. Do you need us to pick you up?"

Owen quickly glanced at the nearest sign post; he was crossing through Twenty-First and Morgan. Much of Brewster was laid out in a simple grid fashion, with numbers moving sequentially and letters alphabetically, meaning he was twenty-two blocks up and four blocks over. He'd never had a super-speeder's abilities, but he did have powerful legs and a cardiovascular system that could go for days.

"No, you guys go ahead. I can run there faster."

"Understood. Let me know when you're getting close and I'll give you directions to meet us. This is a large scale evacuation, so other PEERS teams will be on site assisting, as well as Heroes with appropriate abilities."

Galvanize didn't have to spell it out for him: a lot of people would be there, and so would cameras, which meant he'd better make sure to keep on his best behavior. Increased media scrutiny was going to be part of their lives now, at least for a while, and they needed to make it work for them. Like a wild horse, you either held on and rode or fell off and got trampled.

"I'll seek you out as soon as I arrive." Owen turned and reoriented himself, pausing long enough to check the traffic. He wouldn't be moving as fast as a car, but if he accidently hit one then it wouldn't make any difference. As important as it was to get to the scene, it was just an important not to hurt anyone on the way there. Not for the first time since he'd re-donned the mask, Owen dearly missed having a teleporter on call.

*   *   *

Owen's mouth hung open as he drew closer to the section of city scarred from battle. Even blocks away he could see the wreckage: shattered glass, overturned cars, huge dents in the ground where large objects had clearly struck. No wonder this was a large-scale evacuation; he was only at the fringes and the place looked like hell. The gang they took down must have been incredibly powerful.

"Dispatch, this is Titan." He didn't slow down as he spoke, easily hurdling minor obstacles without so much as missing a step.

"Dispatch recognizes Titan." She was there, ready as always, just waiting for him to say her name.

"I'm meeting my PEERS team and heading to respond to the evacuation caused by some dickhead Supers and Wild Bucks."

"So they reported in." Dispatch wasn't particularly curt with her reply, or even sarcastic. Like nearly everything she said, it was factual and detached. Strangely, it made her one of the easiest people most Heroes had in their lives to talk to.

"I'm getting first sight on the level of destruction and it's a damn wreck. What were the Class Assessments on the gang they fought?" Owen jogged by the remains of what had probably been a small storefront, but was now so crushed it was impossible to say for sure.

"The Supers that Wild Bucks faced were ranked as follows: one NTC Class and three Standard Class. Abilities were determined to be: one healer, one advanced mind, and two shifters."

Owen put his foot down so hard with the next step that he accidently shattered a piece of already broken street. He must have heard her wrong; that was the only viable explanation.

"Dispatch, confirm, did you say an advanced mind and two shifters, all Standard Class, caused this much destruction in their neutralization?"

"Correct." Her voice held no judgment in its calm, slightly-accented tones, but only because that's who she was. For someone like Owen, looking at the devastation caused, it was impossible to remain quite so detached.

Owen was getting closer now and beginning notice things like smashed out corners of buildings, ones that had thankfully already been tagged as clear. The big white spray-painted "X" was an easy visual marker, saving him from having to radio in about every leaning structure he came across.

"Dispatch, what was the civilian causality count from this operation?"

"Final tally will not be available until the evacuation is completed."

"Give me current total."

"Five confirmed, with three more in critical condition."

"Thank you, Dispatch."

Owen nearly panted out those last words, his breath suddenly short for reasons that had nothing to do with physical exertion. Five dead in taking down four Supers who didn't rate above standard class, not to mention countless dollars in destruction. This wasn't like with the robots, when everyone was doing the best they could just to neutralize the threat. Three Standards and an NTC, none with particularly rare abilities, should be a breeze for *any* Hero team, regardless of their composition.

Five dead, three hanging on, and God only knew how many people trapped or in danger, waiting to be evacuated. There was no way the DVA wouldn't be digging into this one, and with good damn reason. Topsy's team had fucked up royally, and they had to be held accountable for it. As Owen glanced around one more time, surveying the wreckage around him that had once been a neighborhood, he was struck with a single overwhelming sentiment:

The DVA was going to have to get in line behind him.

That would come later. Right now there were people in danger, innocents who had nothing to do with the situation currently threatening their lives. They mattered more than anything, and it was time to finally start using his powers like a Hero.

Titan put on an extra burst of speed, bearing down on the destroyed area with all the unstoppability of a derailed freight train.

32.

Titan found his team just as Galvanize was returning to them from a small cluster of men also wearing masks and capes. The number of unfamiliar uniforms and intensity of the situation made it impossible to determine who was a Hero and who was a corpie, but Titan realized that for the first time, he honestly didn't give a shit about the distinction. Everyone was here to help. That was the only thing that mattered.

"Listen up," Galvanize said, addressing his team with clear, ringing authority. He might be a nice guy, but now was not the time for kindness. Now was the time for straightforward orders and prompt obedience. "Afterthought is currently sweeping for minds of people who are trapped, and Scope is using his senses to find the ones who are unconscious. They're on point for this recovery and directing all efforts, so if they give you an order, you carry it out. Understood?"

Most of the team nodded, except for Titan, who said, "Yes, sir." In another situation, one of the others might have ribbed him a bit for the over-enthusiasm, but now each was focused on receiving his or her assignment.

"Hexcellent, you and Huggles are needed to help open up cars with people stuck inside. Switch to Big Henry if the situation demands it, but when you run low on juice, stay with Huggles. We've got plenty of heavy lifters but a pair of blades is always handy." Galvanize pointed the leather-clad girl toward a group gathering near a flipped food truck, and she took off without a word.

"Bubble Bubble, you're helping with evacuating people from higher floors of unstable buildings. Airborn is coordinating, so go to her and follow her directions. If she finishes her operation, come to me for a new assignment."

"Absolutely," Bubble Bubble replied, moving briskly off toward a nearby woman who was hovering a foot or two from the ground.

"Zone, you're with Titan on rubble-clearing duty, and I'm going to stay with Scope and Afterthought to direct us."

"But-"

"This is not up for discussion," Galvanize said, eyes hard as he stared at the muscular young man. After a moment, he spoke again, and this time his voice had softened just a touch. "Zone, we need someone who's on our radio with them so they can tell us where to dig people out. I've only got moderate strength, nothing beyond the human spectrum, and no one who is out there needs my enhancing ability. I know you two don't get along, but right now I don't care about your feelings. Real people are out there waiting for us, and if we piss away time on petty bullshit, we might not get to them in time. Do we have a problem?"

"No. . . sir." Zone didn't break eye contact with Galvanize, but his shoulders dipped and his chest moved inward as he conceded the battle.

"Good. Move to that building immediately," Galvanize said, pointing to a five-story brick building with a massive hole in the center. "The insides have been severely damaged, and with the breaks in the exterior as well, we're not sure how long before the whole thing comes crashing down. Zone, you go to the area directly southeast of it; you'll recognize it by the giant pile of bricks. We've got confirmed people in there who need help. Titan, you're going into the building itself to grab a few people stuck in tight areas. Is it an issue if the building collapses on you?"

"Not for me, but I'd only be able to shield so many people nearby," Titan said. Depending on the size of the people in question, he could usually handle anywhere between two and four adults, though tending to that many would make getting out with them nearly impossible.

"Okay, I'll keep your groups small. Get in there and wait for direction. Move quickly. If the building drops, we're estimating it will hit a lot of nearby workers on the way down, so Crush is going to implode it once it's evacuated. Don't be dumb, but don't dilly-dally either."

"On it." Titan headed off toward the building. It felt strangely familiar, drawing close to a place impending collapse. His team might not have spent a lot of time on cleanup, but they made damned sure to clear out everyone put in danger by one of their fights.

The low, simmering anger that Wild Bucks had kindled flared up again. All this damage, and where were those little shits to help? It was possible they'd already been hauled off to DVA questioning, but he doubted it. Powerful as the Department of Variant Human Affairs was, they were still a government agency, and those things were simply not built to run with that much efficiency. No, more likely they were too ashamed to show their faces at this scene. He hoped Topsy was tearing them a new asshole right now. Despite being the guy they called in when they had to take a "scorched earth" approached to a target, Topsy had always been good about keeping the destruction he caused contained. That was a lesson that needed to get passed on to his trainees, and fast.

Titan came around the corner, walking up to the building to find another man standing there, his head tilted in the way common to one listening to an earpiece. He had to be a shifter; he was wearing a skintight costume made of the telltale shimmery fabric designed to accommodate altered forms. It was useful as hell, invented by some tech-genius before Titan's time. The material was able to stretch to accommodate all manner of sizes, but it was a pain in the ass to get any sort of stain out of. That probably explained why this guy had opted for a black version. He might be able to get at least a few wears out of a single suit of the stuff.

The man glanced over his shoulder as Titan approached. "You're the other guy?"

"Didn't know I was, but it seems like I am."

"Just got updated with new orders from Scope. I'm supposed to secure the bottom floor as best I can while you go up to the higher ones."

"I'm a pretty heavy guy," Titan said. If the interior was that damaged then every pound of difference mattered.

"In my shifted form, my weight is measured in tons."

"Ground floor for you it is." Titan stuck out his meaty hand in greeting. "I'm Titan, pleasure to work with you."

The man in black shiny material laughed, even as he shook Titan's hand. "I already know who you are. My name is Granite; I'm the strongman from Elemental Fury."

33.

"That a fact? I didn't recognize you outside your shifted form." Titan kept a close watch on Granite's face as they finished the handshake. Teams were complicated entities; in order to function, every member had to be completely loyal to one another. That didn't mean they had to agree all the time, though. Granite would back Gale in any moves she made against Titan, but that didn't mean he necessarily harbored any personal animosity toward the older Hero.

"I try not to get photographed in human form, even with the mask. If I can pull it off then retirement will be a lot easier." Granite released Titan's hand, his own eyes clearly scrutinizing the other man as well. "Trying to figure out if I dislike you as much as Gale does?"

"Obviously."

Granite laughed, a deep, booming sound so cheerful that it seemed incongruous against the chaos around them. "Don't mind Gale. She's a little tightly wound. In the last few years some high profile Heroes have come out of Brewster, folks who moved up to bigger cities and better merchandising sales. That's great for them, but the fact that they've all come from here means a lot of new or overambitious Heroes have been migrating to our town, trying to use it as a career springboard."

At last, the pieces of Gale's behavior fell into place for Titan. When a city had a lot of well-known Heroes coming out of it, it was considered "hot." Hot cities were a double-edged sword. Not many truly skilled criminal Supers tried to start shit in them for fear of meeting too strong of opposition, but it also drew the sort of Heroes who were desperate to get bigger in the public eye. Those were the Heroes who made dangerous mistakes and took stupid risks, doing things that got innocent people killed. No wonder Gale had been on such a hair trigger about him coming to her town; if she was already dealing with a bunch of upstarts, the last thing she needed was someone with his profile doing the same thing. It would validate their behavior, invigorate them, and lead to even more reckless choices.

"Should I bother telling you that's not what I'm here to do, or is it wasting my words?" Titan asked.

"I already know that you aren't in Brewster for anything PR-related," Granite assured him. "For one thing, you're fucking Titan. You were back in the public eye as soon as you put the mask on. For another, Brewster is hot right now, but you don't need hot. You could have walked into any city in the continental USA and been huge. And lastly, I mean, come on. You're shepherding a team of corpies around. That is not the action of an overly ambitious man."

"Glad at least someone on your team believes me."

"More than you might think. Of course, you know that won't affect anything."

"Of course," Titan said. Whether Granite believed him to be an attention-seeking ass was irrelevant. Gale was going to order her team to come at him hard during the ability assessment, and they would all obey. She was their leader, they were on a team, and short of a severe moral conflict with her orders, they would follow her without question. Titan not only understood that, he respected it completely.

"Titan, stand by for entry. You've got a third en route." Galvanize's voice crackled over the radio in Titan's ear, more strained than it had sounded when they'd last spoken.

166

"Looks like we're almost clear," Granite said. He tapped his own ear as he spoke and gave a small nod. "I just got word to shift."

Without another word, Granite changed; the suitability of his Hero name became immediately apparent. His dark skin altered, growing lighter but with a distinct gray hue. The outfit on his body sprang and stretched as his form expanded, widening and rising in nearly equal measure. An audible crunching sound, like a tumbling bag of rocks, filled the air as his entire body's composition altered itself.

In the span of ten seconds, Titan went from looking at a muscular young man to a nine-foot-tall monster composed entirely of stone. It towered over him; Titan had to look up to see the thing's face, a strange sensation for a man his size.

"More familiar?"

"Much," Titan replied. He'd studied up on all of Gale's team ever since she put out the possibility of an ability assessment. Granite was large, strong, and durable, which would have effectively classified him as normal strongman in combat, but his transformation also had a handy side-effect. Granite could reform his stone body easily, even if the individual pieces were shattered. This made him functionally unstoppable by brute means, though he'd previously suffered serious injury at the hands of powerful elementalists. Titan had an idea for how to handle him in the ability assessment, but now that he'd actually met the guy it seemed a cruel method to use.

"Hey you two, ready to go in?"

These words came from a tall, willowy woman who floated over to them. She was adorned in a white and blue costume with a cape that fell nearly to her calves. If she was a Hero, then she was the type who didn't do straightforward combat, because a cape like that would have gotten her killed already. "I'm Aether from Transcendental Justice."

"Granite," the large being of living rock rumbled.

"Titan," Titan said. "Granite is supposed to hold the bottom floor while I go up and grab anyone trapped. What assignment are you on?"

"I'm with you, Titan," Aether replied. "I can make myself and other people or objects incorporeal, so I'm supposed to help you search and handle the delicate extractions."

A wave of relief washed over Titan. He'd been seriously worried about accidently bringing the building down when trying to get to someone. Having a Hero with a light touch would make the extractions dozens of degrees more effective. Whoever was coordinating this effort had a solid head on their shoulders; they were allocating resources in a way that maximized their usefulness. Corpie or Hero, when this was over, Titan meant to shake that person's hand.

"Scope sent me over with word that we have survivors on the third and fourth floor confirmed, and Afterthought is scanning the fifth floor as we speak. Granite, your orders stay the same. Titan, I'm on point to survey the area as we go, so hang back a few steps behind me. I'll make sure the floors in each section can bear your weight. Once I get you up to the third floor, I'll leave you to extract while I grab people from the fourth. If you hit a situation where you're not sure you can get someone out without knocking things down, just give me a holler. I'll be listening." Despite her lithe frame, Aether's voice was authoritative and certain as she doled out the orders. Whatever role she filled for her team, Titan had a hunch she did it well.

"Sounds good," Granite said.

"Glad to hear it, because we just got clearance," Aether announced. "Let's get in there and save some people."

34.

Titan stepped through the area that had once been the front door of the apartment building, carefully surveying the landscape as he moved. In a situation like this where the building's stability was in question, someone of his strength could accidentally bring the whole thing down with one misstep. The ground floor was, thankfully, almost completely bare, save for the easy-to-spot support columns. So long as he steered clear of those and load-bearing walls, he should manage to get through this rescue mission without causing some collateral destruction of his own.

There was just enough time for Titan to stop and wonder how Granite was going to get past the small front door before the giant rock-man sauntered calmly through the wall. Aether maintained a gentle but firm grip on his shoulder, releasing her hold once they were completely clear of the entrance. Granite seemed to shimmer for a moment, and the subtle sound of wood groaning beneath his massive feet told everyone he was solid once more.

"Handy. I don't know many density changers who can affect others so easily," Titan said.

"You still don't," Aether replied, floating carefully over to him. "What I do is more akin to shifting us to another plane of existence, one that interacts visually and audibly with ours, but not physically."

"Damn." Titan had been around a long time and had worked with dozens, if not hundreds, of Supers. Aether's ability wasn't wholly unique, but something that powerful was strikingly rare. He'd read up on the local Hero teams, including Transcendental Justice, but if there had been anything especially remarkable about their records, he'd missed it. If a woman with this ability was playing second string then Granite may have understated just how hot Brewster was for Heroes at that moment.

"Damn is right; I am quite incredible," Aether agreed. "Granite, Scope believes the south wall is currently the weakest, so that's where you're needed. Keep your radio on; you may need to change positions as Titan moves around the upper floors."

"Oh great. . . as if I don't get enough of being bossed around from Gale." Granite's words were glib, but he still headed over to fulfill his assignment. Titan understood the reaction; sometimes in stressful situations, making bad jokes was a small way to combat the sense of seriousness that often felt overwhelming. It was why so many Heroes ended up quipping through a fight: they were trying to mentally push back the terror and violence so they could function.

"Titan, you're with me on the first few floors. They should be stable, but there's no reason to risk it unnecessarily." Aether's hand landed on his shoulder. There was a light tingling sensation, and for a moment Titan's stomach lifted as though he were at the crest of a rollercoaster's tracks. Then, as suddenly as it started, the sensation was gone. He was still firmly standing on the floor.

"That is. . . unexpected," Aether said. "I didn't expect you to be a nullifier."

"I'm not, but I did fight a guy with phasing powers a few decades back. He could trap people in this dark existence without light, sound, or touch for hours at a time. Bastard managed to sneak up and get me on our first encounter."

"Fascinating, but it doesn't explain why I can't phase you."

"I was getting to that," Titan said. "Next time I fought him, he got a hand on me and then received the shock of his life when I stayed right there in front of him. The same tricks don't work on me twice, and I think your power is similar enough to his that my resistance countered it."

"Can't you turn it off? What if you need healing?"

"My body handles its own healing, and while I can suppress it if I really need to, it takes real focus so it's an imprecise process. I don't think either of us wants me slipping back to solid while suspended in the air," Titan said.

"A fair point." Aether floated down to the ground, rippled momentarily, and became solid. "I suppose all we can do is go slowly and let me test the stairs as we move."

"That was pretty much my plan from the get-go," Titan replied.

The two set off on the careful climb, checking each of the stairs as they went. Luckily, the building had been constructed in a more industrial era, long before cheap cost-cutting measures had given rise to staircases that were barely anchored at each level. Within five minutes they had passed the first two floors and made it to the third without incident. The floor there was less solid than on the lower levels, and a part of the back wall had been blown out, allowing them to see the cleanup going on outside.

"This is as high as you can go," Aether told him. "Everything above is too unstable. Scope and Afterthought finished the scan while we were climbing. I've got three targets on floor four and one on floor five. You've got two here: one in room one-three-two and one in room four-two-one. Got that?"

"Got it," Titan might not have had the world's best memory, but he had long ago mastered the art of quickly memorizing short bursts of information. In the field, it often made the difference between people saved and lives lost.

"Good. As soon as you've got both, get them out and get clear. Crush is in position to implode this building the moment we're done. The sooner we can bring it down, the better for everyone around it."

"What if you need help with all of yours?"

Aether rolled her eyes in an exaggerated motion. "I can fly through matter, remember? Smart money says I'll get all four of mine out before you finish your two."

"Five bucks?"

"Fine. First one to have all their people on the ground, safely outside the building, wins," Aether said.

The two Heroes shook briefly, then Aether lifted off the ground and floated through the ceiling to the floor above. Titan watched her go, noting the seamless way she phased herself through the various barriers. The woman was clearly hiding some aspects of her abilities, not that Titan blamed her. Even among other Heroes, it was prudent to keep a few bits about one's power close to the vest. It wasn't an everyday occurrence, but Heroes did fall from grace. Fighting someone who knew all of your limits and weaknesses was a worst-case scenario for any Hero.

Titan started tentatively down the hallway, listening carefully to the groans of the floor for any signs that something was about to give. In a situation like this, Heroes like Aether definitely had the upper hand. Still, there were people depending on him to get to them, so Titan was determined not to go crashing through the floor.

He hoped.

35.

The man in the first apartment was young, single from the looks of the décor, and trapped under a dresser. Titan didn't even bother knocking as he entered; pleasantries were for people with more time and less at stake. He shattered the lock and pushed the door open, revealing a panicked young man pinned under heavy furniture. Extricating him was easy; Titan lifted the dresser as though it had as little substance as a banker's promise. Once the man was free, it became clear that the falling furniture had fractured, if not broken, his leg. This actually made things easier as far as Titan was concerned. Carrying someone was much simpler than trying to have them follow him through an unstable building.

In the second apartment, Titan and his new passenger found a woman whose refrigerator had tumbled over and blocked the door. With a quick call of caution, Titan slowly pressed the thin wooden door open, sending the sizable fridge sliding across the carpeted floor. He'd just finished moving it when a loud cracking sound filled the air, accompanied moments later by a shudder than ran through the entire building. He barely had time to wonder what had happened before Galvanize's voice crackled to life on his radio.

"Titan, Granite just reported that the southern wall came down. From what we can see it's causing a ripple effect that's going to send the whole thing crashing. You need to get your people clear immediately."

"Was Granite trapped under the collapse? Did Aether finish hers yet?" As he spoke, Titan grabbed the recently-freed woman around her midsection and lifted her up, holding her at his left side just as he was holding the man with the broken leg on his right.

"Granite is perfectly fine; it would take more than one wall to encumber him. Aether is above you retrieving her final survivor from floor five. Since she's unaffected by things like falling buildings though, you need to worry about you and yours."

Another shudder rocked the building, this one causing the floor at Titan's feet to buck slightly. The man let out a yelp of terror, while the woman seemed to draw closer to Titan's massive frame.

"Evacuating now. Any guess on how long I've got?"

"I'm watching the western side of the building crumble as we speak. You have no time. Get out of there any way that you can."

"Was afraid you'd say that," Titan mumbled. He turned down the hallway and took off at a sprint, no long concerning himself with the integrity of the floor. If he went through it now then it would just put him closer to the ground, which would make escape easier. As it was, he was already in a time-crunch. If it had just been him then he could have blasted through the walls and crashed to the ground, no problem. Having humans with him complicated matters. They could get seriously injured if he went smashing through bricks. Of course, they were still going to be in harm's way even with his current plan, but better a few broken bones than a building's worth of rubble coming down on top of them.

He rounded a corner just as the building gave up a shake so powerful that the walls around them momentarily buckled. It was going to be a close one, but Titan at least had his goal in sight. At the end of this hallway, directly in front of them, was the busted wall that he'd seen when first reaching this floor. Through it, Titan could already see the other rescue workers retreating from the collapsing building. That was good, because he needed a clear landing area. As he reached the end of the hallway, Titan pushed himself off with the tremendous powerful in his sizable legs, pulling his people in as close as possible.

Titan rocketed out of the side of the collapsing building, hurtling through the air as both of his rescued citizens screamed bloody murder in his arms. He paid them no mind, all his focus on getting his body's orientation right. The landing was key: it would determine if these two ended the day facing lumps, bruises, and bad memories, or life-threatening injuries. Titan lifted them both, one in each arm, while tilting his legs downward. He needed to absorb as much of the fall's force as he could with his legs and try to dissipate the rest by letting his arms stay flexible. This was a technique he'd developed many years ago for rapid evacuations, but it had been a very long time since he'd used it.

Dust and rocks flew upward as Titan came smashing down, long legs sliding a bit across the terrain as he tried to bend them upon landing. Once or twice he nearly lost his footing, but old habits and a steely will allowed him to stay upright. When he finally came to stop his charges were shaken, coughing, and clearly scared out of their minds, but alive and relatively unscathed.

"Everybody okay?" Titan asked. Both the man and the woman gave weak but recognizable nods to the affirmative. He'd probably have them checked out by a healer just to be safe; however, for the moment, self-diagnosis would have to suffice.

Behind them, a loud crackling sound filled the air. Titan turned around just in time to see the building he'd just been in collapsing in on itself like a film strip on fast-forward. Dark swirls of energy surrounded it as it fell, and within moments the building was nothing more than a pile of rubble in the center of its former slab. The energy dissipated, and a small-statured man in a black and white costume headed back toward the area where Scope and Afterthought were coordinating things.

"That was pretty cool," said the man still clutched in Titan's hand. His voice finally snapped Titan back to the situation. The large Hero lowered his passengers gently to the ground.

"Galvanize, do we have any healers on hand? I've got a citizen with a busted leg, and after the day he's had, a patch-job seems the least we can do."

"We've already got two heading over. You just sit tight and they'll come to you. Nice job with the exit, by the way."

"Well, the elevator was out and I just can't stand the tediousness of stairs."

"You did good work, plus I'm sure Mr. Greene will be happy that the press was on hand to document your efforts."

Titan had to bite back the urge to groan out loud. He hadn't been showboating in the slightest, but once the media started playing the clip of him leaping from the building, Gale was going to be impossible to deal with.

As he ruminated on his poor fortune, Titan noticed Aether floating down a few feet away, a young man holding onto her like she was. . . well, like she was the one keeping him afloat after escaping a collapsing building. Their eyes met as she landed, and Titan flashed her a wide grin.

It might not have been the most graceful exit in the world, but it had won him five bucks.

36.

Though Titan's high-flying exit did mark a high point in the rescue efforts, it by no means signaled the end of them. Before the work was considered complete, several more buildings were evacuated, dozens of cars pulled open or moved, and two more unstable structures had to be collapsed. Cleanup would be a whole other ordeal, one that the city's services would have to handle. PEERS and Heroes were willing to pitch in on small scale things downtown, but one glance at the ravaged cityscape made it clear that this was work for professionals.

Despite the many hours it took, Titan was feeling fairly upbeat as they arrived back at the penthouse. They'd managed to save nearly everyone still alive in the rubble, and he'd personally only encountered one person that was already gone. Titan had done his best to get put on the jobs with a high likelihood of encountering a dead body, so the one poor soul represented a surprisingly decent ratio. He didn't, by any stretch of the imagination, enjoy discovering corpses, but he'd been a Hero for a long time. Better he did it than someone who'd never experienced a thing like that. The first time could be traumatic, and was best handled in private, surrounded by teammates and friends. After all his years, Titan could hide the way seeing the bodies affected him; he just couldn't stop their faces from haunting his most terrible dreams.

His team stepped into the penthouse, everyone too worn out, physically and mentally, to bother talking. Instead of finding an empty place to relax in, however, they found Mr. Greene waiting with his arms crossed. Galvanize immediately pulled himself up straight and stepped toward their boss.

"Evening, sir. What can we do for you?"

"Most of you can go take the night to unwind; you did exemplary work this afternoon. Titan, however, needs to have a discussion with me."

"She called, huh?" Owen said. Deep down he'd been hoping Gale's last outburst had been nothing but bluster, even after hearing Granite's reasons for her concerns.

"If by 'she' you mean Gale, the leader of Elemental Fury, then yes 'she' most certainly did. Why, exactly, would you think to agree to a publicized power assessment without taking it through us first?"

"I knew it! I fucking knew it!" Zone whirled around, all exhaustion suddenly absent from his face. He thrust a long finger mere inches from Owen's eyeball. "You were just using us to get your profile up, log a little good will, and now you're trying to jump ship to the most popular team in Brewster. I told Galvanize you'd pull this shit!"

"Calm down there; you can walk to conclusions instead of jumping at them." Owen greatly disliked having Zone's finger so close to his face, but if he knocked it away then it would seem like a sign of aggression, and right now he needed to appear as peaceful as possible. "Gale insisted on doing a power assessment on me. I never once asked to join her team, nor did she offer. The woman is almost as suspicious of me as you, thinks I'm here to grand-stand at the expense of doing the job right."

"So she indicated on the call," Mr. Greene confirmed. "But that doesn't explain why you agreed to it without proper clearance, let alone upped the ante to a public event."

"The event part was my agent trying to call her bluff and get her to call the whole thing off," Owen said. "I'll be the first admit, that one sort of backfired on us. As for why I didn't get clearance. . . why don't we go to your office for that discussion?"

It was a simple request, one that Owen tried as hard as he could to phrase as a mere bit of propriety. Unfortunately, as he watched Greene's face and the looks of his team, Owen knew they'd all read it as a power play. They thought he was trying to force Greene off balance and shift the field of battle to his own terms. Of course, this left Greene only one response, which was a damned shame. Owen really hadn't meant it as some sort of verbal dick-joust, but no one would believe that once he actually answered Greene's question.

"Right here is fine, Titan, or do you not feel like your team deserves to hear your reasoning?"

Owen shook his head. Damned fool had held his ground and brought team loyalty into this. Greene left his caged Hero only one way out, and it was not a pretty one.

"No, I just thought it would be more respectful to bring this up in private," Owen replied, keeping his voice as even as he could. "But since you want to go there, right here and now, I'll tell you why I didn't get clearance from you: because I don't need any. I don't work for you."

"The pay and accommodations we're providing tell a very different story."

"Recheck your contracts. You're providing all that as part of compensation for the time I spend working *with* you. Heroes aren't for sale; we're for rent at best. An active Hero, in fulfillment of his duties, is only beholden to one entity: the people he protects. The Department of Variant Human Affairs is the proxy representative of that group, and they're the only ones we have to get clearance or permission from to do our jobs. Jobs that, sometimes, include working with other Heroes or teams and doing things like power assessments. You may have sway over how things are handled on a PEERS operation, but I'll say it again: I don't need your clearance for anything Hero-related."

Mr. Greene's normally composed face was flushed red. Whatever he'd been expecting Owen to offer up, it had not been an open challenge to his authority. He stayed silent for a moment, glaring at the mountain of a man and undoubtedly wishing their physical capacities were reversed.

"I could terminate your contract and have you kicked out of this building faster than you could pack your masks in a makeshift sack."

Owen was tempted, for the slimmest of moments, to back down and let Greene save some face. Unfortunately, that time had already passed. He'd tried to give Greene an out where they could talk this through peacefully and the manager had rejected it. Owen was a fan of peaceful resolution whenever possible, but if someone was going to push him into a fight, they were going to get everything he had to throw. And Owen Daniels, much like Titan, could throw damn heavy.

"That's your right as overseer of this team, but what you can't do is tell me how to do my job. If you can't square with that, then go sign whatever you have to sign to end this deal. I'll tell you right now, though: the next Hero you bring on payroll is going to draw the same line that I just did. We fight goddamned monsters and keep innocent people safe; there is no time in our world for anyone to try and impose extra bureaucratic bullshit on that process. I'll try to keep you in the loop on things, as a *courtesy*, but if you expect me to run and ask permission for what I have to do to fill my role as Hero, then we're going to have a problem. So, Mr. Greene, do we? Do we have a problem?"

The entire room seemed to hold its breath as Owen and Mr. Greene stared at one another. Either this would end, right here and now, or it would be allowed to fester in the weeks to come. One thing was certain, though: the relationship between these two men had been fundamentally altered in a way that could never be undone.

"Everyone go to bed and rest," Mr. Greene said at last. "It was a long, very disturbing day for all of you, and I'm sure we can have cooler discussions once your emotions have calmed."

Placating as his words were, the ferocity in his eyes as he glared at Owen was unmistakable. He'd been called out in front of his employees, and he'd backed down. Mr. Greene might be willing to let that slide for now, but it was only a matter of time until he made a play to turn the tables.

Owen shook his head and walked toward his room. He seemed to be pissing off everyone he met lately. If he had the self-control, he'd have resolved to just stop talking. Instead, he took a very long shower and tried not to think about all the pitfalls he'd already manage to surround himself with.

37.

The first thing Owen did upon waking the next morning was to call Lenny and officially get the ball rolling to set up the power assessment with Gale. Much as a part of him was inclined to hold on to the hope of getting it canceled, after his stand against Greene the night prior, Owen either had to do it or look like he was giving in to what the company wanted. That was a precedent he refused to set, for himself and for any new Hero Liaison that might ultimately get his job when Greene finally decided to toss him out.

The second thing Owen did was try and reach Topsy to talk about the carnage his team had caused, but Topsy proved to be impossible to contact. He didn't pick up his phone or answer e-mail. Even Dispatch couldn't patch their communications together, saying he was registered as inactive for an indefinite period of time. If Dispatch couldn't reach someone, it usually meant they were dead, held prisoner by someone who *really* knew what they were doing, or dealing with the DVA. Given what had happened, Owen's money was on the last option. He'd been in more than one of those meetings himself, and truthfully, he'd probably pick going toe-to-toe with an Armageddon Class over being in another one. All the same, he hoped the DVA was putting the fear of God into those kids, because from the damage he'd seen, they clearly needed it.

With his calls made, Owen suited up in his Titan outfit and headed down to the common area. With the previous night's chaos, he hadn't gotten the chance to see what was on the schedule for the today. He walked in to the kitchen area and found all of his team there eating breakfast. Galvanize took one look at him and gave himself a small thump on the forehead.

"Titan, I'm so sorry. In all the confusion of yesterday I completely forgot to tell you: we're off today. No PEERS team is allowed to work more than six days consecutively, unless there are extenuating circumstances on par with a national emergency. Mordent gives us Sundays totally off: no appearances, no promos, no emergency response work. As Hero Liaison, there's nothing for you to supervise, so I'd assume you're off as well."

"You guys get regular days off? That's a pretty nice perk." Owen was accustomed to the Hero system, where one simply didn't go active or report to Dispatch if they needed a personal day. Most Heroes tried to take them semi-regularly, but it was often very difficult. Each time one went off-duty, they were left to wonder who their friends and teammates were fighting, if everyone would be there the next day, and if they could have made the difference in keeping someone they cared about alive.

"We're not machines," Hexcellent said. "Supers, sure, but we still get tired and worn out. The last thing anyone needs is a PEERS rescue team too tired to do their job well; we'd just be in the fucking way. Probably why the DVA made that rule."

"If they didn't, you know Greene would have us running all over the place three hundred and sixty five days a year," Zone muttered between bites of organic oatmeal.

"I'm sure *Mr.* Greene would use our time wisely, even without oversight from the DVA," Galvanize said quickly. "However, I know we all enjoy our day off and are grateful to have it. Personally, I'm going to head upstate and visit some friends from college. What does everyone else have planned?"

"Dicking around," Hexcellent said with a shrug. "Maybe buy some new video games, hit up a comic shop, the usual."

"I've got an audition for a spot on a local commercial," Bubble Bubble said. She was eating a bowl of what appeared to be fresh strawberries and drinking a cup of green tea, taking each bite with a practiced delicacy.

"You're not supposed to work," Galvanize reminded her.

"No, the company cannot *compel* me to work. What I do with my own time is my business. I booked this audition through a non-Mordent representative and Mr. Greene approved the role as image-acceptable."

"I guess that's fine then." Galvanize didn't look particularly fine with it, but without a point to actually object to, he seemed resolved to not starting a fight. "How about you, Zone?"

"Gym, training, then maybe heading down to the lake," Zone replied. "My cousin's renting a house out there and says it's a good place to relax. Plus, why bother having a body like this if I'm not going to show it off?" Zone accentuated his point by lifting his arm and flexing his bicep, which was indeed large and well-defined.

"Try to behave yourself. After the last pregnancy scare you know Mr. Greene is keeping abreast of your extracurricular activities," Galvanize cautioned. Zone gave a half-hearted nod and went back to eating his oatmeal, so Galvanize turned to the final member of the team.

"How about you, Titan? I know you're new in town, but is there anything you think you'll do with your day off?"

"You're welcome to tag along with me," Hexcellent offered. "You know I hate carrying shit, and Big Henry isn't exactly crowd friendly."

"Much as I appreciate it, I think I'll have to decline," Owen said. "If I have a day off I should probably use it trying to dig into what's been discovered about those robots attacks."

"That sounds more like a day working a side-job than a day off," Galvanize told him.

"Heroes are generally shitty at taking days off. We're the type of people who need to be up in the action constantly, otherwise we wouldn't have chosen this sort of career." Owen left out the other aspects of it: the guilt, the fear, the constant unease. At least when a Hero was doing something, they felt there was a certain amount of control. After taking a decade off, Owen wasn't really itching to get back to a life of leisure.

"Try and rest a little bit, if you can," Galvanize said. "I know physically you're always in tip-top shape, but mental health is important too."

"Oh, don't worry about that. See, I don't have any real resources for research, which means I'm going to have to bum information off other Heroes. Since I don't really know any here, at least none that don't actively distrust me, there's only one way for me to make those connections and get that info."

"You going to tease us with this shit all morning or you going to tell us what mysterious Hero technique you're going to employ?" Hexcellent asked.

"Nothing fancy or mysterious. I'm gathering information the same way people have been doing it for centuries," Owen said. "I'm going to a bar."

38.

A rookie Hero might have been surprised by the amount of people in Brin's Gate despite the early afternoon hour, but Owen had been around enough to know that Heroes didn't live on set schedules like people working normal jobs. They worked as needed, slept when they could, and took time to socialize whenever they could manage to find the opportunity. To someone who worked a nine-to-five, the idea of having beers with friends at one in the afternoon was scandalous, but to a team coming off a twenty-hour patrol shift, it was a chance to unwind.

The bartender greeted Owen's entrance with a familiar nod. Even having only come in once before, having Gale vouch for him had effectively set up Owen as a known customer, and that meant he'd be able to get real drinks and service. When he was younger he'd worried about going to the bars where Heroes congregated unmasked; after all, what if someone managed to get hold of the staff and torture out information? That was when his mentor explained that these establishments tended to be owned and run by former Heroes, people who weren't quite so easy to coerce. Even with that, there was still a certain amount of risk, but it was one most Heroes made peace with. No one could be the job full-time. Owen had learned early on that if you didn't make time for the person under the mask then both identities quickly burned away.

Owen got a beer, dropping a few bills on the counter to pay for it. These places didn't take cards or checks: too easy to create a paper trail of clientele. It was cash-only, though some establishments let the more trusted and frequent patrons run tabs. He leaned back against the bar and scanned the room, taking note of each patron.

In one corner was a group of four people leaning in and talking in hushed voices. A team no doubt, and probably discussing some matter they should have dealt with at their base. Against the far wall was another cluster of people, this one so large it needed two tables to seat everyone. This group was laughing and seemed to be enjoying themselves. Owen guessed they were either all old friends who had met up or a group that just finished a successful team collaboration. Either way, he wasn't likely to find anyone in there he could talk to.

His best bet was a solo drinker, someone who wasn't already encompassed by the shell of a conversation. At the bar were two such people. One sat near Owen nursing a glass of scotch, while the other sat several stools down sipping on some light blue cocktail. Scotch was an older man, face a bit haggard and eyes a touch sunken. He was a man who'd been in the life for a long while, and it had taken its toll on him. Cocktail was male too, but he was younger, with a bit of cheer still shining through as he texted on his phone. It seemed a good bet that Scotch was here just to drink, while Cocktail was waiting for people to join him.

Owen took his time deciding which one to approach. Scotch would be skilled and smart, not to mention open about sharing resources with a fellow Hero. The problem was, Scotch had the look of a man who'd seen too much, and wasn't eager to get any more action than he had to. That meant he probably wasn't proactive; more likely he just took calls from Dispatch and did his job. While Scotch was probably the better overall resource, Cocktail still had vigor and optimism. That would make him a better connection to have in the long-term.

"Mind if I ask what you're drinking?" Owen said, sliding a few seats down the bar. "I don't recall the last time I saw that shade of blue in anything non-toxic."

"This might still qualify as toxic; it's got enough alcohol in it to turn me flammable," Cocktail replied. "It's called an Adios Mother Fucker, basically a Long Island except you add Blue Curacao, switch the Coke for Sprite, and double up on all the booze measurements."

"Damn, sounds like somebody named that thing well. I admire your courage putting that in your body."

"I'm heartier than I look," Cocktail replied. That was probably saying quite a bit, because he looked hearty to begin with. Every Hero worked out constantly—that part of HCP training was never forgotten—but even by Hero standards Cocktail had a wide set of shoulders and well-defined arms. He struck one of them out to shake Owen's hand. "Name's Jeremiah."

"Real name? You're a trusting fellow."

"No, Jeremiah is my code name. Long story."

"Aren't they all?" Owen chuckled. He reached over and took the younger man's hand, giving it a gentle but firm shake. "Pleasure to meet you. I'm Titan."

Jeremiah's eyes went wide, but thankfully he didn't jerk his hand away or recoil. Instead, his smile deepened and he stared at Owen more carefully, clearly trying to imagine the man before him in costume. "I'd heard scuttlebutt that you were back in the life and setting up shop in Brewster no less, but I didn't really believe it." They finished shaking hands and Jeremiah picked up his cocktail again. "Then again, that's assuming you're really him."

190

"I'd offer to lift something heavy, but I just started coming to this bar and I'd rather not piss off the owner. Besides, who would really want to fake being Titan?"

"Someone trying to scare the crap out of villains, probably. Or trying to win respect. But I'm inclined to believe you; you definitely have the stature of Titan. Pair that with the rumors, it seems to add up nicely. Tell me something: are you really running around with a group of corpies these days? I assumed that part had to be people making shit up."

Owen resisted the urge to tell Jeremiah that the official term was PEERS; he needed to stay on his new friend's good side if he wanted to start asking for favors and information so soon. "That part is completely true. They're all good kids, doing the best they can to give back, and I'm enjoying working with them."

"Of course you are." Jeremiah took a long draw from the glass of blue liquid. His voice had been somewhere between sincere and mocking, just between the two enough that it was impossible to pin down which had been intentional. "Tell me, Titan, what brings you out today?"

"Can't a man want a beer?"

"Certainly, but that's not why you're here. You cased the room as soon as you walked in, then spent two and half minutes debating whether to approach me or the other gentleman down there. Now you're trying to ingratiate yourself to me. Obviously you're either after new friends, teammates, or information; I just thought I'd save us some time and cut to the quick of it."

Owen looked the man over once more, with newfound respect. "Telepath?"

"Not even a little bit. Let's just say I majored in one of the less respectable options for people in our careers."

Owen didn't need any more than that: Jeremiah was a Subtlety Hero. That explained the keen observational skills. They were the Heroes who focused on code cracking, information gathering, and certain unsavory activities that were necessary for Heroes, but not quite as respectable or flashy as punching out a bank-robber. Many Heroes treated those who focused in Subtlety as inherently untrustworthy, at least until they'd been around long enough to see what the Subtlety Heroes brought to the table. To Owen, however, this was the best possible profession for his new acquaintance to have. Subtlety Heroes were all about information, and that was exactly what he'd come out looking for.

"How about I buy you another one of those blue drinks, and you tell me what you know about robots?"

39.

"By my count, we're up to number five," Jeremiah said after slowly draining a portion of his bright blue drink. "Of course, that's a bit of speculation; whoever this is certainly doesn't have monopoly on robots. But going by style and evolution of their design, it seems safe to say we just put down the fifth generation."

Owen nodded and took a sip of his own beer. "Seeing as that's hardly common knowledge around town, I'm guessing the others were easier to beat?"

"The first few were, but the fourth generation gave us a bit of trouble. That's why some of us started doing the research and keeping a log of when these showed up. Each time is always the same: robots show up, cause enough destruction or disturbance to draw out some Heroes, then go to town on them. For those of us with some wits and experience, it's not a giant issue, but this time they got hold of a team of rookies. That upped the collateral damage considerably."

"From what I saw yesterday, Wild Bucks going down early in the fight may have been the best thing for everyone," Owen said.

"Maybe so, but it made the rest of us a lot more cautious. These things were a big leap ahead from generation four. Learning as they fought was bad enough; add in the healing abilities and you get a bot that can catch even a seasoned Hero off guard."

"Five generations, all with no other goals than fighting Heroes. Has to be a refinement game then," Owen said. It might be a criminal organization training new members or tech-geniuses testing out designs; either way, there was no shortage of people who used Heroes to refine their abilities. It was a dangerous game to play; every asset lost could put Heroes closer to the main inventor or organization. The flip side was that such a trial-by-fire method could significantly increase the power and knowledge of those pulling the strings.

"That's what we're hoping," Jeremiah said. "The other option is that someone is trying to get enough information on how each Hero in Brewster fights so that they can try and do a purge."

"In a town this hot? They'd have to be more than crazy, they'd have to be stupid, and whoever built those things is far from stupid." Owen had only personally witnessed one attempted purge in his lifetime: a coordinated effort by nearly every criminal, Super or mundane, to simultaneously kill off all the Heroes in their city. That had been when he was starting out, fresh off his internship, in a city smaller than Brewster where The Gentle Hammers were one of only three Super teams. To their credit, the criminals had been smart, prepared, and well-coordinated. What they hadn't been, however, was counting on the new team to be as unstoppable as they were. The effort was foiled, though each of the other teams lost people in the process. It had been a hard, bloody introduction to the world of Heroes, one that Titan had never forgotten.

"There are all different kinds of smart. I've got a cousin that can't remember what he had for breakfast but can quote Tolstoy without missing a beat. Building a robot doesn't mean someone can't overestimate their own chances at taking down Heroes."

"But you don't think it's likely," Owen replied.

"Hell no. Shit, with all the upstarts in this town, not even I can keep track of the Heroes flowing through, and half my damn job is information," Jeremiah said. Owen doubted the truth of the statement; most Subtlety Heroes tended to undersell themselves when dealing with those they didn't completely trust. It was one of the many ways they stayed a step ahead of everyone outside their team. "Anyway, if this bot-maker is aiming for a purge, they'll need a lot more generations to make it viable. Once Elemental Fury took command, the Heroes put those little fucks down hard."

"Speaking of Elemental Fury, what team do you work for, Jeremiah?"

"Not one that a Hero like you would be familiar with, just a small collective of like-minded Heroes who operate under the name Modus Operandi. Nothing too fancy or flashy; we never even make the top lists of popular Hero teams."

"Modus Operandi. . . isn't that the team composed entirely of Subtlety Heroes?"

Jeremiah tilted his head ever-so-slightly and looked at his drinking buddy with new respect. "You actually did enough research to know about us? I'm genuinely impressed. Every story I've heard paints you as a sheer brute with little mind to speak of."

"Gee, what a compliment," Owen sighed. "I swear, just because I can throw tanks people assume I'm a muscle-headed idiot. I researched most of the Hero teams after I met with Gale; the last thing I wanted to do was rub anyone else the wrong way and end up dealing with unnecessary problems."

"From what I hear about your upcoming power assessment, you did a fairly shitty job of that."

Owen shot Jeremiah a hard glance, but he just shrugged and drank more blue liquid. Jeremiah was a Subtlety Hero, after all; it was essentially his job to be plugged in to every outlet of information he could. New Heroes in town, and any friction they might be causing, would certainly be part of that.

"Well, in a few days you'll get to see firsthand just how bad I am at handling these kinds of situations. The assessment is officially scheduled and set up so that everyone who wants to can see it. Makes me miss the days when all people did was try and kill me in my sleep."

"Worried you'll get trounced?"

"Nope, other direction."

"Ah, a man who at least believes he lives up to his legend," Jeremiah polished off his drink and motioned to the bartender for another. "Look, don't fret about it too much. Elemental Fury is a legacy team with outstanding stats and a reputation that deserves respect. That said, we all know Gale has a bit of a stick up her ass. No one is going to hold it against you if you manage to knock her down a few pegs. Well, no one aside from Gale, I mean."

"Maybe not, but this wasn't really how I wanted to come back on to the Hero scene."

"From what I know about you, you sure as hell didn't leave Hero work under the circumstances you would have chosen; I don't see why your return should be any different."

"Has anyone told you that you're terrible at cheering people up?" Owen asked.

"Chin up, Titan. What I'm saying is you're disgraced and tons of people hate you. You're already in the shitpile. So what's the worst that can happen here? Some people like what you do, some hate it, either way nothing really changes. That's the upside of being disgraced and hated: you've got more freedom than the rest of us. You're the only one who can truly say and do what he wants without fear of image repercussions. You're free, Titan. Stop moping about and enjoy it, for fuck's sake."

40.

The next week was a tame one; Mr. Greene kept his distance as Owen continued to get more familiar with his team. They weren't called on any rescue jobs, which struck Owen as a touch odd when he watched the news and saw what was happening the city, but it wasn't his place to push on that front. After the lines he'd aggressively drawn with Greene in their fight, he didn't have any right to go stepping into the other man's territory.

When Owen woke up on Wednesday, however, it was not with any questions about what the day held in store. This was the day of his power assessment. The details had been finalized on Monday; he was going to Elemental Fury's base at noon (the symbolism wasn't lost on him one bit) to be formally tested by the Hero team. There would be an almost-live feed of the event (slightly delayed in case someone said something unHerolike or a mask came lose and censoring was needed) fed to every person who had purchased the pay-per-view. From what Lenny had told Owen the day before, that was quite a large number of people. On the plus side, when all this was over, Owen would be getting a considerable sum of money no matter how it played out. If he could still get drunk, he likely would have put every cent toward enough whiskey to wash away the memory of the whole ordeal.

Owen suited up in his Titan gear that morning. There was no need to lie about and pretend this wouldn't dominate his day. He was officially off the clock as a Hero Liaison until Thursday, leaving him the whole morning to worry about the fallout from this test. Owen shook it off as he slipped on his mask and pressed the button to activate his earpiece.

"Titan, reporting in."

"Dispatch recognizes Titan. You are shown as inactive today for a power assessment with Elemental Fury. Do you wish to change this status?"

For a moment, Owen was tempted to do just that. If he went active in the morning, it might give him the chance to clear his head and work off some nerves. Best case scenario, if he got pinned down in something big, it could give him a valid reason to skip the assessment altogether. Sadly, tempting as it was, he had to decline the option. Someone in trouble deserved a Hero with their head in the game, and even if he did postpone the assessment, it just meant more time to dread the damn thing. Better to meet it head on and be done.

"No, that status is accurate," Owen replied, just a touch of regret in his voice. "Checking in to see if there have been any more robot attacks, ones that the news might not have covered."

"None so far." Dispatch didn't have to specify things like "that I know of" or any such nonsense. If Dispatch didn't know of it, then it hadn't happened. "In the current suspected pattern there are several weeks between attacks."

"I know, just making sure," Owen sighed. Jeremiah had given him wonderful intelligence, more than Owen could have rightfully asked for, but it didn't change the fact that he still had no idea what to do next. Nothing frustrated Owen more than being aware of a problem but not being able to deal with it. He was a physical man; he liked to be in the thick of trouble rather than standing around with his thumb up his ass.

"There's little need to bother checking in. You've been moved to priority response when their next attack occurs."

This was news to Owen, and it showed on his face. Not that Dispatch could tell. Actually, given how much she knew, Owen really couldn't be sure that she didn't have some way to watch him when they talked. Priority on a response was which Heroes were tapped first, something he didn't technically have the right to. For general incidents they went with whoever was closest, but sometimes certain Heroes were tracking a case or had a proven track record against a threat, and it made the most sense to call them in first.

"Who moved me to priority?"

"Unfortunately I am not at liberty to release that information," Dispatch told him.

Now that was something interesting. Plenty of Heroes had worked their way up to get some say in priority management, but very few had the sort of clearance to move people around without it being on official record. That spoke to someone who was deeply connected, probably with ties to the DVA. With all the noise Owen had been making about his interest in the robots, it was going to be tough to figure out just who had shuffled him into the queue.

"Thanks for letting me know. Even if I'm off the comm, please try to reach me for that. I really want a crack at those things."

"Of course. I will follow priority protocol as required," Dispatch said. "Do you have anything else you wish to ask about?"

"No, guess I may as well grab breakfast before my damn assessment."

"There is no need to worry. Assessments are safe, carefully monitored procedures."

"Mine's a bit different than most," Owen said.

"I'm fully aware of that; yours comes with political ramifications in the Hero field. May I offer some advice to your predicament?"

"By all means, I'd love to hear what you have to say."

"Be polite, be careful, and be gracious in either victory or defeat."

It was exactly in line with what Owen had expected her to say. That was Dispatch: always detached, always appropriate, always controlled.

Except. . . she wasn't quite done talking yet.

"Also, make sure to really kick some ass."

Owen nearly dropped one of the gloves he'd been slipping over his sizable hands in surprise.

"Beg pardon?"

"You heard me. Titan has been more myth than man for many years now, but some of us remember who you used to be. We've been waiting for you to come back to us. Don't make your first true performance a lackluster affair. The world still needs a Titan. Remind everyone who's forgotten exactly why that is."

"I. . . um. . . yeah. Yes." Titan felt his resolve strengthen. She was right. He hadn't come back to this world to play politics or patty-cake with an insecure Hero. He'd come back to make a difference, to ensure that every time a criminal said his name they used the same terrified whisper that children used to ask who was there in a dark room. The more scared of him they were, the more often they surrendered, the less people got hurt. It was Heroing 101, and it was time to remind people why entire gangs would once throw down their weapons at the mere mention of the name Titan.

"Thanks, Dispatch."

"I have no idea what you're referring to. It is merely my duty to relay all relevant information as needed." There might have been a touch of snarkiness in her voice, but with Dispatch it was nearly impossible to tell. That was okay, though. She'd already given him enough for today.

41.

When Owen emerged from his room, he found the rest of his team already waiting in the kitchen, clustered together near the breakfast table. Zone looked grumpy and Bubble Bubble seemed bored. Owen barely had time to register their presence before a wave of tantalizing scents hit him at the same time they realized he was there.

"Surprise!" Galvanize announced. "We made you a good luck breakfast."

The scent was becoming more defined now, and as it sank in Owen realized it was both familiar and delicious.

"Is that. . . did you all make actual waffles and bacon?" The rumble from his stomach nearly overshadowed Owen's words. Aside from a few hastily grabbed meals from street vendors, he'd been eating at the penthouse since arriving in Brewster, and each of those meals had been a balanced blend of nutrition and terrible.

"Snuck in the ingredients myself," Hexcellent said, a not-small amount of pride in her voice. "We're still eating the usual stuff—God knows Greene will shit a kitten if we gain an ounce. But we thought you deserved a real meal before your throw down."

"I envy your ability to put down such food and retain such a svelte figure," Bubble Bubble said. From her, it was about as involved and nice a compliment as he could expect.

"Wow. I, um, I didn't expect this. Thanks. All of you. I mean it." Sometimes Owen hated his difficulty expressing emotions. It wasn't like it came from some macho complex; his damned tongue just went dumb when he got overwhelmed by sentiment. When his sons were born, he'd barely been able to string three words together.

"We wanted you to know we support you, as a member of our team," Galvanize said. If there was any guile or subterfuge in his words, it was too well-hidden for Owen to sense. No, this was just the sort of thing that Galvanize did, because he was a good man and a damned fine leader. Owen found himself thinking that if only the young PEERS had been born with a better ability, he would have made a fine Hero.

"I appreciate i-" Owen was cut off by another rumble from his stomach; this one actually managed to overtake his words.

"We get it, you're thankful. Now come eat before the offices downstairs start complaining about the noise," Hexcellent instructed him.

Owen did just that, walking into the kitchen and piling up a plate of lopsided waffles and slightly overdone bacon. Good as their intentions were, the fact remained that none of them had much experience cooking this kind of food. Not that Owen said a word about it; he was so touched by the gesture that everything could have been burned to charcoal and he'd have devoured each bite with gusto.

"Tell us about what this trial of yours involves," Hexcellent demanded once they were all seated at the table. "Us little shits have never gone through such high and mighty rituals."

"Be thankful; they're just overgrown pissing contests that the DVA sanctions." Owen shook his head even as he stuffed it with a mouthful of waffle. They'd brought in legitimate syrup to go with it, the kind that was more sugar than substance. It was perfect. "Basically, they'll be testing the various aspects of my ability using their own team. Technically this is to get a sense of what I'm capable of handling, but a lot of times Heroes use it as a chance to prove they're better than someone else."

"Heroes acting like dicks, imagine that," Zone muttered as he stirred around his bowl of gray-looking oatmeal.

"What kinds of tests will they be doing?" Galvanize asked, quickly skating over Zone's comment.

"Offense, defense, and adaptability," Owen explained. "The first two are straightforward: they just see what you can dish out and what you can withstand. Supers have too much variety of powers to try and break it down more granularly than that. Usually they'll have you square off against someone who's strong in what you're trying to break. So for offense, they'll put me against Granite, to see if I'm able to crack him. For defense, I'll probably have to deal with some of Gale's most powerful attacks."

"You said there was a third one, too," Bubble Bubble pointed out.

"Yeah, that one is the fucker." Owen barely stifled the urge to let out a frustrated sigh. "Adaptability is where they hand you a hypothetical scenario and see how you deal with it. Shit like 'you have five minutes to defeat a teleporter before he successfully sets a bomb off' or 'there are two citizens in the building behind you and a rock elementalist is attacking your team.' The one condition is they obviously can't be tests that require lethal force to solve, because the people doing the testing will be playing the villains. Even in a power assessment, killing is pretty strongly frowned upon."

"Damn, that does seem like a bitch," Hexcellent agreed. "Any clue what Elemental Fury will throw at you?"

"At this point, I think they'll go with a classic: the ambush. I'm doing basic patrol and a gang of criminal Supers jumps out and tries to bring me down. It's not fancy, but it lets them use every member of their team against me at once, and since I don't have any travel powers, I'll have to fight each of them to surrender." Owen took a bite of the overly crispy bacon, which helped calm his nerves a touch.

"Given the nature of your abilities, it seems like that would actually favor you," Bubble Bubble pointed out. "After all, you are renowned for your indestructability."

"That's exactly why I think they'll pick it," Owen explained. "It lets them get every one of their people in play, and they can fight me on what's supposed to be my home turf. If they can beat me on that count, it will say a whole hell of a lot about their skill. If they fail, then they have the deniability of it only being because my power is so strong. Besides, there are more ways to incapacitate someone than just by knocking them unconscious."

"Well, whatever they pull, we'll be there to see it," Galvanize said. "We've all been given the afternoon off to watch your assessment."

"Greene was okay with this?"

"Mr. Greene insisted, actually," Galvanize told him. "He sees the benefits in showing a united front and cheering one of our team members on to victory."

Greene was smart; Owen had to give him that. No matter how much he might dislike Titan at the moment, the fact still remained that tying the team to his image was good for the brand. The man could put business over personal feelings, a skill that made him especially dangerous. Regardless of the reason why they'd gotten permission, Owen was glad to have his team at the assessment. It would be nice to have a few people cheering for him.

Especially since they might be the only ones.

42.

Unlike the PEERS team, Elemental Fury didn't have the luxury of living in the middle of a high-rise. No real Hero team could ever have gotten away with such a location for a base. Aside from defense concerns, of which there would be plenty, putting a base in a shared building broke one of the core tenants that Heroes lived by: it endangered civilians. It took a special breed of stupid to try and hit Heroes where they lived, but unfortunately, stupid was never in short enough supply. When the attacks came, there would be collateral damage, and that meant anywhere that a Hero laid his or her head had to be as isolated as possible.

When Owen first saw Elemental Fury's base, he was surprised that they'd taken such an old-school approach. Their base was located in the middle of a sizable lake, built atop an island that was almost certainly crafted by some skilled Super. It was several stories high with ample cameras in view; Owen could only imagine the arsenal housed within that wasn't so easy to spot. He spent a while marveling at the place until he remembered that they were a legacy team: the base had been passed down with the title. With a legacy team there would have been at least a dozen Heroes, each with their own skills and connections, who had contributed to the defenses over the years.

For today, a metal walkway ran from the edge of the lake all the way to the base's front door; a few folks in capes and masks were currently making their way across. Owen headed over to the walkway with his team trailing several steps behind. Though they'd come to offer support, they also understood his need to focus before the actual brawling began.

As Owen drew close to the walkway, he spotted a familiar form and felt an unexpected sense of relief wash over him.

"Lenny, it's good to see you." The massive Hero shook hands with the small, round agent. "I thought you might still be pissed about me accidently pushing Gale into this."

"Come on, now, why would I ever be mad about that? You know I get a cut from your end of the profits, and have you even seen the pre-order numbers? I could take a month-long vacation on one of those islands where they carry you around everywhere."

"Except you don't take vacations," Owen pointed out.

"That's no reason to ruin my fantasy," Lenny said.

The rest of the team caught up to Owen and Lenny, most of them looking at the bald man speaking confidently to Titan with blatant curiosity.

"You must be my client's team," Lenny said, piping up before any of them had the chance to. "Great job you've all been doing keeping him in line. Galvanize, loved the way you played on camera at that last rescue. Bubble Bubble, that recent magazine spread was fantastic; wouldn't be surprised if they call you for a centerfold gig. Zone, congratulations on the new Punch Juice commercial, I hear it's testing fantastic in the Asian markets. Hexcellent, don't be surprised if a new makeup company tries to open negotiations with you next week. Word on the grapevine is that you're turning into a hot commodity and a lot of folks are interested."

Lenny paused for a moment as the four momentarily-dumbstruck Supers stared at him. "Oh, my apologies. I'm Lenny, Titan's agent."

"You certainly are. . . thorough with your knowledge," Galvanize said, finally managing to find his words.

"It's my job, my passion, and my pleasure," Lenny replied. "Why don't you four go on ahead while I take my boy over to the assessment area? He's never been here and gets lost easily. The people working the door know to show you to my viewing area; funny how no one noticed I worked VIP seats for myself into the contracts they signed."

"There's really no need-" Galvanize began, trying to protest.

"Nope, none of that. You're with one of mine then you're with me. Hustle along, now; if I don't deliver this meathead on time everyone has to wait for the show."

With little choice and no idea how to protest, the PEERS team headed down the walkway towards the entrance. Hexcellent paused to glance back and throw Owen a "Rock On" hand signal, which he chose to believe was her version of a thumbs up for luck.

"Nice kids," Lenny said once they were gone. "Sure you wanted to bring them along for this?"

"They demanded to come. Said we were a team and they were going to cheer for me."

"That a fact?" Lenny glanced up at his old friend. "Still having that trouble with thinking they're not as good as you?"

"No. I think that problem is good and dead."

"Fantastic. Now that you've found your humility, let's go remind everyone else why you actually *are* better than them."

*   *   *

When Owen emerged from the elevator adjacent to the training arena, he wasn't surprised to find the entire Elemental Fury team waiting for him. Though the walls were solid, with no windows in sight, he could still feel the familiar tingle of eyes upon him: cameras embedded all over the place, no doubt, picking up everything he said or did. No movement would go unseen, no gesture unrecorded. He was under the public eye once more, and the pressure from their scrutiny was like a dull pain jamming into the back of his head. Much as he loved Hero work, he'd managed to forget how much he hated this part.

"Welcome to our training grounds, Titan." Gale's voice was loud, well-enunciated, and authoritative. She'd clearly had ample experience playing to the crowds and cameras. It was no surprise; being the leader, the face, of a team this popular demanded some theatrical skills. "You are here for a standard power assessment, to determine your skill levels in case we should ever need to call upon you for assistance or a team up."

"Yeah. Sure. That's exactly why I'm here." There was no attempt to disguise the biting sarcasm in his tone. Lenny was going to give him shit for this, and honestly, at this point Owen didn't care. They might have corralled him into this situation, but they couldn't make him dance like a good puppet.

"Excellent." If Gale was flustered by his response, she kept it completely off her face. The woman was a pro, no question about it. "Let me introduce you to our team. You've already met Granite, I believe."

Granite was in rock-monster form, but he gave Owen a small wave that seemed out of character for such an intimidating being. It was a nice reminder that not everyone on the team hated him.

"To his right is Spring and Birdsman," Gale continued.

An older man wearing a costume that looked oddly arcane gave a bow, as did the lean young woman next to him. She wore a tight costume of bright greens and yellows, although there was a silver sash wrapped around her chest that didn't quite match the motif.

"And on my left you will find Misdirection."

It was hard to tell if Misdirection was male or female; the flowing costume was topped off by loose black sack of a mask that obscured any details about his or her head. Thankfully, Misdirection actually spoke a greeting instead of bowing.

"A joy to meet you," said a distinctly female voice from within the hood.

"Same here," Owen replied. "I've heard great things about your entire team, and I have nothing but respect for what you've accomplished." That part he was able to say with sincerity. Stupid politics aside, these people saved a lot of lives, and that was always going to be worth admiration.

"As do we you," Gale said. "Now that introductions are done, shall we commence the assessment?"

"This is your party; just tell me where you want me to dance."

"Of course. Let's keep it standard and start with offense. Granite will serve as your sparring partner."

Owen nodded and headed into the center of the training arena. So far it was going like he'd expected, but it was unlikely that would continue. In real battle nothing ever kept to plan. All he could hope for was that he'd be able to roll with the changes, and the punches, as they came.

43.

As Owen and Granite got situated in the center of the room, the others moved behind a clear barrier that had been erected in one of the corners. While each was probably capable of handling themselves in case of danger, there was no need to take silly chances. After all, when two strongmen went after each other, there was bound to be some shrapnel and collateral damage.

"Listen, before we get started: you're basically invulnerable to raw force attacks, right?" Owen whispered. The censors should bleep out any discussion of power weaknesses in the video feed, just as they would an identity slip, but it never hurt to be extra cautious with this sort of information.

"Worried you won't be able to hurt me?" Granite asked.

"No, I'm trying to make sure I won't accidentally kill you." There was no taunting in Owen's voice, no signs of trash-talking. He was being as sincere as he could possibly be, because if Granite was hiding a secret weakness this minor annoyance could turn tragic all too quickly.

The rocky face stared at him for a long moment, reading the big man's intentions. When he spoke again, it was in a softer voice. "If you're just throwing punches and kicks I'll be fine. Breaking the rocks apart, even turning them to dust, that doesn't stop me from regenerating. As long as you're not hiding a way to actually destroy them, I can take whatever you dish out."

"Thanks. That's a big relief." Owen still couldn't exactly run wild in an enclosed space like this, but now he wouldn't have to be extra dainty. Given the size and density of Granite, he wasn't sure he could have pulled that off in the first place.

"Whenever you're both ready, the room is clear," Gale called from her corner. Ostensibly it was her letting them know they were safe to proceed, but in reality it was her way of telling them to get the damn show on the road.

"You good to go?" Granite asked.

"Ready when you are," Owen confirmed.

Granite gave a nod, then stood up tall and began to speak to those watching on the other end of the cameras.

"We will now commence the offense portion of the power assessment. Titan's goal is to break through my durable body as much as possible, incapacitating me if he's able. This portion of the assessment will be timed, lasting only two minutes. Since this is purely testing his destructive potential, I will not be fighting back. If, at any point, I feel I am in genuine danger, I am allowed to call 'stop' and the assessment will be halted. Titan, are you ready?"

"Hell yes," Titan replied, giving his knuckles a good cracking for emphasis. A little showmanship wouldn't be such a bad idea here and there.

"Then let the assessment begin!"

The words were scarcely out of Granite's mouth when Titan's first punch connected. It was a straightforward jab to the massive slab of rock that constituted Granite's torso. There was barely time to register what had happened before the several tons of stone that composed Granite's body were hurled backward, slamming into the wall with enough force to crack both it and Granite.

"Holy shit," Spring said, eyes widening as one of the strongest, heaviest Supers she knew got chunked across the room. "That's a hell of a punch."

"We've always known Titan was strong," Gale replied, working hard to keep her tone neutral. "It's part of what he's renowned for."

"Still. . .."

As she spoke, Titan walked over to the wall where Granite was pulling himself back to a standing position. The big stone man had barely gotten to his feet before he felt another blow to his torso. He was pinned against the wall as Titan drove his fingers forward, burrowing each digit into Granite's chest.

"This doesn't hurt you, right?" Titan asked.

"It doesn't feel like a fucking Thai massage." Granite winced, more at the language than discomfort. Even though it would be bleeped, the bleep would still be there, and Gale was going to ride his ass hard for swearing on camera.

"Just cry uncle if it gets too bad." Using his drilled grip on Granite's torso, Titan lifted the stone giant up and began slamming him violently into the wall, over and over as concrete and pieces of Granite rained down at his feet. He kept this up for nearly half a minute then flung his fractured opponent across the room, slamming him into another wall.

"Okay. . . that kind of sucked," Granite coughed out. Even as his body reshaped itself, he could see Titan's approaching feet. "Credit where it's due: those stories about you weren't all talk. You hit pretty freaking hard."

Titan grabbed Granite's leg, gripping so hard that cracks shot through it. "Hitting hard isn't that big of a deal. Lots of Supers can do it. What makes a good fighter is how well you think through your battles. Also, and I say this as nicely as I can, you haven't even seen me hit hard yet."

With that, he swung the massive stone Super over his shoulder like he was doing little more than hoisting a sack of flour. He smashed Granite into the floor. Like he had on the wall earlier, he continued the assault for some time, creating all manner of craters and debris in the previously immaculate floor. Eventually the leg came off in Titan's hands, so he went back to pummeling Granite's torso across the walls, only to change it up a few seconds later.

At long last, Gale's voice rang through the training arena. "Time's up!"

Titan stopped mid-blow, standing up and giving a small bow to his opponent. Then he handed back the stone arm that he'd been using to attack Granite's head. Granite accepted the appendage begrudgingly, pulling himself slowly back together now that the onslaught had finally ceased.

"You really don't go halfway with your attacks, do you?" Granite asked.

Titan flashed him a smile that made Granite feel uneasy in the pit of his reforming stomach. "You might be surprised. Maybe one day you'll see me in a not-so-friendly environment."

"Well, I hope you can get as well as you give," Granite said. "Defense is next, and I know who you're going against."

"Let me guess: Gale."

"Ha! You wish," Granite said, shaking his large rocky noggin. "No such luck, old man. We're putting you against our heaviest damage dealer. You have to survive Birdsman."

44.

Birdsman stepped forward from behind the barrier while as Granite wandered back that direction. The barrier wouldn't hide his substantial bulk, but given that he'd just survived a two-minute lashing from Titan and knew his teammate's power well, he wasn't too worried about catching any crossfire.

Birdsman moved slowly, a man whose age had slowed him the way that no enterprising criminal had been able to. His plodding pace would have been comforting to his opponent, if Titan had been an idiot. He'd read up extensively on Elemental Fury and knew all too well that this man's physique had nothing to do with his power.

"As you inquired with Granite, so I must now ask of you: do you have any vulnerabilities that I should take care to avoid?" Birdsman spoke these words softly when he drew close, his voice weathered yet still tough, like finely tanned leather.

"Not unless you've got a secret ability you're holding in reserve," Titan replied. For a Hero who had been around as long as Birdsman, it was highly unlikely that he'd kept a hidden ace up his sleeve. Unlikely, but not impossible.

"If I did, I'd hardly show it off over a thing like this." The older man gave him a wry smile then walked back across the room. As he did, he started speaking to the cameras, filling his voice with volume and authority.

"We will now commence the defensive portion of the assessment. I shall attack Titan for two minutes or until he calls for me to stop. He is free to dodge or negate my attacks however he pleases, though he may not counterattack me in any way. When time is up, we shall assess how adept he was at defending against the onslaught. Titan, are you ready?"

"One quick question: I've never fought a Super of your kind in one of these before, so is it just you that I can't attack?"

The older Hero gave a small nod. "You are to move and act purely defensively during this portion of the assessment. No exceptions. Any more questions?"

"No, sir. Ready whenever you are." Titan kept his tone a touch more respectful with Birdsman; the man had been a Hero when Owen was still in the Sizemore Tech HCP, and the number of lives he'd saved through the years was commendable.

"The timer starts with my first attack." Birdsman raised his arms, palms facing Titan and fingers outstretched. "Fire Eagle! Lightning Falcon!"

Bursting forth from the thin air a few inches in front of Birdsman's hands came a pair of glowing avian creatures, each so bright it strained the eyes to look at them directly. They soared through the confined space, one made of flames, the other composed of crackling electricity. Each did a single lap around the room then dove directly for Titan.

In the back of his mind, Titan hoped Hexcellent was paying attention to Birdman's style. The man was an experienced summoner; even a Hero who'd been on the job for years could learn from the way he controlled his creatures. Titan didn't let this sentiment distract him, however, and he sidestepped Fire Eagle, causing the flaming bird to sear the concrete before returning to the sky. Lighting Falcon hit him square in the shoulder, burying its talons in his flesh; it moved too fast for anyone without super-speed to dodge.

Titan threw himself back toward a wall as Lightning Eagle released its grip. He couldn't do much, but he hoped he could at least minimize the angles they'd be able to attack from. The large man bounced off the concrete wall, sending a fair bit of debris cascading down it just as Fire Eagle took another shot at him.

This time it didn't bother diving; instead it unleashed a wide cone of flame from its beak. Titan managed to scramble away, taking another strike from Lightning Eagle in the process. He had to hand it to Birdsman: the man was managing to keep him totally off guard. And this was only with two of his summons.

As Titan put some distance between himself and the avian attackers, he heard Birdsman say something else. Unfortunately, the crackling bolts of energy that Lightning Eagle hurled from its wings made it impossible for Titan to make out the actual words. He was able to put it together a few seconds later when he was struck from behind with such heat and force that he stumbled forward.

Turning around, Titan already knew the back of his uniform was toast. Whatever had hit him was far more powerful than lighting or fire. Given that he hadn't been knocked clean across the room, there was only one remaining summon that could have done it.

Floating in the air, burning too hot to look at dead-on, was Plasma Hawk. It flapped its narrow wings once and a lance of energy struck out toward Titan. He jerked to the side, reflexes stepping in where basic processing failed. The beam struck one of the far walls. It lasted only a second, but where it had hit the concrete was gone, revealing a now white-hot metal reinforcement. Even the area around it was bubbling, concrete dripping slowly to the floor.

"Holy sh- crap." Titan said. "I've seen videos, but that thing is *intense* up close."

"You did say you could handle everything in my repertoire," Birdsman pointed out. "Which makes me wonder, why are you jumping around so much?"

"Because unlike some people, I have to pay to replace these damn costumes." Titan leapt up and back as he spoke, dodging a strike from Plasma Hawk, but falling right into Fire Eagle and Lighting Falcon's clutches. The two tore at him until he hit the ground and recovered himself, just in time to narrowly avoid another blast from Plasma Hawk.

By the time the two minutes had finally passed, Titan's outfit was halfway to shambles. His shirt was more rags than covering, and one of the legs of his pants had burned off below the knee. Only his mask, no doubt at Birdsman's direction, had been left unassaulted. The room itself had taken a few knocks as well; the attacks Titan managed to dodge had scorched and melted the concrete. It spoke great lengths about Birdsman's control that the corner where his team was watching remained perfectly unscathed. The only thing in the room completely unharmed, aside from those hidden behind a barrier, was Titan himself. Despite the birds' constant barrage, he'd come through without so much as mild shock or burn.

Gale had watched his refusal to be injured with the same passively detached face she'd worn throughout the entire offensive assessment. They'd known it was a longshot that Birdsman might be able to do even a little visible damage to Titan, but she'd still held on to hope.

In the end, it didn't matter, though. She'd never counted on showing up Titan in either of the first two categories. No, she'd staked their pride on the final part of the assessment, and as she walked out from behind the barrier, Gale found it hard to keep down her grin.

She was going to break the will of a threat to her city and increase the prestige of her team all in a single blow. This would be a good day.

45.

Elemental Fury followed Gale as she moved away from the barrier, fanning out with each step. Birdsman's summons floated back over to him, hovering a few feet above his head. Titan watched all of this with careful eyes, keeping track of as many Supers' positions as possible. By his guess, when things started, he wouldn't have much margin of error to work in.

"Clearly, you did well on the first two assessments," Gale said. "Your strength and endurance are still renowned to this day. However, there is more to being a Hero than brute force. And there is more than one way to be taken down. For the last portion of your exam, I think we would like to see how you fare against a myriad of threats, ones you cannot simply punch your way through."

All five members of Elemental Fury were facing him, spread out in three quarters of a circle. When their assault came, it would be fast and coordinated. These weren't a bunch of kids or amateurs; this was a seasoned team used to working with and relying on one another. Titan's eyes quickly swept his surroundings. He'd done all the prep work he could; now what remained was to see if it would be enough.

"In order to test how you think on your feet, we've decided to do the trial of AMBUSH!"

Gale screamed the last word, and Titan dove toward the floor. He barely avoided the blast of wind as his fingers raced across the ground. Quickly rolling to his feet, he looked up to see where the next attack was coming from. Unfortunately, it was at exactly that moment that his world went black. There was no light, no shapes, not so much as a speck of movement, despite the sounds of motion he could clearly hear around him.

The darkness meant he wasn't able to see the next of Gale's attacks, which struck him in the chest and lifting him off his feet. No sooner was he in air than the humming clatter of footsteps filled his ears. Too fast for a normal person, which meant Spring was racing around him. Titan's mind darted back to the sash she wore that clashed with her outfit. He thrust his right arm up in the air just as Spring turned his legs, left arm, and torso into a tightly coiled cocoon; thankfully, the arm remained free. Then she was gone. In her place came the thundering sound of wind in his ears. He was being lifted off the ground into the air by what he could only assume was a localized tornado.

Blind, bound, and stuck up in a tornado. He had to hand it to Gale: this was a damn good way to neutralize a strongman. Any single one of these could have slowed one of Titan's kind; all three together was going to bring down almost anyone with that power set.

"According to the rules of this trial, if Titan is immobilized for a consecutive minute, the assessment is over," Gale announced to the cameras and the world at large. She didn't bother saying words like "win" or "lose" since no one technically won an assessment. Besides, there was no need to. If he hung in the air like a trussed pig for all the world to see, there would be a very clear winner here, and it wasn't him.

"Feel free to struggle," Gale said, the wind carrying her whispered words directly to his ears. "It will make for a better show. Fair warning, though: that cloth of Spring's was taken off a tech-genius, and it can hold back a charging elephant. Even if you slip free, you'll still be blind and suspended in the air. You've lost, Titan."

"You know, if I'm being perfectly honest, I really wish I could just let it be at this," Titan said. "I've got nothing against you all, really I don't. Sadly, I can't roll over today. Too many criminals out there, watching, waiting to see if they should still be afraid of me or not. And however small the chance might be, there's also the possibility that my boys will see this. Sorry, Gale. Really I am."

Titan didn't know if the words would reach her; he had no power that let him transmit speech through tornados. All he could do, all he'd ever been able to do, was hit harder than everyone else.

Of course, that didn't mean he hadn't picked up a few other tricks about how to do that well.

First and worst was the cloth. He really hoped Spring had a way to repair it, because otherwise he was going to feel downright guilty about what was necessary. That's what happened when you brought tools into battle, though.

Titan stretched his limbs, slowly spreading the fabric apart. He was as gentle as he could be, but the sound of a metallic ripping still reached his ears once or twice. There was definitely some angry shouting coming from the ground as the cloth fell away from him, that much he could tell.

Next came the wind. If it were an advanced mind he was facing, he'd have been in a much worse position, but tornados were easier to handle. Gale couldn't just grab and hold him up like someone with telekinesis. She had to buffet him with wind, a force which was inherently imprecise. Sure, if he were constrained it was doable, but once he was free it was different ballgame. Titan stuck out his limbs, catching different parts of the winds that sent him spinning about. His rotation increased as his stability fell; he was jerking and dancing about in the tornado, bobbing up and down rapidly. Gale struggled to maintain control, to keep him centered, but after a few seconds the inevitable happened: Titan's hand made contact with the ceiling. As soon as he felt the rough concrete, he punched, sending him hurtling through the air, across the room, and out of Gale's tornado.

Though he hadn't planned on it, this surprise thrust also had the added bonus of moving him faster than Misdirection's illusion could keep him blinded. Titan landed hard and quickly scanned the room. The large black orb that had been wrapped around his head was making a beeline for him. It was as fast as thought, just not fast enough. As soon as Titan saw Misdirection, he reared back his right arm. He'd filled his grip with debris when he first dove to the ground, which he now threw it at her. Its impact would be hard enough to bruise and bleed, but he hoped he'd held back enough not to seriously injure her.

Misdirection let out a yelp of pain as the rocks struck and her focus was shattered. The rest of Elemental Fury faced their opponent, uncertainty creeping into their faces for the first time since he'd stepped in the room. The man who was supposed to already be out of the fight was standing there, unharmed, with his eyes unwaveringly trained on them. Despite the politeness he'd shown them, each felt a kernel of fear form in their gut.

These five weren't the first to find themselves sensing their mortality as they stared down a man who was called unstoppable. It was instinct, the kind that lived in the primitive part of their brain and told them when they'd drawn the attention of something far more dangerous than them. That kind of instinct was old, it was impossible to ignore, and most of all it was correct. They were right to be afraid.

Titan's counterattack had begun.

46.

Elemental Fury was caught off guard, but recovered quickly. They'd
seen too much action to let one thing going sideways break their focus.
Unfortunately for them, Titan was no rookie either, and he knew how to
capitalize on small windows of opportunity when they appeared. At this point, it
all came down to dealing with the threats in order of their importance, and the
top spot on his list was set long before he'd even managed to punch free of the
tornado.

Bracing his feet against the cracked wall he'd slammed against, Titan
shoved off, firing himself through the room at speeds only Spring could have
matched. This assumed, of course, that she was dumb enough to get in front of
several hundred pounds of super-strong Hero, which she wasn't. He cleared half
the cell in one bound, landing only a few feet from his target. The sound of
crackling energy and rumbling steps filled the air as Birdsman's summons and
Granite tried to stop him, but neither was quite fast enough.

"You're down," Titan said as his mighty hand wrapped around the
mask-hidden skull of Misdirection, who was still pulling herself off the ground
after his rubble assault. In assessments like this, most Heroes were willing to
play by the honor system, acknowledging a situation where they would have
been knocked out or killed and removing themselves from the fight. It was
proper etiquette and saved on accidental injuries, but Titan still kept his grip
until he heard Misdirection's agreement.

"Looks like you got me." Misdirection finished pulling herself up and
jogged back toward the protection offered by the clear barrier. "But the others
won't be so easy."

A streak of avian-shaped electricity descended from the air as soon as Misdirection was clear, grabbing onto Titan's face and attacking with all its might. Damage-wise, the technique was a waste of time, but it did succeed in obscuring Titan's vision and hearing, which he assumed was the real point. They'd clearly formed a backup plan to keep him off-balance in case Misdirection was taken down; Titan's respect for this team was growing by the minute.

Granite slammed into his back, sending Titan sailing across the room. The electric bird maintained its grip, pecking and slashing at Titan's face. Through the crackle of lighting, he heard the wind whipping as Gale prepared for another attack. Getting out of her tornados was doable, he'd already proved that, but getting bound up in one would give the rest of the team time to regroup. That was something he couldn't afford, not at this juncture, so Titan steeled his resolve. It was time to do some damage.

He grabbed the summoned creature in front of him, ignoring the shrill screech that tore from its beak. Like he'd explained to Hexcellent only weeks before, for something to be able to touch you, you had to be able to touch it. Bouncing around the room like a pinball during the defensive phase hadn't been fun, but it had given him the chance to verify that these creatures were making contact with him; they weren't just bird-shaped energy. They had a physical presence, and while he was barred from countering during that part of the exam, no such restriction existed anymore.

It took a lot more effort than he was expecting, but Titan managed to keep a grip on Lightning Falcon and tear it in half. They was a boom and a burning crackle that washed over him as he landed, so loud it nearly drowned out the painful yelp that Birdsman let break through his lips. Summoners had it better than a lot of Supers in that they didn't have to get their own hands dirty;

however, their power still had a risk. Destroying one of their summons caused mental feedback that hurt like hell; it could even knock the weaker Supers out entirely. Birdsman wasn't quite that frail; he shook off the pain and focused on the other two circling birds, planning his next attack.

Bad as he was, Birdsman wasn't the next target in Titan's list of priorities. That honor fell to Spring, the super-speed Hero who'd tried to wrap him up like an early Christmas present to her team. Her attacks wouldn't do anything to Titan, but she wasn't functioning as offense in this battle. No, she'd clearly been given the same task as Misdirection: field control. Just because wrapping him had failed didn't mean she didn't have other tricks up her sleeve. In fact, after reading up on her reputation, Titan would have been genuinely offended if that was all she brought to the party.

Granite had reoriented from his charge and was barreling toward Titan, just as Gale unleashed a blast of wind that would no doubt take him off his feet and send him hard into a wall. The attacks were good, clean and focused in a way that theoretically left him nowhere to go but back, which was a delay at best. In fact, it was how polished the maneuver was that tipped Titan to what they were trying. At this point in the battle, things should have been more chaotic. Any tactic that clean was rehearsed, which meant the real goal wasn't to hit him with either; it was to pressure him in to making the move they wanted. Titan had no idea what was waiting for him if he stepped back; he just knew it wouldn't be fun.

At the last moment, Titan made his choice, breaking left, away from Gale's attack and right into the massive stone monster know as Granite's crushing path. The Hero's rocky eyes widened as he realized Titan had caught on to their plan, but no amount of realization was going to stop the momentum of a charging creature whose weight measured in the tons. He tried to defend, but it was already too late. Titan slammed his fingers into Granite's chest and flipped the stone monster over his shoulder, right onto the spot where he would have stepped if he dodged their attacks per the plan.

No sooner had Granite hit the ground than he was knocked a few feet upward by an explosion that coated his back and the floor in green goop. He tried to free himself, but whatever the substance was, it seemed to be difficult to break away from.

"If it had been you, that would have been enough force to stick you to the ceiling," Spring said, suddenly behind him. "Pretty smart, realizing it was a trap. Course, you did leave yourself open during that throw."

Titan barely had time to register the explosion that came from a small device stuck to his back before it sent him stumbling headfirst into a far wall. In the brief time he spent with his head smashed against the concrete, he felt hands moving impossibly fast, placing more charges against his body.

"This is for tearing my capture sash. Mending that thing is a bitch."

This time Titan barely even heard the explosion; his ears were filled up too quickly with the green goop as it cascaded over him. One of these bombs had been enough to lift Granite's massive body off the ground and stick him to the floor. The five that Spring had stuck on Titan drove him half a foot deep into the wall and coated his back from head to toe in the stuff.

Even for someone like him, it was a less than ideal situation.

47.

Titan couldn't hear what they were saying on the other side of his gooey tomb, but it was no doubt Gale re-explaining the one minute rule to those watching, maybe adding an addendum about the limitation being for his own good, lest he suffocate. He tested the goop carefully and found it stronger than he was expecting. It was well-designed, a material that was both flexible and tough. Spring used the charges freely, as if she weren't concerned about the supply. These were probably either made in house by some retired team member or purchased from a freelance tech-genius. One of the countless benefits of having a legacy team and a budget.

Of course, even if it were the most powerful binding goop in the world it still had a fault: it might be indestructible, but the material it bonded with almost certainly wasn't. If they'd caught him in midair with this stuff, it very well could have been a different story, but they'd trapped Titan against a solid wall, and that gave him leverage.

He began pulling himself backward, keenly aware of the resistance that the goop was imposing. It was strong stuff, no doubt about it. Pity the same couldn't be said for the concrete it was fastened to. When he'd gotten far enough away to move his arms, Titan pressed his hands carefully against the surface in front of him and gave an open-palmed shove.

A tremendous cracking sound filled the air as Titan tore himself and a considerable chunk of concrete free from the wall. Spring was nearby, glaring at him with a mix of shock and annoyance, Birdsman seemed focused on keeping his summons ready to act, and Gale was flat-out glowering. That last expression told him he'd made it before time was up, though he doubted it was by a lot.

229

Titan didn't waste a second now that he was free. What he had at the moment was just a hunch, but it was better than nothing in a situation like this. He charged through the room, goop on his back and concrete stuck all over him, on a path straight for Birdsman.

"Cocky." Birdsman made a quick motion. Plasma Hawk soared through the air, putting itself between Titan and his target and lashing out with a beam of energy. Titan barely had seconds to act: only the fact that he'd been counting on the interruption let him move in time. He quickly twirled around on his heel, a move more graceful than many would have suspect the large man of pulling off, and turned his goop covered back to Plasma Hawk. He drew his left arm in to his chest just as its beam hit.

The bad news was that the rest of Titan's shirt was effectively decimated in the hit, the force of which caused him to stumble forward, but the upside was well worth the tradeoff. That burning hot plasma had seared right through the green material coating his back, scorching it off into liquid and an almost-certainly toxic green mist.

"You're smarter than I was expecting," Spring said. "Most of your type just know how to smash and get punched."

"I've picked up few critical thinking skills during my years as a Hero," Titan shot back. "Using an enemy's assets against them is a good one, but my personal favorite has always been field advantage." At that, Titan lifted his leg and slammed it down, striking on of the many half-melted sections of flooring left from his earlier battle with Birdsman. The weakened concrete fractured, splintering off several feet in three directions. His next attack sent more tremors out, widening the already broken gaps and creating four new ones.

"Cute, trying to make it hard for me to run. Don't think we'll just let you do what you want, though."

Spring had barely gotten the words out before the column of wind struck Titan from the side, hurling him against the far wall. This time, he twisted in midair, making sure his back slammed into the concrete. This meant he was face-to-face with Spring as she tried to catch him from behind once more. Unlike Granite, she was more than capable of redirecting her speed and swerved off to the side rather than be caught in a clumsy grab from the giant man.

Normally, being backed into a wall was a bad thing, but at the moment it was actually one of the better places Titan could find himself. Gale wouldn't be able to batter him about so easily with a solid surface right behind him, and Spring was smart enough to avoid getting close enough to be caught. That only left Birdsman to attack, which would be an annoyance at best. Sadly, this situation also meant Titan had almost no opportunity to bring them down either, since moving away would destroy his defensive advantage. Were he the type of person to worry about defense, that might have actually worried him.

Bracing his feet against the wall, Titan shot himself forward, replicating his attack from only moments earlier as he barreled toward Birdsman. The old summoner wasn't the most important threat to stop at the moment, but he'd have to go down eventually. Taking him out would leave Elemental Fury with only two pieces on the board—three if Granite pulled himself free—and Titan was confident he could bring them both down given enough time. It would be easier without those damn bird distractions, though.

Plasma Hawk darted into Titan's path again, but this time the charging Hero didn't bother to turn, dodge, or avoid the creature in any way. He kept right on going, taking the beam of energy that shot from its beak head on, his chest smashing into the avian energy creature only seconds later. As it swiped at him, Titan grabbed Plasma Hawk in his right hand and squeezed as hard as he could. This one was smaller than Lightning Falcon, and he just barely managed to get its body engulfed between his fingers. As it turned out, barely was still enough.

A wave of heat washed over Titan as the summon was crushed into non-existence. Birdsman let out a grunt as he staggered back. A small bit of blood trickled down from the older man's nose, falling to the broken floor as the he tried to keep from swaying on his feet. With enough time, he might have been able to get Fire Eagle in place as defense, but Titan showed zero sign of slowing down. There was no time for anyone to act. Anyone save for a person with super-speed, of course.

Spring appeared on his left, keeping pace as she reared back with what appeared to be another bomb. She thrust forward, her coordination incredible given the speed she was moving at. Just like few people could throw a well-aimed punch while sprinting, super-speeders also had to slow down to attack a foe. Their slow was still fast, it was just in the range of humans. That was most super-speeders, anyway. As Spring's hand drew closer, Titan realized he wouldn't be able to grab her, no matter how quickly he moved. It was all he could do to flip his arm around, but flip it he did, and as Spring's hand smashed against him, Titan's face lit up in a victorious grin.

"What the hell!" Spring pulled against the green goop that was binding her hand, and the bomb still clutched in it, to his arm. "This got burned off!"

"I kept a little safe. Thought it might come in handy." Titan jerked to a stop, feet sliding against and cracking the already-shattered concrete, then grabbed Spring's head in his hands as he'd done with Misdirection. "By the by, you're out."

"You dick," Spring muttered. She reached down and undid the fastening on the yellow glove that clothed her hand, leaving it and the bomb still on Titan's forearm but releasing her arm from its imprisonment. Then she was gone, zipping over behind the safety barrier and leaving no impediment between Titan and Birdsman.

"Do I need to do the theatrics?" Titan asked

"No, you've clearly got me. I can still concede when I'm bested," Birdsman admitted. "Good show, Titan. Nice to see you haven't lost your touch. Next time we should play on a bigger stage, though. I think my fourth bird might just have changed the outcome of this assessment."

"Well, it isn't over yet," Titan said. He looked into the air, where Gale was hovering as she waited for Birdsman to get clear. She was one of the biggest threats on the field, but he'd purposely saved her for last. In a small cell like this, with teammates around, she wouldn't really be able to cut loose. Now that it was just the two of them left, he hoped Gale would finally come at him full force.

No matter how it went, he was settling this matter for good.

48.

The small pieces of debris near Titan's foot began to move first, followed by the larger chunks as the wind picked up. Across the room, he saw the remaining members of Elemental Fury pulling the clear barrier to the wall and anchoring it firmly. Whatever Gale was conjuring up, her team knew enough to take precautions, which meant it was likely to be a doozy.

"You're powerful. More powerful than I expected, I'll give you that." Gale wasn't bothering to use her wind-whispering or whatever she'd done when he was in the tornado. She belted these words through the air, for all those watching at home to hear. "But you're reckless; you take too many chances that could get people hurt."

"No disrespect meant, but sometimes we have to take risks to get the job accomplished. It's not something I do lightly; it's just something that occasionally has to be done." Titan noticed that the roar of the wind was still increasing; he'd had to raise his voice midway through the reply to be heard. His already-burned and torn pants flapped against him furiously.

"I disagree; well-laid plans and execution can minimize risk and overcome any obstacle."

"Looks like we're going to have to agree to disagree." Titan readied himself as he saw her eyes shift about the room. She was buying time with the conversation, which had been fine for the first few moments, but Titan had no intention in getting swept up in whatever she was planning. If he went into the air on her terms with no bystanders to worry about, there was no telling when he'd finally hit the ground again.

As quickly as he could, Titan raised his right foot high off the ground, pointed the toe of his reinforced boot downward, and thrust it into the concrete below. Unlike with his shattering stomps against Spring, Titan wasn't trying to spread the force out to ripple through the stone. He wanted it all concentrated in a single point.

A mighty crack of splintering concrete filled the air, audible even over Gale's storm. Titan's foot sank through the floor past his ankle, effectively anchoring him. Fast as he'd moved, he was still barely in time. The blast of wind that struck his chest was tremendous, so powerful he nearly slipped out of his boot as he was lifted up. Thankfully, his foot covering held and he remained rooted in place.

Gale struck again and again, furious blasts coming at Titan from nearly every direction. He managed to lower himself down to the ground, digging his fingers into the floor to help solidify his hold. Even with appendages literally jammed into the concrete, it was all he could do to stay in place. If they'd built their training room from weaker material he'd have been airborne already. The assault was incredible, which meant it also had to be taxing. Using abilities didn't come free; they wore a person down like any activity. Even someone like Gale would only be able to keep it for so long.

Of course, the ground would also only hold for so long, so neither of them was in a perfect situation.

Finally, Titan noticed a steadily-increasing lull between attacks. He chanced a look and saw Gale, eyes still blazing, but with a noticeable sheen of sweat on her forehead. As a trained Hero, she surely had plenty more left in the tank; however, the all-out assault had definitely left her drained. She was probably trying to think of another way to come at him, to negate his strategy of rooting himself. At that moment, she was more focused on what she should do

235

than on what was actually happening, and that was what Titan had been waiting for throughout the entire match.

His left leg, the only appendage he had not thrust into the concrete, shifted back as he braced his foot against the corner where the wall and floor met. The first two times he'd used his trick of blasting off the walls he'd been sure to keep the range very limited. Gale was smart, she had a keen eye, and given her powers, she was probably great at visually gauging distances. She'd floated high into the air and far enough away that she'd be out of range if he replicated the technique. Which was precisely the reason Titan hadn't let her see how strong his jumps could really be.

Titan released his hold on the concrete and soared through the air. His right boot fell apart in tatters; it had been dug in too deeply to get extracted when he propelled himself up. Only his near-indestructability had saved his foot from a similar fate. As he flew toward Gale, he saw the shock in her face as she realized he was easily going to reach her. With her abilities, she might have still been able to redirect him or dodge; that was why he'd waited until her mind slipped away from the battlefield. It probably made a difference of less than a second in her reaction time.

One second that secured her loss.

His arms grabbed her before his body could make impact, bending slowly to cushion his momentum. As soon as Titan had a grip on her, he spun around in the air so that his back smashed into the wall, sparing her from a very painful, and likely bloody, sandwiching. The two tumbled to the ground, where Titan landed on his back, Gale still clutched in his large hands, saved from yet another impact.

"Unless you've got some kind of ultra-resistance that would stop me from squishing you, I think we can both agree that you're down," Titan said.

"That was a beyond idiotic maneuver," Gale snapped. Her voice was firm, but Titan could feel the slight shivers racing through her body. It was no doubt a mix of nerves and adrenaline dumping through the body, a sensation that he was all too familiar with. "If I'd managed to stop you, you'd have been completely in my domain."

"It was a risk," Titan admitted. "But it paid off."

"That is not the *point*! It doesn't matter that it happened to work; it was a stupid, dangerous maneuver. You would have lost if it didn't."

"No, I'd have just been in a shitty position. I'd have figured something else out. I've got a lot of practice. Now are you going to admit that I got you so we can be done with this ridiculousness?"

Gale's face reddened beneath her mask, but she gave a small nod. "I concede that you could have taken me out of the fight. You successfully subdued every member of Elemental Fury in the ambush and provided a strong showing in your assessment. Should we every require someone of your. . . talents. . . we will contact you."

Titan smiled and set Gale carefully on the ground. He pulled himself up next, giving a polite nod to the others that were emerging from the barrier. "You guys put up a hell of a fight."

"That means so much coming from you." Gale barely managed to slip enough false-sincerity into her tone to cover the venom in her voice.

"I get it; you still don't like me, or you think I'm dangerous, or whatever." Titan lowered his voice to a point that he hoped wouldn't be picked up by the audience at home.

"I worry that you're reckless, and that you take unnecessary risks. Our town already has enough Heroes doing that; the last thing they need is an idol to hold up as an example of how that type of thinking works." Gale's own tones had lowered as well. This no doubt looked suspicious to the viewers but was still better than them being overheard.

"You know, I'm getting real sick and tired of you making all these assumptions about me. First it was that I'm a media whore, then it was that I was reckless; I don't even want to know what you'll come up with tomorrow. Let's be real clear: *you're* the one who pushed this event into being, so think hard before you accuse anyone of being spotlight hungry. As for the reckless thing. . ." Titan grabbed her shoulder and pointed across the room, where Spring was freeing Granite with some sort of spray-can solvent.

"I brought down every member of your team, and not one of them has more than light bruising. My entire power is built around hitting so hard I take people out of the fight, and none of you need so much as aspirin, let alone a healer. Think long and hard about that fact next time you want to call me reckless."

Titan released his grip and walked across the room to help with Granite, leaving a silent Gale staring at him from behind.

49.

Owen had just finished changing into his backup pants when he heard the door to the locker room open. He sat down on a bench and began to lace a pair of fresh boots, moving with a deliberate precision. Owen had snapped many a pair of laces before getting his strength under control.

"How'd I do?"

"Not bad, not bad at all." Lenny took a seat next to him, his short legs almost dangling in the air from the height of the bench. "Your offense and defense portions reminded everyone that in a contest of pure might, always bet on Titan. Obviously we expected that part, though. What really impressed me was the show you put on with that last section. You let those folks shine pretty bright."

"I didn't want to walk in and decimate them; they've got criminals to stop too. Hell, given my other duties, they've got a lot more than I do." Owen finished his first boot and moved on to the second. He'd hoped that he wouldn't need a backup costume from this assessment, but practicality and experience had both demanded he bring one along.

"You struck a nice balance. To the untrained eye, it looked like things could have gone the other way if a few things had broken differently. They showed off their skills against a legend, and you reminded them why you have that term associated with you in the first place. Overall, it was a win across the board." Lenny leaned forward and stared at his client. "So why do you look like someone just stole your ice cream and kicked your puppy?"

"I don't know," Owen replied. "Honestly, I realize this is about as good an outcome as I could have hoped for; I guess I'm just a little miffed that I had to be here in the first place." With the second boot done, he planted both feet on the floor and turned to meet his agent's eyes. "When I came back, I said I was doing it to make a difference. To help people and stay out of the petty politics and bullshit that took me out the first time. Here we are, not even a month later, and I'm in a stupid pissing contest for no reason other than a Hero thought I might cause some trouble. I let myself get roped back in; now I'm pissed at myself for allowing it to happen and for the system for bringing me to this point."

"It's a wet mess of shit, but that's the life," Lenny replied. "The reputations, the media stuff, it's all important. Come on, Titan. You've been at this for a long time; you're not some HCP senior who just got the speech. You know what Heroes are really here for. Coming back in meant you were taking that burden on along with all the others."

"I'm fully aware of what I committed to. Just in one of those moods, I guess."

"Ah yes, 'those moods,' what fuckers they are." Lenny pulled himself up from the bench and reached into his pocket. He pulled out his cell phone and began tapping on the screen. "Might have something that will pull you out of that funk, though. Here."

Owen took the phone from Lenny; its screen was already playing a video file. It took him a moment to realize what he was seeing, until he noticed the familiar costumes of his PEERS team right before a loud cheer burst forth from them. He could just make out the shape of the giant television in the corner, which all of them were watching with rapt attention. They let another scream, and Hexcellent clapped like someone had just complimented her tattoos.

"They were cheering for you so damned loudly I was half-tempted to kick them out of my VIP accommodations," Lenny explained. "But in the end I thought doing this might be more helpful."

Owen wasn't sure what part of the fight they were watching; he only knew that they all suddenly grew very quiet. Moments later they all jumped up from their seats in excitement, even Zone and Bubble Bubble, though the latter did manage to seem more composed than the others.

"That was when Spring stuck all those weird goo bombs on you. Poor kids really thought you might be down for the count." Lenny reached over and took his phone back as the file finished playing, then patted Owen on his enormous shoulder. "It's easy to lose sight of what matters when you're entrenched in all the bullshit, but there are people out there who are happier for seeing you succeed. You are making a difference by being back in the life; I bet some kid out there has already hung a new Titan poster over his bed. So, you still having a mood?"

"I think I'm good." Owen pulled himself off the bench, pausing only to make sure that his costume was on straight. There were going to be reporters and cameras when he stepped out of this locker room; he wanted to make sure that Titan looked his best. Just in case fans were watching. "Hey, Lenny, did I ever thank you?"

"For the generous portion of the profits I got us from this whole clusterfuck? No, you didn't, but nothing says thanks quite like a bottle of fifty-year-old scotch."

"Not for the money, though I'll be watching for a check. I meant for making me join up with a team when I came back. As hard as I tried to fight it at the time, it seems so obvious now that you were right. Those kids have probably kept me more centered than anything else since I've gotten back in, and I wouldn't have them if not for you."

"Any agent worth his salt knows what his client needs to stay in peak condition. For you, it's a network of people who depend on you. For others, it's ego-stroking sycophants or more drugs and sex than a seventies rock festival. Yours involves a lot less blowback, which means a lot less work for me, so it's my pleasure. Now let's get out there already, and remember to pimp the fact that we'll have DVDs for sale next week."

"Whatever you say, Lenny."

50.

When Owen finally got home that night, he was worn out. Not physically, of course; even as respectable a fight as Elemental Fury had put up wasn't enough to drain his body's reserves. No, this was a mental weariness that came from shaking hands, smiling for cameras, and just generally schmoozing. He'd have skipped all the post-assessment junk if it was at all viable, but even ignoring the fact that there might be people looking up to him, it was necessary damage control.

Seeing their Heroes fight against one another could be rough on those who looked to them as a united front, especially children. The interviews and smiles between Titan and people who'd just been trying to bring him down showed everyone that it was all good-natured, nothing more than a game people with super powers played against one another. The truth of what motivated the match in the first place was irrelevant; all that mattered was making sure everyone outside the combatants thought it had been their version of a hard-fought baseball game.

Once he was finally safe inside his sparse bedroom, Owen peeled away the layers of Titan, thankful to be simply himself again, if only for a short while. Lenny was already talking about a few new meetings and perhaps a sponsorship deal, opportunities that had come in so fast there was no way the small agent hadn't already been working on them long before the bout. Lenny was the best, but that also meant being his client could get a bit tiring from time to time.

A long, hot shower washed away enough of Owen's fugue that when he stepped into his room, he quickly noticed a small light blinking on his bedside table. It was his Hero earpiece, letting him know that he had messages. They were non-vital; otherwise Dispatch would have found a way to contact him. No, the light only came on when one Hero wanted to relay something to another who was considered offline. They'd probably been sent when Owen was doing all his interviews; he'd made sure to let Dispatch know he didn't want any non-emergency interruptions.

With a weary sigh, Owen picked up the communicator and slid it into his ear. "Titan, checking in for message relay."

"Dispatch recognizes Titan, and congratulates him on his showing today."

Neutral and flat though her words were, Owen felt a smile tugging at the corners of his lips. He remembered her encouragement from earlier in the day with a fond glow. Dispatch tried to keep herself permanently neutral, but every now and then a touch of her true self shined through.

"Thank you for the congratulations, and the encouragement," Owen replied.

"No thanks required. Are you ready for your messages?"

"I am." There was a slight click on the other side of the line as a recording started up. A few seconds of silence rolled and a familiar voice began speaking in Owen's ear.

"Titan, this is Topsy. Wanted to say I caught the show today, and you did us old-timers proud. Way to remind them what the Gentle Hammers were all about. Anyway, we've known each other too long for me to beat around the bush: I'm sure you know what happened with my team a while back. I could use your help, if you don't mind coming on to do a little freelance consulting. Every remaining member of the Wild Bucks saw what you did today, and I think they'd listen to whatever advice you offered. I understand if your plate is too full, just let me know."

Silence returned as Topsy's message ended. Owen would no doubt accept his friend's request; that much was a mere trifle of what was owed between them. However, he had no intention of saying anything inspiring to these young Heroes. Instead, he was going to lay down the kind of law that was etched into stone by prophets.

"Titan, this is Zero." A new voice was speaking on the communicator, and Owen realized that the next message had begun to play. "We've met once or twice, though I've never had the pleasure of working with you. You may or may not be aware, but I am no longer working active Hero duty; I have retired to be the dean of one of the Hero Certification Programs. There is a small matter I'd like to discuss with you, should you have the time. Feel free to call through Dispatch; she can plug you in to my usual line of communication. Thank you."

Well, that couldn't be good. Owen knew very well who Zero was: the Hero who had retired to run the Lander Hero Certification Program. The same HCP that had accepted five former-Powereds into its ranks, one of them with the same last name as Owen himself. He was all too familiar with the Lander HCP, and whatever reason Zero had for calling him, it almost certainly had to be a bad one.

"Salutations and congratulations, my good oaf." It took Owen a minute to place this voice; it was familiar, but not excessively so. He realized who it was only a second before they gave their name anyway. "This is Jeremiah, in case you've already forgotten my voice after our long discussion on theoretical robotics. I'm calling because while you were knocking the stuffing out of the biggest team on the block, I may have found a bit more interesting information. There's no need to try and return my call; in fact, you won't be able to if you try,

245

not for a few days. Instead, you can meet me tomorrow night at The Sleek Minx around seven. Have your costume ready, but come in wearing civvies. Or don't, if you aren't all that curious. Up to you, though I will say this much: I do not expect tomorrow night to be boring."

"That concludes your messages," Dispatch said. "Would you like me to patch you through to anyone?"

Owen considered his options. The one he most wanted to talk with was Jeremiah, but Subtlety Heroes rarely joked about being unreachable. It was the smart move, too, luring Owen in with the subject that interested him in order to have extra muscle on hand. Jeremiah was clearly good at what he did, which made the prospect of seeing what lead he'd caught all the more tempting. Still, he'd said he'd be unreachable, so there was no point in trying to call.

Topsy was the more obvious choice, but Owen wanted to mull things over a bit before he called his old friend. They needed to be clear on what Owen would be doing if he went over to talk to the Wild Bucks, and there was no way for Owen to do that until he'd actually figured out what he *wanted* to do with them. Details would change as he learned the situation, but he still needed to go in with limits and an outline.

That left Zero, the one Owen was dreading the most. If the Lander HCP Dean was calling him, then it had to be something bad. Save for one week together last spring, Owen hadn't seen his sons since he left his family, and even that reunion hadn't exactly been heartwarming. No, the only reason the dean would call him instead of their mother was if it was something to do with their powers. Owen was the closest match to Hershel and Roy's abilities that he knew of, so if an issue came up then he was likely the best resource for fixing it.

At least, that was what he hoped. There was also the possibility, no matter how small, that something really bad had happened. The sort of bad that required parental notification. The boys had been doing better and the HCP ran a tight ship. . . but accidents did happen. Owen's voice was heavy as he gave Dispatch her orders.

"Please connect me with Zero."

51.

Owen exited the town car as it idled at the curb. When his sizable form departed, the frame lifted up several inches, free of the burden weighing it down. A valet rushed over, but the driver waved him off. Say what Owen might about Mordent Holdings, that town car policy wasn't always a bad thing. It meant that after a long day, Owen didn't have to drive or jog to meet up with Jeremiah. Plus, he was able to stash some of his costume's bulkier components in the town car's back seat.

It was the first true break he'd caught all day. Dealing with last night's messages had necessitated several calls to Lenny, who was less than thrilled by Owen's request, as well calls to Zero and Topsy. While it was nice to speak with his old friend, Owen couldn't help noticing the weariness in Topsy's voice as they'd gone over their calendars to find a mutually open date. It hurt to hear his former partner so drained, and it was made all the worse by the fact that Owen knew he very well might be adding to Topsy's stress.

Dealing with Zero, at least, was a straightforward affair. Things with the boys were fine, thankfully; what Zero needed was a favor. The man was professional through and through: he said what he wanted then immediately entered negotiation mode to get it. That in itself wasn't impressive, but it spoke to Zero's understanding that this was the strategy Owen would respond best to. Knowing how to come at people was nearly as important as what was said when the dealing began. Thankfully, Owen wouldn't have to deal with Zero for a little while, so it meant he didn't have any conflicts for dinner.

The Sleek Minx was an upscale restaurant, though not so refined that they actually imposed a dress code. It was the sort of place where one who underdressed was browbeaten and silently shamed rather than flat-out refused service. Owen drew a few looks as he walked through the front door; he'd donned a button-down and a nice pair of slacks but refused to trade in his boots for something more appropriate. If there was a chance this night might end in a fight, Owen wasn't going to be caught trying to maneuver in some slick-soled wingtips.

No sooner had the host looked up from his podium than a knowing look spread across his gaunt face. "You must be Mr. Micah's guest. Please, follow me." The host turned and began heading down a hallway, barely even waiting for Owen to realize he was being led.

As the two walked, Owen took in the ambiance of the restaurant. It was an older building, lots of molding along the walls and ceiling, with every wall painted the same shade of ivory. The large tables had white sprawling cloths and ample space between them; this was not the sort of establishment that crammed in as many diners as possible. Each table was a small island, and no doubt the cost of eating at it reflected that. Here, they clearly courted guests of high quality rather than quantity.

Jeremiah rose as Owen approached, reaching over and shaking his hand. "Nice to see you again." Before the handshake was even done, the host had melted away, resuming his place at the podium down the hall.

"You, too." Owen took a seat, which Jeremiah mirrored. He felt pleased to notice that his chair was a touch larger than the others in the restaurant. It was nice, being able to sit comfortably for a change. "Also, Mr. Micah? Got a thing for prophets I take it?"

"I simply like to commit to my themes," Jeremiah replied. "I feel many of our kind are too lax in that practice. You have to find the fun where you can. Wine?" He gestured to the open bottle which was chilling in a bucket next to the table. From the level remaining, Jeremiah had already gone through a fair bit by himself.

"No, thanks," Owen replied.

"Ah right, where is my head? You're a beer man. We'll have to get you a menu when the waitress comes by. They have some excellent craft choices."

"I'm not really here for the beer," Owen said.

"Yes, I'm perfectly aware of why you're here, but if you'll recall I had you show up incognito, which means we are ostensibly two friends sitting down for dinner." Jeremiah's tone never lost its cheerful tone; his smile never wavered. All the same, Owen took the hint.

"Right. Maybe I'll try a glass of wine after all."

Jeremiah smiled, plucking a glass from the table and pouring Owen a generous helping. Once he tasted it, Owen was surprised to find it wasn't all that bad. Not a beer, but not terrible.

"Now then, would you like to know why we're here?" Jeremiah asked.

"Is it safe to talk?"

"That's my job to worry about, and I assure you we're fine. I called you here for two reasons: the first being that there was an interesting break-in at a cutting edge lab two days ago. That in itself isn't so strange—thievery and corporate espionage do occur—but what's fascinating is that the robber didn't loot the place. Only a few easily-replaced prototypes for a new type of high-powered portable battery were stolen, along with a generous amount of data. This speaks to someone stealing knowledge, not equipment."

"You just said corporate espionage," Owen pointed out. "Maybe someone is trying to get a leg up on their competitor?"

Jeremiah shook his head. "This was a facility under government contract, one of those that technically don't exist. Any technology replicated or gleaned from their research will have whatever company releases it brought up on charges ranging all the way to treason. Adding in that the technology didn't have many weapons-level applications, at least none that trump what's already out there, and it seems to me like someone was looking to build a better robot. This is largely conjecture, of course, but you did request to be kept in the loop as much as possible. My loop often includes speculation and dead ends; such is the burden of those in my field."

"No, I appreciate it," Owen said. "You never know what clue is going to be the one that cracks things open. I assume that's why we're here tonight? A lead on someone that might be able to confirm some link?"

"Hmm? Oh, no, nothing like that. We're here because of the second reason I wanted to meet you for dinner," Jeremiah replied.

"Which is?"

"Which is simply that you likely wouldn't have come if I'd just asked you out on a date."

52.

Owen pushed his chair back from the table carefully, making sure not to destroy either one of them and inadvertently cause a scene. "Cute trick, but I have real work I could be doing."

"I know perfectly well that you do, just like I know that you've got the scent of those robots and aren't likely to let it go. You hardly became renowned for being the kind of man who backed down or gave up. Seeing as I'm the one who is most likely to actually run them down, and I do have a few more tidbits to share, perhaps you should at least be polite and hear me out." If Jeremiah was at all bothered by Owen's reaction, it didn't show.

"You tricked me. There's not much more I need to know."

"Come now: of course I tricked you. For one thing, that's my job; it would be like me getting mad at you for lifting weights. Anyway, we both know you wouldn't have come if I'd been upfront, and for all the wrong reasons. Let me make a new proposal: hear me out on why I used subterfuge. If, at the end, you see no truth in my reasoning, then we'll part ways and I'll keep you in the loop on your prey. If, however, you can acknowledge that I might have been just a bit right, you stay and finish dinner."

Owen wavered for a few seconds then slid back up to the table. Much as he disliked being kept in the dark, Jeremiah wasn't entirely wrong about that being what Subtlety Heroes did. Sometimes they needed to move others into position without being able to share information on why. After a few years, most of them thought nothing of light trickery and manipulation. One had to look at their intentions to get a measure of them, and the only way he'd know Jeremiah's was to listen.

"Talk."

"Very well." Jeremiah plucked the wine bottle out of the ice bucket and topped himself off. "I tricked you into coming here, in this context, because we both know you'd have turned me down if I was upfront. Now, my ego is quite healthy and I don't mind rejection, but only if I'm actually the thing being rejected. Ever since you came back you've clearly been shutting away your personal life, trying to make all of who you are about the job. The reasons are obvious: you don't want to give the media any fuel and you're probably a bit gun-shy after what happened with your last public tryst. I'd bet you even emotionally abstained during those years running the bar, keeping your heart locked away."

Owen's eyes, trained on Jeremiah's face, narrowed. He'd never given Jeremiah his real name. Even if he had, the bar, Tartarus, was run under so many fake identities and shell companies that it should have been impossible to trace back to him. Being a Subtlety Hero was one thing, but this was a step beyond.

Jeremiah raised his brows and smiled in response. "What? Did you really expect me not to be a bit curious? Even before I actually met you, the rumors of your return were more than enough to provoke a touch of research. I couldn't make sense of it all, however, until that day in the bar. That was when I figured out what would motivate such curious, seemingly single-minded behavior. That was when I saw all the guilt that's weighing you down."

"I'm not. . . I feel bad for leaving others in the lurch," Owen replied. "People probably got hurt because I wasn't there. I should feel guilty. That's what you feel when you fuck things up."

"And I have no doubt your penance will be a long one," Jeremiah said. "But you're allowed to be more than just the servant of the masses, you know. It shouldn't be the only aspect of your life. You get to be a person, to have a life. If all you are is the job, then you lose touch with the things worth fighting for. This is a talk we usually give rookies; I shouldn't have to remind someone like you."

"I know the talk, and I know the points." Owen reached over and actually took another drink of the wine. It was better than nothing. "I'm just not there."

"Let me guess: you're afraid if you do find romance and the media gets wind, it will kick up the same shitshow as before? No, that can't be all of it. You're the type that always takes on a challenge from others. Hmmm." Jeremiah drummed his fingers on the table, gaze never wavering from Owen. "You're scared that it will break you again. You don't even have a reason why you think it would, but the idea that you might run a second time, that *you* might be the one who destroys you, is probably one of the only things you still feel genuine fear over. That's why you're just the job. If nothing else exists, nothing can make you run."

"Do people really go in for all your psycho-analytical bullcrap?"

"Some do, most don't," Jeremiah admitted. "Few people find the truth palatable. Perhaps that was why I found you worth pursuing: you do not strike me as one to shirk easily."

"Yeah, about that pursuing. I'm flattered, but I doubt this will work out," Owen said.

"So sure already? We have barely scratched the surface of getting to know one another. It certainly can't be a physical rejection; I still keep a fit shape and my handsomeness is objectively undeniable. Or perhaps you simply prefer men more rough and tumble like yourself, rather than the stuffy intellectual types." Jeremiah grinned.

Owen had to admit the young man was handsome, if a bit cockier than was warranted. Still, it didn't change the fact that there were serious obstacles in their way.

"You forgot to add in that you're at least ten years younger than me, and that we both work in jobs that are incredibly demanding, not to mention dangerous as hell."

"I see. You're afraid to get close to me because you're afraid you'll then lose me." Jeremiah finished off his wine and set down the glass. "Very well, I think that's enough offense for this meeting. Since I assume you'll have to yield my words held some truth, and as such you are now obligated to stay for dinner as a man of his word, let us make another new deal. I promise to keep the dinner on friendly terms, sticking to platonic subjects and business at hand, if you'll make me a promise in return."

"What's the promise?" Owen asked.

"Promise me that, should you actually find that I'm not your type, you won't make the next man whose eye you catch jump through so many hoops to win your affection. Self-denial is all well and good, but no matter how strong you might be, you're still human. Don't neglect a whole part of who you are out of fear or guilt. Besides, the next fellow to fancy you likely won't be as dauntless as I am, so your rebuffing might actually hurt."

"I'll do my best." Owen kept his tone neutral, but the conversation had definitely stirred up questions he'd been avoiding. To say nothing of the fact that Jeremiah was right: he was trying to do nothing but live the job. How many rookies had he watched burn themselves out like that? And what made him think he'd be any different when he'd already folded once before?

"I suppose that will have to suffice," Jeremiah said, breaking Owen out of his thought spiral. "At least until I think the time is right to ask you out properly."

53.

It was getting late in the evening by the time Owen finally made it back to the building's massive penthouse that he'd begun to think of as home. True to his word, Jeremiah had shifted down the over-the-top advances and focused on delivering pertinent information about the robot attacks. There hadn't been anything groundbreaking, but that was to be expected at this point. If those running down the leads found anything juicy, there would have been a call to action, even if Owen wasn't included on it.

Still, the food had been excellent, and Jeremiah was right about the quality of the restaurant's craft beers. Overall it would have been a pleasant night out if not for the whole awkwardness of the dinner's beginning.

Owen tried not to dwell on said awkwardness, or on how right Jeremiah might have been, as he walked through the front door. Most of the lights were out, save for a small one in the kitchen and the massive glow thrown by the television screen. On it, a virtual character in a skimpy outfit was striking an overly-muscled man with her sword. It only took Owen a few seconds to recognize the male character, and the moment he did, a long groan escaped his mouth.

"Really? You found a copy of a *Hero Team Battle Force 5*? Lenny swore to me that they'd stopped making new copies of it years ago."

"Yeah, welcome to the age of the internet," Hexcellent said, maneuvering her scarcely-clad character around the battlefield, blade still in hand as the avatar slashed away at Virtual Titan's health bar. "Someone put up all the games forever ago, and people have been tossing on their own mods as well. It took me less than five minutes to get this baby hooked up."

Owen just shook his head as he saw the pixelated version of himself go into an animated death swoon. It seemed Hexcellent was pretty good for having just downloaded the game: Titan was one of the boss characters. It had been specified in his contract.

"I'm going to bed," he announced.

"Aw, don't be like that. Grab a controller and show me if you can make your avatar kick as much ass as you did the other day." Hexcellent held up a spare controller, and to his surprise, Owen walked over and picked it up. He'd never been much for arcade games, but right now doing anything besides marinating in his own thoughts seemed appealing.

"Awesome, now A is punch, B is kick. . ." Hexcellent continued explaining the controls to him, then gave Owen a few minutes to practice before they started their first battle. The two round match lasted less than thirty seconds.

"You are not great at this," Hexcellent said, clicking the button to start a rematch.

"Give me a break, I literally just started playing."

Hexcellent laughed softly, a sound more personal and delicate than the showy boisterous chuckles she put on when the crowd was around. "No, I'm actually kind of glad you suck. I was starting to wonder if there was anything you weren't impossibly good at."

"Trust me, I'm bad at loads of things," Owen assured her.

"Really? Not from where I'm sitting. You stroll in here out of the past and proceed to pretty much kick ass at everything you do. You saved a girl on your first night here, and then went out of your way to make sure she was taken care of. You get a call about some incoming robots that took down a whole Hero team and you smash them to pieces. The minute you start dealing with the media again it's all they can do to stop talking about you, and yesterday you took down the top Hero team in this whole fucking city. So far this is the first thing I've seen that you really blow at." To illustrate the point, Hexcellent delivered a killing strike, finishing the first round of their rematch.

"Well, I've also managed to act like an ass when I first arrived and piss off our boss multiple times, not to mention alienate one or two members of the team. I'm clearly not great at this job."

"Look, Zone's stuff is his own. He's not dumb; he understands that even if you'd played things a different way there's no guarantee things would have been easier on his brother. He's just pissed at how things went, and you're the only tangible thing he can point at and blame. Sooner or later he'll get over it. But who is the other person you think you've alienated?"

"Bubble Bubble seems largely indifferent to my presence," Owen admitted.

"Oh, yeah, she is, but that's true for all of us. B.B. isn't exactly what you'd call a team player. She tries not to get attached; makes moving about easier on her. I tried a lot to connect with her when she first joined but she was having none of it. Now I mostly just trade insults with her. I like to think it's affectionate, but even I'm not totally sure at this point."

The digital version of Titan began his final death animation again as Hexcellent's blade-wielder took him down. Before Owen could object, she'd clicked on the rematch button and a new battle was beginning.

"I guess it's reassuring, in a way, to know that she at least acts the same toward everyone," Owen said.

"Yup, total ice queen. Don't let it get you down. For what it's worth, I'm really glad you joined our team. It's kind of neat, having a legendary Hero with us. Instead of just being the dorky corpies, we get to see what it's like around the cool kids. Plus, you know, you aren't so terrible as a person either."

Owen smiled, attacking with his character and being summarily driven back by Hexcellent's superior skills. "I think you're easily the coolest kids I've dealt with since getting back. But honestly, if you ever wanted to go Hero, you've easily got enough power to get into the program."

"I appreciate it, but they don't let people with my kind of criminal record in the HCP," Hexcellent said. "Trust me, I tried every last one of them before I took this job."

"Oh." Owen had been wondering almost since he arrived why this powerful, courageous, tenacious young woman had opted for private response instead of trying to be a Hero. This made sense, though; having a criminal record was almost always an automatic rejection from the HCP. She would have needed someone to really take an interest in her to get offered a shot, and even then it still might not have happened. "Sorry, I didn't mean to-"

"Relax, I know you meant it as a compliment," Hexcellent assured him, killing his avatar for the sixth straight time and ending their third match. "When I was young I got caught up with the wrong crowd. A few years and a drug addiction later I finally hit rock bottom and decided to clean my life up, but it didn't change what I'd done. There's a price for fucking up that badly; my chances at an HCP career were a part of it."

She held up her controller and glanced over to Owen. "Want to scamper off to bed, or are you itching for more of this sweet, sweet punishment?"

Owen regarded her for a moment, impressed by her maturity. Most people couldn't own their demons like that. They had to push off what they'd done onto circumstances or others. She'd taken her responsibility without hesitation, and Owen found his respect for her growing yet again. It truly was a shame she'd taken a bad road; he thought the world would have benefited from Hexcellent the Hero.

"I'm down for a few more matches, but I'd like to switch characters first," Owen said. "Between you and me, this Titan guy kind of sucks."

54.

After the battle with Elemental Fury, things in Brewster grew quiet. It was a peace that left Owen on edge, the sort of thing he never really trusted. Even so, the sudden arrival of chaos only took him off guard because it came while he was unconscious.

When the alarm yanked Owen forcefully from sleep, he very nearly destroyed the floor in his attempts to get out of bed. For a split second his muddled brain forgot every change that it had undergone in the last two decades. Instead of being roused to help with a rescue or cleanup effort, Owen's head was screaming that he was in his old base and that they were under attack.

He slammed his feet through the carpet and into the concrete so hard that the force left nearly perfect footprints. It was only when he reached for his mask, which should be resting on the bedside stand, and found nothing more than a desk lamp and a picture, that Owen finally pulled himself out of the fugue and realized where he was. Years of training was good most of the time, but on occasion it outlived its usefulness.

As he pulled on his costume and tried to think of a way to hide the cracked floor lest Greene charge him for it, Galvanize's voice came over the intercom system. Owen nearly didn't recognize it, however, as the young leader's voice was filled with something he'd never heard there before. Galvanize, the calm rock of their chaotic team, was doing all he could to fight back panic.

"This is an all hands situation, repeat, all hands. Anyone not downstairs in five minutes will be left behind, but will be expected to find their own way to the scene as soon as possible. The I-287 overpass in North Brewster was severely damaged in a fight between a criminal Super and Heroes. Current estimates put at least two hundred cars stranded in deteriorating positions with civilians blocked in by debris. The fight caused damage in several other areas as well, so resources are stretched thin. We are needed, people. *Now*."

Owen took a deep breath, then slapped the rest of his costume on so quickly that he nearly ripped it in half twice. That overpass stretched across a large area of residential housing, which meant they needed to evacuate the people under it just as much as the ones on top of it. Depending on who else was there, they might be able to help prop the thing up, but with thin resources, odds were they had to race the clock.

Tearing out of his room as fast as he could go, Owen dashed down the hall, through the living room, and just made it to the elevator as Bubble Bubble saw him coming and held the door. He sprinted through it, barely stopping before he slammed into the back wall, and heard the oddly inappropriate gentle ding as the elevator began lowering them to the basement.

"We're the last ones," Bubble Bubble informed him. Unlike Galvanize, she had not lost her seemingly infinite amount of quiet composure.

"How do you know?"

"Hexcellent was up playing video games; I saw her paused screen when I left the living room. Galvanize would have gotten the word before any of us and therefore been prepping to go. As for Zone, he prides himself on his speed and reflexes. Losing to either of us would be a point of wounded honor for him."

Owen nodded, watching as the red digital numbers ticked away, marking their descent. It struck him as curious that as much as Hexcellent seemed to think Bubble Bubble wasn't interested in team, the red-haired young woman appeared to have a keen eye for details and a strong grasp of her teammates' habits. At any other time, it would have been something he dug deeper on, but as the elevator slowed, all he could think of was the situation demanding their aid. It wouldn't be until much later that Owen realized this marked the first occasion when he looked at the problem as a PEERS first and a Hero second.

Perhaps that was why it wasn't until he'd leapt into the SUV and slammed his door shut that he finally remembered to touch his right ear and get a full assessment of the situation. Before he had the chance, however, Galvanize began to fill them in.

"There was an attempted murder roughly twenty-five minutes ago, over in North Brewster." Galvanize's foot didn't leave the pedal as he spoke. The siren's muffled roar could be heard overhead. "Some gang's strongman was sent to take out a rival gang's leader. We don't know if the first gang was dumb, or just working off bad information, but their guy never stood a chance. The target was a fellow Super, an energy manipulator whose energy had highly corrosive properties."

Owen winced inwardly. Energy manipulators were bad enough; those with talent could create all manner of constructs or obstacles to utilize. Some of the really gifted ones could even coat themselves in their energy, like a suit of armor. If the energy itself destroyed most matter it came into contact with that upped the destructive potential considerably. Just from knowing those two facts, Owen would estimate that sort of opponent to be a Demolition Class, minimum.

"The fight drew the right kind of attention, and a team of Heroes stepped in," Galvanize continued. "I don't know the details, but they were able to bring him down. Unfortunately, he doled out a lot of damage on his way to getting killed. Right now, every emergency service that can is scrambling to get the people to safety."

"What about the Heroes who stopped this guy?" Zone asked. "Aren't they helping?"

"The ones who can are currently containing and evacuating a section of the city he managed to partially cave in to the sewers," Galvanize snapped. He paused for a moment, and Owen watched him carefully. The rise and fall of his chest betrayed the deep breaths he was taking, no doubt in an attempt to keep an even keel. "Some are getting healed; they'll jump in wherever they can. We don't have time to play jurisdiction jockeying right now. Once we get there, it's going to be a madhouse. Follow my orders as best you can, but put protecting the civilians first above all else. Everyone clear?"

The vehicle's passengers all nodded, too well-trained to try and talk over one another while their leader was giving direction. Galvanize appreciated them all the more for it. He pulled up to the boundaries of a massive traffic jam, the sun's early morning rays glinting off the metal tops of seemingly countless stopped cars. They were going to need every bit of that discipline to pull of the sort of miracle they needed to.

"Good, then this is where we get out. Everyone, please do your best. Lives depend on it."

55.

Titan had seen worse.

He'd come upon battlegrounds after Armageddon Class Supers were
taken down. He'd seen entire streets run thick with blood and bodies, the latter
often wearing masks that he recognized. He'd seen what happened when Heroes
were too slow, when civilians were piled like kindling after a maniac's rampage.
He'd seen truly horrible things in his time as a Hero, the sort that woke him in a
cold sweat some nights, desperately groping for someone nearby to remind him
that it was going to be okay. As he surveyed the scene before him, he did so
with a sense of perspective, and concluded that the situation was bad, but not
horrible. Of course, all of that perspective just lit a fire in his gut, driving him to
make sure this morning didn't turn into another one that would live on for
decades in his nightmares.

The overpass was badly damaged; part of it had been sheared off
completely and several of the support columns were broken. Since it was a
flyover that stretched across a residential area, bits of the debris had already
come down and crushed several houses. Titan dearly hoped they'd been
evacuated first, then immediately put it out of his mind. It was key to focus on
the people he could still help, not dwell on the ones already lost. That was how
he'd keep himself moving if things took a turn for the terrible.

A massive jam of cars stretched before him, most of which were
already emptied. The impromptu parking lot stretched up to the section of the
overpass where at least a dozen vehicles had been flipped and scattered, creating
an unintentional barricade for all the civilians still stuck on the elevated
concrete. Some of the cars had caught fire, which meant he had to worry about

266

the slim, but still real, chance of a gas tank exploding on top of everything else. It was bad, but not hopeless.

"Hexcellent, I want Huggles on that overpass. Reports show some people trapped in their cars; get them out now. When that's done, help clear the debris. Zone, you and Bubble Bubble start evacuating people from the broken end of the bridge. She can only take so many at a time, which means you have to keep the order between trips. Titan, I want that wall of cars cleared out, at least enough to make a path that I can lead people through. Be careful, but be quick. B.B. might have to chip in on helping keep the overpass up, which will make your exit point the only one we can use. I'm going to help Hexcellent and Huggles get people out of cars and try to organize them as best I can. This is a fluid situation, so be ready to change in a moment if needed."

Galvanize didn't waste any more time with words; instead he took off at a dead sprint through the sea of empty cars that led up to the barricade, the others hot on his heels.

Titan was with them, moving carefully to avoid knocking one of the vehicles aside and causing a domino effect. By this point, he was used to the precise way that Galvanize deployed his team, but he was still impressed by it. In his Hero days, he'd have never imagined a team purely devoted to rescue would require such careful coordination; several weeks actually doing the job had shown him how essential it was. More than once it had made the difference in saving someone's life, which meant it was a skill damned sure worth having.

They all reached the barricade at roughly the same time, though Zone started moving over it first. He leapt up the pile of shattered concrete and twisted auto parts, only needing a single sphere from Bubble Bubble to finish his climb. Hexcellent and Galvanize waited as Bubble Bubble produced an orb that engulfed them and soon began its slow, but steady, trek over to the other side. Her ability wasn't quick, though it was certainly useful.

For his part, Titan wasted no time once his team was clear. Surveying the warped barricade with an experienced eye, he looked for the spot that could most easily be turned into an opening. He'd have to be choosey, since he had very limited space to accommodate whatever he moved. Add that to the slope of stopped cars descending behind him and it would be all too easy to start a steel avalanche. That meant either just shifting the vehicles or having to try and stack them, both of which had their cons.

With a slam of his shoulder, Titan grabbed the nearest car by its axle and pulled it forward, moving slowly so as not to send the rest of the debris tumbling uncontrolled in all directions. It was akin to playing a very high stakes game of *Jenga*, and as he felt several other cars shudder, Titan would have traded two tons of lifting power for the ability to disintegrate matter. Thankfully, the barricade held, and he squeezed the first car into an open spot near two sports cars. It was a start, but there was still a lot to clear away before he could escort anyone without super-human endurance through it.

"Titan, this is Dispatch." He heard the voice in his ear as he hefted up a slab of concrete and dropped it unceremoniously on the first car, smashing out the one remaining window but otherwise doing little to the already-battered automobile.

"Dispatch is heard, Titan responding."

"Titan, you are currently showing in the recently damaged North Brewster area on a rescue operation, and your PEERS team shows as present too. Is that accurate?"

"Sure is," Titan said. He tried to ignore the growing knot of worry in his stomach. If she was checking everyone's position, not just Heroes, then it meant something bad.

"That zone has been reclassified from contained to active," Dispatch said. He wondered how she could stay so calm, even in moments like these. Maybe that was her ability, wherever she was. "The gangs involved in the initial dispute have begun fighting in the streets. Based on information at hand, we have at least four confirmed Supers, with many more suspected. PEERS teams are permitted to remain and continue evacuating civilians at the discretion of their Hero Liaisons, but all active Heroes in the area are to focus on containing the brawl before more destruction occurs."

Titan let out a long breath as he lowered the car clutched in his hands. Supers fighting in an area already on the brink of destruction meant lives were hanging in the balance. He released the car and looked around, trying to spot where the fight might be going down.

"Give me coordinates, Dispatch. And what's the containment protocol on this one?"

"With so many civilians already in danger nearby, the DVA has ordered that Damage Class evaluation protocol be temporarily suspended. First priority is neutralization before any more innocent lives are lost. The lives of aggressors are considered low-priority."

"Understood," Titan said, and he did understand. In a perfect world, the Heroes could stop people without having to resort to lethal force, but some Supers just wouldn't go down unless it was in a permanent fashion. It was messy, and hard, and ugly; but it was better than letting innocent people pay the price instead.

Titan listened to the coordinates Dispatch rattled off in his head, then he began to run.

56.

"Team, I need everyone's positions. Now." Titan tapped his left earpiece as he ran, wedging it back into place. Unlike his Hero one, this radio hadn't been tweaked and updated by every tech-genius to have to worn one in the last several decades, and as such it didn't quite sit nestled in his ear with the same ease.

"Little busy." Zone's voice sounded like a forced whisper, as though he under tremendous physical strain.

"As Hero Liaison I am informing you that we have a hostile situation with multiple rogue Supers, and I need to assess if your position is safe or not. Now sound off, and hurry up with it." Were there more time, Titan might have bothered with diplomacy, but time wasn't extending him such luxuries. He had skulls to crack, and it would be a lot easier to fight if he knew his people were clear.

"Holy shit," Hexcellent muttered in his ear. "Um, yeah, Galvanize and I are on the overpass; right now he's pulling people free while Huggles cuts off the back of their car. We're about halfway between the barricade and the part that's just open air where B.B. is evacuating people."

"Confirmed," Galvanize grunted, clearly occupied with his rescue effort.

"I'm lowering my second batch of people to the ground now," Bubble Bubble chimed in. "Once we land, I'm sending them west, where police and ambulances are waiting on standby."

"That's all fine, the disturbance is to the northeast, and I plan to make sure it stays out there," Titan told them. "But you should be ready to move if-"

"Hang on, you said it's to the northeast?" Bubble Bubble asked. "Northeast of where the collapsed portion of the overpass is?"

"Affirmative."

"That's not good. We had a kid in the first batch of rescues get confused and run off in that direction. Zone went to retrieve her, and he hasn't come back yet."

Titan realized he hadn't heard anything from Zone since he'd made what Titan had taken to be a snide comment. When he replayed the words in his head, he wondered if perhaps there had been furtiveness in Zone's whisper, as if their missing teammate were trying to speak without calling attention to himself. Then he remembered that Zone, like all the other PEERS, wore a damn costume, which an angry criminal wouldn't realize wasn't on an actual Hero.

"Zone," he called into the earpiece, picking up his pace. "Zone, if you are near the conflict, I need to know. That spot is about to get very hot, very fast, and every Hero dropping in is expecting civilians to be out. Give me some sort of sign, even if it risks you being discovered."

"We're here." This time the words were so thin that Titan wouldn't have heard them at all if he weren't specifically listening for them. He bounded across a street; already he could faintly make out the sounds of fighting going on. It had been a rough situation before. Now, it was downright horrid.

"Understood," Titan said. He stopped his charge a block away from the coordinates Dispatch had provided. Once he was in, things would be sheer chaos, which meant all plans needed to be laid out before he entered the fray.

"When you say 'we,' I assume that means you have the child with you. You should see me in less than a minute, and I'm pretty sure that everyone there is going to care a lot more about me than you. If you can get clear, do it, and let me know as you go. If you can't, then get to me. I'll keep you safe."

There was no response this time. . . not that Titan was particularly surprised. Whatever was happening a mere block away was more than enough to keep Zone, one of the team's most mobile members, completely pinned down. It was certainly a shitshow, and since Titan couldn't suppress it fast enough to get people clear, he'd just slap himself into the center of the storm.

With a mighty burst of power from his legs, Titan leapt up onto the roof of the nearest building, carefully controlling his landing to avoid anything more serious than a few damaged shingles. He'd barely set down before he was in the sky again, heading for higher ground. As the air whistled by him, he spoke, trusting his communicator to pick up the words.

"Dispatch, this is Titan. I'm about to begin engagement, but there's a civilian and a member of my team pinned down somewhere in it. If there are any other Heroes in the area, please let them know."

"We've got two more en route; I'll brief them on the situation. Currently, you will be the first to arrive," Dispatch informed him.

"Well then, at least I get to make my entrance as showy as I want." He landed on the third building, a four-story number composed of lifeless gray brick. It was an apartment complex, one in which he imagined all the residents were locking their doors and calling the cops. From its roof, he could see the fight below; several people still scrapping while others were motionless in puddles of blood. The brawl had probably started in the alleyway and then spilled into the street as things grew more frantic. Titan saw one man hurling bolts of gray energy, another taking gunfire without so much as a wince, and a third zipping about in a blur. Two others had shifted into quasi-animal forms that looked like a bear and a boar, respectively. The rest probably had some abilities as well, but Titan couldn't loaf around and wait to see what they were. He needed to get a handle on this situation, and fast.

The whistling sound reached a few of the more attentive criminal's ears first. It came less than a second before impact, however, which meant even if the bullet-proof thug had taken the time to look up at the noise, it was unlikely that he would have had time to dodge. As it was, he didn't even see the several-hundred-pound mass that landed on his shoulders and shattered the bones that had born countless attempts at injury as easily as dry spaghetti. The thug let out a strangled cry from the ground, which was heard by almost no one, as all attention was on the massive man who had just dropped out of the air and taken out the toughest person left in either gang. This mystery man took two steps forward and spoke in a booming voice that echoed through the streets like a bomb's aftershock.

"My name is Titan—yes, *that* fucking Titan—and the next person who moves to do anything besides get on the ground will be broken."

For a moment, the gangs looked at one another, uncertain of what to do. They had, after all, been fighting each other. Eventually, survival instinct manifested, and all present realized that the Hero was easily the greater threat. Every last one of them charged, and Titan readied himself to make good on his word.

57.

What Titan had entered in with Elemental Fury was a fight. It required strategy, restraint, planning, and cunning all piled on top of his already-impressive physical abilities. Titan was good at fighting; it was why he'd been able to take down such powerful enemies in the past. He enjoyed a good fight, but what followed after the two gangs merged into a single force dedicated to bringing him down was nothing like a fight. It was a brawl.

Even after all these years, Titan could still feel the adrenaline surging through his veins as he stared down over a dozen opponents, all coming at him together. His fingers tingled. Time began to feel a bit slippery. When it was over, he wouldn't remember many of the fine details. Those would be lost in a sea of snapping bones and anguished screams. But as it was happening, Titan took in everything without exception.

As he grabbed the bear-shifter's arm and snapped it in half, he could smell the man's cologne when he fell, hitting the ground with a painful thud. When Titan caught the speedster's clumsy punch, he noticed the young boy's nose piercings just before he drove a foot down and shattered those speedy legs. At the moment that three of the gang members leapt on his back, he caught sight of their terrified but determined faces in one of the few unshattered windows on the street. That moment would stay with him, making him wonder if there was a better way than coming in full force. He almost hesitated, then he remembered that Zone and a child were somewhere in the area trying to stay safe. Titan's resolve hardened. As he stripped each person from his back and hurled them into the concrete wall, he tried to keep from killing them, but he made certain that none would be rising anytime soon.

A bolt of gray energy hit Titan's side, and he glanced up to see the culprit staring at him, eyes wide with surprise. Evidently, he'd been expecting a different result. Either these punks didn't watch the news or they didn't believe the hype. Those that survived sure as hell would from here on, though.

It was funny: all the money and time spent on PR by Heroes and their agents, yet nothing spread true fear in a Hero's opponents like being in the middle of a Hero's path of destruction.

Titan closed the gap to the blaster, knocking aside a pair of men in leather jackets who tried to take a swing at him. He reared back, ready to put the young man down, but a gust of wind made Titan suddenly aware of a hole in the side of costume where the energy had hit him. It was perfect erosion: no shredded cloth or scorched material. Titan let his battle-drunk brain work for a moment, remembering the original report he'd been given about a dead Super with corrosion energy, and noticing how this fellow had puffy circles around his eyes, as if he'd been crying. Supers weren't inherently more likely to have Super children, but those in the same family often had somewhat similar abilities.

Instead of punching him in the head, which could potentially result in brain death even if he was only aiming for a knockout, Titan shattered the man's legs, leaving him to howl in the street. Technically the kid could still use his powers, but without HCP-grade training, it was unlikely he'd be able to focus through the pain. If he did, then Titan would finish the job, but it felt wrong to kill someone who was acting out of grief more than anger. At least, not without giving them a chance.

The effortless defeat of their energy blaster seemed to have broken some of the criminals' spirit, as they now looked at Titan with a new sense of awe and dread. They'd clearly thought that he'd be taken down by one good shot. Faced with the reality of a Titan utterly uninjured by what was presumably their most powerful remaining offense, their willpower began to fracture and break. Several dashed away, running for the alley where the fight had started.

"Goddamnit! I just stepped out and I've got a fucking wave coming at me," Zone panted frantically in Titan's left ear, no longer bothering to whisper.

There was no time to think, no opportunity to concoct some cunning plan. The span of seconds it would take would likely mean the difference of life and death for Zone, to say nothing of the child in his care. Spinning in the direction of the runners, Titan could see Zone and a young girl in his arms, halfway emerged from under a pile of trash in the alley. In front of those two were five fleeing criminals, one of whom was the shifter in boar form. Zone was standing directly in their way. If the gang hit his teammate and the civilian, especially knowing Titan was at their backs, chances of casualties were high, if not completely certain.

Pressing his boot into the concrete so hard that cracks spiderwebbed out from under it, Titan pushed off in a charging leap. He stayed low: the goal this time wasn't to get a better location, it was to play human bowling with himself as the ball. Arms spread out wide to catch all that he could, Titan hurtled through the air, slamming into four of the five would-be-escapees with such force that he could feel their bones break as he made contact. Just before he was about to come to a stop, he twisted in midair so that his back hit a nearby brick building before the four already-battered bodies clutched in his arms. Titan let them drop to the ground; now that they were gone, he had a more important target.

The shifter was still getting up from the ground where he'd thrown himself to avoid to Titan's charge when the Hero stepped forward, putting himself firmly between Zone and the boar. A pair of piggy eyes darted back and forth, locking on Zone, or perhaps the child crying in his arms, and lingering there for a moment. Titan could practically see the wheels turning, trying to figure out if he could get there fast enough to take a hostage.

"Ah ah ah." Titan wagged his finger in the air, drawing the boar's gaze back to him. "You'll never make it. And if you try, I'm going to be less gentle than I have been with your friends. A *lot* less gentle."

"Maybe so," the boar-man snorted. "But I bet one of us will make it."

"You want to know one of the most important rules in battle, BeBop? Always be aware of your surroundings. And maybe you should have noticed that I'm no longer the only Hero on the scene."

The pigman quickly turned around, barely getting a chance to see the new uniforms tearing through his fellow gang members and enemies before he felt a powerful hand grip him by the collarbone.

"Another good rule in battle: don't take your eyes off the fucking enemy."

Titan was quick with crippling the shifter, and luckily the criminal quickly passed out from the pain of his broken limbs. That attended to, Titan jogged back over to Zone and the young girl.

"You should be clear now. Get her to safety and then rendezvous with the team. I have to keep helping clean up here."

"No problem," Zone said, slightly readjusting his grip on the sobbing girl. "And thanks for the assist."

"That's what teammates do," Titan replied, turning back to the fray still going on.

"Also, why the hell did you call that guy Bebop?"

"Didn't watch many cartoons as a kid, I take it?" Titan shook his head and allowed himself a small laugh, despite the horror of the day so far. "I'll explain when things are done."

"Good enough for me."

Zone darted off, racing through the alleyway and back toward what one could only hope would be safety. Unfortunately, unless someone else had shown up to unblock the bridge, that area was also a rapidly deteriorating situation waiting to turn into a tragedy.

Titan scanned the scene, noting that a Hero in blue shooting white fire and one who had shifted into a ten-foot-tall spiny creature had picked off most of the stragglers. As he looked, his eyes fell on a fallen, weeping form, and an idea surfaced in the sea of his thoughts.

"Dispatch, I need you to patch me in to a DVA representative. I may have a way to help our overpass situation, but I'm going to have to make some promises."

58.

Titan crouched down by the young man with the shattered legs. This kid wasn't the only one with such injuries dotting the fractured city street. The legs were the best place to go for, usually. It made it impossible to run away, crippled mobility, and put people in too much pain to focus enough to use their abilities. Titan had broken more legs than he could count in his years wearing the mask, and as such had become reasonably adept at gauging the severity of a wound just from looking at it.

"It'll heal," he said, drawing the young man's attention to his presence. "Not well, mind you, but it will heal in the sense that you'll have two legs. You might be able to get around without a wheelchair, if you don't skimp on physical therapy, though your days of running marathons are pretty much a thing of the past."

"Fuck you," the criminal grunted from the ground.

"Now now, I'm not saying all this to be cruel. We've got a healer currently heading to this area to patch up people hurt in the overpass accident, the one your. . . I'm going to guess brother. . . caused."

The criminal looked up from the concrete for the first time, his still-red eyes widening as he locked met Titan's gaze. "How did you know?"

"The reports from the fight said the energy projector had a corrosive property. Your attack burned through my costume in less than a second, and these things are made of pretty sturdy material. It seemed like a reasonable guess that two men in the same gang with similar powers were related. Let me guess: you both got the same energy type, just one as a projector and one as a blaster."

"My brother and I have. . . *had* the same energy." His eyes darkened, and Titan could practically see the resolve building as he tried to gather up enough focus for another attack.

Titan reached down and flicked the young man on his earlobe.

"Ow!" The young man rubbed his ear, all focus scattered in the brief shock of pain.

"Listen. . . I'm sorry, I never got your name. I'm Titan, in case you missed it the first time."

The greeting was met by a hard, sullen stare.

"Giving me your name isn't going to get you any more in trouble than you already are, and it will make it easier for me to try and dig you some of the way out of this shit heap. I understand you're upset about your brother, but you have to at least partly realize that this was something he brought upon himself. So you can lie here, be pissed, then go to jail and live with hobbled legs for the rest of your life, or you can hear me out and see if you might like what I'm selling before turning me down. You've already seen what's behind door number two, why not at least take a peek behind number one?"

He kept on staring, and Titan shifted his weight, preparing to get up. As he moved a single word slipped out of the young criminal's mouth. "Eli."

"That's progress," Titan said. "Listen, Eli: right now there is a very rare, once in a lifetime opportunity sitting before you. We need to get people off that overpass as quickly as possible, and your power could make that happen. And we're prepared to compensate you for it."

Eli snorted. "My power can't help anyone. All I do is destroy stuff."

"Today that's exactly what we need. The Super world is a funny place; you never know which ability will save the day. This time, it's yours, so be grateful. Few people ever get the chance to really make a difference."

"You want me to just forget about the fact that you all killed my brother, and that you broke my damn legs into pieces? You and all those Heroes can go fuck yourselves."

Titan leaned back a touch, a feat that was actually quite impressive in his crouched position. "Honestly, I don't blame you for that sentiment. If the tables were turned, I'd probably feel the same way. But there's a flaw in your logic, Eli. Those people stuck out there aren't Heroes. They're just regular folks. Families going to work or school who got caught up in a battle of beings that exist on a scale they can't even comprehend. Now when I look at all the bodies that were dropped around here, I don't see any with big corroded holes in them. That tells me that you, Eli, are not a killer. Even when you shot at me, you went for the side, an attack that would injure but probably not kill. Maybe I'm wrong and you don't mind letting dozens of innocent people die out of spite, but I don't think I am. I don't think you want all that blood on your hands. But make no mistake: if you do nothing and let people die, you will feel the weight of their loss for the rest of your life. Trust me."

"It's your job to help people, not mine," Eli protested.

"It's everyone's job to help people. I just get to do it on a bigger scale. Today, so can you."

Eli stayed silent for a long moment, before pushing himself up a few more inches. "You'll fix my legs?"

"We'll have to. You're going to need your focus for what's ahead," Titan told him.

"What about jail?"

"Like I said, it's pretty obvious you didn't kill anyone, so that's in your favor. I've already gotten word from the DVA that if you're willing to pitch in on saving those people, they're willing to be lenient on you. You may even be able to get on some sort of work release; there's bound to be plenty of people who could use your abilities. And on top of all of that, I'll personally speak on your behalf if your case goes to trial. I might not be the most popular Hero around anymore, but people tend to listen when we say someone isn't beyond saving. So you tell me, Eli, are you too far gone?"

"N. . . no. I'll take the deal. Patch me up then show me what you want destroyed."

"Wonderful. Oh, and Eli, this probably goes without saying, but I'll say it anyway: if you try and double-cross me or hurt anyone, I'll break a lot more than your legs."

"You're right, it did go without saying," Eli replied.

"Glad to hear. Dispatch, this is Titan. I need Fix-It brought to my location as soon as possible. We've got a way to get this situation under control."

59.

"Get everyone back from the debris," Titan ordered into his comm. It had taken longer than he wanted to meet up with Fix-It then get back to the barrier of cars and concrete, but he'd finally arrived with a freshly-healed Eli in tow. The young man had borne the journey better than others that Titan had leapt around with before, though his skin was slightly blanched as Titan set him back onto solid ground.

"Heard," Galvanize replied. "Pulling back as far as we can safely go. What's the ETA on opening up a way out for us? Reports from below say they won't be able to keep the overpass suspended much longer. Supers are pretty much the only things keeping us aloft right now."

"If this works, then we should have a clear path in less than a minute. If not, I'm going to have to be sloppy in opening up a hole."

"I'll cross my fingers for Plan A," Galvanize replied.

While they'd been talking, Eli had walked up and down the length of the barrier, assessing which places to target first. Titan kept a close eye on the kid, watching for any sign that he was thinking about running. Thankfully, Eli was either a man of his word or he was smart enough to know that Titan wouldn't let him go; regardless, he made no movement to bolt. Instead, he turned back to the man who had beaten, crippled, and then helped fix him all in the span of less than half an hour.

"I'm going to try and start around the black sedan," Eli said, pointing to an area thick with car parts and concrete.

"Seems like it will take longer to get through there." Titan didn't contradict the assessment; he merely waited to see how Eli would justify it.

"Only a bit, and it's far more stable than some of the other parts. If I get rid of a different section, it will cause another piece of the wall to come tumbling down. This is the only area that seems solid enough to carve a path through."

"Then go to it," Titan instructed. He'd reached much the same conclusion when he first assessed the problem; it was interesting that Eli had a keen enough eye to spot the potential hazards. Then again, for a kid whose ability eroded matter into nothingness, that was probably something he'd needed to master out of sheer self-preservation.

Eli raised his hands toward the chunk of barricade and took a deep breath. Gray, crackling energy manifested in his palms. Twin orbs steadily grew until they were roughly the size of softballs. The one from his right palm flew forward, washing over the front door of the sedan and quickly vanishing, along with most of the door.

"Going to have to go bigger," Eli muttered to himself. The orb in his left hand began expanding, filling with more power until it was bigger than a basketball and barely fit in Eli's grip. This time when the orb struck the debris, it wiped out the rest of the sedan and a large chunk of concrete behind it.

"All right, that's the size." Eli's hands filled with two more orbs, more quickly this time that the first. He fired both shots in short order, quickly destroying a vast chunk of the barricade. Titan could already see through to the other side; there were only cursory obstacles left in place.

"Tone it down for the next shot," Titan cautioned, which earned him a contemptuous glare from Eli.

"I know how to use my power." Eli demonstrated just that by lobbing two smaller orbs at the remaining debris, opening up a path to the other side with unexpected precision. Before Titan could comment, Eli charged up another pair of shots and went to the task of widening his hole in the barricade so more people could fit through.

"Galvanize, we're got an opening. Bring everyone this way, but keep them orderly. This is still a dangerous area if things get out of control."

"Don't worry, Huggles is really good at making people stay in line," Hexcellent replied.

"True, though I won't be surprised if at least a few parents try to bill us for the therapy their children will doubtlessly need," Galvanize replied. "Hexcellent is heading to your location. I'm going to hang back and make sure everyone gets through."

"We'll be waiting here to guide them along," Titan said. He looked around, trying to see any early arrivals through the newly opened hole, and noticed that Eli had stopped shooting orbs.

"This is as big as I can get it without risking another section spilling over," the young criminal said.

"Then it's what we've got to work with." Titan scanned the path; it was large enough for him to stand comfortably in, though he couldn't raise his arms from his sides without smacking debris. It would be a deathtrap if the people panicked, but with Huggles around, hopefully they would be more scared of the blade-armed demon than the tenuous safety of their surroundings.

"So is this it? Did I earn my freedom?"

"You earned your legs," Titan shot back, motioning to the functioning limbs that had been crushed bone fifteen minutes ago. "I'll hold up my end as far as talking to the cops like I promised, but there's no way you're going to skate out of this completely scot-free."

"Worth a shot," Eli said, allowing himself a defeated shrug.

"Don't get too down. You're in a much better position than you were when I snapped your legs and you were lying in the street. If nothing else, you just helped save people. That matters. . . at least it should to you."

Their conversation was interrupted by the rumble of dozens of voices. Civilians were trudging across what remained of the overpass, heading toward the gateway to safety that Eli had managed to open up before. Titan stepped forward, waving his arms so that people could see where to head.

"Stay close, and be good," Titan said. "We've still got a lot of people to help before this morning is over."

60.

The sun was halfway through the sky before the situation was officially considered stabilized. After clearing off the civilians, the weakened and tottering overpass was finally allowed to collapse. Several of the Heroes who'd been using their efforts to keep it aloft did the same, mentally or physically strained by the considerable effort. Sadly, the end of the bridge did not mark the end of the day, as there were still hundreds of vehicles stuck on a road going nowhere, all of which had to be turned around and rerouted. Every Super who could still work pitched in, some going so far as to physically lift cars with passengers still inside and take them to another street. A few days later a picture of Titan carrying a sedan on each shoulder would surface, a single still snapped by a fortunate photographer. As the morning finally came to a close, however, none of the responders were thinking about pictures or press. They were all just exhausted. Even the ones whose bodies rebuked such sentiments could feel the weariness in their minds.

"Team," Galvanize called through their earpieces, gathering their collective attention. "I just got word that the last stranded civilian has been relocated. What follows is a lot of cleanup and debris removal, but our team is being released with the city's thanks. Meet back at the SUV and let's go home."

His people didn't need any more encouragement than that as they made their way across the concrete dusted landscape over broken bits or homes or cars. It was a depressing place to walk through, made better only by the fact that each Super knew that it would have been much worse if they hadn't been there. Houses could be rebuilt, cars replaced, overpasses reconstructed. Those people who'd been trapped, on the other hand, were each one of a kind. While everyone was spent in some capacity, it was the good kind of worn out, the sort that came with a sense of accomplishment.

"Where's your little buddy?" Hexcellent asked Titan as they arrived at the car. It had been moved more than once on Titan's back as they made room for evacuating the other stranded motorists, but he'd been sure to keep the team apprised of its location.

"Turned him over to the Heroes who were collecting gang members a few hours ago." Titan didn't mention that he'd been sure to tell said Heroes about how much Eli had helped, even after the primary evacuation was done, and that he was *not* to be treated with hostility. Thankfully, the Hero Titan talked to had been on the job long enough to understand a good asset when she saw one. If it had been a younger Hero, Titan would have had to put a little fear into them to get the point across, and that was just pointlessly exhausting.

"Too bad he rolls with the bad guys. That power of his could come in pretty handy doing our line of work." Hexcellent popped open the door of the SUV and sank into a seat, resting for the first time in hours.

"He'll catch a decent break for all the help he gave us. Who knows, after that he may make himself into a useful member of society."

"I don't know who you're talking about, but I can guess it's not me." Zone came trudging forward from a small alley, his whole body coated in the white chalky dust caused by collapsing concrete.

"Nah, someone with an actual future instead of a downhill slide of crappy endorsement deals and hosting local cable television shows," Hexcellent replied, her voice oddly cheery in spite of the words she chose.

"At least I won't be fifty and still trying to sell that goth sex-symbol vibe," Zone countered.

"Good enough for Elvira, good enough for me," Hexcellent shot back.

"So glad to know that if I ever lose track of my team, I can just follow the sounds of verbal abuse," Galvanize said as he and Bubble Bubble approached. "I'd tell you to keep it indoors, but honestly I doubt anyone is paying us much attention by this point. Most of the press has packed up and gone now that the thrilling part is over."

"If they're going to take what they want and run off that quickly they could at least leave us cab fare on the dresser."

Everyone turned to Bubble Bubble whose pale, freckled skin immediately began to blush as she realized that she'd spoken aloud what had clearly been intended as internal dialogue. "Sorry, I'm just. . . I've been making energy spheres for hours. I'm pretty wiped upstairs."

"Don't you dare apologize, that might be the best thing to come out of your mouth since you joined this team," Hexcellent said. "Though, yeah, I think we're all drained enough to have goofy-brain."

"I actually still feel pretty wired, despite my body screaming for sleep," Zone said.

"Happens to most people after a really big job," Titan told them. "Even though you're tapped out, your brain is still on high alert. My teams and I used to go to a bar afterward. A little beer and relaxation helps shift your gears down, letting you actually get the rest you need. But I'm sure you lot have some sort of meditation yoga vegetable enema way to decompress after one of these."

"I know that was meant to be a joke, but it's so close to the truth that now I'm depressed." Hexcellent swiveled to Galvanize, whipping out her best innocent expression, which was pretty awful. "Can we do the bar thing instead? Pleeeeeeeeeeease?"

"Absolutely not," Galvanize replied. "You know how Mr. Greene would react if pictures of us drinking surfaced—let alone in costume and in public—don't you?"

"What if you did it at one of Mordent Holding's restaurants?" Titan asked. "They own a bunch of bar and restaurant chains. After a big, publicly visible thing like this, if we went and downed a few at one of their places, it might make for good advertisement. Get it on the news, bill the place as a watering hole for local do-gooders, all that stuff."

"That is an oddly business savvy suggestion, coming from you," Bubble Bubble noted.

"Former small business owner." Titan thumped his chest with unabashed pride.

"I will consent to calling the idea in while we head back," Galvanize said. "If Mr. Greene gives the okay, and we all want to go, then I'd be all right with it."

"Oh, we all want to go," Zone said. "I haven't been allowed to drink anything with that many carbs and calories in so long that my mouth is literally watering at the thought."

"I would like to second the sentiment, though very pointedly not echo Zone's exact word choice," Bubble Bubble said.

"Then it will be up to Mr. Greene," Galvanize replied. "Everyone pile in, and be quiet while I make the call. This is already a long shot, so let's make as good of a pitch as we possibly can."

61.

To Galvanize's great surprise, Mr. Greene actually agreed with Titan's suggestion to let the team be seen dining in one of Mordent's chain restaurants. While the two men might not see eye to eye on many a thing, Mr. Greene was not the type to let a personal distaste for someone skew his ability to spot a money-making idea. After a brief back and forth, it was decided that the team would stop off at Mealtime Jamboree, a family-friendly restaurant with appallingly bright colors and various knick-knacks on the walls. They were to sit in the bar section, though not at the bar, and were allowed two alcoholic beverages per person.

Despite the strict rules placed on their outing, the mood in the SUV couldn't have been more boisterous as the team pulled up in front of the garish yellow and red sign. They piled out quickly, partly in excitement and partly because five bodies that had been deprived the chance to shower and then worked for several hours did not make for a pleasant environment when crammed together. Galvanize led the charge into the restaurant, speaking briefly with the hostess, who led them directly to an already-prepared table in the bar area. Mr. Greene had clearly called ahead to give the staff a heads up, as evidence by the fact that was an extra-large stool to accommodate Titan as they sat down at the chest-high table. He'd also given the press a tip, at least gauging by the number of patrons sitting about with actual cameras, all of them keeping their distance yet watching the costumed team with laser focus.

"Feels weird to be just. . . out here," Hexcellent muttered as they settled into their seats.

"You do appearances all the time," Titan said.

"Sure, but then I'm in my element. Those people know who I am; some of them even came to see me. Being in full gear, just sitting around in public view. . . I don't know, it feels different."

"I'll second that," Galvanize chimed in. "But I don't think it's different in a bad way. I'm rather enjoying getting to let this side of me out on the town instead of vanishing once the work is done. Now then: we each only get two drinks, all of which is going on the company tab so that Mr. Greene can verify that, so I suggest you choose them wisely."

By the time the bartender, who was doubling as a waitress, came by, the team had perused the menu extensively to make sure they got the best options available. Most went with their favorite drinks, the ones they'd been banned from for so many years now, but Hexcellent decided to take Titan's recommendation on a local craft beer, which he also ordered. Their waitress, a pleasantly bubbly woman named Muriel, wrote everything down and quickly scampered away. Despite the fact that only one of the people at the table was a certified Hero, Muriel was clearly cape-struck by serving so many people in costume.

"Check it out." Zone pointed to one of the multitude of televisions suspended around the restaurant, this one playing scenes from the rescue effort they had just been part of. Amidst the wreckage and turmoil, there were clear shots of people being hauled to safety, sometimes even by one of their team. Titan got the most screen time, which surprised no one, but Bubble Bubble, Galvanize, and Zone were also featured relatively frequently. Hexcellent made the fewest appearances, which seemed unusual to Titan until he remembered that she'd been paired with a large demon that had blades for arms. Family-friendly imagery, it was not.

By the time they finally looked away from the television, their drinks had arrived and Muriel had made herself scarce once more. Everyone reached for their respective glasses and started to drink, but Titan held up a hand to stop them.

"If you don't mind, I'd like to do a toast. I realize this probably isn't the best place for it, but hell if I know whether another chance for us to all have drinks in our hands is going to come around." Titan cleared his throat softly then raised the frosted mug holding his beer.

"You all did great work today, just like you do every time we step out there. I don't think it's a secret to anyone that I was reluctant to sign on with a group of PEERS when I first came back, and that was due to nothing more than my own stupidity. You four are as brave, determined, and good-hearted as any Hero I've stood beside, and I am damned proud to be a part of this team. Cheers."

Everyone took a small sip of their drink, nodding appreciatively at both the sentiment and the wonderful flavor touching their tongues. Silence descended on the table, no one quite sure what to say to follow Titan's kind words, until Bubble Bubble finally spoke.

"For what it's worth, you've certainly turned out to be far less a burden than we were expecting."

"Glad to hear it," Titan replied. He was slowly beginning to get a feel for the most stoic member of their group, and he had a hunch that she was fonder of him, and the others, than she might like to let on.

"We could have done worse," Zone agreed. From him it was as good of an olive branch as Titan was likely to receive, and he nodded his head in appreciation.

Hexcellent sighed and rolled her eyes. "I guess if we're all going to have this emotion-fest then I'll say that yes, it's not terrible having you on the team. You damned sure have a knack for making things more interesting, I'll give you that. I can't say I remember a single time Mirror Fog whipped the shit out of Elemental Fury on pay-per-view."

"Oh right, that happened before you joined the team," Galvanize said, taking a small sip of his dark beer.

Everyone at the table, save for Titan who had never met the former Hero Liaison, stared at Galvanize in wide-eyed confusion. It wasn't at the suggestion that Mirror Fog had pulled the same stunt as Titan; that was patently ridiculous. No, their shock stemmed from one simple fact about what they had just heard: Galvanize had made a joke while in costume.

"What?" Galvanize said as their stares began to make him fidget in his seat. "You guys are the only ones who can kid around?"

"Not the only ones who can, just usually the only ones that do," Zone pointed out.

"Though I loathe to admit it, it seemed Hexcellent was righter than she knew," Bubble Bubble said. "Titan's presence truly does keep things more interesting."

62.

As much as Owen would have liked to lie down in his bed once the team got back to the penthouse, such luxuries would have to wait. Instead of passing out and finishing his sleep that had been so suddenly interrupted, he stripped off the costume that was coated in chalky concrete dust and grime, laid out a fresh one, and hit the showers. It took a long while and a lot of strong-handed scrubbing to get all the dirt off of him, but when eventually he emerged he at last felt clean.

Silly as it seemed, Owen had learned over the years that whenever he had to go into a place as an authority figure, he felt it put him in the mood to make himself presentable. Owen had never much been one for leadership roles during his Hero days. There were always smarter people than him on the team, ones who could look at a situation and immediately see where best to deploy every asset they had. Those were the people that took up a leadership role, and Owen was more than happy to give it to them. He might be one of the most lauded strongmen in the world, but he was still just a strongman at the end of the day. Melee was his bread and butter, where he shined and where he felt most at home. Given a choice between having his boots on the ground, staring down a hundred enemies or having to make the calls that would determine who lived or died during a fray, Owen would have taken the hundred enemies any time.

Still, as his star had risen all those years prior, it had brought with it a certain amount of prestige. Titan had become a role model, an icon, one that many people, including other Heroes, looked up to. With that had come public speaking gigs, being chosen to chair meetings, and even getting called upon by other Hero teams to work with their own strongmen. Owen didn't relish such roles, but he accepted them at the time as the price of fame.

Over a decade later, Owen Daniels was no longer certain if such a price was worth it. Time off had given him the perspective that perhaps fame itself was the price of fame. If he'd been asked by nearly anyone in the world to make an appearance as Titan for anything other than helping his team, saving people, or punching bad guys, then Owen would have likely told them to go fuck themselves. Topsy was different, though. He was an old friend, one who'd been with Owen back when they were doing all they could to survive in the insane world where Heroes fresh off their internships roamed. Even beyond that, Topsy had been one of the people who stuck with him during the Titan Scandal. Owen had spent two weeks on the man's couch as the media hunted him and he tried to think of what he could possibly tell his wife and sons to mend the relationships. More than one person he'd counted as a friend turned their back on Owen Daniels during those weeks, but never Topsy. Which meant if he was the one who needed help, then Owen was damned sure going to deliver.

Before leaving the peace of the penthouse and heading out on the town, Owen paused to put in a quick call to order more costumes. He'd thought that doing a job with less direct battle would mean he wouldn't go through so many of the things, but it seemed the strongman's clothing curse was still at work. His supply was dwindling dangerously. At least his supplier cut him a break on bulk orders, a formality they extended to most of the Heroes that got down in the rough and tumble with real frequency.

That done, Titan took the elevator down and stepped out into the last rays of the setting sun. He could have taken the town car or just used his own vehicle since it was stored in the garage, but tonight he felt like walking. A lot of Heroes didn't care to do street patrol; they felt like it lowered the sense of terror a criminal felt at the sight of them. But Owen had always thought it added a sense of danger to the punks' daily lives. Seeing a Hero exploding out of the sky or bursting from a portal was one thing, but to just be walking along and

298

suddenly find one's self in the presence of such power was jarring, and served to remind them that Heroes could appear at any time. Owen liked the idea that he was making sure everyone out there was always on their best behavior.

His jog was a long one, but nearly-endless stamina and powerful leg muscles meant he could close the distance with haste if it was called for. Since he'd left early enough, Titan took his time running through Brewster, nodding and waving at civilians as he passed them. The Wild Bucks' base was in what had once been an industrial area, before the primary company's illegal environmental practices were brought to light and they were fined out of existence. Despite the area being certified by the city as safe, not many people wanted to live on land associated with terms like "contaminated" and "biological hazard." Bad as it was for property values, it was perfect for Hero teams that needed an isolated area to set up shop that was still in decent proximity to the city they watched over. Legacy teams like Elemental Fury might have had fancy mid-lake accommodations, but most Heroes were just trying to find a spot that could be rebuilt cheaply after it was attacked.

As Titan jogged past thick iron gates that were half-rusted and half-knocked down, he spotted a familiar figure standing in the middle of what had once been a private road. Topsy smiled at the sight of his old friend, and the two men shared a brief hug after Titan closed the distance between them.

"Really appreciate you coming out," Topsy said as the hug ended. He looked tired, even more so than the last time Titan had seen him. No doubt the DVA was putting his people through the wringer, and him along with them. Titan didn't exactly disagree with the need for that, though he wished they'd taken more care to leave his friend out of it.

"Don't worry about it. I owe you a lot more than this." Titan did a quick scan of the area, noting that there was a large building with better upkeep than most of the others to his right: either their actual base or the entrance to it, by his estimates. "How bad are things?"

"They're pretty shitty," Topsy admitted. "The DVA finally made its call last week, and I lost two of them. One has been busted back down to intern and had heavy restrictions put on how he can use his power, while the other is all the way out."

Titan nodded, but otherwise kept his face stoic. Being a Hero was a privilege that came with a lot of responsibility. If one couldn't live up to that responsibility, they didn't have any place being a Hero and damned sure wouldn't be once the DVA got a hold of them. For the amount of destruction he'd seen, only one person being tossed out on their ass was actually pretty restrained on the DVA's part.

"That means you're down to a three-person team then?"

"For the moment," Topsy replied. "I honestly think if the whole team wasn't pariahs right now they'd have split off and joined up with other Heroes. Problem is, after all that mess they caused, no one would want them and they know it. Rock and a hard place."

"Well, I can't change their situation, but hopefully I can help them find the best way to handle it," Titan said. It was the sort of thing he was supposed to tell his friend, even if they both knew it was largely bullshit. "Take me in so I can meet the tykes."

63.

Owen was surprised at how nostalgic he felt as he tooled around the nearly-abandoned building. The beaten exterior concealed a fair amount of furniture and creature comforts within, but it was still an overall sparse space. In fact, most of the interior had been left bare, save for a few weights in the corner. From the dents and broken pieces of concrete in one section of the building, Owen immediately recognized the sparring area. All in all, the Wild Bucks' base felt a lot like the one he and Topsy had shared once upon a time: the base of a new Hero team just starting up, trying to do their best on a barebones budget.

Several mismatched chairs had been pulled together in this central space, only a few feet away from where a large throw rug marked the entrance to what appeared to be the living room where three costumed Heroes were waiting for him. They hopped to their feet as soon as Owen stepped into view. Two were men, one wearing the familiar black fabric of someone whose shape would be drastically changing, while the other sported a simple black and blue costume with some interesting swirled patterns. The last member was female, and her costume was red and silver with curiously empty spots on her shoulder and outer thighs. They all stared at Owen, at Titan, with silent admiration as he and Topsy walked through the empty space to their chairs.

Enjoyable as Owen found nostalgia, it didn't blind him from the fact that Topsy had clearly left something out when he talked about training these kids. His old friend had said he was hired on to coach them, but Owen doubted this team could afford take-out more than once a week, let alone the training of a Hero from someone as experienced as Topsy. More than likely, that meant a family relation of some kind. It at least explained why Topsy was sticking around even after the colossal fuck-up. Most Heroes who'd lived that many years understood a lost cause on sight.

"Let's start with introductions," Titan said at last. "You'll forgive the presumptiveness, but given the events of the last month or so, I'm going to assume you all have a pretty good idea of who I am. Since everyone in the room is familiar with Topsy, we'll go ahead and skip him too. Tell me your names and what you can do." It was a faux pas to ask any Hero how their power worked, since the exact mechanics could often betray a weakness in it, but asking what they could do was usually general enough to get a sense of one's capabilities.

"I'll start," said the young man in the blue and black costume. "My name is Deadlift, and I am, or was, the leader of this team." His voice was crisp and strong, but there was enough doubt hidden in his blue eyes to betray the uncertainty that had to be weighing on him after all that had happened. "My power is that I can lift and wield pretty much anything."

"Super strength?" Titan asked.

"If I may, sir, it's easier to show than tell," Deadlift said.

Titan nodded, and Deadlift closed the gap between them. The young Hero reached over and grabbed Titan's meaty triceps with a firm grip. To Titan's surprise, he felt himself rise from the ground as Deadlift raised his arm, effortlessly lifting the man who weighed hundreds of muscle-heavy pounds in the air as if he had the mass of a cloud. There was no strain on Deadlift's face, no visible effort in his muscles. In that moment, Titan understood: it wasn't that Deadlift had super strength, it was that his power affected the weight of whatever he held.

Deadlift set Titan carefully back down and walked back to rejoin the others. Next to speak was the shifter, a thickly built young man with a freshly shaven head. When he spoke, his voice was friendlier than Titan was expecting, lots of energy and pep, despite their dire circumstances.

"My name is Kaiju, and as you can probably guess from the costume, I'm a shifter. If you've seen video or pictures of us, I'm the fourteen-foot-tall dark red one. I can shift if you need me to, but I'm not the quickest, so it will take a bit for me to get in and out of form."

"That won't be necessary. I've seen your shifted form already," Titan said. He had indeed taken note of the massive, scaly creature shown with the Wild Bucks during the footage he'd found. Shifter had been obvious, but it was still impressive. The bigger a form someone shifted into, the longer the process took. For this kid to have made it through the HCP he must have been impressively quick on the shifting draw.

"That just leaves me," said the woman in the red and silver costume. "My name is Juiced, and there's really no way to tell you anything about my power without giving away the whole kit and caboodle. Let's just say I'm a strong woman." Juiced had the vague remains of an accent that Titan placed as from somewhere in the northeastern United States. Maine, if he was guessing.

She reached down to the floor and picked up a water bottle that had escaped Titan's notice before. Twisting off the cap, she gulped down several swigs of the beverage, and as she did her body changed visibly. Her already well-defined HCP-grad muscles swelled and she grew at least an inch and a half taller. The gaps in her costume suddenly made much more sense, as it became clear that her movement would have been rapidly hindered by constricting fabric in those spots. Juiced lowered the bottle from her lips, and Titan noted that she hadn't even drunk a quarter of what was inside.

"I'm a metabolic converter. When I drink a certain liquid I get stronger, tougher, bigger, and can even heal faster. Diminishing returns kick in, of course, and pretty quickly at that, but I can still get powerful enough to hold my own."

Titan nodded and watched as Juiced set the bottle down. She had pointedly avoided mentioning what was inside of it, and he made certain not to ask. The Hero had already given away much of her secret out of formality; there was no way he would be so rude as to try and uncover the part she clearly kept under strict guard.

"It's a pleasure to meet you," Titan said. "All of you. It's clear that you have some interesting abilities, and from the fact that you're HCP graduates, I'm certain you know how to use them. That said, I'm not here just for fun and socialization. Given what you've been through in the past weeks, I'm sure you're all keenly aware of the situation, but I'm going to say it anyway, because harsh truths need to be met head on if you're going to conquer them." Titan paused for a moment, and made certain to look every Hero there, Topsy included, directly in the eye.

"The Wild Bucks are on the verge of being dissolved, and I'm not sure that anything can stop it from happening."

64.

"I'll be honest, that's a little less optimistic than we were hoping for," Deadlift said, filling the silence that had descended after Titan's declaration. "Don't get me wrong: we all know we've screwed up. But the team members deemed responsible for that were handled by the DVA. We just want to make a fresh start and put that behind us."

"There is no such place as behind you, no such thing as a fresh start." As he spoke, Titan felt old, his years weighing down those massive shoulders in a way that not even hundreds of pounds could. "Even if you could purge the record, change your mask, begin with an all new identity, the mistakes you've made will still carry on with you. No one else might know they're there, but you will. And the more that get heaped on, the heavier each one becomes. Your team's mistake caused hundreds of thousands, if not millions, in property damage, and that's something the DVA won't likely ever let you forget. But more importantly, it cost nine people their lives, and that's something *you* should never let yourselves forget."

Juiced began to speak hurriedly, words tumbling over themselves to get free of her mouth. "We were cleared-"

"Maybe you didn't make the big mistakes, but those two who got held accountable were your teammates, people you put your trust in," Titan said, interrupting her for both of their sakes. Talks like this were hard enough when everyone was receptive. Odds were that if she got the chance to dig into a position, it would make her more stubborn and unlikely to listen, and they had to hear this if they ever wanted to rise above it. "Sometimes innocent people get hurt in what we do. It's inevitable, because if we don't step in then a lot more would be affected, but it doesn't change the responsibility we bear for those actions."

"I. . . I thought it was eight." Kaiju was staring at the ground, and Titan could make out the slight glisten of tears through the sides of the eyeholes in his mask. His voice, only moments ago full of life and humor, sounded beaten.

"Eight at the scene," Titan said, lowering his own voice by several degrees. "A ninth killed himself when he heard what happened to his wife. The DVA didn't tell you about it because it wasn't directly linked to your actions, though I think we all know better than that."

"Titan. . ." Topsy was staring hard at his friend, clearly struggling between protecting his team and having them hear the truth. He was invested in these kids and obviously didn't want to see them get broken by one bad call. At the same time, he had to know that what Titan was doing was necessary. Casualties were part of the job for any Hero. If one didn't find a way to deal with it, they'd be buried under the guilt, and if they never acknowledged it. . . well, that was how the true monsters were made.

"There is no fresh start," Titan repeated. "Not in that perfect world where no one knew about your mistakes and especially not in this one where your entire team's reputation has been run through the shitter. The other Heroes don't trust you; they think you're all half-cocked liabilities, and not without good reason. That's not even mentioning the DVA, who are probably only looking for one screw up to pull the rest of your certifications."

"So. . . that's it? Topsy brought you all the way over here to tell us that no matter what we do, we're fucked?" Deadlift asked.

"No. Topsy brought me over to lay down the harsh truth in a way that no one who is close to you ever could. You want to keep going in the Hero world, want to work with people who don't trust you and a public that hates you? Then you need to go in with your eyes wide open. Don't waste time thinking about forgiveness or redemption; those are fairy tales we use to make the world more palatable for children. What you're walking back into is going to be shit. Shit so deep you'll have to fight to keep from choking on it. There is no light at the end of the tunnel; there is no undoing what's been done. If you hope for something other than the shit, then the shit becomes unbearable."

"Then why would we go back in?" Juiced asked. Of the three, only her tone remained unchanged. Titan had a feeling she was more personally vested in what had gone down than the others, at least in her innocence at the scene.

He prepared to tell her why, but Kaiju beat him to the punch.

"Because we can still help people." Kaiju raised his head, making the guilty tears in his eyes all the more apparent. There was nothing wrong with crying over lives lost. Heaven only knew how many times Titan had broken down in his early years when he heard how many people he'd been too late to protect. Titan didn't judge Kaiju for crying, but he decided he liked the kid based on the fact that he lifted his head. Of them all, Kaiju seemed to feel the guilt the strongest, and he wasn't letting it stop him.

"We can still do what we spent so many years training for," he continued. "It doesn't matter if no one trusts or likes us, we can still make a difference. And we should, because even if Titan is right about there being no such thing as redemption, I still want to end my life saving more lives than I cost. Maybe that's selfish or stupid, but right now it's not something that I can say I've done and I hate myself for that."

Another fog of silence fell upon them as Kaiju's words faded, and once again it was Deadlift who ultimately broke it. "If we press on, we do it knowing that things will be awful, and that we'll be a single fuck up away from being out on our asses. But we can press on. Is that what you wanted us to understand?"

"It's a start," Titan replied. "Logistically, you lot need to work like hell on your training to make sure you minimize casualties and damages. Getting rid of your problematic members will likely go a long way toward making that better. Training is important, it's vital, but all the effort in the world wouldn't make a difference if you didn't have a firm grasp on what was waiting for you outside these walls."

"Thank you," Kaiju said, a bit of the former life returning to his voice as he unashamedly wiped his eyes. Titan couldn't be sure, but he suspected that whatever link Topsy had to this team was through Kaiju. The kid had the sort of aura that made people want to help him.

"I have a question," Juiced said. For the first time, she seemed quieter, less certain in her words. "And I don't want you to take this the wrong way. I'm not trying to turn the tables or invalidate what you told us; I just want to understand a bit better."

Titan nodded, and Juiced continued. "Have you ever. . . made a mistake? Maybe not as big as ours was, but. . . you know."

"Three hundred and forty seven people." Titan said. His voice didn't waver or soften, because this wasn't a thought that suddenly sprang to mind at her question. That number was with him every day, in everything he did. There was no change as Titan talked about his number, because the usual Titan was always thinking about it, in some form or another.

"That's how many people I wasn't strong enough, or fast enough, or smart enough, or sometimes even ruthless enough, to save. I have a list with all their names on it. Some of those were from dumb mistakes I made; some I still look back and can't think of any way that I could have saved them. It doesn't matter why it happened, though. At the end of the day I fell short and people died. That's why you train, that's why you push forward, that's why you always have to be better. So that the next time you go out, just maybe you can come home without having to write another name on that goddamned list."

65.

"You came down on them hard." Topsy pulled a beer from the mini-fridge in his room, then grabbed a second and offered it to Owen.

"No one out there is going to be gentle with them. Better they face what's ahead with one foot already in their ass so they don't forget what's waiting for them." Owen accepted the beer and sat in one of Topsy's old chairs. He was pretty sure it was one that been around at the Gentle Hammers' base so long ago, and now it had made the trip to Topsy's sparse quarters with the Wild Bucks. "Besides, they've got you for the kid gloves."

"I think I may have used those too much." Topsy fell into his own chair, a more recent acquisition that almost would have looked at home in the penthouse. "Maybe if I'd been a bit sterner things wouldn't have gone the way they did."

"None of that," Owen said. "All we can do is guide the young ones. Set a good example. Teach them what we learned through our own mistakes. How much they take from it is on them. You're no more accountable for their fuck-ups than the older Heroes we got advice from were for ours."

Topsy snorted and shook his head. "The one I remember the most was them telling us we shouldn't try to form a group out of just physically-gifted Supers. Said we needed a little variety if we wanted to be of any use at all."

"Well, that was different. They were dipshits." Owen took a swig of his beer to punctuate the point. He keenly recalled all the older Heroes saying a team needed diverse skill sets to be of any use at all. Even back then, he knew they were wrong. There was something to be said for specialization, and a team full of coordinated heavy-hitters would be useful in all kinds of situations.

History had proven him right in the end, though the many teams that tried, and failed, to emulate their strategy also showed that conventional wisdom hadn't been entirely off base. Specialty teams were doable, they just weren't easy.

"Maybe so, but part of me wishes I'd given these kids the same advice instead of agreeing to coach them."

"Topsy, if you hadn't helped them who knows how much worse things would be? They might all be stripped of their certification, or up on trial for gross negligence. I'm sure you helped, though I do wish you'd tell me why you were doing it. There's no way this team can afford you."

"That obvious, am I?" Topsy sighed, but it was clear he'd known from the beginning that Owen would figure it out. Unlike many idiotic criminals, Topsy knew better than to judge a man's brains by the size of his muscles. "Deadlift is the nephew of a Hero who interned under me. He was a good man; we even teamed up on several occasions after his internship was over. Poor guy passed about two years back."

"Died in the field?" Owen asked.

"Cancer. Still burns my ass that we've got people who can turn mushed bones whole, but we have to lose good people to disease."

"We've all got limits, Topsy. The healers are no different."

"I don't blame the ones who couldn't fix it. I blame the ones who can but would charge half a nation's economy to do it." Topsy took a long draw from his beer to calm down. "Anyway, Deadlift came to me after his internship was over, said he'd heard how highly his uncle spoke of me and wondered if I'd be willing to coach a team he was planning. Another group of heavy-hitters, like the Gentle Hammers in their prime."

"Makes sense." Perhaps from someone else the words would have been patronizing, but Owen was completely sincere. He knew how deep the bond between Heroes in the field went, doubly so for the ones who shared an internship. His own mentor had been a huge part of his early career, and Owen had visited the man frequently long after his teacher's cape was hung up. "All of that's in the past now. Any ideas about what you'll do with them in the future?"

"The ones who want to keep going, I'll teach," Topsy replied. "If anyone decides to bail out. . . well, this life isn't for everyone. Can't say I'll blame them. Those that remain are going to be drilled six ways to Sunday, though. I'll be damned if I'll have another incident like this on my conscience."

"I can't speak on the ones that are gone, but I think those three have their hearts in the right places. And after what's happened, they have a firm understanding of the consequences of their actions. With enough training and direction, they may just be able to pull themselves out of this hole, one day."

"I truly hope so," Topsy said. "Of course, you know what would help a lot? If an older, more experienced, still-active Hero joined the team. Someone who knows how to deal with adversity from the media and can watch out for them in the field."

"Topsy, I've already got a team," Owen said.

"A team of corpies, of which you're the babysitter. I'll admit this team might be bottom of the barrel right now, but they're still Heroes. You could be back out in the field, stopping real criminals. I know you must miss it, that's why you came back."

"I came back because I wanted to make the world just a little bit better," Owen corrected. "And yes, I wanted to make sure I was around for the big threats that might get other Heroes killed. If you'd made me this offer a few months ago, I probably would have jumped at it, but that was before I got to see what it was like working with that team of corpies. You know what I discovered in that time? I *like* working with my team. We're out there saving lives, helping people, and at the end of the day I have a lot less blood on my hands. I'm still around for when the big problems pop up, but I'd rather spend my days making a difference like this. At least for now."

Topsy nodded his head, then polished off his beer. "I won't say I don't get it, because I do. You don't even realize how much weight you're carrying around as a Hero until the day you finally get to set it down. Still, even if you're around for the big fights, it's a waste of your potential to have you pulling kittens out of trees."

"Maybe so," Owen agreed. "But it's my potential to waste, and I'm going to stick with my team. Who, speaking of, I need to get back to. Thanks for the beer."

"Thanks for giving them the talk," Topsy said, rising to escort his friend out. "And just keep the offer in mind. In case things change."

"If they do, you'll be the first to know."

66.

"Thank you for coming by," Kaiju said, shaking the large man's hand one last time as they stood at the door to the base.

"We truly appreciated your advice," Deadlift added.

"It helps to know what we're facing," Juiced said.

Owen smiled at the kids and did another round of handshakes. Maybe they'd manage to pull themselves out this, maybe they wouldn't. All he knew what that it seemed like they were going to do their best, and that alone was something of a triumph.

"Just glad to-"

"Titan, you are being formally activated under emergency protocol Thirty Two C."

Owen wasn't sure what was worse, the fact that Dispatch's voice had spoken in his ear, or the fact that every member of the Wild Bucks had clearly just gotten a similar interruption.

"Titan acknowledges. Wait, a Thirty Two C. . . that means I've got hostiles incoming on a base."

"Correct," Dispatch confirmed. "The robotic hordes you've been interested in have resurfaced. Currently tracking one pack moving toward you, one moving toward Elemental Fury's location, and one approaching what we're speculating is Transcendental Justice's base."

Owen wracked his brain on the last name, certain he'd heard it before. Finally it clicked: Aether, the woman who'd helped him and Granite with rescue work, was on that team. From the outset it seemed to support Jeremiah's theory that the bots were using Heroes for refining their abilities. After all, why not go against heavy-hitters? The issue there was that he'd come to the Wild Buck's home unofficially, so that meant they were the targets, which was odd given their disgraced status. Plus, Transcendental Justice was a middling team in both power and popularity. The only one of the three that made sense to go after was Elemental Fury.

"Do we have any clue as to what they're after?"

"The Subtlety Heroes have been contacted and are doing what they can; however, at the moment we must assume they seek more destruction and engagement. Assets are being redirected to you as we speak."

"Wait, how many are heading toward my location?" Owen asked.

"We've been able to confirm that each squad is made of nine robots," Dispatch said.

"I took out four on my own last time, seems like nine is doable. Put the assets toward something more useful. Have them help Transcendental Justice, or keep watch to make sure this isn't a diversion."

"There are already assets allocated to those tasks, Titan, and you receiving help is not optional. Every incarnation of these machines is exponentially stronger than before. While you might be fine, you are limited in your capabilities to contain damage."

"Sorry, sorry. I wasn't thinking." Owen was fairly certain he'd heard a slight tremor of annoyance in Dispatch's usually calm and steady voice. Since she was both a key asset and one of the few constants in his life, he saw no reason to upset her. "Can I get ETAs on the hostiles as well as backup?"

"Certainly. Hostiles will be at your location in less than three minutes. Backup will arrive within seven. The Wild Bucks are being ordered to assist you, but you are to take the lead on engagement until the extent of the robots' new abilities has been ascertained."

Even in a group of tanks, Owen was still the one getting shoved to the front lines. He'd have been a bit annoyed by it, except that he would have made the same call, given the choice. After all, he was the least likely to be injured. That was why he'd become a Hero in the first place: to shake off the blows that would cripple or kill others.

"Understood. I'll have them hang back and focus on keeping the bots contained." Owen swung his head around to tell the team to get ready, only to find they'd beaten him to it.

Kaiju was no longer recognizable in his shifted form. Fourteen feet of red, scaly lizard towered above everyone. Just glancing at the thickness of his armor and sharpness of the claws made Owen feel sorry for whatever poor tin can the kid got into it with. There was going to be a lot of scrap metal when the day was done.

Next to him, Juiced was setting down a milk jug full of clear liquid, her body already swelling with power as she picked up a second jug. Owen didn't know how much she could put down before diminishing returns kicked in, but he was looking forward to finding out.

Deadlift was the only one not changed physically, unless one counted the giant steel beam he was casually holding over his head. From the looks of it they'd salvaged the thing out of one of the abandoned warehouses. If his power let him swing that thing at full force even though it was weightless in his hands, it could turn out to be an interesting battle.

Owen glanced down and saw the ground at Topsy's feet had cracked, one of the telltale signs that his old friend was warming up. He walked over and calmly put a hand on Topsy's shoulder. "If you can avoid going in, do. Obviously keep them safe as needed, but don't jump in unless there's cause for it."

"Afraid I can't hack it anymore just because my body doesn't ignore aging?"

"My body doesn't ignore aging. It just sort of. . . tunes it out a lot of the time. Anyway, no, that's not why I want you to stay on the sidelines." Owen lowered his voice a few degrees and hoped none of the Wild Bucks had enhanced hearing. "I just came through here and told them how screwed they were, after the DVA no doubt spent weeks grilling them about their mistakes. Right now, there's no way they see themselves as anything more than fuck-ups. What they need at this moment, more than any nice speech or spark of hope, is to put one in the win column. They need to remember what it is they're good at, and in a team like theirs that's only one thing: kicking ass."

"I notice you still plan to go ahead and enter the fray," Topsy pointed out.

"That's different. For one thing, I'm not their coach, so it feels less like a parent keeping them safe. Plus, Dispatch tasked me with handling this. I'm still active, after all." Owen patted his friend on the shoulder reassuringly.

"And last, but far from least, I'm fucking Titan. That means if there's a fight, I'm in the middle of it."

317

67.

When the robots burst into view, Titan could feel the Wild Bucks tense behind him. It was no wonder: they'd been knocked on their asses by the last iteration of these things and that was with two more members on the team. Of course, last time Topsy clearly hadn't been there; Titan knew that just from the fact that any robots had managed to walk away. And he hadn't been there either, which meant that this was going to be a very different fight than the last time.

A pale, salmon-colored beam of light tore out of one of the robots, lancing across the concrete on its way to the Heroes standing forty feet away. As the beam struck the ground it left cracks and scorch marks, causing enough damage to make for rough driving terrain but not so much that a tire would get stuck. Titan calmly angled himself in front of the team and took the beam across his chest before it petered away to nothing. In truth, he doubted something that weak could have hurt anyone besides Deadlift, but it didn't hurt to start things off with a nice show of force. Titan found it interesting that the robots had upgraded their ranged attacks. Part of him wondered if that was in the hopes of taking out Supers like him before they could get in close.

"I'm heading in," Titan announced. "Kaiju, circle around to the northeast; that's the easiest exit they've got so I want you to make sure they don't use it. Deadlift, as I recall you can throw those big objects, so give me some ranged support. Juiced, from what I've seen on tapes you're pretty mobile; run along the outsides of the crowd and pick off the distracted ones. Topsy. . . well, you'll know what to do if it's needed."

Titan burst forward without even waiting for a single member of the team to confirm their orders. Part of this was so he could surprise the robots and hit them before they were ready, but he also wanted to show the team that he

318

trusted them. He'd told them what to do and left them to do it, just as though they were competent Heroes instead of recent screw-ups. Only they could prove which of those definitions truly suited them.

As he drew close the robots tried to spread out, clearly expecting his charge after their last battle. Titan let them. There was no way he could keep all of them wrangled in a single spot without support from a Hero using some sort of crowd control powers. He instead focused on the two nearest to him, grabbing each robot with one of his hands and lifting them into the air. Titan could hear the crackle of charging weapons and see the robots shuffling to encircle him. No doubt about it: this was a tactic they'd developed for dealing with strongmen. Trying to overwhelm his resistance to damage by attack simultaneously on all fronts was actually a pretty good plan, in theory. Hell, it probably would have even worked. . . against someone else.

It was impossible to see through the series of multicolored flashes that struck him from all sides, so Titan didn't bother trying. He focused on the two robots in his hands, smashing them against the ground and each other over and over until there was nothing but metallic shards to be collected. If the last generation had been able to self-repair, he had to assume these could too, so he wanted to make good and certain these things stayed down.

The group attack died out at last. Titan blinked away the spots in his eyes as he swept the battlefield for fresh targets. One of the robots that had spread out was pinned between two massive pieces of concrete. Another was trying to pull itself up as Juiced hammered it over and over again with her fists; each blow shattered the concrete under its head. Kaiju still stood ready but untested, as none of the robots had made any attempt to flee. Fifty feet away, Topsy was watching patiently as Deadlift hefted up another slab of concrete and took aim.

Four out of nine in the first scuffle and no casualties save for another of Titan's costumes. He quickly made note of all the burns and tears in the fabric and shook his head. If that order didn't come in soon he was going to be fighting crime in sweats and a T-shirt.

Titan leapt forward to grab two more of the robots, hoping they would circle up around him once more. He'd already suspected he could take what they could dish out, but now that he knew for certain keeping them trained on attacking him was the best case scenario. Unfortunately, it seemed the robots had also realized the futility of trying to gang up on him, as they scattered the moment he moved. The three he wasn't reaching for simply bolted, but the closest robot threw itself forward, directly into Titan's path. It was such a strange action that it took him a moment to realize what it had done.

The robot had sacrificed itself, and in doing so it had allowed the other bots Titan was reaching for to elude his grasp. He blinked in surprise as he tightened his grip against his struggling metallic opponent. Titan had dealt with many a mechanical creation in his Hero days, and he couldn't think of any that were programmed well enough to respond to a threat with a sudden act of self-sacrifice. All of their tactics were rooted around attack and defense coordination. Either this one had been programmed by someone with the brains to set up default responses to an incredible number of scenarios, or it had been given enough agency to make complex calls on the fly. Whichever one it was didn't actually matter: they both spoke to a creator that was *much* smarter than Titan had been expecting.

He quickly scanned the field, taking stock of what the other robots were doing. One had charged Kaiju, another had been snared by Juiced, and two were running toward Deadlift and Topsy. Titan began dismantling the robot in his arms quickly, but not as quickly as he could have if the need were dire. He was the one who had told Topsy these kids needed to score a solid win.

Time to see if they'd be able to pull it off.

68.

Titan was a bit surprised to see Juiced in action. From her swelling of muscles and size, plus the small amount of fight footage he'd witnessed, Titan assumed she would be a straightforward damage dealer like himself, punching and smashing through opponents with enough power to render their defenses futile. As it turned out, though, Juiced had more finesse than that. She was a grappler, bringing her robot to the ground as soon as she had it in her grasp. The robot scrambled wildly, trying to free itself or turn a weapon on her, but Juiced was in complete control from the moment they hit the ground. Locks that were generally used against human opponents to force submission were employed quickly and efficiently to break the robot's limbs and limit its mobility. Juiced wasn't as fast at dispatching her opponent as a true heavy-hitter, but she was more precise than almost any strongman Titan had even seen work. She probably wouldn't fare well in a giant brawl, but one-on-one, the woman was a force to be reckoned with.

Kaiju fell more in line with what Titan had seen on the tapes and expected. His robot managed to fire off one of the beam attacks while closing in the massive reptilian beast, a blast of energy that struck Kaiju right on his scaled flank. The one part Titan hadn't been expecting, however, was that Kaiju's red scales didn't simply hold up under the attack: they reflected the beam upward into the sky. Clearly the robot hadn't been expecting that either; it stopped in mid-motion while still firing the beam from its wrist canon. Most likely it was trying to calculate whether to risk another ranged attack or to try and deal with its opponent in melee. Kaiju didn't give it the chance to make that call, however. He barreled forward on all fours and skewered the robot with one set of sizable, sharp claws. They slid through the robot's tough exterior shell like knives cutting into a very silver cake.

As someone who was in the process of manually ripping apart one of those robots, Titan had a good appreciation for how tough they were. These things had been built to take a beating, and they lived up to it. But Kaiju shredded his opponent like a fourteen-foot- tall food processor bent on destruction. Titan glanced down and saw that Juiced was finishing up with her robot and spreading the pieces she was snapping off in all directions.

Deadlift was the last one to deal with his opponent since he'd been doing ranged work. Unlike the others, he didn't merely stand in place when one of the robots fired at him. Instead, he quickly rolled to the side, snatched up a concrete column, and hurled it at the reorienting robot like it was made of foam. The robot dodged easily, through the resounding boom that resounded when the column landed was enough to startle anyone, man or machine. Deadlift wasn't bothered, though; he sprinted forward, grabbed the robot quickly by the shoulder, then threw his opponent up into the air.

Titan watched the metallic dot soar through the sky until it broke through the lowest layer of clouds, at which point he lost track of it. Deadlift might not be technically strong, but whatever he did was still damned impressive in its own way. When he glanced down, Titan couldn't help but let himself smile. The last robot, having seen its counterparts be destroyed one by one, had decided to try and attack the only untested opponent still on the battlefield. It was making a rush for Topsy, who stood calmly as it raised an arm to fire one of the beam weapons at him.

The beam of light crackled through the air, racing toward Topsy with incredible speed. When it was only inches away from the older man's body, his defense kicked in. What appeared to be a black tornado encircled Topsy's form, casting wind in all directions and tearing up the ground under his feet. The beam was shredded the moment it touched the swirling mass, whittled away to nothing under the relentless assault.

While most of the Gentle Hammers had been strongmen, there had been a few whose abilities fell outside those bounds. Topsy, with his power to creating swirling energy vortexes, was one such example. The man might not be able to lift a car or shrug off a bullet, but when it came to taking and dealing damage, there were precious few who could outpace him. Sadly, it was also why he'd never risen as high as he deserved in the public's eye. When one had a power of pure, unrestrained destruction, it made people uneasy. Too often they would look at him and anticipate what he might do if he went evil rather than appreciate his efforts as a Hero.

As the beam died out, Topsy let the defensive tornado fall away. The robot raced forward, determined to handle this old man in melee since range was ineffective. As it extended a fist toward Topsy's stomach, he reached out and carefully placed a hand on its metallic forearm. The robot seemed to swell for a moment, like a silver balloon being overinflated. Then it exploded outward, pieces flung all over as the vortex Topsy had placed inside of it came roaring out. The only part of it that remained even remotely unscathed was the fist and forearm Topsy was still clutching in his hand.

Titan was impressed: not by Topsy, who he'd always known was a force to be reckoned with, but by the strength of the Wild Bucks in combat. Even with him and Topsy pitching in, they'd handled themselves smartly and with skill. It didn't make sense that this team had been completely crushed by the last generation of robots. This group was tougher than the last ones Titan had fought and seemed a bit smarter too, so they certainly hadn't downgraded. Something else had changed, clearly, but whether it was removing the other members or the remaining three getting a sense of what the stakes really were, Titan didn't couldn't be sure. He just knew that they had real potential.

As he finished crumpling up his robot, the one Deadlift had hurled into the air became visible once more as it careened toward the ground at an incredible rate. Deadlift was already there, column hefted over his shoulder, and when the metallic man came in range, Deadlift took a steady swing. The robot wasn't quite as demolished as Topsy's had been, but there was no way it would be putting itself back together. Not without a lot of time and buckets of super glue.

"Dispatch, our hostiles have been resolved. No injuries, no need for healing, but we could do with a little cleanup." Titan walked over to the robot still pinned under the concrete slabs. It was struggling, but seemed to be losing power. "Even got one in somewhat decent shape, so tell the tech people to sharpen their scalpels. Or. . . I guess wrenches in this case."

69.

Titan and Deadlift rode the elevator, accompanied by a generic rock ballad that seemed familiar yet impossible to place. Walking into a hotel in full costume had been strange enough, but odder still was how the staff had seemed unsurprised to see two Heroes casually saunter in and request to use the penthouse elevator. When Dispatch had given them the meeting location, Titan had almost, *almost* asked her if she was sure it was correct before coming to his senses. If she said this was where everyone was gathering, then it was the spot. Trusting Dispatch was as ingrained in a Hero's life as trusting themselves.

An elegant chime filled the air as the elevator's doors opened, showing not a hallway like Titan had been expecting but rather the foyer of a luxurious suite. Already standing there, tapping his foot impatiently, was Jeremiah, whose handsome face broke into a grin as he saw his guests arrive.

"Titan, good to see you as always; Deadlift, a pleasure to meet you. If you could both come this way, the others are already here." Without waiting for their reply, Jeremiah turned on a heel and walked briskly down one of the halls jutting off the foyer. Titan and Deadlift quickly followed suit, the younger Hero struggling not to marvel at the opulence around him.

Titan had been surprised when Dispatch reported that the other robot squads had been effectively handled, and he'd bordered on shocked when she told him a post-battle meeting was being held less than half an a hour after the attack. Obviously, someone had been ready for this, or at least expecting it. Technically only Deadlift was required to attend since he was the leader of the attacked team, but Titan had been invited along for a multitude of reasons, most important of which was his vocal curiosity about why this attack seemed to deviate from the established pattern.

Jeremiah opened to the door to a large room with a projector and a finely-crafted conference table. Already seated were Gale and Aether, the representatives of the other two attacked teams. Both looked more or less unaffected by the skirmish, unlike Titan, who was wearing a borrowed sweatshirt that barely fit him.

"My fellow Heroes, I have called you here to discuss the robotic attack you all suffered today," Jeremiah said, gesturing for Titan and Deadlift to take seats.

"Can we also talk about why you're in a freaking hotel penthouse instead of a base?" Deadlift asked. "How much does this place cost to rent?"

"No idea, we bought it outright," Jeremiah replied. "Subtlety Heroes often have to move about, so having multiple locations rather than a static one suits our needs better. Most of my team's hidey holes are less opulent than this, but they're also closely-guarded secrets. Consider this place the equivalent of our guest room."

"Our guest room is a corner where we store our extra weight bench," Deadlift grumbled.

"Lovely as it is, I'd rather talk about the matter at hand," Gale interrupted. She and Titan shared a brief look that, while not exactly warm and friendly, at least didn't dip so cold as to be called frosty. "Namely, why did the robots come after us this time? And why with such paltry numbers? That last wave had no fewer than a hundred units attacking half a dozen different targets, most of them civilian."

"Quite accurate," Jeremiah said. "But you left out the fact that this attack also came much earlier than their others. Usually there's at least a three month gap between attacks, presumably so that more units can be designed and built. Only about a month and a half has elapsed since the last attack, which I believe speaks to why the units we dealt with weren't nearly as refined. By my estimations, this was not the next generation of robots. I believe they were the same generation of units with some additional features and programming slapped in."

Aether was hunched forward, fidgeting with the corner of her glove while her forehead creased in thought. "That doesn't make any sense. Why come after three Hero teams with nothing in common, using already-beaten units and low numbers?"

"That it makes no sense tells us the real reason for the attack," Jeremiah replied. He produced a remote from his pocket and clicked one of the buttons, causing the projector at the back of the room to hum with life. Moments later an image displayed on the white wall across from the projector, one immediately recognizable to all present as a map of Brewster.

"As soon as I heard that the robots were attacking Wild Bucks, Transcendental Justice, and Elemental Fury, it was obvious that they had nothing to gain from such an assault. I took this to mean that they weren't out for gain at all. . . they were just pawns, calculated losses."

Titan let out a weary, frustrated grunt as understanding kicked in. "Decoys. They were all decoys."

"No fair getting ahead of me." Jeremiah glared at Titan for a moment, then sighed and clicked his remote again. "Delpham Technologies and Pharmaceuticals." Jeremiah paused to point at the building's location on the map, which was marked by a large red X on the new slide. "At exactly five minutes past three, an alarm was tripped, indicating that a robbery was taking place. Police responded within four minutes and noted robots fleeing the scene.

They put in a call for Heroes to deal with them, but no one was close enough to reach the robots before they somehow dropped out of sight. Now, here's where the ingenious part comes in."

Jeremiah clicked again and new slide appeared. This one still marked Delpham's location, but it also had colored dots representing each of the bases attacked by the robots. Before he said a word, it was evident what had happened. Those three bases formed a misshapen triangle around the company—not especially close to it, but probably nearer than any other Hero bases.

"As you can see, your teams would have been the first to respond to the call, were you not under assault. Additionally, having those three squads make such a ruckus let the fourth one slip through town unnoticed, and ensured most of our Heroes were playing defense rather than offense. From stem to stern, this whole play was never about sticking to their pattern. It was about keeping our hands full while they stole prototypes from Delpham, and damn if they didn't pull it off perfectly."

"Bastards," Gale swore, grimly staring at the map before them. "How did we not see this coming?"

"Why would we have? They've never done anything remotely like this. If I didn't know better, I'd guess that they spent all those other attacks training us to look right, just so they could completely catch us off guard when they went left," Jeremiah said.

"Let's focus on the matter at hand," Titan said. "If they went to all that trouble to successfully rob some place in the middle of Brewster, it must have had something they wanted pretty badly."

"That was my first thought, too," Jeremiah agreed. "Sadly, the company was not particularly compliant in giving us a list of stolen goods.

Something about copyrights, industrial espionage, technology thieves, blah blah, you get the idea. It will take me time to get a full list of everything that was taken, but before the meeting I was able to. . . let's call it *liberate*. . . the details of one item."

Jeremiah clicked his remote once more, and a detailed schematic for some cylindrical device popped up on screen.

"Yeah, if we're supposed to know what this is. . . we don't," Deadlift said.

"Nor would I expect you to. This device is a highly experimental gravity distortion field generator, based on the work of a long-dead tech-genius who attacked San Francisco. From what my smarter teammates have told me, it seeks to circumvent the size restrictions inherent to building large machines. Giant robots, for example, currently weigh too much to be able to move on two legs unless the higher pieces were made of far less dense materials. So, unless someone is a tech-genius who finds a workaround, robots must either be small and durable or large and vulnerable. With this device, however, the weight could be compensated for by a weakened gravity field, allowing for almost no limitation on the size of a robot's construction."

Jeremiah paused to make sure the others were taking his message; the worried expressions greeting him made abundantly clear they were. Still, he felt it was good to really send the point home, just so they understood the severity of what faced them.

"To put it simply: the next wave of these machines we face may not come through downtown. They might be the size of downtown."

70.

Owen was expecting a bit of a circus when he returned to the top floor of the Mordent Holdings building; after all, the city had just seen another attack by robots, albeit a small one. He was not, however, prepared for the utter chaos he walked in on as soon as the front door opened.

Mr. Greene was on the phone, shouting loudly at someone about defamation and lawsuits, while a myriad of people clustered and scuttled around him, all on phones or laptops of their own. From down the hall came an occasional bout of shouting, which quickly died away into what Owen thought might be sobs or angry screams; often the two were hard to distinguish at a distance. The only member of his team in the living room was Hexcellent, who was playing one of her video games in spite of the people who kept darting in front of the television. Given the expression on her face, Owen wouldn't have been shocked if Huggles or Big Henry soon made an appearance to enforce the sanctity of the screen.

"There is no way I fucked up bad enough for all of this," Owen said, standing next to Hexcellent as the crowd parted and ignored him.

"For once, my favorite scapegoat, you are not the cause of today's drama," Hexcellent replied. "That honor goes to Bubble Bubble, who has had the dubious honor of an internet scandal all her own."

"Did she scowl at the wrong person?" Owen asked.

"If only. Seems someone might have made a little whoopee with one of her commercial directors, and a very incriminating tape leaked online. Since he's done movie work and she's actually becoming well-known, the media decided to run with it. Probably doesn't help that, at the time, he was supposedly dating a well-known actress as well." Hexcellent scowled as a dark-haired woman in a pantsuit strolled in front of the television, causing her to miss the jump to her next platform. "Also not helping that she's on a team with you. Let's just say parallels are being drawn."

"You have to be fucking kidding me." Owen heard another bout of shouting, though this time he had a more accurate guess as to what might be the cause. "I assume Zone and Galvanize are comforting her?"

"More like trying to coax her out of her room, which she locked herself in," Hexcellent corrected. "I thought it best if I stayed out of the way for now. She and I don't have the best dynamic anyway, and I wouldn't want to see someone as bitchy as me during all this."

"Good intentions," Owen said. "But unfortunately, the wrong strategy." With a single motion he scooped Hexcellent off the couch, knocking the controller to the ground and sending her character off to die. It was enough of an event to draw attention from Mr. Greene and the suits, though only the former bothered addressing it.

"What are you doing?"

"Fireman's carry, I think," Hexcellent chirped from over his shoulder. "Also, holy shit you are tall. I never really noticed looking up at you."

"I'm going to help my teammate," Owen replied. "And we all need to be there. Don't worry about it; you stay out here and keep doing damage control. If there's anything I can do to help, let me know."

Mr. Greene didn't even bother to conceal the sneer on his lips. "I'll certainly keep that in mind."

"Please do, because I mean it." Owen rested a meaty hand on Mr. Greene's shoulder, sending ripples of confusion across the leaner man's face. "You and I might not get along, but if there are some PR hoops I can jump through to make this easier on Bubble Bubble, say the word."

"I. . . I will actually keep it in mind," Mr. Greene said, this time with exponentially more sincerity. He still didn't seem to trust Owen in the media's eye, but the man was too powerful of a tool to ignore entirely.

"Thanks." Owen adjusted his grip on Hexcellent and waded his way through the sea of people and into the hallway.

"You know, I would have just come along if you told me to," Hexcellent said from flopped over his shoulder.

"I know. I just thought you'd have more fun this way."

"You're like the big gay older brother I always wanted."

They quickly arrived at Bubble Bubble's door, where Zone and Galvanize were pleading their case. Since the door was firmly wedged closed, he could see how well that tactic was going.

"Owen, we're glad you could make it back," Galvanize said. "Things are a bit hectic right now-"

"I brought him up to speed," Hexcellent said as Owen set her carefully on the ground. "Even told him B.B. had locked herself up."

"We've tried everything to get her out," Zone told them. "She just keeps yelling at us to go away, so maybe she wants to deal with this in private."

"Oh, I don't have any doubt that's what she thinks she wants," Owen said. "But as the only one here to have been on the other side of that door, I also know how important it is she have people reminding her that she's not alone in all of this. Now pay attention: if you ever have kids one day this is a technique you'll want to use when they inevitably try to lock you out of a room."

Owen leaned in and tapped lightly, but firmly, on the sealed door. "Bubble Bubble, it's me, Titan. I'm here with the rest of the team, and just the rest of the team. We're here to talk things out with you."

"There's nothing to talk about!" Bubble Bubble's voice cracked halfway through the scream, a telltale sign she'd probably cried herself partially hoarse. "I'm packing up and quitting. My career is ruined."

"If that's what you decide to do when you calm down, then we'll help you pack, but first you need to get some perspective and let the initial wave of panic wash away. That's what we're going to help you with."

"I'm not opening the door!"

"Suit yourself; I'm sure maintenance can get a replacement in the next couple of days. You might want to stand back, though. I'd hate for you to get clipped by any debris." Owen reared back and closed his hand into a sizable fist.

"What are you. . . are you breaking my door down?!?"

"Or you can open it, but we're not going to let you be alone. I've been where you are, kid. I mean, almost exactly where you are. I know firsthand that right now you're scared and ashamed, and the idea of talking about it literally fills you with stomach-churning dread because it will make it all become real. But you have to talk about it. If not with us, then with someone we can bring here. You can't sit alone and let it fester, because you're going to make snap choices. Decisions that will have much bigger impacts than you expect. You'll do things that, years from now, when you finally do get that clarity, you'll realize you regret even more than the thing that stirred you up in the first place."

For a long moment no sound came from the other side of the door. Owen pulled back his punch a bit further, then a small click came from the door and it opened several inches. Bleary- faced and red-eyed, Bubble Bubble stared back at them from the small opening to her room.

"You can come in, but only for a few minutes."

71.

"Let's start at the beginning," Owen said. He scanned Bubble Bubble's room, having never been invited in before, and noted that it was significantly larger than his own. She'd decorated it tastefully, save for the fact that most decorations featured her promoting some brand of product. It reminded Owen of the rooms a new Hero usually had when getting their first taste of fame and public adulation.

"There's not much to tell." Bubble Bubble shut the door behind Hexcellent as the tattooed girl scurried past. "It was two years ago when I was just getting real endorsement deals. Corbin Calhoun was charming and handsome, plus a real director to boot. After we wrapped the commercial he asked me out for dinner and one thing led to another. Two days later I was reading a magazine that talked about him and his girlfriend, who he'd failed to mention existed, going on a vacation to Paris. I never took his calls or worked with him again. Of course, whoever leaked the hotel footage of us making out in an elevator and going into a room didn't add in those details."

"I'm going to make a wager that he isn't telling that version of the story," Owen said.

"Sadly, no," Galvanize said. He settled into a computer chair Bubble Bubble had left out while the others settled cross-legged on the floor. "According to Mr. Greene, the story is that Bubble Bubble seduced Corbin, leading him astray. There have even been some sources trying to claim that as a Super, she had some unnatural sway over his actions."

An all-too-familiar vein throbbed in the back of Owen's neck, but for Bubble Bubble's sake he kept his face neutral. Despite decades of research and a well-controlled government program, people still liked to trot out the "who knows what a Super can really do" card if it made life easier on them. Heroes were usually spared the indignity, if only because no one wanted to piss off the people stopping the real bad guys from laying waste to a city. Other Supers weren't quite so lucky.

"From what I heard, Mr. Greene is launching defamation suits against every news outlet that tries to report that angle. Bubble Bubble's powers have been on record and used in public for years, so there's no foundation for such claims," Galvanize added.

"He can sue whoever he wants to, as long I don't have to show up at the hearings," Bubble Bubble said. "It doesn't matter how this shakes out. No matter what, I'm fucked. All my brands are about being upscale, desirable, and classy. Screwing some director makes me look like a desperate slut. I'd be amazed if most of my sponsors haven't already dropped me." She lowered her head and leaned against the far wall, small droplets of tears running down her face anew.

"The ones owned by Mordent will probably stick with you," Zone said. It wasn't terribly helpful, but at least he was trying.

"It's just so unfair. I made one mistake when I was younger and now everything I've been working so hard, so *damned* hard, to get is going to burn up right in front of me. I'm so careful, I'm so good, I'm. . ." She turned her head and screamed toward the ceiling, "I'm the perfect pristine fucking mascot!" Her shoulder slumped as the anger seemed to leave her as quickly as it came. "All those years posing, holding my tongue, being demure, all of it is going to be forgotten. . . just because of one stupid mistake."

"You're wrong," Owen said, standing and walking over to his teammate's hunched form. "Not about all the bad shit coming—you've got a pretty firm grasp on that—but about the mistake. You never made one. You're an adult who had consensual sex with another adult. The only mistake anyone made was this Corbin guy for lying about being single. These next few days are going to suck, and the weeks to come will be rough, but don't you dare think for a minute that you're to blame."

"Maybe not, but I'm going to be the one who pays for it," Bubble Bubble said. "Corbin's a successful director and a human. I'm nothing but a corpie and a genetic freak. Who do you think people are going to side with?"

"Probably the wrong person, as they often do," Owen admitted. "But we can't control them. No Super can make the world think the way they want it to. All we can control is who you think is really responsible here. Some of the blame goes to whoever leaked that video; most belongs to Corbin for making this a scandal-worthy incident. Tell me the truth now, do you really think you did anything wrong?"

Bubble Bubble didn't answer. Instead, she began to cry again, leaning forward and pressing her already tearstained face against Owen's borrowed sweatshirt. It was coated in a thin film of concrete dust, but she didn't pull back. She wrapped her arms around his sizable torso and pulled herself closer. He hugged her back carefully, marveling at how slender and delicate this woman he'd seen save dozens of people truly was. She was just a damn kid, only a few years older than his sons, and this was what the same media that had torn him down was reducing her to. Anger tried to well up in him, but Owen forced it down. There was no place for rage right now. It might make him feel better but it wouldn't do anything for Bubble Bubble.

"I once crapped myself during a skateboarding competition."

Zone's words broke the melancholy spell that Bubble Bubble's tears had cast, as everyone in the room, Bubble Bubble included, turned to stare at the chiseled, spiky-haired man who was staring at the floor in red-faced shame.

"Whaaaaaaaaat the fuck now?" Hexcellent's eyes were so wide they seemed to have physically grown.

"I had the flu, but I was just starting out and it was my first paid gig. I *really* needed the money. After I did my tricks, and I mean *right after*, my body let me know that the floodgates were opening no matter what, and I could do with that information as I pleased. I managed to duck behind some bushes, but. . . things happened and then there I was, standing around in a competition with my jeans ruined. I was sure my life was over, so I decided to go big. I stripped naked, fastened my helmet over my junk, and streaked past the stands. I lucked out and people thought I was a bad boy instead of realizing what had really happened." Zone finally looked up from the floor to find the entire room staring in rapt attention. "I just. . . my point is that we all have things that are embarrassing. Like, career-wrecking embarrassing. It really blows that the media got yours, so I thought it might help if you knew one of mine."

Bubble Bubble stared at him for a long moment, then snorted out a snotty, half-cough of a laugh. It was a bit disgusting after all the tears, but it was also beautiful to hear. Owen realized it might be the first time he'd ever heard Bubble Bubble laugh, or do anything, without carefully measuring her response.

"I was in a porno," Galvanize said slowly. "Not as an actor—well, I mean, I acted but. . . I was the guy who found the real performers in the ball pit, and no, that is not a play on words."

"Holy shit!" Hexcellent yelped. "Mr. Fly Right was in a skin flick. Please tell me you used a fake name."

339

"I didn't choose one, but they listed me as Rock Thruster." Galvanize hung his head in shame while the rest of the laughed and hooted nearly uncontrollably. "It was before I decided to do rescue work, and I had a friend on set. You all get the idea."

Eyes turned slowly to Hexcellent, who was enjoying her chuckles so much she didn't notice until the stares had gotten awkward. "Oh! Um. . . shit. You all pretty much know my dark and dirty secrets. Drugs, sex, rock-and-roll, all paired with a nice side of petty crimes." She looked at Bubble Bubble who, was, in spite of everything around her, smiling just a touch.

"But. . . oh fuck it. Like most Supers I got my powers when I was a kid, so my first summon wasn't Impers. It was a bunny I named Hopcules, because he was strong and brave, and I called him up because I was afraid of the dark."

"You are shitting us," Bubble Bubble said. "You, *you* had a summon that was a fluffy bunny? I have to see this to believe it."

"Sorry, but I can't call it up anymore," Hexcellent said. "Summons are pretty tied up in who summoners are mentally, and I haven't been that naïve little kid for a long time. I swear on my tattoos and vintage albums, though, it's the god's honest truth."

"As for me, everyone here knows my big secret: destroyed my own marriage because I couldn't be honest about who I was, even to myself," Owen said. "I wasn't like you, Bubble Bubble. I fucked up my own life; you're just caught in someone else's blowback. If it's too much and you have to go, I definitely understand. But if you want to stay and fight to keep that image you worked so hard for, know that everyone in this room has got your back."

Bubble Bubble looked around to see all of her other teammates nodding and a fresh set of tears came to her eyes. It had been so very, impossibly long since anyone had ever looked out for her. Ten minutes earlier she would have bet all her money that no one cared about her beyond what she offered business-wise. Now that she realized she might be wrong, Bubble Bubble wasn't quite so keen to give these people up just yet.

72.

"I need a favor."

"Are we going to just replace 'hello' with that now? First you're trying to set me up on a public speaking gig at Zero's behest, what can be worse?" Lenny sounded tired, which surprised Owen even with the late hour. Given that the city had seen some actual Hero action during the day, he imagined Lenny would still be up, wheeling and dealing and making sure his clients came out looking great.

"That one wasn't even for me; I was just passing along the message since you don't take phone calls from retired Heroes."

"Now, now, be fair. I take them if they're from my old clients," Lenny reminded him. "But I can't go returning every message I get during the day. I'd spent all my time talking to wanna-be clients instead of working for the ones I've got."

Cold as it seemed, Owen knew Lenny was actually being more honest than arrogant. There were tons of agents in the Hero world, some okay, some awful, and a few tremendous. As a man who fell into the third category, Lenny was in high demand. He could have taken on every Hero that was willing to sign. Others before him had. But it would have dropped the amount of attention he could give each one. Lenny had chosen quality of clientele over quantity throughout the years, and his reputation had flourished for it. Unfortunately, that meant if he actually did grant Owen's favor then Owen would owe him *huge*.

"It's actually kind of about that," Owen said, gathering up his nerve to charge the verbal hill. "I'm assuming you saw what happened to my teammate, Bubble Bubble, on the news today?"

"Sadly, yes. Scouring tabloids and skeevy news sites is one of the many fringe benefits of my illustrious job. Give the gal my condolences, by the way. She's getting a raw fucking deal and anyone with half a brain in their head knows it."

"Maybe so, but I want to drill it in to the ones with less than that half." Owen idly ran his fingers over the battered sweatshirt he'd taken off, getting more concrete residue on his hand. It was now or never; the worst Lenny could say was no. "That's the favor I need. I want you to take her on as a client."

Silence screamed at him through the phone for several long, lingering seconds. When Lenny finally spoke, it wasn't with annoyance, as Owen was expecting. In fact, even the weariness seemed to have disappeared from his agent's voice. If anything, he seemed to be barely holding back chuckles of mirth as he responded.

"Sometimes, just sometimes, I honestly forget how big a pair of brass ones you've got swinging down there. To be clear: you want me to take on as a client, for the first time ever, a corpie. And not one that's prime real estate, but one going through a media shitstorm that will likely end up torpedoing her career."

"She's probably toast," Owen agreed. "Unless someone with real skill, a legendary level of talent, were to take her on and steer her to safe shores."

"Flattery, a nice touch. Little overt, but that's about what I expect from you." Owen could hear Lenny sigh. He imagined his agent pacing about, weighing the pros and cons while time was pitted against potential income in that balding head of his. "Listen, Titan, you and me go back a long way, and there's not much I wouldn't do for you if needed, but that's for you. This girl is going to need a hell of a lot of work to keep afloat, and even more if she wants to come out ahead. Truthfully, that might not be a bad thing, though. I've been thinking about taking on a few of the corpies with real earning power out there, and pulling her from the fire would be the best exposure I could ask for to show them what I bring to the table. That said, this one isn't going to be free."

"Tell me what you want," Owen said.

"You know damned well what I want," Lenny shot back. "This year's Intramurals have two of the supposedly heaviest hitters to come out of the HCP in a decade squaring off against each other. I want what no other agent gets: a seat at the show to judge them for myself."

"This year it's being held at Lander, I've got almost no clout there. If it were Sizemore, sure, I could swing a few things, but all I've got at Lander is kids who won't talk to me. Why not do the talk for Blaine? He's more likely to be able to get you in."

"Already agreed to that, but he's not sure he can swing it. All he could promise was support. Now, if someone still active in the field, someone who might still have a few markers to call in were to ring old friends in the Intramural Committee, that could give me the extra push I need to watch this firsthand."

"I. . . can make some calls. That's the most I'm able to promise, Lenny. A lot of people voided their chips to me when things went south and you know it. I'll do everything I can, and I'll take on some favors if needed, but that doesn't mean I can make you a promise." Owen had once been a man who prided himself on never breaking his word. Despite the fact that this character feature had ultimately unraveled along with the rest of his life, he still made it a point not to make a promise unless he truly believed he could keep it.

"Tell you what: you promise me that you'll do your best and I'll let it ride for now." A soft *fwump* of sound filled the receiver, and Owen knew that Lenny had just let himself fall into his favorite easy chair.

"Really?"

"Really. I'm not dumb, I know you can only do so much. Still, you're a determined guy. If you say you'll give it your all, then that's the most I can ask for. Make me that promise, and you can send the girl by tomorrow morning. I doubt she has any other pressing appointments to make. I'm not agreeing to take her on whole hog just yet, but I can at least help get her through the rough patch."

Owen let out a long sigh of relief. Just knowing Lenny would help made the whole situation less scary and more manageable. He wondered if this was how people felt when they saw a Hero drop in on a scene, like suddenly things might just be okay after all.

"I promise, Lenny. Anything I can do to get you a seat, I'll do it. Calls start going out tomorrow."

"Then tell your girl she has a new ally. It'll be a hard road, but I've got a few ideas for how to spin things. Now if I can just make that damn dean push from his side, I might get treated to a real spectacle."

"These kids supposed to be that strong?" Owen asked.

"Remember Hank Rhodes? One of them is his son."

Owen indeed remembered Hank Rhodes; while the man hadn't become a Hero, he was a Super of incredible power and often helped train Heroes when asked. He'd never met Hank's son, but if his power was close to his father's, he would be hell to defeat.

"Who's the poor bastard going up against him?"

"Graham DeSoto's granddaughter," Lenny replied. "Both, by the way, undefeated in their entire time at the HCP. That's something that, correct me if I'm wrong, not even the great Titan managed to accomplish."

"No need to be mean about it," Owen said. "I came a long way in those four years, and it's not in how you start a race. It's about how you finish."

"Heh, well, you definitely finished strong. That was another Intramural I had to scheme, bribe, and favor my way in to watch. Worth it, though. You made for one hell of a show."

"I like to think I still do."

73.

Owen was faced with a problem, one he wasn't quite sure how to deal with. Despite having come up against this dilemma several times before, he still found himself semi-flummoxed each time it reared its head. In fact, it occurred with such regularity that it was amazing he managed to continue being surprised by it.

Sunday had arrived once more, and with it came the team's mandatory day off. Even after several weeks with them, Own still wasn't comfortable just dicking away an entire day. Sometimes he went active, pitching in as best he could as a Hero, but that was off the table this time. After the previous day's robot battle, he had exactly one lone Titan costume remaining. Delivery for his next batch was scheduled for Monday morning. Until then, he couldn't risk losing his last outfit in case he needed to suit up for a real emergency.

Most of his team was busy, with Bubble Bubble off to see Lenny, Galvanize catching up on paperwork, and Hexcellent having a date day with Spyda. She'd offered to let him join, but a picnic in the park seemed a touch too romantic for him to intrude on. Still, Owen had to give her man points; despite the tattoos and hard rock persona, he seemed to be a real softy. Given how protective Owen was starting to feel about his team, Spyda's dutifulness as a boyfriend was as good for him as it was for Hexcellent.

The only one who didn't seem to have plans was Zone, who had settled into a semi-peaceful silence where Owen was concerned. Old grudges were slow to die, even when one realized the foundation might not be as solid as once believed. Owen understood; the kid was lugging around years of confusion, resentment, and anger that had ended up aimed toward people like Titan. Given the circumstances, Owen was actually very happy they'd managed to get this far. He didn't intend to push it by intruding on the spiky-haired young man's personal time.

Owen briefly considered calling up Jeremiah to see how things were going with the robot hunt, but thought better of it. Pestering him wouldn't make the information come any faster, and at worst, it might give Jeremiah unintentional encouragement. Owen still wasn't quite sure where he fell on his fellow Hero's romantic advances. The man was confident, skilled, and capable; all traits Owen found desirable. However, he was also young, brash, and cocky. Maybe in the Subtlety world things were different, but Owen had seen too many Heroes with those traits end up in the ground to dismiss the possibility that Jeremiah might get himself killed. All of which ignored the larger issue of if he was ready to actually date again.

In those years at the bar, when he'd just been Owen, things were simpler. He was merely himself, a muscular entrepreneur who was maybe a bit too strong for what even his large frame implied. Now, things were different. If he started dating again, *especially* with another Hero, he'd be doing it as Titan. Maybe that would be a good thing; owning who he was and moving on with his life publicly could be the catalyst that finally took the sting out of the Titan Scandal. Then again, maybe it would undo everything he'd been working hard to fix since he returned. It was a thorny, complicated issue, and Owen was determined to take his time in choosing the proper course. Rash decisions had taken too much from him in the past. Whatever he chose, whether it was for the better or worse, it would be deliberate. He would own his decisions.

Unfortunately, the decision of what to do with his day off still loomed overhead, and that one was proving to be quite a toughie. He could try vegging out in the living room, maybe pick up a few of Hexcellent's games, but he knew himself well enough to guess that doing so would just lead to boredom and the sense of a wasted day. After five more minutes of thought, Owen decided to give it a go anyway, as he was unable to come up with anything else that might prove better.

Stepping into the living room, Owen was surprised to find not just Zone but also two men in lab coats. Edgar and Kirk, or "the docs", were standing watchfully over Zone while he skimmed, signed, and initialed a large stack of thick papers.

"Trying to requisition extra carbs?" Owen almost regretted going with a bad joke to announce himself, but as soon as they heard his voice, Edgar looked up and smiled.

"Ah, Titan! What a treat. We so rarely get to see you about, but I suspect that's to be expected with your indomitable physique. You don't require our check-ups or assistance."

"Or advice, that you can then ignore," Kirk added. That barb wasn't directed at Owen, though. The shorter man's gaze was fixed firmly on Zone, who scratched his name in the stack of documents even faster.

"Ahem, yes, that either," Edgar agreed, shuffling awkwardly. "Though, if you'd be willing, we'd love to do some basic calibration tests on you. Technically Heroes are exempt from having to fulfill that requirement for the event, but it would still be fascinating to administer."

"I'm sorry, event?"

"The charity show, remember?" Zone's sneer was half-assed as his attention was still on the myriad of paper set before him. "Contests, sports, meet-and-greets; Supers from every public occupation coming together to raise money for those in need. We signed up for it last month, and it starts next week."

"Must have slipped my mind," Owen muttered. Between Gale and her team, hordes of robots, and Topsy's students, the charity event had dropped off the backburner of his mind and fallen under the stove.

"Quite all right, it's not as though you need any additional training to be able to perform well," Edgar noted.

"And you aren't likely to blow your damn knees out, either." Kirk grabbed the stack of papers from Zone as the last signature was put in place, yanking it away angrily. "But I guess that's no one's problem but the participant's."

"It's my body; I'll decide what risks I take. Mordent has its waivers, so leave me alone." Zone clicked the pen shut and twirled it through the air, tossing it to Edgar before getting up from the coffee table and walking briskly past Owen.

"Kirk, you could have been a bit nicer about everything," Edgar chastised. "But I do wish he'd have listened to reason."

Owen didn't have to ask what they were talking about; he'd seen the way Zone winced for himself. The kid was tearing his body apart with all the sports and rescue work, and unfortunately, he didn't have one that fixed itself. Owen had half-suspected he was the only one who knew about Zone's condition, but it seemed the docs had caught on too. Galvanize did once say they were brilliant, after all, mentally-gifted beings who were well-versed in all manners of. . . science.

The realization came crashing down on Owen as the docs were gathering their things and beginning to leave.

"Those calibrations you wanted to do. . . got time for them today?"

Edgar perked up so visibly that Owen feared the wiry man might have tweaked his back. "For you? Certainly we do! Kirk, push everything back. This will be a rare and fascinating opportunity."

"I'm surprised you're willing to do this at all," Kirk said, eyeing Owen suspiciously.

"It's not totally altruistic. There's an interesting work problem I'm dealing with, and I'd love to get your perspectives on it."

"Ah, quid pro quo." Kirk nodded; clearly this fit better into his world view than simple generosity. "In that case, please follow us downstairs."

74.

"This feels. . . risky." Bubble Bubble set down the stack of papers on Lenny's desk. The outline of their counter-strategy to her scandal was in-depth, smartly-worded, and shockingly comprehensive, especially given that the whole thing had only gone down the night before. She'd known anyone who represented Titan would be good, but even she was taken aback at so much planning done so soon. That said, this was a far bolder strategy than she'd been expecting.

"Risky is an understatement. This is outright courting trouble," Lenny corrected. "If done improperly, this strategy will torch what little goodwill you have left, pretty much putting you out of business. Whereas if you just try to lie low and weather the storm, you'll probably end up back to square one, career-wise."

"I take it there's some greater gain to be had by this strategy then, if the chance at loss is so much higher."

Lenny smiled, a surprisingly charming feature on the unkempt, clearly sleep-deprived man. "Smart call. I've still got Heroes that I'd have to handhold to that realization." He reached over and rested a thick finger on the stack of papers resting in front of Bubble Bubble. "Your old image, really your whole character, is dead. No matter what we do, no matter how we frame it, that demure gal who embodied polite, quiet beauty is never coming back. If we sit this through silently, playing it defensive, all we're doing is clinging to the last vestiges of something that's already lost. If, on the other hand, we take this route, then we can create a new image out of the ashes from your old one. But, like I said, that only works if you can play it right."

Bubble Bubble picked up the documents once more, Lenny's finger sliding off as soon as she touched the papers. "What do you need from me to make this work?"

"There will be lots of sound bites, some PR work, and I've got an interview tentatively scheduled for this afternoon to kick things off. But more than anything I need to know if *you* believe you can make that girl come to life. You have to be bold, certain, and unwavering. A lot of people aren't going to like what you're selling. This isn't some milquetoast persona that no one talks about and some people admire. You're going to piss some folks off, and if you give so much as an inch, that's all it will take to tear the whole thing down. Only you can say for sure if you're up to the challenge, and really, only you should make the call on something this dangerous."

"It's certainly a change of pace," Bubble Bubble agreed. "But in a lot of ways, I like this one better. If nothing else, she seems a lot more fun. Tell me something though, if you don't mind. Were I one of your actual clients, a Hero, would this be the strategy you recommended for me?"

"Depends on the Hero, but probably not," Lenny admitted, no sense of shame in his voice. "Heroes need to play it safer; they're civil servants sent in to keep people safe. Making a Hero polarizing is dangerous. Some folks will outright refuse to be saved by someone they disagree with. If a Hero were in your shoes, I'd have to recommend something that was a half-step between this and playing it safe."

Lenny leaned forward slightly in his chair, a wicked gleam suddenly twinkling in his eye. "But in that situation, I'd be silently wishing I *could* recommend this tactic to them. Heroes don't have the freedom that you do, Bubble Bubble. I can't make you use it, or even tell you if it's right to do so. All

I can say is this is the only strategy I can see that has a chance at putting you ahead of where you were before the fiasco started."

"You do know how to sell a pitch, I have to give you that," Bubble Bubble said. She skimmed the documents one last time before setting them down. "This new version, she seems a bit combative. Do you think people will respond to that?"

"In my experience, it's not the fact that someone's aggressive that turns people off so much as what they're aggressive about. And yeah, you're going to alienate the shit out of a lot of folks. But you're also going to draw in a plenty of people who are just as sick of this bullshit as you."

"If I do it right," Bubble Bubble added.

"Goes without saying," Lenny agreed. "Think you can handle being a little more abrasive and mouthy than before?"

Bubble Bubble chuckled, a soft, practiced sound that couldn't hide a touch of harshness. "I didn't make it this far by not having a bit of asshole in me. Honestly, keeping that suppressed was the hardest part of my job. . . far worse than jumping into fires or risking injury. I understand that this has the potential to utterly lay waste to my career, but since that could happen anyway, I think I'd prefer to go out swinging."

With a quick motion, Lenny produced a new stack of documents from under his desk and slid them over. "That was what I wanted to hear. Welcome aboard, Bubble Bubble; if you sign these then you're officially one of my clients."

"Wasn't I already?"

"Yes and no," Lenny said. "Titan asked me to help you, so I was going to do that no matter what. But there's a hefty amount of difference between getting you through one scandal and actually taking you on as a client. To be frank, I dislike working with people that have no guts. Life, at least this life, requires people take chances. If you want the big pay-off, you have to be willing to take the dangerous gambles. You're not obligated to sign on, of course. I just wanted to let you know the offer was on the table."

Bubble Bubble stared at the contract for a long moment, then motioned for Lenny to slide the pages over. "Mr. Greene, the man who manages us at Mordent, wanted me to take the safe route. Hole up, let the team do damage control, try and wait for it to pass. That's the sane move, isn't it?"

"Unquestionably so," Lenny agreed.

"Then I'm happy to sign on with you. I too dislike working with the gutless." Bubble Bubble grabbed and pen and began flipping through the papers, initialing as she read. "Besides, I can't wait to see the look on Hexcellent's face when she finds out I'm challenging her for the title of baddest bitch in the house."

75.

"Can you push any harder?" Kirk peered around the side of the metal box where a single protruding bar was being pressed down on by Owen, who was using only his triceps. It was a pretty standard device in the high-end gyms developed for strongmen, built to figure out how much the user could safely lift using any given muscle group. When one measured their workout equipment in the hundreds of pounds, guesses could lead to injury or worse.

"I can, but in my experience this is around where the machine breaks," Owen warned them.

"According to the reading, you're only moving the equivalent of one and a half tons," Edgar said from his position at the console across the room, eyes unmoving from the screen. "These are rated to go to at least three."

"Yeah, they say that, but given how few Supers out there can even get over one, it's not a claim that they get called out on often." Despite his warning, Owen obliged, easily moving the bar lower through the increasing resistance. Plenty of Supers out there could move more weight than he, but they had to do it using telekinesis or anti-gravity or some other trick. Pure physical force usually capped out around a ton per muscle group for most Supers, though obviously they could move far more when not localizing the effort. Even with abilities, the human body was built to have limitations. Strongmen were plentiful, but those who could break the ton-per-muscle barrier were somewhat rarer. The number who were in the same league as Titan could almost be counted on a single hand.

"Stop stop stop!" Edgar leapt up from his seat and waved his arms in the air, as though his impassioned screeches hadn't gotten the message across.

Owen obliged, forcing himself not to gloat at the slight crackle of snapping metal from inside the metal box as he allowed the bar to raise itself back up. Kirk hurriedly moved a few steps away, while Edgar fell back into his seat and began typing up a storm on his computer.

"I suppose this is the repayment for our hubris. Your strength is well-documented, after all. Tell me, do you have any idea what your actual maximum is these days?"

Returning the bar to its resting position, Owen let go and shook his head. "I stopped being able to use Hero gyms a long time ago, for obvious reasons, and even with a few ultra-dense weights there aren't many other gyms that can do much for me. Working out is more of a way to turn off my brain and relax these days. Luckily my strength never goes down, only up, so it's not like I can get rusty."

"Fascinating." Kirk produced a tablet from his lab coat pocket and began typing furiously. After a few moments, he looked up, glanced at Edgar, who was desperately clacking at keys, and realized he was being rude to their guest. "Since it seems the testing equipment will be down for a while, why don't we use the time to answer the questions you mentioned?"

"It's not so much a question as me wanting an opinion," Owen said. "By now I assume you heard about the robots that attacked the other day. . ."

Owen went through the events as he knew them, sharing the information available to him while leaving out the only confidential bit—the stolen piece of experimental equipment—and otherwise bringing them up to speed. He was nearly done when Edgar walked over to listen in, waving off Owen's attempt to backtrack.

". . .so honestly, I'm not sure what to ask you here. I just feel like we're all busting our heads against the walls trying to figure out what's going on, and maybe some fresh, smart eyes could offer insights."

Kirk and Edgar shared a look, one that was both easy to read and deeply worrying to Owen. As his story had gone on, they'd seemed less and less surprised by each progressive revelation. The stony resolve with which they faced one another now was a poor fit for the perpetually curious men he'd been dealing with.

"You don't think-"

"I most certainly do think."

"But how?"

"Parallel thinking, corporate espionage, simple-"

"Guys." Owen leaned forward and spoke firmly, cutting off Edgar and causing him to jump slightly. "I'd like to be included in the conversation, if you don't mind."

"You explain. I'll go check it." Edgar didn't wait for a reply, he merely rushed out through a glass and metal door into some deeper part of the lab that Owen had not been privy to viewing.

Kirk cleared his throat and shuffled awkwardly, but after a few seconds of hesitation, he finally pulled himself together and began speaking. "Titan, what you've described makes no sense. The way these robots are acting, the strategies in use, sacrificing one unit for another with no time to have received an order. . . It seems like nonsense, if we're viewing these robots as independent, programmed units."

Owen didn't lean forward or shift his weight; he wanted to avoid coming off as intimidating for as long as possible. Still, there was a touch of edge to his voice as he pressed for more information. "I take it you have a theory?"

"A highly unsubstantiated one. Merely a hypothesis based on personal observations from a prior experiment," Kirk warned. "But, all the patterns that make no sense in individual units do hold structure if each unit is viewed as a piece of a greater whole. All working toward singular goal, prioritizing success over conservation of resources or minimized losses."

"Like ants from a hill," Owen surmised. "Their goal is the survival of the queen."

"Similar, but more like cells in a body," Kirk corrected. "Each unit has no inherent value; it is only a piece of the true whole. Ants and bees and the like still operate under an individual consciousness, however primitive it may be. To these robots, it's possible that they have no thoughts of their own, that all share in a single mind. That is to say, it may be that each robot is actually connected to the greater program running them all, thus why they are able to coordinate so perfectly."

"Wait. . . do you think these things are alive?"

"No no, nothing like that," Kirk said quickly. "Merely that rather than running a program on each unit's hard drive, they are all connected to one source that runs remotely and controls the robots like appendages."

"I'm with you now." Owen doubted he was really getting all the intricacies of what Kirk was trying to tell him, but he'd at least grabbed the gist. It was an interesting theory, definitely one that put those metal assholes in a new light. Unfortunately, that's all it was at this point: a theory. "Is there even record of a machine that can do something like this?"

"The creations of Supers with technical abilities are largely classified, so I can't say for certain how many functional units like what I described have existed, but I do know of at least one prototype that was created by those of the more mundane genius." Kirk paused to look up at the mountain of a man before him then plunged onward. "Edgar and I made it years ago; in fact, it was one of our first projects together. There were serious issues, though, and we shelved it in the Mordent laboratory vaults until time and technology advanced to where we could perfect the design."

"Seems like someone felt the time was ripe." Edgar had reappeared though the doors, a vacant, haunted look on his face. "The prototype is gone, no record of it being checked out. Our work has been stolen."

76.

Whatever else Owen could say about Mordent Holdings, they certainly didn't falter in the face of an unexpected development.

Within five minutes of Kirk calling in the missing invention, dozens of privately-employed security officers swarmed through the lab's doors. Owen was briefly spoken to as they uncovered why he was present in a restricted area. Once it was established that he had been with the docs, who had more clearance than nearly anyone else at Mordent, and that it was impossible for him to have taken anything without being seen, Owen was gently escorted out to the elevator and told to return to the penthouse.

He did so a bit begrudgingly; in truth, he felt like there was a lot more he could learn from Kirk about what this prototype machine had done, but it didn't seem like a good time to press the issue. Even aside from the Mordent security picking apart their lab, neither one of the docs seemed to be taking the news well. Kirk had been flitting about, desperately coming up with new places were the device might have been, only to come up empty-handed. Edgar had been far worse, though. After announcing that the prototype was gone, he simply sat down in one of the rolling chairs near a computer and didn't move. It had taken multiple attempts from security to get any information out of him while Owen was there; Edgar had seemed largely preoccupied with staring blankly at the wall.

Having accidentally set off a panic in his own home, Owen decided to double down and alert the other Heroes to what he'd uncovered. It wasn't much—hell, technically it wasn't really anything at all yet—but it might lead them to something real, eventually. That job was up to Jeremiah and the other Subtlety Heroes, thankfully. Owen's only real focus was on kicking apart whatever defenses were there when they found these bots' home base. Deep down part of him hoped there would be some tough obstacles. It had been a long time since he'd really had to push his limits. A genuine challenge might be nice.

That challenge wouldn't be coming today, though. After sending his report to the other Heroes through Dispatch and puttering around the kitchen trying to make lunch that didn't taste of grass and terrible, Owen finally gave in to the Sunday laziness and sank into the couch, picked up the remote, and flipped through the channels.

He'd managed to burn through about half an hour when a vibration on his leg caught his attention. Pulling out his phone, Owen saw the recent text from Galvanize about moving the Monday morning meeting back an hour, then noticed one stamped a few hours prior. Evidently it had come when things were more hectic. Owen pressed the small mail icon and saw a message from Lenny pop up.

Channel 44, 1:00 p.m. Don't miss it.

Since the clock on his phone told Owen that it was already 1:23, he grabbed the remote and frantically began clicking through the channels, in such a hurry that the idea of punching in the numbers directly never even occurred to him. Arriving at last, he saw a stuffy, somewhat ruddy-faced man wearing what was clearly an expensive suit. For a moment, he was uncertain why Lenny wanted him to watch this dipshit, then a familiar voice came from off-screen and it all made sense.

"And what, pray-tell, is it you feel I should apologize for?"

The camera turned to Bubble Bubble, who looked as composed and put together as she'd ever been, a sharp contrast to the worn out man sitting across the desk from her. Owen stared at the screen, taking careful stock of his teammate. Something seemed slightly off about her. Same copper hair, same pale, freckled cheeks, same designer costume as she always wore. Then he looked in her eyes and it clicked. She wasn't being demur and careful, wasn't doing her best to be pretty yet inoffensive. Bubble Bubble was meeting her interviewer's gaze head on, her eyes flashing with a confidence and fire Owen couldn't recall ever witnessing in her before.

"Your position makes you a role model to countless little girls," the man said, his voice raised higher than was called for. Owen might have missed the beginning of the interview, but he had a solid hunch that it hadn't been going the way the host expected. "The least you can do is show remorse when you make a mistake."

"I tell you what, I'll be glad to make an apology." Bubble Bubble leaned slightly forward, graceful as a falling rose petal, and smiled charmingly. "Why don't you just tell me which part I should apologize for? Is it being lied to by a man who I only now know has a history of infidelity, or being naïve enough to trust someone I liked at his word? Perhaps you feel I owe everyone an apology for making a sober, informed decision to have sex with a fellow adult rather than stick to a centuries' outdated ideal of feminine chastity. Or do I owe an apology for not being sorry that I was tricked, for standing up and refusing to let myself be blamed for another's actions? You tell me, Mr. Biron, which one I should apologize for. Explain it to me, and the viewers at home, and I'll be happy to say I'm sorry."

The station cut to a commercial quickly, though not quite before the interview's face grew a shade or two redder. As a commercial for dish soap began to play, Owen pressed a button on the still open phone in his hand, dialing up Lenny.

"Thought you'd have called earlier," Lenny said, picking up after only a single ring.

"Just got the text," Owen replied. "What in the hell did you tell that girl?"

"I told her the right call was to be aggressive and proud. She did nothing wrong, so instead of being conciliatory, she had to go on the attack. Show no shame, no fear, and keep calling out people for being assholes. Booked her on Robert Biron's show to test the waters; he's an aspiring talking head with too little brains to make it anywhere big. She's more or less been wiping the floor with him for the last half hour."

"Caught the tail end of a speech, I thought the guy was going to have a damn aneurysm," Owen said.

"This is only the beginning. If she keeps up doing this well, Bubble Bubble might just end up coming out ahead in this scandal. Speaking of, a little bird told me there was a lot of action around the Mordent building today. Anything your agent needs to be aware of?"

"No, for once this isn't my problem." As an ad for Hero-endorsed candy bars ended, Owen saw the now-familiar set reappear.

"Gotta let you go, Lenny. I don't want to miss a moment of this."

77.

"All right team, this is going to be a big week for us."

Galvanize was somehow awake and peppy on Monday morning without the aid of caffeine, a talent more than one person had theorized might be his actual super-power. Around him, the others looked more or less like half-risen zombies, save for Bubble Bubble, who seemed unusually chipper. Despite being pulled in for an "image consultation" with Mr. Greene after Sunday's interview, it was evident she was still riding on high on her small victory and the hope that all was not entirely lost. Only time would tell if the strategy actually paid off, but Owen was content just to see life returning to her eyes. It was more than had been there before, in all honesty.

"The eighth annual Supers Care Charity Spectacular kicks off tomorrow at nine in the morning," Galvanize continued. "Aside from dealing with emergencies, our schedules have been completely cleared out. No appearances, no interviews, no meetings, nothing. All Mr. Greene wants us to do is focus on the event and do our best to represent ourselves, and our sponsors, in a positive light."

"Translation: we have no excuses for skipping out early when we get bored and tired," Hexcellent mumbled, not bothering to try and actually avoid being heard.

"Mr. Greene simply wants to make it easy on us to focus," Galvanize countered, treating her grumbling as though it had been a sincere concern. Owen had realized that this was one of Galvanize's greatest tricks for handling the egos and whining of his teammates. By acting as though every petty complaint was a genuine issue, it essentially shamed the others into somewhat holding their tongues.

Galvanize reached under the kitchen table, which was laden with healthy-eating options brought in specifically for the Monday meeting. He pulled out a paper bag bearing a logo that said "SCCS" woven into a number eight. It only took a moment to put the meaning together, which gave everyone a clue as to what the packets Galvanize was pulling from the bag might relate to.

"These are your schedules for the coming four days. It tells you where to be for the individual events and contests you signed up for, as well as directs you to places on site where we can rest and recover privately." Galvanize began handing them out one at a time. Each team member's name was scrawled in impressive calligraphy across the eggshell-colored envelope. "None of this should come as much surprise to you, as we all chose our activities ourselves; however, there are two exceptions I need to make you aware of. Mr. Greene felt it was important that we show a united presence and as such requested that we be registered for two team events."

"Anyone else worried by the fact that he's just telling us this now?" Zone ripped off the top of his envelope and began hurriedly sorting through pages until he found what he was looking for. "Are you shitting me, Galv? The tug-of-war?"

"It was chosen because all Supers, be they Heroes, athletes, or PEERS, can compete. Plus, it shows all of us working in tandem toward a common goal."

"Yeah. . . do you even need us to call bullshit on that?" Hexcellent jerked a thumb at Owen, who was examining his packet of documents far more carefully that Zone. "They picked it because it's a contest of pure strength, which means Titan can do all the work and we won't look like dumb-asses. It's going to get us far, sure, but no one is going to be fooled into thinking we four did anything other than hold the rope."

"There will be entire teams on the other end pulling against us," Galvanize protested. "Even Titan can't handle the task alone."

"No, I probably can," Owen replied, looking up from his pages at last. "I mean, depending on who they've got on the other teams. Anything is possible, but knowing the Heroes of Brewster, I'd lay pretty good odds that I can win that thing solo." He glanced around at the others and gave a half-shrug of his shoulders. "Look, I didn't ask for this crap any more than you did, but I may as well be honest about our chances of winning."

"What's the other event?" Bubble Bubble asked, her own packet resting untouched in front of her.

"A simple Q&A for those interested in going into the PEERS line of work," Galvanize responded, clearly glad to be even momentarily off the tug-of-war topic. "Titan will be there to field questions from active Heroes who are interested in taking on Hero Liaison roles."

Hexcellent snorted then snickered in a combination so perfect that everyone at the table instantly knew she'd practiced it. "Which means Titan will get peppered with questions for half an hour while we sit around with our metaphorical dicks in our hands. The dudes could probably literally do that, too, and no one would even notice."

Galvanize began to reply but stopped himself. He took a moment to look around the table at the faces of his team, and then sat down in the only open chair remaining at their breakfast table. "Look, the simple truth of this is that Titan is *far* more famous than the rest of us. You know it, I know it, and

Mordent certainly knows it. So they want to put him out in front of the cameras as much as possible, with us right there alongside him to make sure the logos get seen. I'm not saying it's going to be great, but it's only two events. The rest of the time we get to do our own things."

"Galvanize, chill," Hexcellent told him. "No one's actually pissed about the extra events. We know Titan is a fucking legend, and at this point, hanging out in his shadow can be kind of fun. We just didn't want you trying to sell us shit by pretending it was chocolate."

"Not how I would have put it, not even in the slightest, but I second the general sentiment," Bubble Bubble said.

"I'm in for whatever the team wants," Owen told them. "Technically, Mordent doesn't have the right to sign me up for events I don't agree to, so if you all aren't feeling these two then I'll drop out. Pretty sure they won't try and force you four to handle them without me."

"No, we should do them." Zone lowered his packet, and, in a rare display, actually looked Owen in the eyes. "Who cares if it's really all about you? That's business as usual for us corpies. At least there's the chance some good will come of these. And besides, I think we might not entirely hate the idea of spending a little time together at this thing. You know, as a team."

Owen scanned the table, watching for dissent but finding only agreeable smiles and nodding heads. Personally, he wished they had asked him to call it off, at least the tug-of-war. He had a feeling that SAA members and Heroes weren't going to take well to losing to one washed up Hero and his team of corpies. But what his team wanted, Owen would deliver.

"Tell Mordent we're good to go," Owen said, looking over at Galvanize. "And ask them if I've gotten any mail yet today. If we're spending most of the week out in public, I'd better get my new uniforms pressed."

78.

Owen was surprised by the knock at his door. Given the team's busy day of helping out at a multicar pileup, not to mention the upcoming public spectacle, he'd expected everyone to have already hit the showers and be heading to sleep. Getting up from his bed carefully, he walked over and pulled open the door to find Hexcellent standing on the other side.

For a moment, Owen didn't even recognize the thin, pale young woman in front of him, as it was the first time he'd ever seen her face free from its caked layers of makeup. Adding in that she was adorned in a t-shirt bearing Spyda and his band along with a pair of sweatpants, she could have easily passed as a different person. In spite of all the moaning and complaining about Mordent and the rules, she was possibly the most dedicated to never being seen out of character.

She looked younger than usual and a bit more frail, as though he were seeing her without her armor for the first time. The impression of weakness was quickly shattered as she strode past him, scanned the meager room, and let out a sharp whistle. "Man, they really fucked you good on the accommodations, huh? Pretty sure this was a storage room back when Mirror Fog worked here."

"Was it now?" Owen had known from day one Greene was sending a message, but he hadn't imagined the corporate puppet had gone quite so far to send it. "What's up kid, can't sleep?"

"Yeah, they make drugs for that," Hexcellent replied. "I just wanted to see what you had scheduled around eleven tomorrow." Reaching into the pocket of her sweatpants, she pulled out a half-crumpled piece of paper and tried to smooth it out. "I've got a gap in ye olde schedule, and if we do lunch together in public then Greene can't really bitch about me eating from the food stands that will be there. I mean, team solidarity and supporting a good cause, that's two fucking birds right there."

Owen repressed a chuckle and went across to his dresser, picking up the packet and pulling his own schedule out of it. By the time he turned back around, Hexcellent had crossed the room and was now examining the pair of pictures on his desk. She glanced up, stared at him for a long moment, then looked back down.

"Were you wearing a wig in these? Your hair is way longer, but you look almost exactly the same."

"Those photos were taken over ten years ago." Owen moved to join her, staring down at his sons. It was hard to believe so much time had passed. He could still remember watching Roy struggle to get the washing machine off the ground, then slowly moving it higher and higher. By the time he'd managed to hold it over his head, the kid was so proud he may as well have been Atlas holding the earth. And Hershel, nervous as could be to speak in front of all those people at the spelling bee, had still pushed through. What he lacked in strength, Hershel easily made up for in heart and guts.

"Ten years?" Hexcellent looked back and forth again then stood up straight. "Are you a fucking Highlander?"

"Just a Super whose body does not want to play along with the aging process," Owen replied. He tried not to think about his body's rebuffing of something as natural as growing older. It meant that there was no peaceful end in sight somewhere down the line. The only options were to be killed or to keep living until it became a curse. At least there were Supers out there who could kill him. After so many years of being untouchable, Owen actually took a measure of comfort in that knowledge.

"Damn. The kids still that age too?"

"No, they've both grown up into fine young men." Owen smiled, unable to suppress the fatherly pride that beamed within him. Even if they hated him until the end of time, he would never stop being proud of what his sons had made of their lives. "They're my kids, actually. Going through the HCP right now."

"Oh yeah, I saw some videos speculating about what would happen to your family after. . . well, you know, the fucking another dude thing."

"I'm familiar with it, yes."

"So are they like you? Immortal little bad asses destined to whip the shit out of every bad guy who crosses their path?" Hexcellent stepped away from the picture slightly, more interested in Owen's current expression than his photographed past.

"They're similar, but with gifts all their own." Owen shook his head, still looking at the boys as he'd remembered them until they came striding into his bar looking for answers. "But they're better than me by a mile. Those two are going to make the world a more decent place, in and out of costume."

"In costume? Ah, I get you. Titan's kids in the HCP. Bet they're knocking the teeth out of all the other students."

"The HCP isn't as cut and dry as you might think," Owen told her. "Even I got knocked around in my early days. It's not as much about the beatings, but what you learn from them. Actually, I'm hoping to get time off in a few months to go watch their end of the year exam, assuming Greene doesn't find a way to keep me penned up here."

"As long as you put on a good show this week, I bet you'll be able to swing a favor or two," Hexcellent advised. "And if worse comes to worse, ask Galvanize for the time instead of Greene. Fearless leader has a knack for making the suit come around."

"I'll keep that in mind." Owen realized he was still holding his paper, so he pulled it up to check the time Hexcellent had asked about. "Looks like I'm free from ten to noon. Lunch at eleven, then?"

"Kickass, I'll meet you at the entrance to the food alley." Hexcellent pulled out another piece of paper, this one diagramming the different eating options available to those attending the charity event. She skimmed it with a growing expression of delight. "I say we hit the cotton candy and funnel cakes first."

"That's your idea of lunch?"

"That's my idea of what I'm eating with my very rare access to a free pass."

Owen glanced down at his schedule once more, the unmistakable sense that he was being played creeping into his mind. "You're going to get me in trouble, aren't you?"

"Fuck yeah I am." Hexcellent turned and headed out the door, but turned back around and gave Owen a genuine smile. "But hey, you've only got yourself to blame. Before you showed up, there wasn't any trouble to get in."

Then she was gone, leaving Owen torn between whether he should feel complimented or worried by her statement. Ultimately, he settled on the former.

79.

The hectic, half-mad energy of the sprawling grounds felt strangely familiar to Owen as he rode past the few security barriers, crammed with the rest of his team into the Mordent-issued SUV. Once upon a time, Titan had been a mainstay at many such events, putting on displays of strength and signing autographs until his pens ran dry, all in the name of giving back to the community. Many of his fellow Heroes undertook such activities as necessary obligations, something to generate good PR and make their agents happy. And, in total truth, Owen hadn't been so different from them when he first started doing Hero work. That changed when he found out about Hershel and Roy's status as Powereds. Suddenly all those unfortunate souls he'd had the chance to help seemed closer to family than strangers.

As they cruised past various stalls and tents being set up on the Brewster fairgrounds, which the city generously allowed for the SCCS's use, Owen felt pangs of both nostalgia and regret. While it was good to be back in a position where he could make a difference, the weight of all his years pissed away on seclusion and self-pity weighed heavy on his heart. He looked away from the window, turning his attention to the team that was excitedly gabbing inside the vehicle.

To them, none of this was familiar in the slightest. Mordent had put them in charity events before, but never one as big as what they were currently heading into. It just hadn't made fiscal sense; few corpies had any fans that would want to see them, and their powers generally weren't strong enough to compete with Heroes and professional athletes in a meaningful way. Sending them into situations like this was a good way to make a team look foolish while also tearing down their self-esteem. Unless, of course, they had a big wave of public accolades to ride or a very famous Hero backing them up. Even so, Owen knew Mordent was taking a risk putting them out there like this. Most likely, they were counting on him to keep his team looking—and more importantly feeling—good.

Thus far it was an easy job. Zone was listing all the events he wanted to watch rapid-fire, Galvanize was reminding everyone to stay ahead of schedule whenever possible, Hexcellent was almost leaning out the window as she tried to catch sight of food trucks setting things up, and even Bubble Bubble seemed cheery as she spotted the occasional famous Super. Everyone was in costume, under strict orders not to be out of them unless they were safely inside the penthouse. Given that some of their activities were going to be physical, sweaty, and downright dirty, Owen imagined whoever did the team's laundry was in for a hellish week.

At last the SUV angled into a covered parking area near the rear of the fairgrounds. Following the direction of several men in vests, Galvanize pulled into a large parking spot and killed the engine, then swiveled in place to face his team.

"All right, what're everyone's first events? Hexcellent?"

"Fiery Discussion is sponsoring a temporary tattoo booth where I'm going to stand around and help people pick what designs they want." She watched as Galvanize began to open his mouth then cut him off. "And the designs have to be on the pre-approved board. I am not allowed to try and talk anyone into making the artist draw a dick on their face, no matter how funny I think it would be."

"Very good. Bubble Bubble?"

"Cosmetics company is doing a raffle for free makeovers. I'm there to sell tickets and answer basic questions about the products."

Galvanize nodded. "Given your extra burst of notoriety, Mr. Greene approved having some plainclothes security stationed nearby, just in case anyone decides to forget that we're all here for charity."

"I'll stop by when I've got downtime too," Owen promised. Bubble Bubble gave him a grateful look and seemed to relax visibly. In his experience, people tended to use a lot more manners when staring up at a tree-trunk of a man who could juggle cars like cotton balls.

"On that note, Titan, can you remind us what you'll be doing with the morning?" Galvanize asked.

"Private panel for new Heroes, ones still in or only a few years out of their internships," Owen replied. "They're paying to get in and ask some of us experienced folks questions and advice for a couple of hours."

"Hot damn, that sounds cool," Hexcellent said. "Who else is in there besides you?"

"Not a clue," Owen admitted. "I was the first name on the list when we signed up, and I sort of forgot about all this anyway, so I never checked to see who came after me. I'm assuming some people did, though, otherwise they'd have canceled the damn thing."

"I wouldn't be too sure about that," Galvanize told him. "Plenty of people would pay good money to learn from your experience alone. All right Zone, you're the last one, tell me you remember where you're supposed to go."

"Like I could forget." Zone leaned back in his chair and set his sneakered feet up on the SUV's dashboard. "Punch Juice is teaming up with a sports equipment company, so I've got to be on hand demoing what their stuff can do in order to get people to buy it. Which, by the way, I'm logging as work-out hours."

Galvanize reached over and swept Zone's legs down from the dash before responding. "I'm sure Mr. Greene will have no objection to that, since you are burning calories." He looked away from Zone, making sure to meet the eyes of each member of his team at least once. "Now everyone, today is basically a warm-up. All the events are small and simple, with none of the showy stuff scheduled to start until at least tomorrow. Use this time to get familiar with the area and plan your routes for the more hectic days. Remember, we're here on the job, and everything we do reflects on our team and sponsors."

"Hey fearless leader, since we had to be quizzed on our schedules, what are you doing with your morning?" Hexcellent asked.

"I will be spending my morning at a meeting for organizers and team leads. Lots of slides, handouts, and boring details. Anyone who dislikes their plans up for trading jobs with me?"

Deafening silence was the only reply, and Galvanize allowed himself a smug smirk in the privacy of their SUV.

"I thought not. Now everyone get out there and do your best!"

80.

Owen made his trip through the fairgrounds as quickly and covertly as a man made of muscle and bordering seven feet tall was capable. Thankfully, the team had arrived early enough that the majority of others in attendance were either workers getting the booths set up or fellow Supers who were preparing for their own morning activities. Many, some Heroes and no doubt a few corpies, were in costume, but by far the majority of attendees wore uniforms from their respective Super Athletics Association teams. Just in his immediate proximity, Titan spotted several Fort Worth Juggernauts, a couple of the Tampa Atlanteans, and one relatively massive quarterback from the L.A. Crushers.

While Owen took in the crowd, it was also clear the crowd was taking in him. The more polite ones simply glanced in his direction and looked away, but a few felt free to stare at the famous, disgraced Hero hurrying through the grounds. As for the Hero himself, he dearly wished he'd paid more attention to the map in his schedule packet. For the most part, people kept their conversations about him whispered low enough to where he was unable to hear them, thankfully. On occasion, though, a word would rise up to greet his ears, and it was rarely a kind one.

His brisk pace waned as Owen forced himself to slow down. This wasn't a mission or rescue where he could get in and get out. He and his team were going to be here for several days. This walk was likely to be the easiest one he'd have in that entire time; at least these people felt some professional courtesy towards him. If he wanted to get through it, Owen would have to do more than act like it wasn't bothering him; he would actually have to not let it bother him. He'd known this was part of what he was walking back into when he put on the mask; there was no wiggling out now.

Taking his time, moving slowly across the grounds, it took only a few more minutes of searching before he found the small building where he was supposed to do the morning's panel. Old, brick, and no doubt built for some utilitarian purpose long before Brewster converted this area to fairgrounds, it was still a high step up from the open tents that were being set up all around him. Near the front entrance, a small line of people in costumes was already forming. People younger than some of Owen's teammates stood milling about in the morning sun. He was a bit surprised at the number; Brewster alone didn't have this many interns or rookies. Seemed folks from out of town had traveled in for the event, which made Owen worry all this might be a bigger deal than he'd realized.

Pushing that thought out of his mind, he made his way around to the back entrance before anyone spotted him. He gave a polite nod to the lone worker stationed at the rear, a teenaged girl who looked to be in awe of all the famous figures around her, then pushed his way through the door and into the building. Owen had barely made it five steps before he heard a familiar, though not altogether friendly, voice call to him.

"Well I'll be. Seems you really did sign up for this event. Aether was certain someone had put your name down as a joke." Gale, fully-costumed and a bit bleary-eyed from the early hour, stood from her small metal folding chair and walked over to Owen, giving his hand a quick shake as soon as they drew close.

"I wasn't certain. I just said it seemed unlikely that he'd choose to spend time at such an unremarkable venue," Aether corrected. She didn't rise from her seat, but she did give Owen a polite nod and gentle smile.

There were two more open chairs sitting at the long table that stretched across the makeshift stage, one far larger than the others and made of reinforced material, clearly set up with Titan's renowned size in mind. Counting Gale and

Aether, that made for a panel of four: a healthy size given the intimate setting and small room. In just the three Heroes present, there was also a large amount of power and career diversity. Gale was the leader of a team that had been passed down for decades, and a powerful elemental manipulator to boot. Aether could speak about running a team with unusual power sets, as Transcendental Justice was an effective, if unorthodox, composition of Heroes. Owen himself had the experience to talk about what it was to be a strongman, to run a team, to fall from the public's grace, and to work as a Hero Liaison. The only area they'd need help to cover in order to answer all the questions these kids might have was Subtlety.

"I do not, for the life of me, know how you lot put up with arriving early to these things. Time is too precious to be pissed away on waiting around."

Owen did a half-turn, already knowing who he would find. Sure enough, standing there in the sort of simple, unremarkable costume that was the fashion with many Subtlety Heroes, stood Jeremiah. It looked strange on him, and it took Owen a minute to realize that this was the first time he'd ever seen Jeremiah in full gear, out in the field. Every other time they'd met he'd been behind the scenes, not out in public. Having finally seen him in costume, Owen could easily say that the other version suited him far better.

There was little doubt Jeremiah agreed as he tugged at his mask and collar, clearly uncomfortable in the elaborate get up. That didn't stop him from greeting Gale and Aether before finally making his way through the room and arriving in front of Owen.

"Ready to dole out the pearls of wisdom from years of accolades and fuck ups?"

"As ready as I can be when I have no idea what the kids are going to ask me. Haven't exactly done one of these in a while, and I've been out of the field for a long time," Owen admitted.

"Please, the questions out of the newbies' mouths never change. They'll ask about how whether to pick a team or create one, what it was like to fight some criminal that we don't remember but they studied meticulously, and if we have any tips for not dying. Same stuff we asked about when we were doing internships." Jeremiah paused, glancing toward the front door where soon a dozen or so young Heroes would come streaming in. "Just try and make them feel at ease. Nothing we say in these things is likely to make much of a difference in the field, but we can at least give them some hope and confidence. That's what they really came out for."

"I'll keep that in mind." Owen could hear the bustling of moving feet, a clear indicator that the door had just been opened. "Glad you were able to come out as well. All of you, really. I can't remember the last time I saw one of these with three different team leaders on it."

"You're the one to thank for that," Jeremiah replied, heading toward his seat. "We were approached about filling out the empty slots after so many others turned it down. Or did you think it was coincidence that the only people willing to sit on a panel with you, to be publicly associated with such a polarizing figure, were the ones who had personally worked with you before?"

Owen stared at the drably-costumed man as he walked away, then took his own reinforced seat. It was nice to walk slow, keeping his chin up and trying to be strong, but he also couldn't forget how most of the Hero world still viewed him: nothing but a scandal and a fuck up.

He tried to keep that thought out of his head as the first costumed body entered the room and made a beeline for the front row.

81.

"Today, we're here to talk to you about what comes next. While you had ample time to go over the Hero occupation and our world during the time you spent at your respective HCPs, by now you've all gotten at least a few months of real world experience under your belt. As such, the questions and concerns that you have now are likely different from a student's, who had only theoretically delved into what it means to be a Hero." Gale's voice rang through the small building easily, keeping every back straight and ear attentive. Owen had to admit: whatever bad blood had passed them between since he arrived, there was no question that the woman could command a room.

"Now, we are not here to contradict your mentors; they are, of course, the best font of wisdom any of you has access to. But, that said, no Hero has experienced every aspect of this life personally. We may have different answers regarding different specialties or career paths than your mentors did. Please ask anything you like, though I do recommend you keep all inquiries respectful. Regardless of what our individual pasts may be, we are all up here because we have wisdom to share." Speech done, Gale took her own seat and motioned to the event worker who was standing down near the front of the audience with a clipboard.

The woman hurried forward so fast she nearly fell over, scanning down her clipboard and calling out a name. A young woman wearing a bright uniform that seemed to span the entire color spectrum rose from her seat near the back and walked briskly to the front as the worker ticked the name off the list. Ordinarily, this was where the enterprising Hero would have been given a microphone, but in such a small space, utilizing audio equipment was a waste of money.

"Hi there. I'm Lorikeet. Korman Graduate and second year intern. My question was for Aether. Are there many teams out there like Transcendental Justice, or did you found yours because there was no other fit for you?"

Given Lorikeet's odd name and stranger costume, Owen had a hunch that the question was more personal than academic. While many Supers fell into easily classifiable categories where they could be lumped together, the fact that no two were ever completely alike could lead to some strange powers. Lorikeet was either very smart or very strong; she'd have never made it out of the HCP without one of those traits. That didn't necessarily mean her power would easily fit into an existing team's dynamic, though.

As Aether talked about founding her team cooperatively with the rest of her group, being chosen as leader by a vote she had no hand in, Owen's thoughts drifted back to the founding of the Gentle Hammers. Unlike those with odd powers, any of the Hammers could have easily been worked in to any other team's arsenal; there was never a shortage of need for those who could lift trucks and shrug off bullets. Still, they'd decided to band together anyway, opting to go out and try and run things their way rather than being relegated to the role of mindless muscle, a stereotype thrust on strongmen since the earliest days of Hero work.

The sound of applause jerked Owen out of his stupor, and he realized that Aether had finished her response. He joined in the clapping, better late than never, as Lorikeet headed back to her seat and a young man wearing a black and gold color scheme stepped forward. There was something a bit archaic about the design woven into his costume, though Owen didn't have the historical sense to place where it was from. When the man reached the front, he scanned the panel, eyes narrowing a touch when he saw Titan, then continuing on until he was staring Jeremiah dead on.

"My name is Hop-Frog, and yes, it's after the Poe story. First year intern, graduated from West Private University. My question is for Jeremiah. As a fellow Subtlety Hero and a proud gay man, did you find the Hero world a welcoming place once you were out of your intern years?"

"Hell no," Jeremiah replied immediately. "And it started long before I got out of my internship. But if I'm being honest here, the Subtlety thing has been far more a roadblock for me than being gay. Lots of Hero teams out there understand what it is we do and bring to the table, so they'll let us join up, but it's always with that attitude. 'Letting us,' like we're being done a favor by getting the chance to come on board and help save lives while keeping our team safe. I'm not going to paint with a wide brush and say every team is this way; in fact, I know firsthand that the Subtlety Hero on Transcendental Justice considers herself a valued member of the group. That said, it's still the way of thinking in a lot of the older, more established teams. Your options are either to put up with it, find a group that treats you right, or start your own damn team. In case you couldn't tell, I opted for the latter."

Hop-Frog started to head back to his seat, but Jeremiah held up a hand to stop him. "Now, as for how being gay has impacted my career, I won't sugarcoat that either. There have been times when I could have signed on to teams with clout and prestige, and all I would have had to do is put up with some other member who had very firm thoughts about people's sexuality. Luckily, I had enough pull to tell them to go fuck themselves, but that's not the case for everyone. And this has gotten much better as time passed and the older opinions died out. Were I trying to make it as an openly gay Hero even a few decades back, it probably would have been a whole different story. Back then, even admitting a simple truth about yourself cost people their entire life's work. It forced a lot of good people to live lies, all so they could keep doing what they loved: keeping innocent people safe."

His speech over, Jeremiah lowered his hand and let the intern hustle back to his seat. The worker called another up another Hero, who scrambled down the aisle. Up on stage, Owen looked down to Jeremiah, who made no effort to meet his eyes. Though Titan hadn't been mentioned once in the discussion, there was no doubt in anyone's mind what Jeremiah had been really talking about. It was a kind, unexpected show of unity.

And a nice reminder to Owen that not everyone wearing a mask thought the worst of him.

82.

After the panel wrapped, there was a quick flurry of goodbyes as the others had to hurry off to their teams or next events. Unlike Owen, they were still immersed in the life, and that meant downtime was a rare commodity. It was an aspect of being a full-time Hero he remembered fondly, yet wasn't particularly burning to recapture. Perhaps it was age, or more likely the perspective that came with living through the years, but Owen was content to spend a portion of his time outside the field. At least, so long as he had his team to spend it with.

He flipped through his schedule to see what was next on the agenda. Lunch with Hexcellent wouldn't be for another hour, unless she managed to slip out early, which seemed like at least a fifty percent shot. After that he just had some minor personal appearance work until things wound down. Galvanize hadn't been lying; the first day really was set up to be light and let everyone get comfortable. Lacking anything pressing, Owen decided to make good on his word and go check on Bubble Bubble. The guards Mordent had paid for were no doubt top notch, but that wasn't really why he needed to be there. Owen was meant to be a comforting presence for her more than a deterrent for someone with a lot of lip and little wit.

Weaving his way through the myriad of tents and booths that were still springing up like weeds, it took Owen a good fifteen minutes to find Bubble Bubble's booth. Once he did, however, there was no mistaking it for any other. The fact that she was standing in front of it certainly helped, but not as much as the half-dozen reporters holding cameras and swarming around her. She was inexpressive, face well-controlled as she talked to a handsome man wearing clothes that probably cost more than Owen's first car.

Whatever they were saying was lost as Owen moved closer. The other reporters caught sight of the massive man's approach and hurried over; Bubble Bubble and her debate partner were half-dragged along with them. Cameras were raised and small microphones thrust upward as they tried to surround him.

"Titan! Any comment on Corbin Calhoun's claims that your teammate has fabricated her telling of the events?"

"Do you know Bubble Bubble to be a habitual liar, or is this her first time?"

"Have you seen her use powers to manipulate other men?"

Owen nearly took a step back, bowled over by the wave of questions and accusations, especially since it was the first time he could remember that they weren't all barbs aimed at him. To his great surprise, he wished they were. At least he was used to this sort of scrutiny; he'd far rather handle it than let it fall on Bubble Bubble's shoulders. His eyes swept the small crowd once more, and this time they locked on the handsome man with the wide, clearly artificial smile. This no doubt was Corbin Calhoun, the one who made so much trouble for Bubble Bubble, who had apparently shown up to ambush her and undermine her efforts at fixing her image. It was a bold move; Owen had to give him that. Ordinarily, he respected bold moves. Today, he was feeling less charitable.

"Whoa now. Getting in to 'he said, she said' arguments is no good for anyone," Owen replied, raising his hands and gently parting the crowd. He stepped through them, getting between Bubble Bubble and Corbin then laying a hand on each of their shoulders. "I know Bubble Bubble to be an honest, capable young woman who has never given me any reason to doubt her."

Corbin opened his mouth, and Owen squeezed ever-so-slightly, using all the self-control he had to keep from snapping this man's bones beneath his fingers. "But I also want to take this chance to pay my respects to Mr. Calhoun, who is showing the Hero community so much faith and respect with his recent accusations."

"Excuse me, he's *what*?" Bubble Bubble snapped, whipping her head up to stare at Owen, who merely smiled knowingly at her before returning his gaze to Corbin.

"Corbin Calhoun is a brave man, one who clearly believes in the Heroes and what they stand for. Most people would be too afraid to make such bold, viral accusations about Supers keeping their 'secret powers' hidden from the world. Insinuating that a woman who uses her clearly-documented abilities to help save lives is also concealing powers of mental manipulation is, to be frank, illogical and unfounded. Mr. Calhoun, however, has chosen to exercise his freedom of speech, even though doing it like this is likely to draw the ire of every one of the pro-Super organizations and syndicates out there, legal and otherwise. Mr. Calhoun is trusting in us, in the Hero system, to keep him safe from all those people, even as he slanders our very species, and I want to thank him for that. It shows that he completely trusts in the Heroes of this great country, and believes that we will be able to keep him safe."

The blood from Corbin's face had begun to drain halfway through Owen's speech, and as he stared up at the seemingly genuine smile plastered on Titan's face, his legs wobbled the slightest bit. It was only Owen's powerful hands that kept the man from fainting outright. Titan held him up through the dizzy spell until the world famous director had partially recovered.

"Anyway, if you'll excuse us, I just came to get my teammate for a quick briefing. Duty always calls, you know how it is." Owen released Corbin, who was swarmed by reporters as Owen carefully led Bubble Bubble away from the booth. Her guards tried to follow, but he waved them off. She needed some space, and he aimed to give it to her.

"Titan. . . was that a threat?" Bubble Bubble glanced over her shoulder to where the small crowd of reporters had turned on the man who brought them, shaking her head as if she couldn't believe what had just happened.

"It was simply the truth. There are groups out there who take umbrage with Supers being slandered, and not all of them are the type to handle things legally. I doubt any would really have the balls to go after that high profile of a target, but you never know. He's certainly not helping himself," Owen explained.

"Yeah, but it still really felt like you were threatening him. I can't point to a word you used, or anything you did, I just know if I'd been in his shoes I think I might have pissed myself."

"Don't sell yourself short," Owen told her. "You'd have held up far better than he did. Now, let's go duck into the private parking area, then I'll grab Hexcellent and we'll all go get cheese fries."

Bubble Bubble laughed softly and patted Owen on the arm. "You are nothing like the Titan I first expected."

Owen grinned, nothing like the fake smile he'd shown Corbin and the reporters, and gave her a quick side-armed hug. "That might be the nicest thing anyone on this team has said to me."

83.

Lunch was a longer affair than Owen expected, though he really should have been prepared for such: Hexcellent had every intention of eating her way through the fair under the guise of team building. By the time she was finally done, a small stack of greasy paper plates had been collected in her hands like trophies: trophies she quickly dumped into a trash can as she hurried to her next event. Bubble Bubble, having taken the opportunity to down a funnel cake and corn dog herself, also returned to her booth once she got word the reporters had cleared out.

Owen, once again with time on his hands, took the chance to actually stroll through the event and check out some of the various attractions. He was getting accustomed to the stares and whispers, so much so that there were times he didn't even notice them. Instead, he focused on the bevy of booths and tents spread across the landscape, gazing in wonderment at the well-organized attractions meant to wring as much money as possible for charity.

Autograph booths were by far the most popular and frequent attractions, spread carefully across the fairgrounds so that the sprawling lines didn't cause a complete bottleneck. Just as in the morning, the vast majority of these were manned by Supers from various sports teams, mostly younger players of whom Owen was only cursorily aware.

As he walked by an area devoid of people but roped off in preparation for what would be a massive, snaking line, Owen caught sight of a very familiar name emblazoned across the banner stretched above the lone table at the end of the line. The Comet, Jade Norris, was going to be present on the final day for an autograph session. Now retired, she was still a legend in her own right, and Owen found himself flipping through his schedule to see if he had any free time that day. Maybe if he could get here early enough, he could snag the former football star's autograph. One look at the heavily-inked block of activities made it clear that he'd be lucky to squeeze in time to piss; standing in a massive line was way out of the question. Pity. Owen had a feeling that would have been quite the thrill.

Just past the area blocked off for Jade's signing Owen spotted a familiar figure slipping into a white tent with a red cross on it. He contemplated pretending not to have noticed, but then headed toward it anyway. If someone was hurt, he felt like he should acknowledge it, even if that person was Zone.

Owen pulled back the medical tent's flap to reveal a wide space filled with air-conditioning units and cots. Most were empty, though a couple hosted people who looked as though they'd had too much sun, fun, or rum and were trying to sleep it off. In the corner, resting a large bag of ice against his left knee, was Zone, who balked as soon as he saw Owen's massive silhouette in the entrance. Zone didn't bother trying to run or flee; he merely tried to look as sullen as possible while Owen carefully made his way through the tent.

"Hurt yourself already? It's only the first day." Owen didn't bother pointing to the ice bag; they both knew why Zone was here.

"It's preventative, not that this is any of your business," Zone snapped. "I have to ice my knees between events so I can make it through everything. Doctor's orders."

"Uh huh. I'm pretty sure the docs' preference was that you not do any of this stuff, not just keep your knees cold." Owen crossed his arms deliberately and stared down at the much smaller man. "What's the deal with this, anyway? Will Mordent really not spring for a healer? I mean, you've got a lot of sponsors. It seems like a worthwhile investment."

Zone puffed up for a moment, ready to be combative, but as he shifted the bag from his right knee to his left the wind seemed to drift out of his sails. "They. . . they've healed me before. A few times, actually. The problem is that this isn't just one injury that can be easily fixed. It's the culmination of a lifetime full of putting constant strain on my body. Unlike some people, there's nothing really special about my physique, just in how I use it. Little injuries keep piling up, and by the time a healer comes around, the damage is already done."

"And total-body, retroactive healers are as rare as they are expensive," Owen said, understanding setting in. Healers, like all Supers, had highly individual powers. They were already a fairly uncommon breed, and the ones who could do more than just accelerate a body's natural recovery were a step above. Getting rid of injuries after they'd already healed on their own. . . there were probably fewer than ten known Supers in the world with that kind of power, all of them in high demand. Even if it could book one, Owen doubted Mordent was willing to fork over the cash it would take just to turn back the clock on a single asset.

"You've got it. So I'm stuck icing my knees and powering through, at least for as long as this body of mine is willing to hold out." Zone shifted the bag once more; clearly his right knee was the one more in need of treatment.

"I can see that. I suppose asking if you've thought about hanging it up before you tear yourself apart would be a waste of my breath," Owen said.

"Not all of us get to do this for as long as we want," Zone replied. "Getting a taste of what it's like to be out there, making a difference, doing things that only we can. . . for a lot of us it's fleeting. One day, when these things finally give out on me, I'll have to settle for some corporate gig, probably take a job for Mordent helping oversee new corpies. But until then I can still work. I'd rather spend the rest of my time doing the job I love than watching from the sidelines. But I guess you probably wouldn't understand that."

There was no right answer Owen could give, not to Zone, so he didn't bother. Instead, he merely walked across the medical tent, filled up a fresh bag with ice, and brought it over to his teammate. Wordlessly, he took the melting bag away and handed Zone the fresh one. Only when the new bag was in place did Owen speak, and it was with a more subdued tone than Zone had ever heard from the large man's mouth.

"You're not wrong. I've got no place to lecture you on how you spend what time you've got, not after I wasted so many of my years. But I've seen a lot of good people die because they couldn't let go when their bodies were no longer capable of doing the job. It's a damned shame to see that happen. What's worse, though, is that there are people counting on the ones who die. . . innocent civilians who were expecting to be saved but got left in the fire because someone unable to admit their time was up took the call instead of letting it go to a person still capable. Just remember, Zone, your job doesn't exist in vacuum. Your team and the people we go out there to help all depend on you. When the day comes that your body does finally give out, you might not be the only one who pays for that failure."

Before Zone could respond, Owen turned and headed out of the tent. There was no trying to drill the point in, not with someone so stubborn. Heaven only knew how many people Owen had seen ignore the warning before.

All he could do was hope that Zone would be smarter.

84

When the rest of his team headed back to the Mordent penthouse, eager to relax and prepare for the next day's activities, Owen took a quick jog across town to a different destination. The evening air was cool against his face as he ran. He nodded his head to those who waved at his familiar costume as he passed them by. Near the day's end, Dispatch had passed on a message from Jeremiah that another meeting was set to take place. Owen was surprised at how eager he was to attend, and not just because of his curiosity about what the hell these robots were up to, either. Owen was getting a bit of a thrill from the chase. Working with his team was great and rewarding, but Titan hadn't been a legend for no reason. Deep down, Owen Daniels loved Hero work, and hunting the bots was reminding him why.

Instead of a hotel, this time Jeremiah had them meeting in the upstairs of a store that seemed to sell nothing but smoked meats and whiskey. Owen circled around the back, climbing the rickety staircase and easing past the slightly-rotted wooden door. It seemed Jeremiah hadn't been kidding about his team's need to meet in different places; this was about as far from a five-star penthouse as he could get.

Stepping into the surprisingly-spacious room, Owen quickly realized that he was the last to arrive. Deadlift, Aether, and Gale were all sitting in fold-out chairs, staring at the projector's screen that Jeremiah had positioned himself next to. The Subtlety Hero smiled as Owen entered, motioning for him to shut the door.

"And at last, the great Titan has arrived to bless us with his presence. I'd offer you a seat, but the owners only had the three chairs on hand."

"Did you run all the way here or something?" Gale added. "We got the call over half an hour ago."

"Actually. . . yeah, I just jogged over." Owen slunk toward the back, towering over the other seated Heroes and positioning himself carefully so as not to block their view.

"You're joking," Aether said. "I know not every team has a teleporter, but surely you've at least got a car."

"Well, the team does, but I let them take it back home," Owen admitted.

"Wow." Jeremiah shook his head, half in amazement and half in disbelief. "That's something one of us should do something about. If there's a situation where we have to call in Titan, I doubt we'll have time for him to take the shoe-leather express."

"It's worked fine so far," Owen said.

"Ah, but I fear things are about to get more complicated, if not outright dangerous." Jeremiah clicked a button on the remote clutched in his fingers; an image appeared on his projector screen. It showed a map of Brewster, complete with a dozen or so small red dots scattered throughout. "As you all know, the robots we've been dealing with broke their usual pattern last week, using decoys to attack us while they looted technology from a local company. Since then, there have been sporadic break-ins throughout the city, all at places specializing in either high-tech research or materials. No security camera footage has been recovered, not a single witness has come forward, and most distressing of all, the strikes have always come at times when Heroes are occupied or scattered."

"Hold on, if no one has seen the perpetrators, how do we know it's the robots?" Deadlift asked. "All they did before was attack us, and now they turn to petty crime?"

"I assure you, there is nothing petty about the sorts of things they've been stealing," Jeremiah replied. "And as for why we assume the bots are the culprits, I'll admit that part is speculative. That said, it would explain the shift in their behavior. What we assumed were attacks meant to test out new models may, in fact, have been intended to test us. . . specifically, our individual response times and coordination. These robberies are hitting us in the metaphorical blind spots, which either means that someone is using extensive surveillance and planning to estimate our responding abilities, or the Dispatch system has been compromised. My team ruled out the latter possibility as soon as we suspected it."

"Wait, did you actually meet Dispatch?" It was Aether who asked the question, but everyone in the room, Owen included, leaned slightly forward as they stared at Jeremiah. Despite a long, prestigious career as a Hero before his scandal, Owen had never met, nor heard of anyone else who had met, Dispatch. Whoever or wherever she was, it was a complete mystery even from the people she talked with daily.

"I. . . no, I did not," Jeremiah admitted. "But people I trust went through the communication system and assured me everything was still secure. And if the actual Dispatch decided to turn against us, we'd be in for more trouble than just dealing with robots, theft, and assault. Thus, we assume they are avoiding us through the other method, which points squarely at our mechanical opponents."

"What do you think they're doing?" Gale asked. "It's still a month out from the next attack in their pattern."

"Yes, and that's part of why I gathered you all here." Jeremiah clicked the button once more, and a diagram of a small device took the place of the map with the red dots. "Titan has informed us of a piece in the puzzle we were previously unaware of, a stolen machine that allows the machines to act as a single unit split into multiple bodies. That knowledge forced us view their attacks as far more organized than we originally assessed, and from the new perspective, my team has crafted a fresh theory."

Another click, this time showing a familiar model of the robots that Owen had fought on two occasions now. "At their last iteration, the bots were tough enough to injure multiple Hero teams and cause extensive damage. While we don't know exactly what benchmark they were working toward, we do believe that in that attack they met it. Thus, having evolved to whatever necessary point they were aiming for, their methods switched in to gathering experimental technology and equipment. Essentially, the robots reached a baseline, and are now incorporating stolen assets into their already powerful forms."

"Damn." Gale leaned back in her chair as Jeremiah's words washed over her. "You're saying this next fight is going to be a tough one."

"Worse." Jeremiah made another click, and this time all that showed on the screen was a giant red question mark. "I'm saying that, now that their first pattern is broken, we have no way to know when or where the next attack will be coming from. Not only will these things be far more powerful than any iteration we've faced before, but they have already demonstrated the ability to blindside us. Their next strike, the most powerful one yet, will likely come with exactly zero warning or chance to prepare."

85.

"I really hope there's some good news as well, and that you didn't just call us all in to make sure we knew we were helpless." Gale seemed unfazed by Jeremiah's announcement, as did pretty much else in the room save for Deadlift. As the youngest Hero of the group, he'd let out an audible gasp of shock at the announcement, an act he was clearly regretting in the face of the other's stoic reactions.

"Well, it might be good or bad. Sort of depends on how things go. But we definitely know *something*." Jeremiah clicked away the question mark, revealing a diagram of a single red dot with dozens of arrows pointing to blue ones spread across a new map of Brewster. "While running all the robots from one device might allow for incredible levels of cooperation, information relay, and strategy, it does still come with one giant weakness: namely that all of your robots are being run from one single point."

Aether nodded, quickly taking Jeremiah's meaning. "Unlike before, when we thought each unit was self-contained, now we know there's a central command system. Which means if we take that out, we end the entire threat with one blow."

"I can always tell which teams employ their own Subtlety Heroes, even without the research," Jeremiah said. "Aether has hit the nail dead on. Before, we were trying to track the robots' points of origin or uncover their creator, assuming that once an attack started, the only way to end it was to break them all to pieces. Now we know there's another option, as well as some method of remote relay being used to issue orders. One of my fellow Modus Operandi members is currently working on a device that will, in theory, allow us to trace the signal back to its origin point, assuming we can capture a robot that isn't completely destroyed."

More than a few sets of eyes glanced at Owen, who merely raised his wide shoulders in a mighty shrug. "Guessing there are other Heroes who might be able to manage that."

"Speaking of Modus Operandi, when are we going to meet one of these other team members of yours?" Deadlift asked. "You all seem to be spearheading the research, but from what I've heard, you're the only one of the group anyone ever talks to."

"And that is for good reason," Jeremiah said. "The less that is known about a Subtlety Hero, the better. We do our best work when no one is ever certain we've been there at all. That's why I, as the most extroverted member, was chosen to be the face and mouthpiece of our group. It lets the others keep on task while protecting their privacy as much as possible."

"Though if you ever really want to meet them, just hold an event with an open bar," Gale added. "I've yet to meet the Subtlety Hero that won't drink as much of the good liquor as possible if given half a chance."

"Cruel, but not inaccurate," Jeremiah said. "At any rate, you can trust that the man in charge of making the tracking device has the skills to make it work, assuming it's doable in the first place. This means that when the attack does come, we will have Heroes functioning in two distinct capacities. Most will be tasked with bringing down the robots and protecting the civilians, but there will be a few of us whose jobs revolve around tracking their orders to the source. Once there, we'll hopefully be able to put an end to these antics for good."

"Why are we assuming they'll attack?" Owen's voice bounced off the bare wooden walls, no doubt echoing down to the smoked meat shop they were standing over even as the other Heroes turned in their chairs to face him. "Jeremiah said it himself: they've deviated from their old pattern. If all the other attacks were to refine their designs and figure out our weak spots, what does another fight gain for them?"

"That, my giant comrade, is the billion dollar question." Jeremiah reached out and turned off the projector, his presentation having reached its end. "We know another attack is coming because most of the technology stolen during the break-ins was centered around weaponry or national defense. Not exactly the sorts of party favors one stocks up on if the battles are over. As to the why, that I genuinely have no answer for. If I knew, I'd be able to anticipate more and we wouldn't be flying so blind. It's possible Titan is right, with the pattern deviations there might not come any more battles. We may never see or hear from these damn robots again."

"But you're betting otherwise," Gale surmised.

"I am. My team is. And we feel it behooves us to be as ready as possible when the time for action comes," Jeremiah said.

"Then why are there only the five of us here?" Deadlift asked. "Shouldn't you be getting the word out to as many Heroes as possible?"

"What word would that be, exactly?" Jeremiah countered. "That a giant, unpredictable attack may or may not be coming, and that if it does we have no idea when or where it will be from, nor will we know what the attacking enemies are capable of? I've just described every single day that a Hero wakes up to; nothing about that situation is novel. We five are here because, assuming you all accept, our task will be a different one. Should this strike come, I'll be looking to you five to help me run down the device at the center of everything."

"You're picking an. . . interesting lineup." Gale scanned the room with fresh eyes, lingering on Deadlift the longest as she took stock of her allies.

"Someone who can move through anything, someone who can lift anything, someone who can get anywhere, and someone who is functionally unstoppable." Jeremiah ticked off their abilities on his fingers as he rattled them off one by one. "I dislike going into any situation without a veritable filing cabinet full of research and planning, but since I have to fly blind on this one, it only seemed prudent to pick Heroes whose combined abilities were up to any conceivable challenge, the majority of whom were seasoned warriors with excellent decision making skills."

"It's not a bad team, at least for infiltration," Owen agreed. "If you need our help actually finding the place, though-"

"Thank you, but no. That much we'll have well in hand," Jeremiah assured him. "I just need to know if, should chaos rain down on us, you'll be willing to come help me end it. This was what I hoped to accomplish today by making you all fully aware of the situation."

"It'll depend on the exact moment you call; I doubt any of us will leave our people in the lurch," Gale said, rising from her seat. "But if I can swing it, I'll come by."

"Good to hear," Jeremiah replied. "Perhaps you can pick up Titan, so we're not stuck waiting for him to lightheartedly jog across the city."

86.

Owen's team was a touch more subdued as they pulled into the parking lot early for the Supers Care Charity Spectacular's second day. Now accustomed to their activities, they'd realized that, the setting aside, it wasn't really all that different from things they usually did when not on rescue calls: shake hands, pose for pictures, and make nice with the public. Besides, one day of sitting in those tents as guests walked by was all it took to remind them that they were secondary attractions. Between the sports stars and Heroes filling the ranks, few people even noticed that a team of corpies was present. While this should have been disheartening, it curiously had the opposite effect. Being out of the spotlight for a change took some of the pressure off and allowed them to enjoy themselves.

It had been a good call to spend a day getting settled, and Owen mentally tipped his cap to whoever had scheduled things out in such a way. As the crew unloaded from the SUV, however, Galvanize stopped them to deal with the one potential sore spot looming on their day's horizon.

"All right, everyone, you've all got your schedules and know where to head, but I want to make sure we're all clear on where to be at three this afternoon." Galvanize pulled out a printed map of the fairgrounds and pointed to a moderately-sized outdoor pavilion on the eastern side. "The panel starts at half past three, so we need to be there early to get ready."

Hexcellent stretched her hand in the air and waved it about, like a kindergartener racing the clock to get permission to use the restroom. "Can I be excused from that?"

"On what grounds?"

"On the grounds of BOOOOOOOOOOOOO." Dropping her arm from the air, Hexcellent cupped both hands around her mouth as she started to jeer, adding a bit of volume to her already impressive voice.

Galvanize, to his credit, stood patiently and waited until her booing slowly waned and faded out altogether. Only after silence had once again reasserted itself did he speak, and it was with the same calm voice he'd asked the initial question. "Was that you booing me, or an impression of what you think the crowd will do to us?"

"Either or. Pretty much take your pick," Hexcellent replied.

"Despite what you might think, there is an abundance of Supers out there who want to use their abilities in less. . . martial capacities." Galvanize's eyes flitted to Owen, who kept his own face neutral. What Heroes did wasn't always pretty, and sometimes it was downright horrifying; there was no pussyfooting around that. It was the unfortunate truth that, bad as what they sometimes had to do was, it was necessary.

"The chance at fame and money doesn't hurt either," Bubble Bubble added. "I'm sure we'll get a fair amount of people who actually want to talk with us."

"Thank you, Bubble Bubble," Galvanize said.

"Of course, Hex is right too; we're bound to get a few assholes, be they there for us or for Titan." Bubble Bubble patted her massive teammate gently on the arm, not even making his elbow wobble.

"It's a Q&A at a charity event. Anyone who can't conduct themselves appropriately will be removed from the pavilion," Galvanize told them. "Some of the burlier players from the SAA are also volunteering their time as security."

"Guess we better hope they're tougher than anyone who starts shit." Zone made his way around the SUV more slowly than any of the others, giving his joints as much of a break as possible.

"I think things will be fine," Owen said, breaking into the conversation at last. "It's only a half-hour panel. We'll take a few questions, snap a few photos, and maybe at the end a couple of Supers will leave here ready to apply to be PEERS. Galvanize is right. This is a charity event. No one is going to make a scene." Owen wasn't entirely sure he believed that; there were those who still had extreme opinions about the Hero known as Titan. Either way, he was sure his team would be fine, though. If security couldn't handle a problem, then Titan would.

"Anyway, that's not until this afternoon," Galvanize reminded them. "For the morning, we've still all got our own work to do, which means we should get moving. Remember: on time is ten minutes late."

This phrase was met with muttered grumblings from the rest of his team, Owen included, as they spread out and left the parking lot. The others were no doubt going to work booths for Mordent again, toiling their days away until the inevitable panel. Owen, however, was off to something slightly different.

When signing up for his activities all those weeks ago, one particular option had caught his eye. A booth had been set aside for recruiters, sometimes ones that were Heroes, to talk with potential applicants about Sizemore Tech's Hero Certification Program, and try to convince those with the right skills to try and apply. It was something he'd done many years before and in truth would have enjoyed doing again. Just jumping in didn't seem right, given how his reputation had changed, though. Instead, he'd reached out to the booth's organizer and set up a meeting. If it went well, he might pitch in. If not. . . well, Owen hadn't ever really expected to be able to go back into that world anyway.

Despite the early hour, there were already at least a half-dozen high school kids clustered around the front of the tent. They whispered as he passed by, a sound Owen was quickly growing accustomed to, but didn't seem terribly shocked to see him walking around. By now, word had doubtlessly spread that Titan was on the premises. Moving past them, he walked all the way around to the back, where a white tent was set up. Later in the day, this would be the air-conditioned break area for the recruiters to lounge in between talking to prospective students. Currently, however, there was only a single occupant inside as Owen pulled back the flap.

"Titan, good to see you back in a mask." The man who was standing there was tall, nearly comparable to Owen himself, with wide shoulders and muscular arms. This was especially impressive since a head of white hair and noticeable wrinkles betrayed his advanced age. With one large step he closed the gap between them and took Owen's hand in a firm shake.

"Dean Jackson, it's always a pleasure." Owen shook the hand right back, then took a seat on a couch clearly made for the outdoors and settled in for his meeting with the dean of Sizemore Tech's Hero Certification Program.

87.

"So. . . you're back in."

Dean Jackson sat across from Owen with the same careful, measured expression he'd worn back before the name Titan was more than some boring old piece of Greek mythology. Of course, that had been decades ago, when Dean Jackson still had his dark hair and Owen was comparatively scrawny. Idly, Owen found himself wondering how many years the old warhorse had left in him. It was hard to imagine anyone running Sizemore Tech aside from Herbert Jackson. It always seemed like he'd been there since the first brick was laid and would continue running it until it was rubble.

"I'm back in," Owen confirmed. "For a while now. Working as a Hero Liaison for a team of PEERS."

Dean Jackson nodded, the wrinkles around his forehead bunching together as a thoughtful expression found its way to his face. "A fine job, working with good people. I've always felt the PEERS get shortchanged; they do as much as good as we do, and without having to get blood on their hands."

"I can't say I always agreed, but being with this team has made me realize how vital they are." Owen was a bit surprised to hear Dean Jackson be so positive about PEERS. He could scarcely remember the man saying anything kind about anyone, save for the mightiest of Heroes that had come before. Then again, it had been a long time since they last talked. Perhaps time had tempered his perspective just as it had Owen's.

"To be frank, I was a little surprised to hear from you." Now that the basic pleasantries were over, Dean Jackson was clearly moving things to the heart of the matter. He was a busy man with a lot on his mind, and as such he rarely bothered to beat around any bushes. It was one of the qualities Owen admired most in his former dean. "Getting back into the Hero world is one thing, and make no mistake, I'm sleeping sounder knowing that you're out there, but doing recruiting work is a bit stickier."

"The name Titan tends to earn some polarizing reactions," Owen agreed. "And I understand completely if you don't want me coming around the Sizemore booth. I just wanted to offer, in case it was something you decided would be beneficial. You know I love my alma mater."

"Yet you sent your sons to Lander," Dean Jackson replied.

Owen wasn't exactly shocked that an HCP dean would be in the know about that, though he was taken slightly aback. Before he had a chance to defend himself, Dean Jackson continued, this time with what Owen thought might be a slight chuckle in his tone.

"Relax, I understand why it was the best fit considering their. . . situation. My ego has long ago made peace with the fact that Dean Blaine is far more capable at neutralizing a Super than I am. Were they my students and things went awry, there's no certainty that I could stop them without making it permanent."

"Thankfully, so far things have gone fine." Owen wasn't entirely sure how much Dean Jackson knew, so it seemed prudent to keep things as vague as possible.

"Better than fine; that class they're in seems to be quite the strong one, yet they're hanging in. It's bad enough that all anyone can talk about for this year's upcoming Intramurals is the golden girl from Lander and unstoppable boy from West. Damn thing is still months away and it's like we other three schools are just already assumed to have lost. If I have to put up with another year of it, I might end up popping the other deans in their mouths."

Dean Jackson leaned back slowly in his white plastic folding chair, the worn cushion underneath likely providing little to no comfort whatsoever.

"I'll level with you: Sizemore could use a little help reminding people that we produce just as amazing of Heroes as everyone else. With Globe busting Relentless Steel out of prison last year, all people are talking about is the damn Class of Legends again. I'd love to rub one of our own legends in their faces. If you're willing to do a little work here and there, I think we can at least draw in the students who look up to you for the top-tier ass-kicker you are."

"And what about the people who steer clear because they hate me?" Owen pointed out.

"Fuck 'em." Dean Jackson rested his hands against each other, fingertips pressing on their counterparts. It was a position Owen had rarely seen his dean in when he was a student, but since graduation had come to learn as a signal that the older man was making a firm decision. "I'm not training the kind of milquetoast Heroes that would pass up a good education because an alumnus happened to make a mistake, and I'm damn sure not going to teach someone who believes your orientation affects how good a Hero you are. Even if no one thinks my HCP trains the strongest Heroes right now, I can still make sure I churn out ones that deserve to wear the title."

Owen certainly couldn't argue with that sentiment, especially since he'd seen it in action first hand. Dean Jackson had tossed out more than a couple of students who might have had the potential for greatness simply because they failed to live up to his standards of character. Sizemore Tech might not have as many Heroes who were household names as some of the other schools, but they also had the lowest number of Heroes turn criminal by a wide margin.

"Well, Dean Jackson, you let me know what I can do to help and I'll be glad to pitch in. Sizemore gave a lot to me, I'm happy to give back to it."

"Don't suppose you could re-enroll in time for Intramurals, could you? Now *that* would be an upset worth watching." Dean Jackson chuckled to himself, then shook his head. "Never mind, never mind. We'll just get them next year. For now, if you're willing to stop by the booth during operating hours, maybe help out a recruiter with the more obstinate potential students, I think that will be fine. Likely more work will come down the line, but for now starting small seems best. Besides, according to the schedule you've got a panel to be at this afternoon."

"I'm all too aware," Owen said, sighing heavily. "Why can't every aspect of Hero work just be punching? That's the part I'm good at."

"No argument here." Dean Jackson pulled himself out of the chair with a single motion, no sign of his age present in the way he moved. "But until the world devolves into a dystopian wasteland with nothing but constant combat, our kind will have to soldier on. Want to get some breakfast?"

As it turned out, Owen very much did want breakfast, or at least a breakfast that wasn't carefully calorically calculated. There was no amount of skillful cooking that could replace good old-fashioned grease and salt.

88.

For all the worry he'd had about standing in front of people while publicly representing Sizemore Tech, Owen's morning was shockingly uneventful. He sat around with the recruiter, a nice young man who was paid by the DVA to help potential students understand what the HCP entailed, and occasionally answered a question from a nervous teen.

While Titan might have been a household name a couple of decades ago, the vast majority of the kids he talked to had only a cursory knowledge at best of who he was. Even if he'd been in his prime, though, Owen had forgotten that most teenagers, especially Supers interested in the HCP, were far too nervous about their own future to worry about much else. Owen spent the vast majority of his time at the booth discussing whether or not some particular power could make it in the HCP, since that was the first question out of nearly every potential applicant's mouth.

To nearly all of them, Owen gave the same answer: for admission, the power was less important than the person. These Supers would find their limits in the HCP, and at that time they would learn if it was enough to let them make the cut. Just in terms of making it through the admissions process, however, one's power was almost secondary. Determination, willpower, strength of character, and guts all counted just as much, if not more, than what ability a student was born with. True, those who failed to improve or keep up would quickly be culled in the freshman year, but everyone who applied with at least a decent power had a shot. Save, of course, for those with completely useless abilities and Powereds.

Powereds were heavy on Owen's mind as he finished his time at the booth and began the trek across the fairgrounds. He'd left plenty of time to reach the pavilion before Galvanize's deadline, so he paused to swing by a tent that was sponsored by Shelby's House, the largest charity for Powereds in the nation. The small staff was trying to coax passers-by in to donating their time at any of the local chapters in Brewster. Every one of the workers was young, and a few were charming enough that they'd actually gotten people to stop. Still, it was a losing battle, as it had always been. No one liked to think too much about Powereds: what they were, what they represented, or the problems they caused.

Owen had never taken his sons to a chapter of Shelby's House; being a Hero meant he could have experts assess their condition. Being a famous Hero also meant he had the spare income to take care of them, and to make sure they had the chance to come to peace with their abilities. Titan, on the other hand, had spent a large chunk of his time at chapters of Shelby's House across the nation. He'd given as much time as he could spare to the organization that only luck and career choice had spared him from needing. Of course, knowing what he did about Hershel and Roy, Owen was keyed in to the fact that in the next decade or so, Powereds might become a thing of the past.

"Excuse me; I'd like to sign up to volunteer."

The copper-haired woman stared up at him, visibly craning her neck to take in the giant of a man standing before her. Unlike the teenagers, she definitely recognized him, and the nervous shifting of her eyes made it clear that she wasn't sure what to do with the offer. Heroes usually went through different channels, they didn't sign up with workers on at a booth.

"You. . . know what we do here, right?"

Owen smiled and gave her a large nod. "I very much do. And I'd like to help." Carefully, Owen took the pen and clipboard from her hand and scratched the name "Titan" along with his contact information. It was a message service that Heroes used, one that would see to it he got any actual calls or e-mail and kept out the waves of spam or harassment.

"I'm not trying to do PR work or anything. I can sweep floors if you need it. Whatever helps." Owen handed the young woman back the clipboard, which she accepted limply with her mouth still half-open. Without another word, he turned and started toward the pavilion once again.

Behind him, Owen could already hear the crowd forming around the workers, people who'd been ignoring their calls suddenly desperate to find out what was happening with the volunteers of Shelby's House. If he was lucky, word would spread, and they'd spend the day getting the attention that was really due to their cause. That clipboard would be filled with people wanting to chip in within the hour, that much was a given. It wasn't a lot, in the grand scheme of things, but it was what he could do for now. After all, a cure in ten years wasn't much help to the Powereds just trying to make it through the week.

The rest of the trip to the pavilion was uneventful, assuming one didn't count the usual array of stares and whispers that cropped up as he walked through the fairgrounds. Owen walked past a security guard manning the back entrance, pausing to give the man a handshake, and made his way up a narrow set of stairs. Though, in fairness, the stairs wouldn't have been narrow for anyone else, but that was the curse of carrying around so much mass.

"And there he is!" Hexcellent said, sitting in a small makeup chair. The other three were seated alongside her, being touched up by the staff Mordent had hired to ensure they looked their best. It was, after all, a public appearance, and they were the faces of several Mordent brands. One of the men holding a handful of brushes looked at Owen, who simply pointed to his mask. No need to work on what nobody could see.

"Am I late or something?" Owen made his way over to the side of the room and sat down carefully on a large box, which thankfully held his weight.

"Since you didn't need to be checked over, you're right on time," Galvanize assured him. "Mr. Greene requested the rest of us come a bit earlier than we'd planned to make certain we were the best representation of the company that we could be."

"Personally, I think he just got wind of how many people were coming to this thing and decided to doll us up," Bubble Bubble added, tilting her head back as a staff member applied her eyeliner.

"This might not be that big of a house, but damn if we didn't pack the fucker," Hexcellent announced. "Standing room only."

Owen got up from his box and went over to the edge of the room, which adjoined an outdoor stage in front of a small cluster of benches. Sure enough, there were dozens of people out there, though mercifully almost none in costume, along with beefy security guards walking around to keep order. Deep down, he'd known this was a possibility, but seeing so many faces before him, Owen couldn't help the tickle of nerves in his gut. This time, there would be no other Heroes to protect him if the crowd tried to turn things south.

No, this time he was the one who had to do the protecting. Whatever the world may think of him, his team deserved to be treated with respect. And Owen was damned determined to make sure that happened.

89.

"Got the jitters?" Hexcellent had sidled up to Owen, her goth makeup now done perfectly as she eyed the stage. "It's okay if you do. It just means you're a cowardly pussy. That's all."

"You know I used to do public appearances multiple times a day, right?" Owen said.

"And I used to shit my bed when I was a baby. Doesn't mean I'd feel comfortable doing it tonight," Hexcellent shot back.

"Everyone, it's time." Galvanize's announcement came from behind them, so Owen and Hexcellent both stepped aside. After all, it was only right that their team leader go first.

He walked briskly past them, the usual charming smile affixed firmly in place, and then Hexcellent fell in behind him. Next was Zone and after that Bubble Bubble. Finally, at the end of the procession, was Owen, who stepped out into the public eye for the second time in two days.

The open roof allowed the afternoon sun to pour in, keeping everything on the stage just a touch too warm. Oddly, he felt more at ease as soon as the stares and sunlight hit him. Any actual conflict, be it a fight or a crowd of possible assholes, was never as scary for him as the anticipation. Once the action kicked off, there was no room in Owen for fear. He was usually too busy trying to keep everyone alive.

The others quickly sat in their chairs, leaving Owen the one at the end of the table again. He noted that this seat was extra-large and reinforced, just like the chair he'd sat in yesterday. In fact, there seemed like a very real possibility that it was the exact same seat. Idly, he wondered if some poor staff member was dragging it from event to event for him. Then Owen realized he'd been standing, staring at his chair for a hair too long, so he quickly threw himself into it. The reinforcement turned out to be a good idea, as audible creaks could be heard when Owen settled in.

"Good afternoon, everyone." Galvanize was talking into the small microphone set up before him, his voice completely calm, as if a near-giant hadn't just stared at a chair then collapsed on it so quickly he nearly turned it to debris. "My name is Galvanize, and with me here is the rest of my PEERS team: Hexcellent, Zone, Bubble Bubble, and our Hero Liaison, Titan. We've come here today to answer any questions you might have about what it takes to be PEERS, or a Hero Liaison, if any of you are interested in working in that capacity. I understand the staffers took your questions ahead of time, so please ask them as you're brought a microphone."

Pre-vetting the questions: smart. It was easy to think of his team as just kids, but Owen tried to remind himself that they were media savvy performers who'd been doing this for years without him. None of them showed the slightest amount of worry as the event staff member made his way through the crowd to a muscular man in a tank top. They all seemed completely self-assured, despite the nearly endless complaining about doing the event. Owen, it seemed, wasn't the only one who knew how to put on his game face.

"Yeah, I was wondering, if I got rejected by the HCP, does that mean I'm not qualified to do the rescue stuff either?" Owen couldn't quite place the man's accent, though he did note the way his eyes flicked to Titan's side of the table when he talked about the HCP. It was a fair question, though; getting denied to go into the Hero business was a hard moment for a lot of Supers to swallow, and many didn't want to open themselves up to that sort of rejection again.

"If you all don't mind, I'd love to take this one," Galvanize said, looking up and down the table. When no one objected, he looked back at the man in the tank top and continued. "That is absolutely, one thousand percent not the case. The Hero Certification Program is a great system full of wonderful people, but what they're looking for is a narrow view compared to all the different kinds of Supers out there. Just because you weren't a good fit for them doesn't mean your power can't help someone. That's why I wanted to take this question; I was turned down by every HCP three years in a row when I was younger. It wasn't out of malice; it was simply because neither I nor my power had what they were looking for. Fast forward a few years, and I've been able to do a lot of good on PEERS teams, so much so that they let me run one of my own."

Polite applause filled the room and their first question asker took a seat. The microphone was passed down several rows down to a short girl with mousy brown hair. She reached out slowly, as if she were afraid the staff member was going to smack her with the microphone, before finally starting to speak.

"Hi. Um, my name is Hillary, and I was just wondering if you have to be really outgoing to do this kind of work. My power is solid, but I'm not so good at talking in front of people." Given that she was half-whispering in the microphone, the part about her shyness was already evident. Before she'd really finished getting her question out, Hexcellent was leaning forward and gripping her own microphone like it owed her money.

"Yeah, I got this one." She shot some glares up and down the table, lest anyone dare to object, which no one did. Even Owen, the newest member of the team, knew not to try and stand in the way when Hexcellent got her mind set on something.

"Look, Hillary you said it was, here's the thing no one explained to me until I'd gotten been stuffed into a pink costume and had my fucking roots dyed blonde: there's a brand to fit every personality type out there, and a good company will find it for you. When I came to work for Mordent, one of the first things they did was get a sense of who I was; me, the real person. Upon finding out that I liked heavy metal, dark makeup, and strong language, they paired me with the kind of people who were proud to have that sort of person repping them. If you've got what it takes to do the hard work—saving people—then any manager worth their shit will pair you with people that want you to be the shy gal you clearly are and love you for it."

The applause for Hexcellent was rowdier than it had been for Galvanize, which only seemed fitting given the nature of her reply. As the microphone moved once again, Owen found himself a bit relieved. Despite what everyone on the team had expected, the questions so far were about being PEERS. No one had even mentioned Titan, let alone tried to make the panel about him. Owen wasn't sure if this was based on the folks who had vetted the questions or if they team had all underestimated genuine interest in the field.

All he knew was that he hoped it held out.

90.

"Yeah, I have a question for Titan." The young man standing up near the back wore a yellow shirt that was stained with sweat, no doubt a byproduct of standing directly in the sunlight.

Around him, Owen felt his team stiffen slightly. While he'd fielded a few questions that were tossed up so far, this was the first one directed at him. Showing no fear of his own, Owen nodded for the sweaty man to continue.

"I want to know why these teams need Heroes on them at all. All they're doing is rescuing people, why does a Hero need to get involved?"

"Titan, I can address this one," Galvanize began, but Owen shook his head.

"No, I think I've been on the job long enough to give a good answer." Owen turned back to the one who'd asked the question. "The simple truth of it is that they don't have to have a Hero Liaison if they don't want to. Instead, a PEERS team is welcome to pair up with local law enforcement agencies. They can rent space in the police station and act as a support unit for rescues and emergency services. But I think you were probably asking why they need supervision at all, not necessarily just from Heroes, am I right?"

"Yeah." It was more grunt than word, but Owen accepted it.

"That's because as dedicated and powerful as any given PEERS team is, they aren't trained for engaging with Supers who are hostile." Owen leaned slightly back, taking his microphone with him, and allowed his eyes to scan the crowd. "It's an unfortunate but real truth that in many of the cases where emergency services are needed, Supers or Powereds are involved. Sometimes it's unintentional, an incident involving a young kid still learning to deal with their abilities. Other times it's less innocent. I'm not saying every fire or busted building is the result of our kind, mind you, only that the risk is constantly present. That's why we pair teams of PEERS with Heroes or law enforcement: to make sure they're properly protected should such a situation arise."

A light applause swept through the crowd, nothing like Hexcellent had managed to garner during her answers, but enough to signify they liked his reply. The staff member with the microphone tried to move on to the next guest; however, the man in the yellow shirt kept hold of it, clearly not happy with the answer he'd received.

"That's bullshit and you know it. This is just another way for so-called 'Heroes' to get more influence and control over the lives of real human-" The remainder of his rant was cut off as a burly staff member physically separated the yellow-shirted man from the microphone. Already, two others working security were heading over, no doubt to toss him from the pavilion, if not the fairgrounds as a whole.

Owen tried to think of something to settle the crowd, who were visibly unnerved by the unexpected verbal attack, but he wasn't nearly as quick-witted as another member of his team, who grabbed hold of her own mic and addressed the crowd.

"Whoa there, asshole, I'm not exactly a big fan of Heroes either, but that doesn't change the fact that we see some dangerous shit out there." The security guards, troublemaker firmly in hand, slowed down slightly to let Hexcellent say her piece. "Titan here has kept us safe from fires, collapsing bridges, and even a bunch of dickhead gang members. Before him, Mirror Fog made sure we never went into situations too dangerous to handle. There are a lot of Heroes out there with god complexes and enough ego to choke a donkey, but the ones who come aboard to help us usually aren't in that lot. And even if some are, Titan damn sure isn't among them."

Hexcellent, ever the crowd favorite, was treated to enthusiastic applause. Owen was a bit taken aback at how quick she'd been, not only getting things back on track but turning what had actually been an attack on Heroes in general into something personal she could defend. If this was what she was like when she actually tried, it was no wonder Mordent let her get away with so much. Hexcellent could deliver when the chips were down and she felt the need.

"Oh, and as for that 'real human' talk you started to spout, I've been around enough to know Purist bullshit when I hear it. Security, throw him out of here. Something tells me he's got a cow to fuck and a cross-burning to start."

The crowd cheered loudly, while across the table Galvanize stuck his head in his hands. Regardless of the amount of leash Hexcellent had, that part might have been a bit over the line in terms of what Mordent would forgive, especially given how many people were recording the panel. If Hexcellent noticed or cared, she didn't show it; instead she threw her arms in the air and encouraged the crowd to get even louder.

For his part, Owen kept an eye on the man they were escorting out of the pavilion. Human-Purists might be the largest and best organized of Super hate groups, but they were far from the most radical. Usually they limited themselves to picketing outside events featuring Heroes, spreading the message that people with powers weren't true humans, and of course trying to pass legislation to strip Supers and Powereds of their basic rights. That was as a group, though; the actions of an individual could never be completely predicted, which was why Owen didn't completely relax until the aggressor was completely out of sight. Given how many celebrity athletes and Heroes were present, security had been top-notch, but Owen had seen too many sure things go sideways to ever trust precautions completely.

"All right, now that the dickhead is gone, let's move on to a fun question. Clipboard guy, pick us a good one," Hexcellent demanded.

The staff member, caught off guard by the request, quickly skimmed through the list of remaining questions and selected one, hurrying over to a woman in a blue cap. She jumped up from her seat and took the mic, grinning from ear-to-ear.

"Aside from Bubble Bubble and that fuckwad director, I wanted to ask: who else among you has gotten to bang a celebrity?"

Around her the crowd began to hoot, and Hexcellent's laughter could be heard ringing through the speakers as she immediately turned to Zone and began trying to extract stories from him. Galvanize did his best to reassert control, but it was a largely futile effort.

The crowd had chosen their own leader, and it was a woman decked out in goth makeup.

91.

"The old ghost of the battlefield let you do a little recruiting, huh? Good for him, I always liked that curmudgeon."

Lenny poured the cold beer from his fridge into two chilled pint glasses while Owen waited in the living room. As a rule, Lenny made it a point to check in with his clients regularly, and this whole charity event had provided a rare moment of predictability in Titan's schedule. Thus, with the panels done for the day, the agent and Hero were having a sit-down to address any problems or opportunities that might have arisen. Lenny found the more often he did this, the less frequently he had drunken people banging on his door at two in the morning.

When Lenny turned around, beers in hand, he found Owen staring at him with an unexpected look of amusement. "You aren't supposed to know that's his nickname. Technically, you're not even supposed to know what his power is or Hero name was."

"Just try doing recruiting in all these schools and not picking up a little information here and there." Lenny walked over, cold beers in hand, and set them down on coasters that were resting on his coffee table. "No one ever worries about an agent betraying HCP secrets. For one thing, we make our livelihood off our talent for discretion, and for another, just getting in the doors of those places means I've signed so many nondisclosures that the government could hurl me into a windowless cell for the rest of my life. Which I am not game for; you think they carry my damn orthopedic insoles in prison? Hell no."

"We've got people who can melt buildings with a glance or punch through skulls like tissue, and that's the thing that scares you." Owen snickered as he reached for his beer, taking a tentative taste. It was good, but not great. Interesting. Lenny saved the great stuff for when he had bad news to take the edge off. Things must be looking up.

"What can I say, you get to my age and the body becomes a lemon in need of constant upkeep." Lenny looked up and down at the giant muscle-bound man who refused to show more than cursory aging. "Okay, maybe not when *you* get to my age. . ."

They shared a laugh at this and sank into light conversation as they worked through their beers. Both knew business would come later, but Lenny enjoyed reinforcing the personal relationship with his clients when the opportunity arose. It helped them to trust him when things got rough and they needed careful steering, plus it made them less likely to jump ship for some schmuk offering false promises and a lower percentage.

Eventually, however, the chitchat came to an end as Lenny set down his half-drunk beer and looked Owen in the eye.

"I think it's time we got down to brass tacks. Namely, how you want to start moving from here."

Owen looked at his agent uncertainly, motioning for the small man to go on.

"I'm saying you need to make a plan, chart a path, start figuring out where you want to go. The public is responding well to you, and your stock is once again on the rise. Hell, didn't you wonder why Dean Jackson was so willing to let you wave the Sizemore flag? After the fight with Elemental Fury, people are starting to remember why the name Titan was a household one even before the scandal."

"It's been nice, sure, but I'm not certain what you're getting at here," Owen replied, nursing the remainder of his drink.

"I'm getting at the fact that you're beginning to have options. Hero teams have started sniffing around, seeing how mobile you're willing to be. Now I'm not saying you need to jump right now; there's still a lot of groundwork to be laid. But if you've got some top picks we can work in that direction and make you as appealing as possible."

"But. . . I already have a team."

Lenny stared at Owen for a long while, leaning back against his couch and taking his drink with him. "Yes, you do. A team of corpies that you didn't want to join in the first place. Maybe we're not on the same page here, Titan. I thought this would be a stepping stone to get you back out there. You get to rehab your reputation a bit, and a PEERS team gets training and protection from a world-class Hero. The long-term hope was that you'd eventually outgrow it and move on to a place where you could do more good."

"I guess. . . I suppose that might have been in the back of my head when I first started this. But now, they're my team. I don't know that I'd feel right abandoning them," Owen said.

"Who's asking you to abandon anyone? There would be a transition time where you trained their new Hero Liaison, a job that plenty of people are interested in doing since you elevated their status. You could see them socially as well, if you wanted. Heroes change teams for various reasons all the time, you know that."

With one swallow, Owen finished off the last of his beer and set down the glass. "Maybe so, but this isn't a Hero team. It's a PEERS one. I like being there, I like watching over them, and I like that a big chunk of my time gets dedicated to rescue work instead of having to get my hands bloody."

"Look, Titan, this is your life, your career, your second chance," Lenny said, his tone gentle as he scooted forward on the couch cushion. "You want to stay with the PEERS? That's completely fine by me. I only brought this up because when you came to me, you said you wanted back in the life because you felt like you could take on the hard jobs, the ones that might get other people killed. As your agent, I took that to heart and have been trying to get you into a position where you can best fill that role. Which, we can both agree, is on a team of Heroes, who spend nearly all their time on the clock. Maybe I misunderstood what the end goal was; maybe things changed along the way. Point is, if we need to change directions, you just give me the new coordinates."

"No, you're right. That's what I came back for." Owen looked down at his hands, wide and strong, and thought back to how many times he'd used them to take another person's life. People that could have, would have, killed other Heroes who didn't have his gifts. Being able to use his power to save without bloodshed, it had been wonderful. A breath of fresh air, a living vacation. But Owen hadn't come back to take a vacation. He'd come back to do penance, to pay for his time wasted hiding from the world.

"Make some inquiries, I guess. Look around. Like you said, we're a long way off from having to actually take any real steps forward."

"I'll be completely discreet," Lenny assured him. "And no promises will be made until you're ready. Take your time, enjoy being with those kids. You do deserve to be happy sometimes, you know."

Owen nodded, not sure if he really believed the words but appreciating them anyway. "Thanks, Lenny. How about another beer?"

92.

Owen could hear the familiar beeping of electronic battle before he stepped through the front door of the Mordent penthouse. Hexcellent, no doubt, playing her games and cursing at the screen. Bubble Bubble would probably be nearby, reading a magazine or surfing the internet. Zone would be in the gym, either exercising or icing his knees. And Galvanize, the team leader, would probably be off somewhere doing all the work that kept things running smooth. It had snuck up on him, how much he'd gotten to know and care about these people, barely older than his own children, in their time together. It had never really struck him that there might be an end in sight; now that it had, he entered the room with a heart that was just a touch heavier than normal.

To his surprise, it was not only Hexcellent smashing on the control as her digital avatar battled a giant woman with a fearsome axe. Bubble Bubble was sitting next to her, controlling said axe-wielder, focusing so hard on the fight that she'd forgotten to wear her usual mask of composure. Nearby, Galvanize sat on the couch, eating some of the butter-and-salt-free popcorn that they kept on hand. Zone was in the corner, doing some light curls as he watched the scene unfold.

"Must be one hell of a game," Owen said, taking in the scene before him.

"Round-robin tournament," Hexcellent spat out, physically jerking her whole body as she angled her ninja with a giant spear around the screen, leaping down to score a hit on Bubble Bubble that took off nearly a quarter of her health.

"Since we had a long day today, and have to do the tug-of-war tomorrow, it seemed like a good idea for us all to unwind," Galvanize said, shrugging as if he'd been bullied along into agreeing.

"Hexcellent and I are in the lead," Zone boasted. "So far we've done racing games and fighting games."

"Those reflexes of yours aren't going to mean shit once we get to the puzzle games," Hexcellent said, slamming her fists into the buttons so hard Owen genuinely feared for the plastic device's safety. "You can still jump in, if you want. Obviously you can't win, but I've seen you play. I think we all know that was never going to happen in the first place."

"Cruel, but accurate," Owen admitted. Part of him wanted to retire to his room, to think about what Lenny had said and what the future held. But that was just dwelling, and if the bar in Colorado had proved nothing else, it was that once Owen started dwelling, it took a hell of a lot to shake him out of it. His time was better spent around the people he enjoyed. "Let me grab a shower first, then I'll come out here and snatch last place away from whoever currently has the title."

"That would be Galvanize," Bubble Bubble supplied helpfully.

"My parents thought video games would rot the mind," Galvanize said, mounting a weak defense to his apparent lack of digital skills.

"Who the hell wants an unrotted mind?" Hexcellent asked as she made her ninja throw the spear, which slammed just below the axe-wielding woman's sternum and took away the remainder of her hit points. "Booyah! Suck my metaphorical dick."

"There are days I wonder about the metaphorical part," Bubble Bubble muttered. "Galvanize, you're up. Hurry before Titan finishes his shower so fewer of us will see your shame."

As Galvanize headed for her seat on the couch, Owen made his way down the hall toward his room. Happy as it made him, it was strange to see them all together like this. He was so sure they'd be off doing their own thing when he got back; how could he have been so wrong? It was just as Owen's hand closed around the doorknob of his room that the answer struck him.

Owen had been predicting their actions based on how they used to be. Between waves of criminals under collapsing bridges, watching their liaison take on a whole team of Heroes, Bubble Bubble's own scandal, and occasionally sneaking beers, they'd actually started to come together. Not only as a team, but as a unit of people who liked one another. It was strangely heartwarming to realize he'd gotten to bear witness to such an event and maybe, in his own small ways, helped contribute to it.

His fingers were just reaching under his mask, preparing to peel it away, when a familiar voice appeared in his right ear. "Titan, this is Dispatch. Are you on-comm?"

"Titan responding; what's going on, Dispatch?" He lowered his hands from the mask, letting it rest in place. Depending on Dispatch's next words, he might need to go right back out into the world, and still being in costume would save him several precious seconds. They wouldn't mean much to him, but for anyone who needed help, those seconds might be a literal lifesaver.

"Modus Operandi has requested a bulletin go out to all Heroes in the Brewster area. Today, several covert attacks were carried out on the communications network in and around all of Brewster. While they did not interrupt phone and internet services, they did cripple them. The restraint was estimated to be intentional. It is expected that one more set of attacks will bring down the entire communication structure, though our own Hero-issue equipment would not be affected, thanks to the alternate systems used."

"Got it. Someone sawed through most of the tree that is Brewster's communications network, so that they can bring the whole thing down with one good blow when they need to. Add a little mayhem, and with no one able to talk to one another it's a recipe for chaos. Damn, that is crafty," Owen admitted. "So what's the plan for fixing it? Since Modus Operandi noticed the attacks, I'm guessing they've got a way to patch things back up. Do they need me to lift anything?"

"I will check, though it is doubtful." Dispatch either had no sense of humor or willfully plowed through jokes, which seemed like the same thing after long enough working with her. "Modus Operandi asked me to pass on this bulletin in order to request that no Hero take any action to repair the damage. They feel at this point showing our awareness would make the attackers wary, perhaps changing their plans. To quote: 'Next time we might not catch their ambush ahead of time.' Therefore, all Heroes are placed on alert to a potential situation in the next week and asked to keep their earpieces in at all times."

"I'll do that," Owen said, beginning once more to pull his mask away. "And Dispatch, would you be so kind as to pass a message to Jeremiah of Modus Operandi back for me?"

"Certainly, Titan. What is your message?"

"Tell him I understand the tactical need for taking this kind of risk, and I get where they're coming from with wanting to capitalize on advanced knowledge." Owen flung his mask onto his bed, where it lay there, staring up at him.

"All the same, I'm not a fan of using a whole fucking city for bait. Tell Jeremiah that he'd better be ready for whatever comes, because if this goes sideways, I'm holding him personally responsible."

"Your message will be passed on," Dispatch replied. "Though it may be a while before he hears it. There are currently twenty other similarly worded messages ahead of yours in his queue."

Owen snickered, and considered the possibility that Dispatch might just have a sense of humor in there after all.

93.

Despite Jeremiah's cryptic warning, the third day of the charity event started off just like all the others. True, Owen might have been a bit more on guard as he wandered about the booths doing some meet-and-greets, signings, and shaking hands. And he might have readied himself just a touch too quickly every time a loud noise met his ears, as if he expected chaos to break out at any moment. As the day wore on, however, Owen gradually let his nerves settle, reminding himself that technically trouble was always around the potential bend. All stressing over it would do was wear him down for when he was actually needed.

By the time the day's main event rolled around, Owen had managed to completely settle, a feeling that lasted only until he arrived at the stadium. It was a run-down relic of times long past, back when Brewster was a small city with little more than a farm league in the realm of professional sports. Across town there was a new, high-tech stadium where actual events were hosted, yet the original field was still here on the fairgrounds, steadfastly refusing to crumble or give way in spite of its age and wear. Owen felt a kinship to the battered building as soon as he set foot on the green, well cared-for turf.

Already several of the teams, the vast majority of them players from the SAA, were out warming up for the tug-of-war. Some were having matches against teammates, others were tossing a ball around, and a few were just slowly curling weights while making conversation. It was a festive atmosphere; everyone seemed in high spirits about the impending event.

For a moment, Owen was taken aback by the jovial ambiance. Years of Hero work had conditioned him to equate using his powers in public with danger, towards others and occasionally himself. But that wasn't the case today.

No one was going to get hurt, unless they turned an ankle or something. Hell, it didn't even matter who won. Aside from bragging rights, the only real prize today was selling the tickets and raising money for charity. Which, if the crowd lined up outside was any indication, they'd already accomplished.

Scanning the field, Owen finally saw his own team, grouped up near Galvanize as he no doubt drilled them on proper rope-pulling techniques. Owen was halfway to them when a familiar voice flagged him down.

"Titan! Hey, wait up."

From across the field, Kaiju jogged over. Though the young man was still in his human form, Owen had seen how quickly that could change. He glanced over to where Kaiju was coming from, noting that Juiced and Deadlift were both chalking their hands and practicing grips. This competition might be more interesting than he'd expected; Deadlift's power alone was bound to have some unexpected effects.

"Afternoon, Kaiju," Owen said as the Hero finally came to a stop several feet away. Around them, a few people looked over, noticing for the first time that Titan had arrived.

"Afternoon yourself," Kaiju replied. "I'd heard people saying you were going to be part of this, but I didn't really believe it. Are you actually going to come tug a rope around with us low-end schmucks?"

While the assessment might have been harsh, it was true that there were very few other Heroes on the field, and of those that were present, Owen recognized almost none. These sorts of events usually weren't appealing to Heroes from a PR perspective. If you were popular and won, pretty much nothing changed, but if you were popular and lost, people might think less of you. It was a poor bet for most Heroes to make, the obvious exception being ones that needed exposure and had little image to lose, such as a disgraced team that had barely held on to their certifications, for example.

"What can I say, I heard you all were going to be here and couldn't pass up that challenge. Who knows when I'll get another opportunity to actually test myself against that kind of power," Owen replied.

Kaiju smiled, a small, guarded one that clearly said he knew Owen was just being polite, but it was still a smile all the same. "Whatever you say, big man. Well, it doesn't change much for us; we were already expected to lose early. This is just one more check in the column against us."

Owen let out a snort that was so loud it startled a nearby man doing push-ups. "Who the hell would expect you three to lose? You're a team of strongmen—and women—plus Deadlift's ability is bound to make things interesting."

"Sure, we've got power, but what we don't have are alternates," Kaiju said. "Every match is teams of three, and while the others have people to change out so they can rest, we're going to have to do each one by ourselves. Since we're going against other strongmen, it's bound to get tiring."

"Maybe so, but I've seen you three fight. Something tells me you're not going to let a little thing like fatigue slow you down." Owen started to say more, but a loud female voice echoed through the ancient stadium, crackling across the speakers with a healthy amount of feedback.

"Attention: all competitors for the tug-of-war please report to your starting areas. The gates will be opened to spectators in five minutes. Again, please report to your starting areas; guests will begin arriving in five minutes."

"Did she sound familiar to you?" Owen asked.

Kaiju shook his head. "Doesn't ring a bell. Then again, over all that static, I doubt I'd even recognize Juiced's voice, and she is not shy about filling the base with it when someone eats her waffles."

"Must be my imagination." Owen looked at Juiced and Deadlift, who'd put down their rope and seemed to be stretching. "Good luck to you all. I'm not sure how the bracket system on this thing works, but if we face each other, I hope it's in the final match."

"Same here. Though ideally someone else will take you out, and we'll capitalize on some fatal flaw in their team dynamic," Kaiju replied. "But yes, barring that, here's hoping we meet you in the finals."

He turned and jogged back toward his team, and Owen headed toward Galvanize and the others. Already he could hear the excited chatter of the large crowd coming from outside the gates. In minutes, they'd come pouring through.

The show was about to begin, and Owen knew he had to be ready. If he was going to leave his team soon, then the least he owed them was a moment in the glorious spotlight of victory.

94.

"Ladies and gentlemen, it is my pleasure to thank you all for coming to today's main event at the Supers Care Charity Spectacular. We, and more importantly, those in need, greatly appreciate all the funds you've helped us raise so far." The voice crackled through the stadium, audible over the static, but not by much. Thankfully, someone had turned up the volume, as the woman talking now had to compete with a nearly-stuffed stadium. Admittedly, it wasn't a very large arena, not much bigger than what would be built for a high school football team, but it was still packed full of people eager to witness Supers testing their might against one another.

"Today's event will be three-person teams in a single elimination tournament, meaning once your team loses, you are out of the running," the voice continued. "There are white painted lines indicating where to start, and where the midway point is. The first team with a participant to cross that middle line immediately loses, and the winners will move on. Since we've got such strong competitors, plus we don't want to see broken ropes everywhere, the contestants will be using specially fortified ropes. They might weigh upwards of ten times more than the usual kind, but they won't break easily, and that means you all will really get to see these Supers strut their stuff."

"I swear I know that voice," Zone said, peering up at the speaker from next to Owen.

"Yeah, I had the same thought," Owen agreed.

"Really? Neither of you have placed it yet?" Galvanize had an uncharacteristically smug grin on his face as he looked between his teammates.

"Come on, now, I know she didn't talk much during her player days, but she's been doing commentary on SAA games for at least five years now."

"Hoooly shit." Zone stared up at the speaker with new found respect, and for once he and Owen were on exactly the same page. The secrecy of their revelation was short-lived, as seconds later the voice spoke once more, this time announcing to the crowd what it seemed only Galvanize had figured out.

"And I'll be down on the field, doing interviews and providing color-commentary throughout the whole event." From a nearby entrance, a woman which short brown hair and an athletic build stepped into view. No sooner was she visible than the ever-present roar of the crowd escalated, forcing her to raise her voice. "For those of you who don't know me, my name is Jade Norris, though they called me The Comet back when I used to-"

The rest of her speech was drowned out by cheering from the stands. While not everyone seemed to know who she was, those who did were clearly overjoyed by the surprise celebrity commentator. She quickly gave up trying to speak over them, instead just waving politely as she waited for the crowd to cheer itself out.

"Damn, is that what it's like to be A-list?" Hexcellent asked, admiring the crowd's reaction more than the woman who had triggered it.

"Pretty much," Owen told her. "Just remember: as loud as they cheer for you, that's exactly how loud they'll be when they're shouting for your blood."

"Well, that's a bummer," Hexcellent muttered.

Owen nodded in agreement. "That's fame."

Eventually, the cheers of the crowd faded and Jade was able to get the event underway. The system was well-organized, with three tug-of-war areas set up for the teams to use. Only one match would take place at any given time, but the other spots would minimize any delay in the action. As soon as a team's match ended, referees would descend on the area, fixing any of the chalk marks that were smudged and dragging the rope back to the starting point. Then the next set of teams would get into position, squared and ready to go as soon as the signal was given. It was a rotation that kept the action constant and the crowd thrilled, never leaving a dull moment in the show.

The team from Mordent Holdings was in the fourth match, set against three players from the Orlando Krakens. Owen recognized two of the three men set on the opposite end of the rope, albeit one was easy, given his distinctive shifted form. The man looked like a cross between a gorilla and a bull. He easily lifted the rope from the ground and handed it to his teammates. While his shifted form wasn't pretty, it did make him an excellent receiver on the field, and he was no slouch in the muscle department either.

Reaching down carefully, Owen lifted the fortified rope. By human standards, it was probably damn heavy, though in his hand the difference was barely discernible. As the other team hefted their side of the rope, Owen matched their movements and pulled it taut. Logic had dictated he take the anchor spot at the rear, since that would allow him to make sure there was no slack in the line. It would have been embarrassing for the rest of his teammates to struggle at even lifting the rope they were supposed to pull. This way, at least, they could hold it and appear to be contributing.

Galvanize and Zone got into position, gripping the bundle of woven fiber as tightly as they could. Galvanize was in the front, of course. He was the team leader, and if anyone was going to bear the shame of being pulled across the line, it would be him. In another life, with another power, Owen imagined Galvanize could have been a damn fine leader for a team of Heroes. Then again, he'd found a calling with a team that helped save people, so maybe Galvanize had gotten the right power after all.

Then, with almost no warning, the referee blew the starting whistle and the match began. Owen braced himself as he felt the pressure increase; all three Supers on the other side of the chalk line were pulling with everything they had. The strain increased steadily, taxing Owen's muscles a bit more every second, until finally it leveled out. They'd reached the point where they were pulling with all of their strength, and aside from a few fluctuations of grip and adrenaline, it wasn't going to get any stronger. That was too bad for them, as they were still nowhere near pulling with enough might to actually drag Owen forward, let alone beat him.

With methodical movements, walking backward foot by foot, Owen dragged the other team forward. They struggled, first shocked, then angry, and finally determined as they realized one man was easily beating their combined strength. Digging in with everything they had, the team managed to eke out a bit more power, which was no small feat given how hard they were already working. Sadly, it made no difference as Owen's steady pace continued. Seconds later the first foot was pulled across the chalk line and the referee blew another whistle. The match was over, and the Mordent Holdings team had won.

As Owen lowered the rope and prepared to shake the other team's hands, he noticed something odd. Though the crowd was cheering, Galvanize and Zone were smiling woodenly, their usual charisma absent as they accepted the kind sentiment. Glancing over to where the others were resting, Owen noted that Bubble Bubble and Hexcellent looked much the same. The act was still there, but that's all it was. None of them were happy to be there. If anything, they were embarrassed.

The more Owen considered their situation, the more sense it made. Everyone knew he was strong. No one was really cheering for them, and they knew it. They were just set-pieces, and much as Mordent tended to prop them up like display models, at least when they did shoots or rescues they were working under their own power, no one liked to feel useless. Especially in such a public venue.

If Owen wanted his team to get any enjoyment or meaning out of the day's activities, he was going to have to think of a new strategy, and soon.

95.

Owen won his team's way through two more matches before an idea finally struck him, and it came from his opponents. In their third match of the day, he was once again up against a hefty shifter and a strongman, but the third member of their team was something a little different. Instead of actually grabbing the rope, he held up his arms and moments later giant energy duplicates of his hands appeared, floating a few feet away. Those massive hands reached down and gingerly picked up the rope as if it weren't even the slightest bit unusual, a wide grin across the projector's face.

"Oooh, and here we see legendary receiver for the Fort Worth Juggernauts, Douglas Fairbanks, using his famous phantom grip," Jade said, hurrying over to be near the action. "For those of you wondering, this is perfectly allowable. The rules state that a Super can use any method at their disposal to move the rope, so long as they move with it and don't interfere with the other team. We thought it would keep things interesting."

She certainly wasn't wrong about that; people's excitement was rekindled as they prepared to watch the strange showdown. Credit where it was due, Owen had to admit this team was probably the strongest they'd faced so far, though it was impossible to tell how much was due to the energy hands. Still, they weren't strong enough, and he dragged the rope backward just as he had all the others before. This time, when he won, the cheers seemed a bit muted. They'd been rooting for the guy with the interesting power, not the one who was slowly plowing through every opponent without putting on a spectacle.

Well, if the crowd wanted to cheer for something unique, they were about to be in a whole mess of luck. Owen headed back over to where the rest of his team was waiting, Zone and Bubble Bubble trailing behind since they'd come out for this match. They were rotating through, not because anyone was getting tired, but because it gave everyone equal time for camera exposure.

Owen motioned for everyone to gather around him, which they did, although there was little enthusiasm in their steps. All wore fake smiles, even Hexcellent, which were obviously as much for his benefit as the cameras. They knew he hadn't chosen to be here and make them suffer through being glorified props; Mordent had forced this upon them, there was no point in throwing blame around on one another.

"Okay, we've got a few minutes until the next match," Owen said, keeping track of how things were going on the field. "Time to figure out who is going in."

"That's not really difficult," Galvanize said. "Zone and I were first, then Bubble Bubble and Hexcellent, followed by Zone and Bubble Bubble, which means it will now be myself and Hexcellent."

"That's a good start," Owen agreed. "But what about your third?"

"Uhhh, that would be you, dipshit," Hexcellent said, jabbing a finger into his oversized chest.

"Nah, I've gone in for the last three matches. I think it's time to switch things up." Owen looked his teammates up and down, ignoring the perplexed stares they were shooting him. "Bubble Bubble, I think you should be their third. With your spheres you can create some solid footholds for everyone."

"Titan," Galvanize said, lowering his voice as understanding finally sank in. "What are you talking about? You play in every match. You're the only way we win this thing. That was the plan all along."

"That was Mordent's plan, sure," Owen said. "But we only agreed to show up and compete. No one said I had to be a part of every match. And, come on, do you really want to keep doing more of this shit?"

"Fuck no." Hexcellent looked surprised by her own words; evidently they'd been meant as inner monologue. Having released them into the world, even if by accident, she steeled herself and opted to own them. "This is embarrassing as hell. We've all got our own strengths, but from just watching this contest, you'd think we were fucking useless dickbrains that you carried along everywhere."

"But we're winning," Zone pointed out.

"No, Titan is winning. We're just there." Bubble Bubble turned to look up at the crowd, all cheering for the current match and ignoring those on the sidelines. "He's the only one here they care about."

"And, if you haven't noticed, that's starting to wane," Owen added. "This isn't any fun. Not for them, and sure as hell not for us. So I say we change things up and actually try to enjoy ourselves."

"You realize that we're going to lose the moment we try to compete." Despite the pessimistic words, Galvanize actually seemed rather cheerful at the prospect of public defeat.

"Maybe you will, maybe you won't. Like Hexcellent said, you've got your own strengths. Really though, it doesn't matter. There's nothing on the line here but pride, and we might be the team with the least of that to lose. Besides. . ." Owen paused and pointed to the stands and the cheering people within them. "Everyone loves the underdog. Win, lose, it almost doesn't matter. Just put up a good fight, and the people will clap for you. You might even get some decent publicity out of this."

"Mr. Greene still won't like it," Galvanize said. "But he can't say we didn't do as the company ordered, so perhaps he can just deal with it."

Hexcellent let out a long whistle. "That was about as close as our fearless leader gets to telling corporate to go fuck themselves with a pineapple. Well damn, if Galvanize is willing to piss off the handlers, then I don't see any reason why the rest of us would turn down the chance to stir the pot. Just tell me you've got some sort of plan, Titan."

"Plan is a bit of a stretch," Owen admitted. "More like an idea, or a series of partly-formed ideas that might form a whole one. We'll probably still lose, you all know that going in, but I think you can hold out long enough to put on a good show."

"You're in luck," Bubble Bubble said as she leaned in, prompting the others to mirror her movement and collecting them in a makeshift huddle. "Putting on a show is one thing this team definitely knows how to do."

96.

The whispers started softly, mere confusion, not yet fully-formed. Soon bewilderment turned to speculation, and as it did the whispers grew, snaking about in the silence between cheers. Eventually, the whispers began to overtake the yells as more and more people stared down at the three figures approaching the rope, none of them a near-giant of a man with legendary strength.

"You really think they have a shot?" Zone asked, carefully watching the crowd as they scrutinized his teammates.

"At winning? It's not likely. The people here haven't exactly been wimps. But this kind of event isn't just about raw power. Footing and grip also come heavily into play. On at least one of those, we're going to have a clear advantage, plus a little oomph of our own pulling. The odds that it will allow them to snare victory are slim, but they shouldn't go down easy. That might be enough." Owen tried to sound more optimistic than he actually felt; the truth of the matter was that without having tested the other team himself, there was no way of knowing how powerful they were. It was entirely possible they could win the match in seconds, humiliating everyone on his team. That was life, though. There were always risks, always unknowns. At least the others knew what they were getting in to.

"Oh, what's this? It seems our local **PEERS** team has pulled their Hero Liaison out of the rotation for this turn," Jade announced. She skittered over to where the next match was being set up, ignoring the one currently in progress. No one in the crowd seemed to object, as their attention had also been stolen by this unexpected roster change. "That's a. . . bold strategy. Can one of you tell me what prompted such a decision?"

"What do you mean? We saw everyone else switching people, so we just thought that was what we were supposed to do. Did we make a whoopsie?" Hexcellent's voice was dripping with both sarcasm and an almost infantile naivety. A few titters of laughter could be heard as the crowd tried to pair the sickly sweet voice with the smirking girl in heavy makeup. There was no telling how long she would have milked it, but Galvanize stepped in before she got a chance.

"We just wanted to give the people a good show so they got their money's worth," Galvanize replied. "And while Titan is unquestionably the strongest of us, he's also only one member of our team. We decided it was time to spice things up a bit."

"Interesting. I'm assuming one of you also has enhanced strength then?" Jade sounded polite but skeptical as she looked the three competitors over.

"Not directly, no, but since you made the rules so flexible, we do have a way to fill that need." Galvanize gave a nod to Hexcellent, who couldn't quite resist rubbing her hands together with glee.

Slowly, she parted those hands and lifted them into the air, muttering softly under her breath. Owen knew she could use her ability without all the showboating, but he didn't begrudge her a little theatricality in this sort of situation. They were, after all, trying to win the crowd, not the match.

A familiar burst of smoke suddenly appeared, and when it dissipated many members of the crowd let out gasps and a few half-muffled shrieks. Big Henry was a bit unsettling the first time anyone saw him. Hexcellent's demon paid the crowd no mind as he reached down and picked up the end of the rope. He didn't seem to grimace from the effort, and Owen let out a small sigh of relief. If Big Henry couldn't even handle the rope, they were pretty much done for.

"See, we've still got a strongman to pull for us." Galvanize was flashing the pearly whites and turning up the charm, waving to the crowd as they tried to figure out what to make of a demon suddenly appearing on the field. "And not to worry folks, he's harmless. Or he's as harmless as Hexcellent, so you can all make your own judgments there." More laughter this time, as the crowd's nerves settled and they got used to Big Henry.

"Anyway, I think we're about to begin, so if you don't mind, we'll all get in position." Galvanize turned away from Jade to where his team was clustered together. It was far enough away that she almost didn't catch his next words, but they still managed to crackle through the intercom.

"Okay everybody, remember: **do your best**."

Owen was glad Galvanize could target his power; otherwise he'd have just brought everyone in the stadium, opponents included, to their peak level. Instead, only Hexcellent, Bubble Bubble, and Big Henry got the boost, each of them standing a little straighter as his words worked their magic. Galvanize took his spot at the front of the rope while Hexcellent went to stand next to Big Henry. She couldn't pull with him, that would be more than three people, but she did still need to stand near her proxy.

Bubble Bubble, however, made no attempt to grab the rope. Instead, she walked around her other teammates, summoning spheres of energy on the ground directly in front of them. Foot by foot, Galvanize and Big Henry braced themselves against her orbs, until she called forth a final pair on the ground for herself. Pressing her feet against them, Bubble Bubble took hold of the rope and flashed the audience a brief, measured smile.

"Well folks, this match will certainly be different, no doubt about that," Jade said, finally moving away from the team of oddballs. She walked across to the match still in progress, a hard-fought one where neither team had been giving or gaining more than a few inches at a time. Fatigue, however, had finally set in, and bit by bit one team was dragging the other forward.

Owen watched, not caring who won the bout, only knowing that as soon as their match ended his team's would begin. None of the ones holding the rope spared any glances for what was happening around them. They were all braced, ready, and focused completely on the task at hand. Even if they couldn't win, they were going to fight like it was still on the table.

It was one of the many stubborn qualities he admired about his team.

97.

The first tug of the match nearly cost Owen's team everything. Their opponents put a lot of power into the opening move, clearly intent on throwing the weaker Supers off balance and claiming an early lead. It nearly worked, too. Only Big Henry's stalwart readiness coupled with Bubble Bubble's footholds kept them in the game, as the lumbering demon halted their movement forward and brought the match to a state of momentary equilibrium.

Now that they had a chance to react, Galvanize and Bubble Bubble both dug their heels in, pulling with all they had, using their whole bodies as wedges. The match would ultimately depend on Big Henry, but, unlike when Titan was at their backs, they knew every little bit they could add would make a difference. In seconds, both were sweating from the effort of staving off a team of strongmen, Bubble Bubble's makeup smearing around her eyes as she gritted her teeth and continued to pull.

"Well now, look at this. Seems like the team of PEERS is able to hold their own even without their Hero Liaison. But how long can they keep it up?" Jade stood near the center line, the point which would mark the failure for one of the teams. It seemed she was going to be there at the exact moment this match was decided, and from the way the crowd seemed to be leaning in, they no doubt wished they had her vantage point as well.

Every member of the Mordent Holdings team was visibly shaking with effort. Even Hexcellent, standing on the sidelines, had her eyes narrowed and fists clenched as she willed Big Henry to pull with every ounce of power he could muster. By contrast, the other team seemed to be giving it quite a bit of effort, but they weren't exhausting themselves. Owen couldn't blame them; why would they? From the outset, it was clear that all the PEERS were doing was buying time, going down with a fight. At their very best, giving all they had, the most they could manage was to hold the rope steady. No, the other team would wait until the PEERS tired themselves out then drag Galvanize across the line for a simple victory, preserving energy for their next match. It was the smart move, tactically.

Of course, there were always more than one set of tactics at play in any engagement.

The first cheers came less than a minute after the match had started. It was a mishmash of syllables as people tried to yell the names Galvanize, Hexcellent, and Bubble Bubble on top of each other all at once. Eventually, someone hit upon the idea of just chanting "PEERS," and in seconds it had caught on like wildfire. Soon, whole sections of the crowd were cheering for the straining, sweating figures that were barely holding on. They hadn't exactly won over everyone, but it was a far cry from what had happened when Titan was on the rope.

Owen smiled to himself as he watched uncertainty ripple through the players of the Cincinnati Cyborgs that were holding the opposite end of the rope. It was a hard and fast rule every Hero learned in their first years on the job: people always liked to cheer for an underdog. It was what they identified with, what movies and television had taught them to believe in. David was always more fun to root for than Goliath, which was precisely why Titan had made such a boring competitor to watch.

True as that was, though, underdogs were underdogs for a reason, and life didn't often echo the fable-like stories of triumph people adored. Slowly but surely the stalemate ended and Owen's team began to move forward. Bubble Bubble pushed her orbs along with them, allowing them to keep their footholds as they were dragged, but even that wasn't enough to turn the tides. Their opponents were stronger: always had been. But they'd put up a good fight, and Owen was proud of them now that it was over.

Except. . . it wasn't over. They were still being dragged, there was no doubt about that, but not a one of them seemed to have accepted their fate. Galvanize leaned back, straining with every fiber of muscle contained in his body. Bubble Bubble was pulling so hard that her pale, freckled face had gone completely flushed. Sweaty red hair was matted to her forehead, the sort of sight she would have never allowed cameras to glimpse before. Even Hexcellent was right next to Big Henry, whispering encouragement in the demon's ear as it grunted and strained against the combined might of its opponents. They were losing and they knew it, but each one of them was still fighting like they had a chance to turn things around.

The crowd, fickle though it could be, had taken note of their efforts, and the cheering in the stands reflected it. Everyone knew the eventual outcome, yet the harder Owen's team fought to deny it, the more those in the stands loved them. Even Owen felt impressed and surprised by the depth of their determination. This was more than he'd expected them to give, to be capable of giving, and if it hadn't been in bad taste he would have cupped his hands to his mouth and screamed for them right along with the crowd.

Owen was seconds away from saying to hell with bad taste and cheering anyway when the match finally came to an end. Galvanize, moving his leg backward to adjust his stance, slipped, and was dragged several inches forward, sending his foot across the line. A whistle blew, and the rope fell to the ground.

"Looks like our winners for this match are the players from the Cincinnati Cyborgs!" Jade announced. Their triumph was greeted with applause, a dimmed sound compared to the yelling that had been taking place only moments prior. Luckily for all involved, Jade wasn't a novice. She knew the importance of keeping a crowd pumped and exactly how to make sure they stayed that way.

"And let's have one more round of applause for their competitors, the team of PEERS-"

Jade was cut off by the screaming enthusiasm of the crowd. Yes, they still did and always would like Heroes and sports stars better, but for that moment it didn't matter. In this coliseum, all that mattered was who put on the better show. And in that regard, a demon, energy orbs, and visible effort definitely made for more interesting entertainment.

"Well, that went exactly as expected," Hexcellent said. She was the only one of the three who could speak without panting, as Galvanize and Bubble Bubble were both trying to catch their breath. "Greene's going to be pissed."

"I don't know about that," Owen replied. "Let's see how the coverage comes out before we assume we're in trouble. Worse comes to worse, we'll tell him I refused to go out and you all did the best you could."

"You know he won't buy that," Zone said.

"Probably not, but he already dislikes me, so he'll happily let me be blamed." Owen nodded to the field, where Wild Bucks were getting into position for their next match. "Now let's be good sports and watch the rest of the contest. Some of these are bound to be interesting."

98.

Only four teams were left, Wild Bucks being one of them, but Owen would not be around to see the results. He had his eyes trained on the field when he heard a familiar voice tickle his right ear. He betrayed nothing as it spoke, though his eyes turned across the field to Deadlift, who met his gaze. Owen gave a slight, nearly imperceptible shake of his head, and then turned to face his team.

"I have to head out for a bit. There's a situation, I'm tough, you all know the drill." He kept his tone neutral, almost bored, as if he'd forgotten to pick up milk and was now saddled with making a trip to the store.

"The duty of a Hero is never done," Galvanize said, giving Owen a knowing smile. "We'll be sure to make apologies for you in any post-event interviews."

"Ten bucks says he's faking it just to ditch the press," Hexcellent ventured.

Owen said nothing, merely rose from his spot on the bench with his team and jogged off the field. Only when he was safely below the stadium did he speak, and this time it wasn't to anyone nearby. At least, not so far as he was aware.

"Dispatch, this is Titan. I'm clear from being overheard. Deadlift and his team are staying at the tug-of-war to keep from panicking the crowd. What's the situation?"

"Three companies of robots, all approaching the city from different directions," Dispatch said, somehow still calm despite the news she was relaying. "One seems to be en route to Brewster's downtown, one is moving north with destination unknown, and the third. . ." Her voice, always careful and detached, wavered for the barest of moments. "The third is on track to arrive at the charity event within fifteen minutes."

"Sweet Jesus, we've got a couple thousand people here," Owen muttered, turning back to look at his team. "Give me their coordinates, I'll intercept that one."

"Negative, those are not your orders," Dispatch replied. "You are to group up with Jeremiah, Gale, and Aether to meet the robots heading for downtown. Modus Operandi has begun efforts to track the central signal that controls the robots; getting closer to them will expedite the process. Once the target is located, your team is to move immediately to take out the controller."

"I'm not leaving my team or these civilians unprotected." Owen stood in the bottom floor of the stadium, listening to all of the people moving around above him. There were more outside, a thousand or so individuals with no idea what danger was marching toward them.

"Nor would anyone ask you to," Dispatch told him. "We've got three other Hero teams already heading to your location, plus Wild Bucks will be on defensive duty after Deadlift leaves to join up with your group. They will easily be in place long before the robots arrive, and I should add that many are better suited to protection and handling multiple enemies than you are." She wasn't quite snippy—Dispatch never veered that far off course—but it was clear from her tone that she didn't appreciate being questioned.

"That's. . . fine. I mean, good. Sorry, Dispatch. I'm just worried. Can I at least tell my team to evacuate?"

"You need to be moving, Titan. Your team is safer there, under the protection of trained Heroes, than they would be navigating the streets. All other communication networks have already gone down, just as expected. Jeremiah believes that we are only seeing their first move of the day. We have no idea where the next one will come from, or what it will be."

"Shit." Owen began moving once more, jogging forward out of the stadium and into the bright afternoon light of the fairgrounds. "Do we even know what they're after yet?"

"Currently, there is only speculation," Dispatch said. "However, as downtown is a location where an attack will draw immediate response, and given the current composition of people in the fairgrounds, Modus Operandi has put forth the theory that they are seeking out situations that have the greatest concentrations of Supers."

"More refinement?" Owen jumped to the side to avoid a small crowd as he hurried through an exit gate. In spite of the need to move, he made sure to give them an apologetic wave and reassuring smile. If people panicked or caught wind that things were wrong before the other Heroes were in position, the whole place could fall into chaos. That was why Deadlift had to finish the contest: they needed to keep people from realizing things were headed south.

"It is possible. The second most likely possibility is that the refinement has been finished, and this is the end-game."

"No way. . . someone is trying to purge Brewster? That seems spectacularly ill-advised." Owen raced down the streets, now officially out of the fairgrounds and able to stop pretending he wasn't rushing for all he was worth.

"True, but no logical strategy makes sense with these tactics so far," Dispatch agreed. "The DVA is calling in as many Heroes as possible to Brewster to assist with the attack. Currently, the orders are to protect the civilians, destroy the robotic troops, and try and discern what their main objective is."

"In that order?" Owen asked.

"For everyone else, yes. Your team is to prioritize location of the controller and its destruction above all else," Dispatch informed him. "Though, until that location is found, you are to work in the same way as all the other Heroes."

"Guess that's something." He understood the need for the greater good; no Hero could save everyone, so they had to prioritize saving as many as they could. That said, Owen had never found peace with ignoring people in need. He still did it, because that was how he saved thousands at the cost of dozens, but it still ate at him every time he had to do so. At least he could do his part for a while. Hopefully, by the time they were supposed to split off, things would be under control enough that the other Heroes could handle it.

Owen sprinted down the street, hurdling intersections with the barest of effort, doing his best to ignore the stares as he leapt over cars and people. All thoughts of discretion went out of his mind as he barreled across the roads. There was no telling how long it would be before the attack started, but every moment of delay had the very real risk of costing someone else their life. He refused to be too late to help.

No matter what, when the robots arrived, Titan would be there to greet them.

99.

Downtown Brewster, while not fully recovered from the most recent battle, was in substantially better shape than Owen had last seen it. Whether it stayed that way for long would depend in equal measures on luck and the costumed men and women who were already gathered in front of him, many transporting civilians out of the area in large groups. Seeing the humans being evacuated eased Owen's nerves a touch; he'd been in enough metropolitan battles to know that sheltering in place wasn't always a safe strategy. With the normal people gone, the Heroes would be free to focus on neutralizing the threat, and that would be safer for everyone.

Most of the other Heroes were familiar to Owen in that he'd seen them in his research, though he couldn't always pair a name with a costume. Several, however, he was certain didn't usually work Brewster. It appeared that Dispatch was right: the DVA had decided to swell their ranks. Were he a younger man with a more vulnerable sense of pride, Owen might have felt slighted at the idea that what Brewster had on hand wouldn't be enough. Instead, he merely thanked whatever divine force was watching over them for the extra help. These robots could be a handful, and the presence of every able body available would mean less death and destruction.

Spotting his temporary team was easy enough, since Gale was hovering in place ten feet off the ground, eyes closed and hands lifted skyward. While he didn't know exactly what she was doing, Owen could still read the mood well enough to approach slowly, lest he disturb something important. Aether and Jeremiah both turned as he approached, the latter holding up a finger to his lips, then whispering, "She's trying to get a sense of where they're coming from."

"How?" Owen's tone matched Jeremiah's, as soft as he could make it while still being heard.

"Feeling the air currents, seeing if they hit unnatural obstacles," Jeremiah explained. "Can't do it for people, but a giant herd of robots would be distinctive."

"You both know I can hear you and that I don't actually need silence, right?" Gale opened one eye and glared down at them before turning her face skyward once more.

"Huh, you don't? I sort of just assumed." Jeremiah shrugged and went back to a normal voice, forgoing the gentle whispers. "Anyway, Dispatch has been tracking the robots' general movement, but there are limits to how much detail she can get us. Once Gale determines exactly where the attack is coming from, we smash up the first wave since the damn things always come in multiple waves, but try to keep at least one functional. My people are doing their best to track the signal, but so far they're not having any luck, which means our best shot is to tap into one that's still active."

From his pocket, Jeremiah produced a device that looked roughly like a ballpoint pen someone had covered in glue and rolled in electronic debris. "Assuming I can figure out which part of the robot is the receiver and jam this in, we'll have our location in less than a minute."

"Can't you just sift through the wreckage of one?" Aether asked. "These things don't go down easy and keep fighting as long as they've got limbs and power."

"Wouldn't do me any good. As soon as the robot is down it deactivates itself, burning out its receiver," Jeremiah said. "We've gone through the remains

459

of nearly a hundred and it's the same every time, nothing but a burned out box of circuits. Hell of a self-preservation mechanism, I have to say."

"Then how do you know it won't self-destruct when you try and jam that pen in it?" Owen asked.

"We don't. Shit, given how well they're built, the damn things will almost certainly do just that. But if it does work, then it makes our job way easier and saves a lot of people. Seems like a gamble worth taking, don't you think?" Jeremiah seemed oddly sincere with the question, as though he'd listen to whatever objections Owen could voice. The big man had none, however, because Jeremiah was right. Even if it would probably fail, there was little risk to trying, and the payoff was high enough that it justified the time spent.

"When the first wave is broken, I'll snap the limbs off one and hold down its torso," Owen offered. "It might still have some tricks up its sleeve, though, so be careful."

"Don't worry, I'm a lot tougher than I look," Jeremiah replied. "Might even be tougher than you."

Before Owen could call into question the likelihood of that, Dispatch's voice sounded in his ear. "Titan, I wanted to let you know that the first defensive teams are in place at the fairgrounds, and that Deadlift is headed in your direction. He's being brought by a Hero with flying abilities, so arrival should occur in less than three minutes."

"Thanks, Dispatch." His team was safely under the protection of fellow Heroes, and the last member of their hunting party was en route. It wasn't ideal—no situation where masses of destructive robots were about to attack could be—but it was as good as he could hope for. Part of him wished he could be with the PEERS to make sure they were safe, but they were in good hands.

Aside from the Heroes present, they were plenty strong and smart themselves. He trusted in them to survive and to help where they were needed. If the tug-of-war had shown him only one thing, it was that none of those kids were the type to just roll over and die. Which reminded him. . .

"Hey Dispatch, you don't happen to know who won that tug-of-war event, do you?"

"My understanding is that the Wild Bucks took the final win of the competition, although it was a tough one."

"I'll have to congratulate Deadlift when he gets here," Owen muttered.

"Yeah, that might need to wait a bit." Gale's eyes were open again, and she was lowering herself to the ground. Cupping her hands to mouth, she yelled her next words, which were miraculously carried on the burst of wind she sent out at the same time.

"Everyone! Robots are approaching from the southeast and will probably break into view around Eighth Street. If you're a Hero, prepare for battle. If you're a civilian still here, start running north. There's a lot of them coming and they'll arrive in less than two minutes!"

"That is a damn handy trick," Owen told her, shifting his view to the street where robots would soon be appearing.

"It's useful, but a little more imprecise than I'd like." Gale, always confident and sure in herself, chewed on her bottom lip and glanced at the sky nervously. "Dispatch, are we seeing any movement besides the robots? Something big coming from the east?"

Though he hadn't been the one to ask the question, Dispatch's reply still crackled in his ear. "Negative, based on our surveillance and satellites everything is clear. Do you have other information?"

"No, I just thought I might have felt something," Gale replied. "It was only for a moment, though. Like I said, trying to use air currents as a sensor is imprecise."

A high-pitched whine filled the air, and the unmistakable sound of metal feet pounding on pavement echoed toward them from the southeast. All eyes turned as muscles tightened and abilities were made ready.

"Imprecise or not," Owen said. "It looks like you got this part right."

The explosion from behind him, to the northwest, took everyone by surprise. A horde of robots erupted upward from under the streets, immediately attacking the Heroes nearest to them. Seconds later, the wave they'd been expecting burst into view, and just like that the collection of Supers was flanked on both sides by their enemy.

No one had time to curse or throw blame or even try and understand all that had happened. In moments, their entire plan had been shot to shit. Now, all they could do was fight to survive.

100.

It was supposed to be controlled, safe, and defended. That was what the Heroes had told them as they arrived, assuring everyone that if they all grouped together in the small stadium, they would be protected from the impending robots. No one really believed they'd be perfectly secure, of course. Living in a world with Supers and Heroes had taught them that safety was a fleeting, impermanent thing. But they also knew the Heroes guarding them would lay down their lives to protect everyone. It would be scary and dangerous, but there would be control. Then the second group of robots had appeared, breaking out from underground with an explosion and pouring up like ants from a freshly-stomped hill. And just like that, it all turned to madness.

Bubble Bubble was forming spheres around groups of civilians, offering what meager protection she could from the sudden onslaught of mechanical monsters. It would have been a futile effort, save for the fact that the robots seemed uninterested in humans. They set themselves directly on course with every Super in a costume or SAA uniform, almost entirely ignoring those without powers. Bubble Bubble soon had to pop a sphere around herself as she tried to fend off a trio that set their sights on her.

Help quickly arrived in the form of Big Henry. Hexcellent was clinging to the creature's back as he smashed his mighty fists into the metallic flesh of those trying to break into Bubble Bubble's sphere. Strong as he was, these things were no slouches either, and as he drew more of their attention, they began to swarm him.

Hexcellent barely had time to cry out before Zone, holding a javelin he'd likely dug out of some supply closet, leapt into the fray and speared a robot through the neck. It turned to strike him, which was just enough of a distraction for Big Henry to grip its head and tear it off the mechanical torso. The other two robots began to attack Big Henry once more, but a giant scaly hand wrapped around each one and lifted them upward. Before either could counterattack, they were bitten clean in two by the crushing jaws of a lizard monster who tossed them to the side.

"You okay?" Its growl sounded like the sort of thing one heard in the darkest nightmares before waking in a cold sweat, but at that moment it was easily the most beautiful voice any of the three could remember. They nodded, trying to get their bearings and figure out what was happening around them.

The stadium was a sea of chaos, robots and Supers duking it out everywhere. While the Heroes had clearly been taken by surprise, they were managing to regroup bit by bit, wiping out the robots in wide swaths as they worked to get the humans to safety. In one corner of the stadium, a man in a simple gray mask who looked about retirement age had been left alone. It would have been worrying if not for the fact that a veritable graveyard of smashed robots littered the ground at his feet. Those that remained were approaching him very carefully.

"My name is Kaiju," the monster said, drawing their attention back. "I'm a friend of Titan."

"I have never been so thankful for his schmoozing as I am right now," Zone muttered.

"Hang on, where's Galvanize?" Bubble Bubble said, eyes sweeping the field as she realized they'd lost their leader.

"Making the rounds," Kaiju informed her. He stretched out a claw and pointed across the stadium's field. "And probably making a hell of a difference."

Sure enough, there was Galvanize, darting in and out of battle with such recklessness that Mordent's insurance people would have shit a chicken if they'd seen him. He was bounding between groups of Supers and humans alike, pausing only long enough to speak briefly to them before moving on to the next cluster of people. Wherever he went, the effects could be seen, as blows became heavier and dodges more precise. Galvanize couldn't make people any better than their best, but there was still a lot to be said for having every Super in the stadium fighting at peak form.

"He's how I knew where to find you all," Kaiju explained. "Though Juiced and I were already looking. Titan helped us out when no one else would, so we're sure as shit not going to let anything happen to his team." Another robot turned to face them, but before it could contemplate an attack, Kaiju was on it, turning the thing into scrap before there was even a chance to react. "But damn, I love what that Galvanize guy can do. Wish we had an enhancer on Wild Bucks."

"Don't put any ideas in his head," Hexcellent said. "So what's the plan, oh mighty Hero? Just keep fighting the robots here all day?"

"Too dangerous," Kaiju replied. "They always come in waves, and since they seem to have found a way to move underground, we can't risk staying clustered together like this. Current orders are for us to take out as much of this wave as we can and then begin evacuating all non-Heroes. Their attacks are pretty focused, at least for the moment, so if we can get you out of the hot zones then you should be okay."

"Sure, you just have to crush a whole wave of robots that took you by surprise before the next one gets here, piece of cake." Hexcellent was all but clinging to Big Henry, even as Kaiju worked to keep the area around them clear.

"This looks worse than it is. We've got a lot of people here whose powers are built for handling groups of attackers. Plus, the brunt of the attack seems to have hit downtown from what we're hearing. And, in the mother of all fuck-ups, the robots didn't realize that one of the HCP deans was here. Trust me, within ten minutes we'll have cleared a path out. It's the others you should be worried about; they've got three times this many robots attacking them."

"Is downtown where Titan went?" Bubble Bubble asked.

"Yeah; seems they were called over to stop one wave and got taken by surprise just like us," Kaiju told her.

"Then why bother worrying?" She released the sphere around herself and pulled in Hexcellent before creating a new, larger one. "If he's there, they'll be fine."

Kaiju turned his giant reptilian head toward her and cocked it slightly to the side. "Look, I know Titan is strong and all, but even he has limits."

"Spoken like someone who hasn't worked with him for the past few months," Zone said.

"My thoughts exactly," Hexcellent agreed. "Downtown is going to be fine, so let's just focus on getting this place clear and moving everyone to safety." Big Henry reached over and lifted the sphere in one hand, setting it on his shoulder.

"Zone and Kaiju, lead us out," Hexcellent ordered. "We'll bubble and carry as many people as we can along the way."

"You know, I'm the one who's a Hero," Kaiju pointed out.

"And I'm the one who does rescue work every fucking day. Which does this look more like to you? Now either take out your scaly cock so we can have Zone get the measuring tape out to formally settle this or help us get clear." Hexcellent put her hands on her hips and stared Kaiju down, nearly eye level from her spot atop Big Henry's back. Eventually the giant lizard monster let out a snort and began lumbering forward.

"I was just making a point, no need to be mean about it." In any other situation, they would have laughed mercilessly at the massive creature growling out a passive aggressive grumble. But that would, hopefully, come later. For now, there was only the job at hand.

101.

In battle, everything was madness. Maybe it was different for other Heroes, the ones who could soar above and see the whole field or those with minds quick enough to calculate every variable as it entered their awareness. But Owen wasn't that kind of Hero, or Super, or man. He'd always been the type with his boots on the ground, slogging through the blood and chaos one heavy step at a time. Only when guided did he have any objective beyond moving forward. There was no greater plan at work, or if one existed, he hadn't been let in on it. Today, Owen didn't try to calculate or scheme or even bother with thought. He simply did what seemed most appropriate: destroy every robot he could get his hands on. Much as he might be lacking in the grander abilities, when it came to that task, he was *damned* good at what he did.

Two robots jumped on him from the left, one with an open mouth full of teeth like needles and the other with arms crackling with energy. The designer had changed things up this time around, giving the robots different specialties instead of making them interchangeable. While it meant every bot wasn't the best fit for every situation, it also made fighting them more dangerous, as one never knew what the next opponent was capable of. Case in point: the ones with needle teeth had managed to tear through the flesh of many a Hero's armor and extra-durable skin already. The teeth were probably some sort of high-tech gizmo specifically designed to cut through even the densest of materials.

Owen threw his right forearm into the needle-filled mouth as his left grabbed the energy wielder by the torso. If the thing was going to get a piece of him, better it be a non-vital chunk. As for the energy bot, Owen had taken every burn, disintegration, and jolt that the Super community could throw at him during his Hero days. Odds were good that this wasn't so new that it would get past his existing defenses. The needles shredded through his costume easily, and while he could feel them scratching at his skin, they failed to pierce the barrier of flesh.

"Too bad, looks like someone beat you to it." Owen could have sworn he saw a look of surprise in the robot's fixed facial features, but an instant later he'd whipped the needle-filled head into the bot crackling with energy, smashing both up and then tearing them to small chunks. The one trait these did all seem to have was the ability to self-repair, which not a single Hero present was giving them the chance to do.

All around Owen the battle raged. Beams of energy tore apart metal frames, explosions rocked the streets and buildings, and all manner of costumed combatants could be seen bounding to and fro as they spotted new targets or friends in need. The familiar form of a hawk made out of plasma caught Owen's eye as it dipped and dove, carving through the robots like they were formed from wet sand. Granite wasn't too far off, tearing apart every robot that stepped near him while protecting the summoner guiding the energy bird. In the center of the sky, surrounded by a hurricane of robot debris, was Gale, whose blasts of wind broke enemy formations before they could fully form.

There were plenty of others who Owen didn't know, but they were holding their own nonetheless. A Hero with red hair had pulled out a pair of swords and was slicing up her opponents without missing a step. A duo in matching costumes was taking turns throwing one another, leaving a smoking trail in their wake that reminded Owen of Bullrush. A woman in a green and black costume was somehow freezing clusters of robots in place while a man wearing a purple suit calmly stepped through them and touched their torsos. The moment they unfroze, every bot he touched exploded into scrap, leaving charred husks behind.

The Heroes were better and stronger, there was no doubt about that, but the robots were seemingly endless. For every one the Heroes downed, three seemed to burst out of the ground. If they were being swarmed, that would be bad enough, but the situation was actually worse. Owen had personally seen several units split off and run away from the battle, which meant there were probably a lot more he'd missed. With so many Heroes just dealing with the horde, the ones that escaped were free to run amok and tear up the town. Of course, that was presuming that destruction was their end goal, which Owen knew was a pretty big assumption. It was maddening how little they actually knew. Luckily, Owen had plenty of easy targets to vent that annoyance on.

Three steps brought him to another robot, this one trying to sneak up on a Hero already dealing with two others. Owen grabbed it by the waist and ripped it neatly in half, then reached over to pop the head off another. The Hero, a short woman whose costume bore a skull on the mask, gave a quick nod of thanks before finishing off her remaining opponent with a single kick. It began to rust at her touch, corroding and collapsing into nothingness within seconds. She didn't bother to talk as she rushed off to find more robots, nor did he expect her to. There was nothing to be said, unless it was strategic. In a fight like this, everyone did their best and looked out for one another when they could. Maybe later, when things were finally settled, there would be time for gratitude and buying each other rounds of drinks.

Another robot stepped forward, but before Owen could so much as touch it, a breeze blew past him. Along with the gust of wind came a dozen of those needle teeth, crudely pried from their owner's jaws, shredding the other robot before it had a chance to react.

"I've got to get a stockpile of these," Gale said, floating down next to Owen as the needles made their way back around, landing lightly in her hand. "They cut through anything."

"Almost." Owen held up his arm showing her the torn costume and the red, but unbroken, patch of skin.

"Why am I not surprised?" Gale muttered. Around them, a new tornado began to form, whisking up all the chunks of beaten robot and turning them into projectiles that would smash apart anyone who tried to get too close. "Anyway, I wanted you to know that as soon as this wave slackens, we're going to make the attempt to crack one of these things open. You need to start fighting your way north toward Jeremiah so that everyone will be in place when it's time."

"That's fine, but why didn't he just tell me through Dispatch?" Owen asked.

"Because at this range, he thinks the robots can overhear us talking and adapt their strategy based on what we say. Hence my noisy little barrier." Gale held up her hand and gestured to the swirling storm engulfing them, as if there were any question of what she was talking about.

"Got it. Anything else I need to know?"

"You've probably already noticed, but the fucking things are spreading. Dispatch has already had to peel some Heroes off to deal with the ones that left this fight. They're doing their best, but. . . well, you can count. We can't leave this scene, obviously, but if you see any trying to escape, do everyone a favor and discourage them."

"I like to think I can be an excellent demotivator when the occasion demands," Owen replied.

"Then show them what you've got. I need to go find Aether and pass along the message. Remember, go north and stop the rogues on the way." With that, the tornado suddenly came to an end and Gale was gone, racing through the sky as she searched for the woman darting through solid objects.

With the wind wall removed, Owen could see how the landscape had shifted and that new clusters of robots had gotten near them in the brief window of concealment. Flexing his hands, he set his sight on the nearest ones and bolted toward them, not bothering to try and land properly. His body was a weapon in itself, and he planned to use it as one, leaving a trail of destroyed robots in his mighty wake.

102.

Hexcellent wasn't sure why she'd thought things would be better once they were outside the stadium; it had just seemed like the way these sorts of events were supposed to play out. Someone would have a plan, and they'd be rushed off to safety with the other civilians. Getting out of the stadium and then off the fairgrounds were the first steps toward freedom. Except once they made it outside, following the path cut by Wild Bucks and other Heroes who'd shown up to help, their world made even less sense.

At least in the stadium there had been a sort of order, with limited entrances and only so much ground to cover. The moment they stepped outside people began to scatter, which was made all the more troublesome by the fact that there were robots roaming about. It took less than a minute for their tight, well-guarded unit to disintegrate as Heroes, including Kaiju, were forced to peel off to meet charging robots or rescue civilians. She and Bubble Bubble had to flee the sphere on Big Henry's shoulder, as the large demon simply couldn't move quickly enough while hauling them to steer clear of the more troublesome spots. As she stepped out into the open again, Hexcellent came to peace with the fact that there was no greater plan in place, or at least not one that involved them. If they wanted saving, they'd have to get themselves out of the fire.

"Time to pick a direction, folks," she said, pointing to the several streets, all with at least one squad of robots near the entrances. "As I see it, our best bets are to try and get the hell out of Brewster proper, maybe flee to the burbs, or make a run for the Mordent Building. We might not be a lot safer there, but personally I'd like to die in my own bed, if that's on the table."

"Mordent is actually very secure," Galvanize pointed out. "It's built to withstand all manner of natural disasters, plus the security is top of the line.

Granted, that might not stop all of. . . this." He waved at the robots bounding about and targeting every Super they could find. "But it's a far sight safer than being on the street."

"And what about everyone else?" Bubble Bubble asked. The streets were all but choked with civilians who were barreling out of the fairgrounds, no doubt filled with the same naïve hope as Hexcellent that things would be safer once they were outside.

"We're probably not authorized to fight these things, but given the situation, it would be hard for anyone to argue that we aren't acting in self-defense," Galvanize said. "I'm not the only one who's noticed they only seem to be going after Supers, right?"

"Sort of." Hexcellent had noticed the pattern to, though she'd seen it slightly differently. "They're going after people who mark themselves as Supers. SAA athletes, Heroes, and obviously us. I don't think they somehow invented a scanner to tell humans from Supers; shit, if they had, they could make billions overnight. I think they're just going off the markings we've put on ourselves."

"She's right," Zone said. "They'll knock normal folks aside, but it's only the people in costume or uniform that they target."

"Okay then." Galvanize surveyed the layout of the chaos before them, his mind whirling as he tried to put together what little information they had and turn it into a plan for survival. "Zone, take off your shirt. Since that's where most of your ads are, hopefully you can pass for a normal person once it's gone."

"Why only me?" Despite the question, Zone had already begun to strip down. Much as he wanted an explanation, he'd been in more than enough dangerous situations with Galvanize to trust his leader's orders even before he understood them.

"The rest of us have costumes that are too elaborate; we would never fool them," Galvanize explained. "You're going to scout ahead, finding us the clearest route and hiding spots so we can make our way back to the Mordent building. If we see any civilians in trouble along the way, we do our best to save them and bring them along. As long as they don't stand too close to us, they aren't likely to get targeted."

"Yeah, but how do we-"

Hexcellent was cut off as a giant, demonic hand slammed itself into her back and pushed her to the ground. Big Henry stepped in where she'd been standing, raising its gauntlet-like hands over its chest moments before a blast of red energy struck. Big Henry let out a massive roar as its flesh began to pucker and sear. To the monster's credit, it held out for nearly a full ten seconds before the damage became too great and it disintegrated into a cloud of smoke. Ten seconds, paltry though it was in the scheme of the universe, proved to be long enough for a member of the Cincinnati Cyborgs, one of the very Supers they'd gone up against in the tug-of-war, to slam a powerful shoulder into the robot and knock it to pieces.

Big Henry was gone and Hexcellent rose to her feet slowly, gripping the side of her skull, visibly in pain. Summoners took a healthy bit of mental feedback when their creations were destroyed, and the more powerful they were, the more it hurt. Bubble Bubble was already at her teammate's, her friend's, side as Hexcellent managed to slowly steady herself.

"I was going to ask how we chat with Zone, since no one brought comms to a charity event, but that fucker robot just solved the problem for us."

Hexcellent held out her hand and Impers appeared on Zone's now-bare shoulder, trying not to hook its small claws into his tan skin. "Impers will run relay between Zone and us, so that he can always be scouting."

"Are you sure you wouldn't rather have Huggles on hand?" Zone asked. Big Henry was the best they could ask for, but his destruction meant it would take time and rest before Hexcellent could summon him again.

"Huggles is great, but she's not subtle. I think the more covert we are, the better," Hexcellent replied. She leaned on Bubble Bubble, a fresh wave of pain wracking her skull. Though she didn't tell the others, summoning another creature so soon after losing one intensified the pain. There would be time for beers and bitching later. Right now they needed to survive.

"Okay, I'm going ahead," Zone told them, jogging east in the direction of the Mordent Building. "I'll find a way past all the robots guarding the exit streets, you three just try and stay safe until Impers comes back."

Hexcellent chuckled darkly under her breath, eyes taking in the destruction and bloodshed around them. "I could have created a summon with flying powers big enough to carry us years ago, but noooo, I had to be afraid of heights."

"We'll make it back," Galvanize assured her. "I'm sure the Heroes are already taking control of the situation."

Confident though he sounded, it was somewhat hard to believe him when the sounds of raining debris drowned out his words.

103.

Something was wrong. Owen couldn't quite put his finger on what, but as he smashed his way through the intersection stuffed full of robots, ignoring their bites, swipes, and blasts, he could tell that there was an element off about the fight. Another man or a younger version of himself would have shaken the feeling off as nerves or fear, but Owen had been in the fire literally countless times during his tenure as a Hero. He'd made a name for himself by being the one they could drop into any situation, and as a result had gained enough experience to learn the value of trusting his intuition, especially when it so boldly grabbed his attention. If something seemed off about the fight, then it was, even if he couldn't put it into words quite yet.

It certainly wasn't that the battle was too easy, at least for the Heroes as a whole. Granted, nothing the robots had seemed able to hurt him, but he was just one man. Containing this many threats required the coordination of dozens of Heroes, many of whom didn't share his invulnerability.

Owen grabbed a robot with whirling blades for arms and smashed it down over his knee, then stomped it to pieces on the ground. Maybe it was that these seemed easier to kill that the previous times he'd faced them. Then again, before they'd been in limited groups and focused on defense. Now, there were so damn many it was nearly impossible to stretch his arm out without smacking one. Perhaps the tradeoff to creating so many had been that they were lower quality; maybe the person in charge had switched tactics and decided to simply try and overrun the Heroes. That seemed viable, though ill-advised. At the rate things were going, they'd manage this first wave in five more minutes, and by the time the next arrived they would have regrouped and prepared.

A Hero in gray and crimson zipped past Owen, so fast they were an unrecognizable blur, leaving a trail of severed robots behind them. No, it wasn't his imagination; these were definitely going down easier. But why? Numbers would make things more troublesome and might bring down a few more civilians, but they were far less likely to kill actual Heroes. It felt like he was on the right mental path to solve the mystery, but he had no idea where to go from here. So he focused on moving his body instead, barreling through a set of robots hobbled by the gray and red blur to finish the job.

Roughly a hundred feet away, he saw Gale settling down for a landing near a broken streetlight. Seemed like he was almost to his goal, then. Whatever was hitting him as wrong, it would hopefully get resolved when Jeremiah got a lock on these bastards' signal. If they could shut down the source, the robots' plan would be irrelevant. Still, he couldn't shake the feeling something was wrong, so as he punched his fingers through a mechanical torso and hollowed it out, he decided to check on the lone element he couldn't directly influence.

"Dispatch, this is Titan. Can I get a location and condition analysis for my PEERS team?"

Even in the middle of this fight, which was no doubt only one incident among many she was dealing with across the country, Dispatch's reply was instantaneous.

"One moment, Titan, let me see what I can get for you."

Owen finished coring the robots in his hands and reached for the next nearest one, only to realize it was another Hero in a mechanical suit. He gave a small wave of apology, to which the other Hero responded with a curt nod. It was hard to blame them for being annoyed. There was no way Owen had been the first Hero to see metal and assume it belonged to an enemy. He quickly

478

turned away, grabbing a robot that was taking aim to blast another Hero with an energy beam and placing his hand over the weapon's muzzle. In seconds, the laser gun had melted to scrap as the beam was unable to escape. Owen quickly dismantled the rest of the bot before it could get its bearings.

"Titan, your team successfully evacuated the fairgrounds under the watch of Kaiju from Wild Bucks. However, once they were out he lost track of them as there were other civilians to protect. Based on satellite imagery, they appear to have slipped away from that concentration of enemies and are currently working their way toward the Mordent Building."

Owen remembered his first day walking into Mordent, taking stock of the cannons disguised as potted plants and knowing it was only the tip of their security iceberg. "Good. I know we've got a lot going on, but if you can, keep an eye on them for me. I want to know when they're home safe."

"You will be kept abreast," Dispatch assured him.

With that as settled as it could be, Owen tore through a half-dozen more robots before finding himself in what was as close to a clearing as he'd seen since the fight started. Gale, Deadlift, Aether, and Jeremiah were all gathered together, polishing off a few mechanical adversaries as he stepped into view. Aether finished hers off last, phasing her arms through its chest and coming out with several components that were, apparently, quite vital to its operation. It was easy to forget just how terrifying phasers could be, given the right talent and training.

"There's our big fella," Jeremiah announced. He somehow still looked composed, barely a hair out of place as he whipped the cane-like object in his hand about. With a flick of his wrist it compressed down and he tucked it neatly away in a compartment of his costume. No great shock that a team full of

Subtlety Heroes would have fancy high-tech weapons, though from the smoking remains around his feet, it seemed the cane did far more than just make itself portable.

"We clear enough to do this, or do we need to thin the herd a bit more?" Owen asked. The tide had certainly turned in the Heroes' favor, but the battle was far from finished. He would be damned if he left people hanging when it could be avoided.

"I think this is as good as we're likely to get," Jeremiah replied. "Sooner or later the next wave will show up, better to be ahead of the curve. Gale and Aether, please maintain our perimeter. Deadlift, handle any who get past them. Titan, if you would be so kind as to grab me a subject."

Owen leapt out of the clearing, grabbing a robot that was already short one bladed arm and snapping off the other. He tore off its legs too, just for good measure, and then carried his prize past Gale, who was already calling a fresh blast of wind to surround them. Setting the torso down on the ground, its head still intact and somehow glaring at them, he motioned for Jeremiah.

"You kept the head on?" he asked, pulling a large knife from another compartment. With a single touch of a button on the side, the blade began to glow a fiery red.

"I don't know what makes these things register as 'broken' but being decapitated seemed like a good bet." Owen rested one hand on the bot's metal neck, keeping it pinned just in case it had a trick or two up its sleeve.

"You'd be surprised by how many things that doesn't work on," Jeremiah muttered. As he spoke, his hands worked quickly, slicing into the torso with surprising delicacy, easily piercing the metal hide to reveal the robot's inner workings. He may as well have cracked open a pinball machine for as much as Owen could tell, but Jeremiah seemed to have some idea of what he was looking at. After a few minutes of rooting about, he grabbed a dark box that Owen thought looked identical to four others also in the torso and yanked out his strange pen.

"On the very likely chance that this blows us up, sorry about the costume." That was all the warning Jeremiah gave before plunging his pen into the device. Owen tensed, not because he expected the explosion would hurt, but because it would still be a damn explosion. None came, however. Instead, a pale blue light near the top of the pen flashed on, and Jeremiah let out a long sigh of relief.

"Did it work?" Owen asked.

"Maybe, it will still take several minut- Hang on, what?" Jeremiah touched his right ear, the universal signal for being on comms, and as he listened his eyes grew steadily wider. Worse, the smug expression always present on his face vanished, and for the first time since they'd met, Jeremiah looked genuinely worried. Finally, he dropped his hand and with a single stroke of his knife carved up the innards of the robot.

"Guessing something went wrong," Owen said.

"Not with the device, per se. With the plan as a whole. They saw us coming, the bastards. These robots aren't being controlled by a central signal. There are six signals spread throughout the city, relays to act as redundancies and mask the real source."

"Well then, let's go find those." Owen pushed to his feet, ready to charge back into battle.

"No need," Jeremiah said, rising more slowly and pulling his cane back out. "According to what my team said, one of those signals should be landing right on top of us in less than two minutes."

104.

"What in the tap-dancing fuck is that?" Hexcellent reached out and grabbed Galvanize by the cape, pulling him up short as she pointed to the sky five blocks north of their position.

So far, their plan had been going surprisingly well. The robot forces were scattered enough that Zone was able to sneak the team around the bigger clusters. Between his scouting and Impers running messages, they'd made good progress in getting closer to the Mordent building. For a moment, Hexcellent had allowed herself to feel cautious optimism about their chances of surviving the day.

This was when, almost perfectly on cue, a giant mechanical monster rippled into view and fell from the sky. Hexcellent didn't know how something that big had managed to stay out of sight; then again, the pinnacle of her technical expertise was switching the television's input feeds between game systems. She could tell it wasn't the only one, though. She could see another appear to the south and fall, and she thought she caught a sliver of one to the east. The one nearby, however, she had a perfect view of, and what a view it was.

The thing had a base built like an insect's. It hosted a half-dozen ultra-thick legs which supported the towering torso, which in turn sported four arms, each ending in what looked like various gun clusters or cannons. The torso itself was heavily fortified, with smaller weapons mounted at regular intervals. A head was perched on the very top, eight glowing eyes spaced out to give what Hexcellent had to imagine was a 360-degree view of its surroundings at all times. Worst of all, which was saying a lot when one watched a giant mechanical monster shatter the concrete as it landed, compartments just above its legs were sliding open to release more of the regular-sized deadly robots.

"What I wouldn't give to have been born a tech-controller," Bubble Bubble muttered, stunned as they watched the river of robots pouring out from the massive mother ship.

"Something tells me if that solved the problem, the Heroes would have brought one in ages ago," Galvanize said. "Hexcellent, can you have Impers bring back Zone? I've got a hunch we need to rethink our strategy. I can't imagine anything that big would have the capability of focusing just on Supers."

"Yeah, not an issue. As soon as I saw the building-sized mech falling from the sky, I figured we'd need to change plays." Zone hopped out from a nearby alley, Impers riding on his shoulder, leaving a small trail of blood where his tiny claws had sank into Zone's shirtless flesh.

"So, that thing probably came to clean house," Hexcellent said. "Which means we need to get the hell away from it, and the troops it has, as quickly as possible. Smart money says this whole block will be gone soon if the Heroes don't intercept it, and even if they do, that's not a fight I want to be near."

"She's right, we need to focus on speed now," Bubble Bubble agreed. "Whoever is doing this clearly plans to level all of Brewster."

Again, Hexcellent felt a tickle in the back of her mind. Why? Unless this was the world's most patient sociopath at work, it didn't make any sense. Criminals acted for a reason: revenge, profit, pride, feeding an addiction, there was almost always purpose behind their motives. This, all of this, it didn't really fit. Maybe if there were a ransom demand or banks being targeted, but it just seemed like random chaos.

Except. . . somehow, it was familiar. She couldn't put a finger on it, yet Hexcellent was certain she'd seen something like this before. Maybe in her darker days, the ones hidden behind a cloud of foggy, drug-coated memories. It was there, darting about in her brain, always just a few inches out of reach.

"Hexcellent," Galvanize repeated, snapping her attention back to the moment. "I asked if you'll have Impers scout for us? It's too dangerous to send Zone, but your demon might slip by undetected."

"Yeah, yeah, no problem." She tried to follow the itch in her brain again, but it was gone, scared off by the rational issues she should be handling. Giving a few quick orders to Impers, she took the demon and tossed it into the sky where it pumped its tiny wings and began to rise.

"Okay, he's going to do a wide sweep of the block, then come back when- FUCK!" Hexcellent grabbed the side of her head, her knees buckling from the burst of pain. If not for Zone reflexively catching her in mid-fall, she'd have been splayed out on the concrete. As it was, her breath came in heavy, ragged gasps, and there were spots in her vision.

"Impers?" Galvanize asked.

Hexcellent could only manage a weak nod. Her brain felt like it had blades running across it. She'd never lost two of her summons in such rapid succession before; it was a whole new level of pain. Dismissing them didn't hurt in the slightest, but when they were killed, their suffering channeled through the shared link. Each was a part of her, and she felt their destruction on a visceral level. That was why summoners could only have so many creatures, and why the creation of each one took untold effort. One only had so many pieces of their mind to spread around.

"Damn," Bubble Bubble said. "No more eyes in the sky."

"At least Zone got back before he was stuck out there," Galvanize said. "If they saw and shot down Impers, we can assume everything non-metallic is probably a target. At this point, we'll just have to move fast and hope for the best."

"Not yet." Hexcellent pushed herself off Zone's shoulder, using him as a prop. "We need protection."

"Forget it, you're clearly in no shape to summon anymore," Galvanize told her.

"And will I be in better shape when the robots carve me to pieces?" Hexcellent shot back. "None of us are good in a fight, so we need protection. Something to sacrifice if we need a buffer between us and them. Huggles can be summoned again after I rest. That's not true for anyone else."

"Galvanize, she has a point," Zone agreed. "We might be able to take *one* of those things if we got lucky and worked together. But there's a lot more than one out there. We've got no eyes and no heavy-hitters. We need help."

Galvanize looked at his team for a long moment before shaking his head. "I don't like it. I think it's too risky. But we all know that nothing I say will stop you, so instead of being a naysayer, I'll offer encouragement. Hexcellent, **do your best**."

"Thanks, fearless leader." Hexcellent straightened her back, held out her hand, and set her jaw. "And one of you assholes better carry me if I pass out."

Dark smoked swirled in front of them, expanding slowly but steadily. Sweat began to drip down Hexcellent's face as she ignored the pain in her head, which was now turning to an ache that seemed to echo in her bones. She focused on bringing forth the product of her imagination into the real world. She knew every inch of Huggles, every aspect of the demon's being, and she pushed that image to the front of her mind, then further into the cloud of smoke before her.

It took almost twenty seconds, the longest summon Hexcellent had ever done, but when the smoke cleared, the familiar bladed arms of Huggles were there to greet them.

"And that's. . . how you do. . . that." Hexcellent stumbled as she took a step, but Zone and Bubble Bubble both slid their arms beneath her shoulders. She was still conscious, though clearly not by much.

"Team, we need to get out of here, *now*," Galvanize ordered. "Run as quick as you can, avoid the robots whenever possible, and no matter what, don't let anyone fall behind." Without another word, he turned toward Mordent, made a quick motion for them to follow, and took off in a jog just slow enough for them to keep up with as they helped Hexcellent along.

"He better not try to ditch us," Hexcellent said. Zone and Bubble Bubble both chuckled, even though there was nothing funny about what Galvanize was doing. He'd taken the front position because it was the most dangerous.

If anyone were going to be spotted, it would be him, and with as strong as the robots were, that might be a deadly choice.

105.

"Please tell me there's a backup plan." Owen watched in wonder as the six-legged metal monster fell from the sky. The beast landed with a thunderous crunch only two blocks away from where he and Jeremiah stood over the carved-up carcass of a smaller robot.

"There is. . . sort of." Jeremiah yanked his pen-device out of the robot's chest and slipped it back into a pocket on his costume. "From what my people were able to figure out, the six giant mech-style robots are functioning as relay stations. The universal signal goes to them, and they broadcast it to the lesser robots. It's a good way to make sure people can't use one of the pawns to find the king—basically exactly what we were trying to do—but there are two weaknesses to the tactic."

Jeremiah scanned the area, pointing to two other giant mechs as they fell in their line of sight. "Most importantly, at least for the time being, from the way that the big bots are scattered about, I'd guess there's a range limit to their relay capacity. That means if we take them down, the smaller ones depending on the signal might be cut off."

"Won't be easy, but I think we can swing that," Owen replied. Already, the Heroes around them were shifting focus, taking note of the new wave of bots that was pouring on to the battlefield from the innards of the giant mech. "What's the second weakness?"

"Those big ones must be connected to the master signal," Jeremiah said. "So our original plan is still valid. If I can somehow get access to the receiver inside one of those, we might be able to track down the source."

Owen sized up the massive opponent that was already firing off rounds of bullets and lasers at every Hero advancing on it. "That is a lot of metal to root through for one little box."

"Which is why we should focus on knocking out the first five, especially if my theory on the signal range bears out. For the sixth, we take our time and see what we can uncover," Jeremiah said.

"The presented plan has merit, but current damage potential for Brewster is approaching catastrophic levels." Dispatch's voice came to their ears without prompting. It was easy to forget that, while she usually replied only when addressed, Dispatch was technically listening to everything one said while wearing a comm. That was how she knew every detail of a battle without Heroes having to constantly check in.

"Jeremiah, I can only allow approximately half an hour for you to test your plan. Currently, evacuations of areas near the large robots are being undertaken, but there are too many of the smaller models to be allowed to spread. They must be taken out while they are centralized. Right now, we are saving as many civilians as possible. If you can neutralize the small units by stopping the large ones before evacuation is complete, I can allot more time. If you cannot, then all Manhattan-level Heroes will receive authorization to terminate the army."

Not for the first time, Owen was glad he'd never tried to go into the DVA like some of the other retired Heroes. The call to wipe out entire city blocks wasn't necessarily a wrong one, as those robots could do a lot more damage if they spread out. Still, there was no way to completely evacuate this much of the city, no matter how many Supers the DVA pulled in. Casualties were going to be inevitable, but it might be less than what the city would face if it became overrun with robots. There were no perfect calls, only ones that might minimize the damage.

"Understood, Dispatch." Jeremiah licked his lips as he stared at the mech, eyes taking in every facet and weakness it presented. "Our best bet is probably to focus fire on one of them, show proof of concept. Once we know that destroying the large ones knocks out the smaller bots, we can shift to just taking out the big boys."

"We don't have long, so tell me where I'll do the most good," Owen said.

"There is one more item for Titan," Dispatch continued, breaking into the short silence they presented. "You requested to be kept abreast of your team. They were, unfortunately, in the landing zone of another of the six giant robots. From what I've been able to track, it seems Hexcellent is injured, and they are still attempting to reach the Mordent building."

The ground beneath Owen shattered. He looked down, expecting attack, only to realize that he'd shifted his weight without holding back. A second's loss of focus and the world around him crumbled. "Dispatch, how are their chances? Do they have a clear path?"

"They are near the central point where more of the smaller units are swarming. Even if we could spare evacuation personnel, their situation is too dangerous. I'm sorry, but they have very small, almost negligible, odds of surviving."

Owen's eyes swept around to Jeremiah, who nearly jumped back at the ferocity on Owen's face. "I need to go. I—"

"I know. Dispatch had me patched in, too."

"Can you manage without me?"

"Can I manage? Titan, look around; there are dozens of Heroes for me to work with. I can still easily make this happen. In fact, I'll do you one better. Dispatch, have Gale join Titan and me," Jeremiah said.

Moments later, the wind-manipulator settled to the ground a few feet away, glancing back and forth between Owen and Jeremiah. "What do you need?"

"I need you to take Titan to his team," Jeremiah told her. "Dispatch can give you the coordinates, but time is of the essence."

"I'm sorry; did you just ask me to play taxi while there's a giant robot a block away tearing up my town?" The wind seemed to pick up as Gale spoke, swirling around them in a not-so-subtly threatening manner.

"No, I'm asking you to help me diversify our efforts." Jeremiah pointed to the mech under all-out assault from the other Heroes. "We need to kill one of these things, and soon. But there's always the chance that the one we got is a lot stronger than the others, or has a secondary relay. It's the one that was dropped on the Heroes; we need to assume that wasn't an accident. Titan's team is right on top of another one, farther into Brewster, possibly under attack from it. Now, Titan, what are you going to do if you come upon one of these things trying to kill your team?"

"I'll kill the son of a bitch first," Owen said without hesitation.

"Exactly. So, if I'm going to split off two Heroes to try and topple one of the other big bots, I'd like it to be a pair that actually has a chance of succeeding: the leader of the strongest Hero group in Brewster and a living

491

legend." Jeremiah patted both of them on their shoulders. "Can you think of any other duo with a better shot of pulling it off?"

"There might be others that are a better fit, but I can promise you there are none more motivated." Owen turned to Gale, whose skepticism was beginning to melt. "Please, help me get there. I promise, I'm going to help keep your town safe."

"I'll do it, but I'm not so sure even the two of us can bring down one of those," Gale said.

"If it's attacking my team, it's going down. *Trust me*." For a moment, Owen was gone, all the gentle kindness and tempered power of a man who'd seen too much vanished. In his place was Titan, the Hero whose name was whispered among criminals like a demon's curse, the man who no Super had managed to stop, who'd used his bare hands to rip apart many an allegedly unbeatable foe.

In that instant, Gale did trust him, and she felt a surge of pity for any who tried to get in his way.

"Just don't get motion sick," she warned. "I'm not the gentlest ride when I'm in a hurry."

106.

Things were going okay, until the building collapsed.

While their situation wasn't perfect, so far they'd managed to avoid being caught by any robots. Hexcellent had even started running under her own power as the worst of her headache finally began to ebb. However, avoiding being caught was not the same thing as avoiding detection, and as they ducked and veered between alleyways, the sounds of pursuit could always be heard at their backs. For possibly the first time since joining Mordent, every one of the team members were all simultaneously grateful to Mr. Greene; without his ridiculous exercise requirements, their stamina might have flagged out already. As it was, they were weary, but knowing they were only ten minutes or so from the potential safety of Mordent gave them all the energy needed to push through.

Then, unfortunately, a three-story building next to the alley they were in tipped forward, pushed by an unseen force on the other side. Bricks and debris began to rain, the only warning they got as the building started its descent.

Bubble Bubble reacted quickly; instead of throwing an orb around herself, she made a series of them overhead to create a sort of canopy to protect them as they ran. It wouldn't be enough to actually halt the building, which was already more splinters than structure, but it might let them make it to the other side. Zone was only a few feet ahead of her, not daring to leave the safety of her orb-canopy.

Galvanize, by virtue of being in the lead, was already clear of the collapsing obstacle. He had halted, ostensibly to wait for his team, and was gesturing at Bubble Bubble frantically. At first, she thought he wanted her to hurry, so that was what she did, manifesting more orbs in front of her as she ran, trying not to think about the toll that creating so many was taking. Already, her hands were starting to shake, but she pushed through. It was only when she got closer that Bubble Bubble realized Galvanize had been pointing past her to where she'd been running from. With a heart suddenly full of dread, Bubble Bubble looked over her shoulder.

Hexcellent, who'd been only a step or two behind her when the collapse started, was all the way back on the far side of the building, standing next to Huggles. Maybe she had tripped, maybe the fatigue had gotten the better of her; whatever the reason, she'd been separated. In the chaos of trying to outrun a falling building, neither Bubble Bubble nor Zone had noticed.

Bubble Bubble slowed and turned to try and head back, but even from this distance she could see Hexcellent shaking her head. It was too late, and they both knew it. If Bubble Bubble went back now, she'd get caught in the collapse, already there was too much debris raining down to deflect. There was a chance that she could put an orb around herself to survive it, but the shaking in her hands was getting worse. She'd already drained too much of herself. Even if she did survive, what good would it do? By the time Bubble Bubble got out, the others would be long gone, either safe or. . . caught.

There was no way to save her friend. Hexcellent was clear of the building, but they'd all heard the robots getting closer. She was trapped, and it would be a matter of minutes until they caught up to her.

"Fuck that." Bubble Bubble turned back around and ran toward Galvanize again, Zone right beside her. Maybe she couldn't go back for Hexcellent, but that didn't mean she had to stand around and let her friend die. She would get out of here, double back down the next block, and reunite with the team summoner. Hexcellent had Huggles; she could survive for a little while, even against the robots. Hexcellent was tough. She could do it. She had to, or Bubble Bubble would never forgive herself.

Unfortunately, they made it no further than the mouth of the alleyway before the massive shadow fell across them.

* * *

It was bittersweet, watching her friends run to safety even as the sounds of robots drew closer by the second. Hexcellent wanted to see them make it. It was her own fault that she'd stepped into a pile of loose rubble and gotten her foot stuck. If she'd called out, they would have waited, helped her get free, and turned the delay into five seconds rather than ten. But she hadn't. She'd stupidly tried to struggle free on her own instead of counting on the people around her, and it had cost her a chance at safe passage. That was *her* mistake, though. She'd be damned if she let Bubble Bubble try and pay the price for her, which was why Hexcellent waved her off. It would be a comforting thought in the end, she hoped, to at least know her friends made it out safely.

Heavy steps in the center of the alley revealed three robots, each built like the ones she'd seen from footage shot during the previous attacks. Their eyes glowed as they assessed her, though the sword-armed demon a few feet closer naturally drew more attention. There was no need for blustering. The situation had its entire context laid out before them: kill or be killed.

"Slice 'em up, Huggles."

The demon lunged forward, taking a wide swing with both of her arms. The robots stepped nimbly aside, but Huggles was faster than she looked and pressed the attack. One of those arms made it through the torso of a robot. Hexcellent was about to let out a whoop of joy; however, it morphed into a cry of pain midway up her throat as the other two robots used the opportunity to forcibly tear Huggles' head from her shoulders until she dissolved back to smoke.

As she released a dull, half-choked whimper, Hexcellent fell hard to the ground. In comparison to the pain in her head, the impact barely registered. Her vision was nothing but static and spots, and she was pretty sure blood was pouring from her nose. Every nerve in her body felt like it was on fire. She tried to take refuge in the fact that the pain probably wouldn't last too long. After all, she was about to die.

Despite what she'd expected, that thought provided no comfort at all; it only made things worse. She didn't want the pain to end. She didn't want to die. She wasn't done yet, wasn't ready to walk out of the world. How many years had she pissed away? And only now, when things were getting good, was she going to get killed. It sucked. Hexcellent tried to get angry, to force herself to rise from the ground and die on her feet. All she managed was to tilt her head slightly upward, gaining a view of the approaching mechanical legs.

As fury failed her, fear set in. This was it. There was no last rally in her, and the Heroes were scattered. This was how she died. She wished Spyda was here, to whisper kindly with his poorly hidden accent. Or her team, to remind her that she'd managed to make a few friends in the world. Or Titan, though of course if he were here she wouldn't actually be in danger, now would she? But they weren't. Hexcellent. . . no, Hannah. . . was going to die alone, in the streets of Brewster, and that was what scared her most of all.

The fear stripped away her mental armor, all the defensiveness and walls she'd spent a lifetime building. As she curled up on the concrete, waiting for the end to come, she felt the terror wash over her in a way she hadn't since childhood. She wasn't a corpie or a Super: she was just a helpless person, afraid of the approaching unknown, the coming darkness, wishing with all her might there was at least someone else there to hold her hand.

Somewhere, in the deepest part of her mind, a familiar presence not felt in decades stirred.

Hexcellent's body spasmed, something like a seizure causing her to convulse violently. Her consciousness slipped away—a mercy as this finally separated her from the pain, which was growing even more intense. Above her, the robots stared at the sudden thrashing, unsure of what to make of it. They were so focused on her, in fact, that neither saw the massive, furry, elongated foot as it slammed down on top of them, grinding both to scraps.

A soft paw reached down from the sky, delicately scooping Hexcellent's battered, but not yet broken, body into its grip. Though still unconscious, she nuzzled into the fur, and let out a small, peaceful sigh.

107.

"What in the fucking hell is that?"

Owen followed the direction of Gale's pointing hand, squinting to see through the wind. His jaw dropped. Years spent as a Hero, dealing with Supers of every manner, had exposed him to many a strange situation. He'd seen the rules of reality twisted, if not outright defied, in more ways than he could have imagined back when he started.

He had not, however, previously come across a twenty-story-tall bunny rabbit, standing on its hind legs, wearing a suit of medieval armor and breathing fire on the cluster of robots trying to attack it. As a few tried to run from the flames, it. . . well. . . hopped forward, smashing them and a large chunk of the street into oblivion. Owen took some comfort in knowing that it was apparently on their side, or at least that it hated robots.

"Please tell me that's some Hero I somehow missed in my research of Brewster," Owen said.

"Pretty sure I'd remember someone like that," Gale replied. "By the looks of it, the smart money is either on shifter, summoner, or tech-genius creation."

"That shift would take hours, if not days, to get in and out of. Tech-genius maybe, but we've been on watch for that sort of stuff, so I can't believe we'd miss it. As for summoner, I don't know of any who can pull in something that big. Plus, combat bunny? Who. . ." Owen's words trailed off as he remembered the night that he and the team sat around sharing embarrassing stories. Hexcellent had told them about her childhood bunny, but said she couldn't call him anymore. Granted, she hadn't described him as able to step over buildings, yet Owen's gut still screamed that the coincidence was just a little too much.

"Gale, can you sweep the area and get me coordinates on the big robot near my team? I need a few minutes here."

"Are you going to fight the rabbit? Because even for you, that's a pretty big one," Gale pointed out.

"I really hope not," Owen said. "But I may have just found one of my team. I need to check on her. And, if things go well, I might even get us a helping paw."

"Booooooooooo," Gale jeered. "Fine, but I'm giving you the quick drop, and I'm coming back as soon as I find our target."

"Wouldn't have it any other way."

Owen barely got the words out before a blast of wind sent him hurdling forward. He ripped through the air before slamming to the ground fifty feet in front of the massive rabbit. Its ears twitched and it turned to face him, those beady black eyes gazing down at the sudden new arrival. They weren't natural looking, more like they'd been based on someone's toy stuffed rabbit than one with actual eyes. It had the dual impact of being disturbing and reassuring, as Owen felt like his hunch might be on the money.

"Hopcules, I hope?" Owen cupped his hands and yelled, in case the ears were just for show.

The rabbit, only watching him before, turned further, giving him its full attention. Slowly, the creature leaned forward. Owen could actually feel the hot breath from its pink nose despite the distance between them. If this really was a summon, then it was incredible. To create something this big, this capable of independent action, surely put whoever made it among the top one percent of all known summoners. Even better, if it was still standing, then its creator had to be alive.

"I'm a friend of Hexcellent's," Owen yelled. Talking to a rabbit was a bit odd, though given its size and armor, perhaps it shouldn't have been. "I wanted to make sure she was safe."

Hopcules peered at him warily. Owen had no idea how much it knew about Hexcellent or her life; he just had to hope that as long as she trusted him, it would be enough for the bunny. Moving in closer, the nose sniffed him twice. Evidently, this satisfied some unknown test, and it held up its right paw, uncurling its fingers, which Owen was certain real rabbits didn't have, to reveal the battered but breathing body of Hexcellent.

On instinct, Owen took a step forward, and immediately the paw closed. He started to protest, then thought better of it. What was he going to try that the rabbit wasn't already doing? Owen wasn't a healer; he couldn't fix her wounds. And he'd have to protect her from the robots flooding the city while she was unconscious. Confident as Owen was in his abilities, even he could concede that a giant fire-breathing monster who knew only loyalty might be better suited to the task.

"I'm going to come back with a healer," Owen yelled. He didn't know if Hopcules understood what a healer was, or if the rabbit even had a grasp of the English language, but so far their communication had been going well. Besides, he didn't have a lot of other options. "Someone to make Hexcellent better. Keep her safe until then."

Hopcules snorted, and Owen had to wonder if an imaginary bunny was annoyed with him for trying to tell it to do what it had already planned. That thought alone made him really want a beer, but as Hopcules pulled back up to a standing position, turning to the new robots that had begun to pour into the area, Owen also felt a sense of relief. One member of his team, at least, was safe.

"Dispatch, this is Titan. We've got a giant summon shaped like a rabbit that's probably hitting a few people's radars. Let them know it's friendly, and anyone who attacks it without cause will personally answer to me when this is over. If you can get me a healer to the location, we might be able to start using it as a more precise resource."

"A healer? Is the rabbit injured?" If Dispatch felt at all odd asking such a question, it didn't come through. Much as Owen wanted to chalk it up to her usual demeanor, the truth of the matter was that this probably didn't even register on her weirdness scale. After all, she was in the ear of every Hero across the country. There was no telling what manner of crazy shit she'd witnessed.

"The rabbit is fine. Its summoner is in bad shape, though. All it's doing right now is keeping her safe. Once she's conscious again, she can give some proper orders."

"Titan, please repeat. Did you just say that the summoner who called forth that thing is *unconscious*?" This time, he did hear the shock in her voice, and it only took a second to realize why. Usually summons disappeared when their creators went down. They were, after all, manifestations of their creator's thoughts. When the thoughts ended, so did the summons. At least, that's how it generally went. Every Super was different, after all.

"Confirmed, summoner is out, and the rabbit remains," Owen told her. "So, maybe double time on that healer."

"Resources are tight, but I'll see what I can do," Dispatch assured him. "Also, Gale has requested a direct connection to your comm."

"I accept," Owen said, and seconds later Gale's voice came blasting in his ear.

"Titan! Jump as high as you can right now. I'm en route, but there's no time to waste landing. I found the big bot and your team, which are in the exact same place. We've got maybe a minute or two before they're in deep, and I can't fight one of those on my own. They need our help, *now*."

Without pause, Owen pushed off so hard that the ground buckled under his power as he went flying upward. Nearby, he could see Hopcules smashing apart every robot that came near it. Personally, Owen had always thought dogs to be the best of all pets.

But he was beginning to see the appeal of rabbits.

108.

If having to (they hoped momentarily) leave Hexcellent wasn't bad enough—which it certainly was—the Mordent team found as soon as they emerged that they weren't the only ones moving. The giant mech was also making progress, though it had gone through structures rather than darting around them like the Supers. It had been what caused the collapse, no doubt; it seemed to be chasing a few people that were trying to escape from its sight. The only actual upside of walking into the mech's shadow was that there was so much chaos, a few people in costumes didn't draw much attention.

"Fuck me," Zone muttered, gazing up at the machine with wide-eyed terror. Galvanize grabbed his shoulder and jerked him forward, snapping the shirtless man out of his trance.

"Come on! We either run or die, and my legs can still move." Even as the words left his mouth, Galvanize knew how hollow they were. The street before them was sheer madness with the smaller robots swarming across the ground. Add in that the way behind them was blocked and that the giant bot could easily reach them with one step of its insect-like legs, their chances of surviving the next few minutes were looking slim. But Galvanize had faced death before. Not every rescue they went into was without risk, and he refused to let death take him standing still. Whether by crushing legs or a murderous robot, death would have to at least catch them.

They raced along the fractured city streets, trying to take cover by nearby buildings. All thoughts of direction were gone from their minds; Mordent was no longer their goal. Now, all they cared about was surviving from one footstep to the next. They picked their paths strategically, minimizing their contact with the robots whenever possible. It was a game of numbers, one that was quickly turning against them. More and more of the smaller units seem to rain down from the sky, and the places to hide were quickly running out. Something gigantic could be heard stomping around a few blocks away, which they all took to mean another mech was in the area. It was a bad scene and only getting worse.

Then, almost as if a beam of light from the heavens shone down to show him the way, Galvanize spotted something that gave him hope. A small alley, its entrance almost completely obscured from view, which would take them in the opposite direction of the robot hordes. It might even give them a chance to circle back for Hexcellent, if luck was on their side. . . and since they would have to race all the way around the giant mech to reach the exit, luck would pretty much have to be.

Silently, he tapped Bubble Bubble and Zone on their arms and pointed to the alley down the street. It was hard to see, as the giant mech's legs blocked out so much of the view, but eventually they realized what he was showing them.

"We'll never make that," Bubble Bubble told him. "There are too many small robots on the periphery. We're barely hiding from them as it is; if we try and go all the way around we'll be caught for sure."

"Probably so, but we still have to try," Galvanize said.

"What if we went under it?" Zone motioned to the ample space between the robot's legs. One could drive a bus under there and still have ample clearance, so it wasn't an issue of space. But Galvanize couldn't imagine that the area was undefended, not on a machine built for such destructive ends.

"It's probably more dangerous underneath," Galvanize speculated.

"Seeing as the edges are definitely going to get us killed, I'm weirdly okay with 'probably more dangerous,'" Bubble Bubble said. "Whatever we do, let's just do it soon. Time is against us."

Despite all the preparation and training that PEERS teams had to undergo, the decisions that resulted in life or death often happened in split seconds. Galvanize knew they had to move and the alley might be their one shot at living. His team was right; the long way was basically a guaranteed death. Risky as running under a giant killer robot might be, it was the better choice.

Of course, that didn't mean either choice was actually going to keep them alive, but Galvanize shoved that thought out of his mind as he raced forward, motioning for the others to follow. They sprinted in the one direction no one else was going: toward a mech currently knocking down entire buildings.

It struck Galvanize that the world seemed to go curiously quiet as they ran between two of the six metal legs. All the madness that had been filling their ears was somewhat blocked by the impossibly big structure around them. It was peaceful, though not in a way that brought him comfort. No, this peaceful was like that of a cemetery, or a watery cave left unexplored for centuries. It spoke of darkness buried just beneath the surface, waiting for a chance to arise once more.

That chance didn't take long to surface. They were no more than ten feet along in their journey when Galvanize caught sight of a red glow in the corner of his eyes. No time to think: another split second decision that might cost him, or his team, their lives.

"To the side!" Galvanize yelled, leaping away from where he'd been standing moments before a searing beam of energy struck the concrete. Bubble Bubble and Zone had moved on his orders and managed to avoid the shots coming at them as well. However, now that he'd stopped, Galvanize looked up to the source of the attacks and felt his heart drop.

All along the underside of the robot were at least two dozen glowing red circles, each of which could roast him and his team alive. Another three fired, but before they could hit, a wall of blue energy appeared in front of them.

Bubble Bubble was stooped down, arms held out as she focused on keeping the orb around them in place. With every shot that landed, her body seemed to shake. Maybe if the day had just begun, she might have been able to keep it up for a while, but as it stood, Galvanize knew she was only buying them a few extra seconds. Maybe a minute, tops.

Galvanize wracked his brain, trying to think of something, anything he could do to get them out of there. He considered Zone's abilities, Bubble Bubble's power, and what he could augment. But no matter how he turned their situation around in his head, nothing provided even a glimmer of hope. They just weren't strong enough. Each of them might be Supers, but this was the sort of situation even Heroes would have trouble with, and none of them had power on that level.

Galvanize had been determined to at least die trying, and now it seemed that was exactly what they were going to do.

"Getting. . . tired. . ." More and more beams were locking on to them. Bubble Bubble seemed to be fading. Their time was almost up. All that remained were the few precious seconds she'd bought them, so Galvanize decided to make use of her gift.

"Zone, Bubble Bubble, I just want you to know how proud I am of both of you, and of all we've accomplished as a team. No matter what happens next, try to take comfort in the fact that we are among the few who can say we left this world better than we found it."

Bubble Bubble's arms fell, and the orb around them flickered out of existence. Galvanize, all his bravery spent on surviving this long, closed his eyes. He'd done enough; staring down a firing squad wasn't the way he wanted to go.

Instead of hot, searing pain ripping apart his body, however, Galvanize felt a tremendous blast of wind strike and send him spinning roughly through the air. When he finally landed and managed to pull his eyelids apart, he was no longer trapped beneath the robot.

Instead, Gale was staring at him, at his whole team, who were miraculously unhurt. She floated above them, lit by the afternoon sun which they could once again see. Her wind had blown them some distance from the mech, which seemed to be distracted.

"About time you dropped that shield," Gale said. "I've been trying to get you out for the past thirty seconds. Titan, your people are clear. Time to step it up."

"Titan is here?" Bubble Bubble asked, turning her head in a vain effort to find their Hero Liaison.

"Sure is, who do you think kept that thing distracted?" Gale asked. "But now that you're out, he's going to stop playing so nice. And as soon as I get you three a little higher and safer, I'm going to help."

"Wait!" Galvanize yelped. "Hexcellent needs your help more; she got trapped a few blocks behind us."

Gale merely smiled as a new gust of wind began to lift them up from the ground. "Hexcellent is probably the best off of anyone here. Don't worry, you'll definitely see it from the rooftops."

109

"Titan, your people are clear."

Owen's whole body tingled with relief at those words, aided a bit perhaps by the energy blast one of the robots nearby was trying to kill him with. It had been hard, letting Gale be the one to go save them, trusting her to make sure they survived, but part of being a Hero was accepting that no one was the best at everything. For rapid extraction, Gale's abilities were better suited than his, and he was certainly the superior choice for a distraction. Still, ever since she'd left his sight and he'd begun ripping up robots and throwing them at the big mech, his heart had been filled with worry that something would go wrong. He'd already failed so many people who depended on him throughout his life. Losing his team might be one blow too many.

But that hadn't happened. Gale had gotten them clear and was likely lifting them somewhere safe before she rejoined the battle. Owen grabbed another robot and shredded it into two pieces, then hurled both at the mech. His projectiles weren't doing any real damage, but he was definitely holding the thing's attention, drawing occasional rounds of bullets and energy, neither of which caused Owen to so much as stumble.

"Dispatch, what's the situation with civilians around me?"

"This area was a business district that began evacuations during the first wave of attack," Dispatch told him. "The last stragglers were seen fleeing several minutes prior, though not all were successful. By current accounts, the area is considered fully evacuated."

"Glad to hear it. And my clearance for property?"

"The DVA has ruled that if Jeremiah's theory proves true, targeting the large robots would be far more prudent than fully unleashing Manhattan-level Heroes. They want to see a big one brought dropped as soon as possible, and with the civilians gone, you are in one of the best positions. Clearance is Full Demolition: do what's necessary to bring your target down," Dispatch instructed.

"Understood. I'll still try to minimize where I can." It wasn't always possible to get DVA clearances in the heat of battle, but for a fight this big, Owen knew damn well doing so would make things easier. There was going to be a lot of cleanup and insurance claims when this was all said and done, and the last thing he needed was to be held for reckless destruction. But now they'd given him their blessing, and he knew the area was as clear as possible.

He could finally get down to work.

"You know, I've had to fight robots before. Not this many or this often, but your kind pops up from time to time when some smart Super wants a machine to do their dirty work." Owen grabbed a pair of the robots that were trying to attack and crushed them in his hands, scattering their debris as he moved forward. Another came at him; seconds later it was in pieces. With no other Heroes or civilians around, he didn't have to worry about where the hurled shrapnel might land.

"Personally, I'm not really a fan. I prefer opponents who can think on their feet and maybe use enough wisdom to give up when they know the fight is unwinnable."

This time, five of them ran for him. Owen met them head on. The things were strong, no doubt about it, but Owen had fought stronger, and that was all it took. Raise the bar once and that's where it lived forever on. His power was a brutish, simple one that paled in comparison to some of the more grandiose out there, but it *was* effective. In seconds, the five robots were pieces in his wake, and the large mech was only a few feet away.

"There is one good thing about dealing with robots, though. Especially ones as big as you. It's probably the only time I get to have a fight where I don't need to hold back. And I have to say, from time to time, that is an absolute pleasure."

The mech turned to launch another pointless barrage of projectiles at him, but Owen was no longer there. He'd leapt into the air, turning the ground below him into utter rubble as he soared upward. His course was the center of the mech's torso, but as he'd expected, it wasn't going to let him land so easily. One of the four arms swept through the air, intent on smacking Owen back to the ground. Instead, he grabbed on as it struck, his fingers bending the metal as he pulled himself up, getting into position just above where the massive gun joined to its wrist.

"You big guys always seem tough, but beating you is just about knowing the simple trick. It's the same way you eat a whale. One bite at a time, you bastard." He reared back, spreading out his palm to get as wide a surface area as possible, then slammed his hand through the metal wrist. It took several more blows, but eventually the wrist was so shattered that the entire gun broke away, smashing to the ground and flattening a few robots in the process.

Owen looked up at the six-eyed head. He was pretty sure at least a few of those orbs were gazing angrily at him. If the thing was pissed now, it would be livid by the time he was finished.

He began to climb up the remaining section of arm, slowly making his way closer to the torso. A loud whooshing sound ripped through the air, and suddenly Owen found himself and the arm he was holding in free fall. They crashed heavily on to the street, and before he could react, one of the six legs was above him and dropping fast, clearly intent on crushing him like a bug.

"Detaching parts, pretty clever," Owen admitted as he rolled out of the way. "But you'll run out of arms eventually." The leg kept pace with his movements, and as he pushed off the ground, it slammed into his back, pinning him to the concrete below.

"Holy shit, are you okay?" Gale's voice came through his comm, and even though he couldn't see where she was at the moment, she obviously had line of sight on him.

"Been better," Owen admitted, his voice a bit strained. "But I'm pretty sure the gravity thingie they put in these to make them light enough to function reduced its weight. Normally I'd expect this to be a lot worse."

"Normally? One day we need to have a talk about what you consider normal," Gale said. "Can you get out?"

"Not easily. I'm strong enough to move, but with this much weight, if I try to shove off the ground my arms will probably go right through it, especially given how much we've wrecked the street. Little help?"

"Pretty sure I can hit it hard enough to knock it aside, but you'll need to scramble," Gale warned.

"Even a second is plenty. I just have to flip over. Then I can grab the damn leg and start tearing it apart."

"Yeah, I heard your whole 'one bite at a time' spiel. Personally, if I had to kill a whale, I think I'd rather a harpoon to the heart." Even as she spoke,

Owen could hear the wind picking up around her. He mentally readied himself for the impending attack.

"Those arms are quick, they'll knock me aside if I do a direct run," Owen told her.

"In a hurricane, winds blow so fast that pencils get embedded in trees. I'm pretty sure I can get you past a few waving arms. Now get ready: that leg is about to move."

"If you can do it, I'm in." Owen barely got the words out when a tremendous blast of wind deafened him. It struck the leg at one of its joints and bent it outward. The pressure on Owen vanished. He pushed himself forward, getting on his feet before the leg could pin him again. He'd made it all of ten steps before another blast of wind hit him in the back, lifting him skyward at a rapidly increasing speed.

"Pretend you're doing a cannonball off the high-dive," Gale instructed, yelling to be heard over the comms. "Tuck everything in and prepare for impact. As of now I'm Captain Ahab, except we're killing our damned whale."

110.

It had been a long time since Owen was in a real fight. Picking off stray robots here and there didn't exactly test his limits, and while the work with his team was rewarding, it usually demanded more effort to keep control than to push himself. The assessment with Elemental Fury was the nearest he'd come, and even that was closer to a dance than a brawl since he had to evade and subdue without seriously injuring. He'd been so long outside of a true battle that he'd almost forgotten the thrill of danger and adrenaline that coursed through one's system.

That familiar feeling came rushing back as he tore through the air, moving so fast that he couldn't even see the giant mech's arms as it reached uselessly for him. Gale had built up too much speed for the thing to have a shot in hell.

Owen roared past all its defenses and slammed directly into its chest. Were he human, or even less-established in his career, Owen would have been a smear on the metal surface. Instead, he left a sizable dent and merely shook his head, more dizzy from the ride than hurt from the stop.

Already he could see the remaining arms reaching for him, so Owen didn't waste the time he had. Bending the metal under his fingers to get a solid grip, he reared back and punched directly into the dent he'd made. Unlike when fighting the robot's arm, this time he tried to concentrate the force as much as possible. His fist effortlessly broke through the armored barrier. Grabbing both sides of the hole, he tore it wider and then tumbled through, only a few feet ahead of the metal appendages trying to knock him away.

Truthfully, he hadn't been entirely sure what to expect once he was inside. Robots might be semi-regular occurrences in the Hero world, but the giant type weren't exactly run-of-the-mill. Part of him expected the cavity within to be filled with the smaller bots operating the big mech like some sort of weird puppet. Instead, it seemed like he'd just thrown himself into a gigantic car engine. All around him were motors, pistons, and wires so tightly bunched together that he could barely move without bumping into something.

Owen was a little disappointed, actually. Silly as it might have been, he would have loved to have seen the puppet theory in action. On the upside, however, this made his job a whole lot easier. He didn't know how these things worked or what critical parts would take it down, so Owen was just going to break everything, which was much easier, especially when it was all neatly packed in like this.

Setting his sights on the nearest cluster of moving metal beams, Owen braced himself and threw a punch that he hoped would be just strong enough to send the heavier bits bouncing around inside the armored torso.

*   *   *

No one was sure exactly what came bursting out of the mech's back like buckshot, flying into the air before they could make out so much as a blurry detail, but the PEERS team had a pretty good idea of what had caused it. After all, witnessing Gale fling Titan into the giant robot's chest had significantly narrowed down the need for conjecture.

Despite the large crater in its front and smoking holes in its back, the mech continued moving about, seemingly unbothered by the Hero currently tearing up its insides. More of the smaller bots were still pouring out, though they seemed to slow significantly. Whether it was running out of steam or keeping the bots inside to fight the intruder was anyone's guess, though the latter strategy seemed like it would be pretty inefficient.

"Just like the good old days." The voice came from the rooftop's edge where a man wearing a familiar Hero costume was climbing up from the fire escape. "I mean, not the giant robot part. Tech wasn't quite as fancy as it is these days so they never got them that big. But dropping Titan into the middle of a fray and letting him do his work, now that takes me back."

"A pleasure to see you again, Topsy," Galvanize greeted him. "What brings you to our rooftop?"

"Heard Titan's people were in need of a little help, and seeing as I'm technically just supposed to be a coach anyway, it seemed like a good place for me to lend a hand," Topsy replied. "Besides, Titan looked out for my team; least I could do is watch over his. Seems like it might have been unnecessary, though."

"No, this is perfect," Bubble Bubble said. "You can go help him! Gale just threw him inside the mech without joining. Even for Titan, that has to be dangerous. If you hurry, you two can bring that thing down before he gets hurt."

"The concern is touching, but misplaced," Topsy assured her. "Do you ever wonder why he's called Titan?"

From the battlefield nearby, a huge metal beam suddenly burst out of the mech's lower torso and was dragged upward, like an inverted stabbing. The behemoth's legs began to shake, no longer capable of making the smooth, controlled motions that it had previously. Slightly higher, a blast of wind shattered another of its eyes, the third one taken out since Gale began her outer assault.

516

"Because he's really strong, like Titans from mythology," Zone said.

"That's probably why Titan agreed to use the name, but I actually know the Hero who suggested it to him, and that wasn't the reason." Topsy paused to glance over the edge of the roof, taking in the shuddering robot with a dark smile. "That fellow was Titan's rival back in their HCP days, and when they first started out he was much more powerful than our friend currently killing a robot from the inside. But every time he lost, Titan kept coming back, stronger and more determined than before. He just couldn't be stopped."

Suddenly, the mech's legs gave out. It came crashing to the ground, the weight of its body clearly no longer being offset by a gravitational anomaly. The arms flailed, now too heavy to move properly, and smoke poured out from the holes in its torso.

"You can never really kill a Titan," Topsy said, nodding to the fallen monster that only moments ago had seemed so indomitable. "Even the gods could only imprison them. That's why the name was suggested. Because if you've ever seen him in a real battle, walking through blood and fire completely unstained, you understand what it is to witness something that's truly unstoppable. The man you've been working with all this time is a good fellow, but he isn't the real Titan. Titan is a destroyer, a force of nature, a monster that only the grace of God has put on our side."

Topsy raised his hand and pointed to the collapsing mech. Flames began to rise out from the many openings punched in the giant body. Around it, the smaller robots suddenly began to twitch, then collapse, like puppets whose strings had been cut. After one last outward explosion from the place where the torso joined to the metal legs, a figure could be seen walking out from within the mechanical beast's belly. Even from so far away they could recognize the

517

familiar red and blue costume as the man strolled, dirty and sooty but unharmed, away from his fallen foe.

"*That* is the real Titan. And as an over-the-hill Hero who's witnessed too much evil in his lifetime, I can't tell you how fucking ecstatic I am to see him again."

111.

The first thing Hexcellent noticed as her eyes fluttered open was the strange man wearing a red and white costume with his fingers on her forehead. The second was Titan, standing over the other man's shoulder and looking anxious. The third, a realization that quickly dwarfed the other two, was that she was lying in the paw/hand of a massive rabbit, which was stooped over to allow Titan and the stranger access. Surprisingly, it wasn't panic that welled in her at the sight of the towering creature, but relief, like something long trapped had finally gotten free.

"Is this. . . Hopcules?"

It nodded, a gigantic gesture that was impossible to miss, staring down at her with those black shiny eyes. He looked much the same as he had when she was a child, armored and human-like, but easy to cuddle. She wondered if he could still cast light from his mouth, like he did when something in her room had made a noise and he lit it up to show her nothing was there. It was possible, though clearly things had changed.

Slowly, Hexcellent pulled herself to a reclined lean, noticing for the first time Galvanize, Zone, and Bubble Bubble were also there, albeit standing farther back from the giant bunny. Next to her team stood Gale and an older Hero that she half-recognized as Titan's friend. Around them were dozens, if not hundreds of the robots, all collapsed lifeless on the ground. There was also a fair amount of damage to the nearby buildings, some in the shape of giant rabbit-like footprints.

"Oh fuck me running. Am I going to be held liable for all this? 'Cause if so, you can go ahead and just kill my ass now."

"Good job, Bedrest," Titan told the man in red and white. "Looks like she's back to her usual cranky self."

"She should still take it easy for a while; healing or not, that sort of damage takes a toll. I have to get going, though, lots of our people need patching up." Bedrest walked away from the paw and Hexcellent, over to where a nondescript man in a rumpled suit was standing. Seconds later they were gone, seemingly vanished into thin air.

"Okay, but seriously, how much of this is on me?" Hexcellent asked, just before Titan wrapped her in a hug so tight that for a moment she worried Hopcules would have to intervene.

"You damn kids are going to give me a heart attack, and I don't think I can even get those." Titan slowly set her down, at which moment the rest of the team swarmed her. Hard as she tried to seem unbothered by the attention, it was impossible not to be a little moved by the influx of warmth.

"Anyway, to answer your question, you're technically clear on all this," Titan told her. "For one thing, it was self-defense, since Hopcules only attacked robots that came after it. Not to mention the fact that you were unconscious, so you had no say in what was happening. I ran everything up the ladder while we waited for Bedrest, and while there might be some hearings and paperwork, you'll come out fine. I'll make sure of it."

Something about his voice made it clear that Titan meant those words, possibly by any means necessary. Hexcellent had a good idea of just how many means the man had. As the others finally let go of her, she turned around to take in Hopcules in all his glory.

"When I summoned him as a kid, he was like five feet tall, tops," Hexcellent said.

"You said you summoned him to drive off your fears, right?" Bubble Bubble ventured. "Well, you've seen a lot more since then. Maybe you've got much bigger fears."

"On the subject of your rabbit, I need to talk with you about something," Titan interrupted. "We've learned that those giant robots are acting as relay points for the smaller ones. Basically, kill the big guys, and the little ones go limp."

Something in Hexcellent's brain wriggled again. Why did that seem familiar?

"Unfortunately, just like with the little ones, once the big bots are damaged to a certain point, they self-destruct everything we might be able to use, signal relays included. Currently, the Heroes have been able to take down four of the large mechs, and they're dealing with the fifth right now," Titan continued. "The sixth will be a special case, however. We're going to try to infiltrate it, find the device that's receiving and relaying the master signal, and trace it back to the source. Brewster can't take another attack like this one; it needs to end today."

"So do you need me to unsummon Hopcules to clear space or something?" Even as the words left her mouth, Hexcellent hated the taste of them. She'd just been reunited with an old friend; the last thing she wanted was to send him away again.

"Actually, pretty much the exact opposite." Titan pointed up at the giant rabbit, who was still watching everything with those glassy eyes. "Your summon is incredible, and right now it might be the most useful piece on the battlefield. If you're willing, we'd like to have you and Hopcules help contain the mech while a team hunts through its insides for the signal device. If the robot is fighting something of equal strength, that will keep it from tearing up the city, which will minimize damage and casualties while we take the time to search. It's dangerous work, though, I won't lie to you about that. I understand if you don't want to take the risk, especially so soon after a close call."

"Risk comes with the turf of being a PEERS," Hexcellent replied. "But you're sort of skipping over a big detail, aren't you? Self-defense is one thing; what you're describing sounds a lot more like picking a fight, and that's Hero work. Giant bunny or no, I'm not a Hero, remember?"

"No, you're not," Titan agreed. "But this work is messy, and it's far from the first time that a Super who had what we needed wasn't wearing a mask. The DVA has protocol for this kind of situation, and with Brewster's predicament, you weren't hard to sell them on. The technical term is Temporarily Authorized Hero Asset, and it means you can fight the good fight until the current threat is neutralized."

"And if I screw up?" Hexcellent had seen what happened to Heroes who made serious mistakes; the DVA wasn't shy about letting the public watch the trials. It was important to show that these enhanced beings charged with people's safety were held accountable. That was part of why people were comfortable trusting Heroes.

"Then that's on me as the one that authorized you." Titan set a hand on her shoulder, his massive palm almost engulfing her whole upper arm. "But you won't screw up. If you decide to fight, I know you're going to kick that thing's ass."

"And what makes you so certain?" Hexcellent shot back, wishing she had as much confidence as he did.

"Because I know you. Because I've seen you work. And because the first time we trained together, your immediate instinct was to try and show up me, a Hero renowned for his strength." Titan smiled down at her. "Half of this job is just having the guts to wade into dangerous, impossible situations and try to fight them back to salvageable. Guts are something you've got a lot of. Guts and a giant fire-breathing rabbit."

"He breathes fire now?" Hexcellent glanced up at Hopcules, as if expecting an explanation, but only received the same endless stare looking back at her. Shit, she'd never given him eyelids, had she?

"Oh good, that's news for you, too. We were wondering how that bunny didn't burn your house down," Zone said.

"He can do a hell of a lot, and so can you, but only if you want to." Titan dug into his pocket and pulled out a small silver device. "This was dropped off along with your healer. It will connect you with all the other Heroes out there trying to save this city. Take it, and until that last mech is beaten, you're one of us."

Hexcellent reached out, her fingers with their chipped black nail polish wrapping around the device and carefully lifting it from Titan's hand. The dream she'd had as a child, the one she'd pissed away with years of bad decisions, seemed to glow in the gizmo's metallic depths. She was never going to be a real Hero, and she'd made peace with that a long time ago. But if she couldn't grab hold of her dream, she would still settle for grazing her fingers against it.

"Tell me how this thing works, Titan. It sounds like we've got some robot ass to kick."

112.

"Hooooly shiiiiit!"

Hexcellent's scream was drowned out by the thunderous boom of Hopcules landing on the street below and launching himself upward once more, leaving only a giant footprint behind. She stood nestled between his neck and shoulder, while Titan and the rest of her team clung to the top of Hopcules's armor a few feet away. Her words seemed to sum up everyone's sentiment; there was no carnival ride in the world that could simulate riding on the shoulders of a giant rabbit as it hopped through town.

With no teleporter on hand capable of moving a twenty-story bunny, there was only one way to get to the final mech's location. Several Heroes had already evacuated a path. Others were driving the mech toward them in an effort to minimize how much damage was done. Word came down from Dispatch, the strange woman relaying everything through the new comm Hexcellent had shoved in her ear, that they were converging on a spot that had already been halfway leveled fighting an earlier mech. Better to rebuild one section of town than two.

Nearby, Gale and Topsy floated alongside Hopcules, her powers keeping the two of them aloft. Though they'd been offered the chance to ride on the rabbit's shoulder, the two Heroes had declined. Hexcellent wasn't sure if it was out of pride or prudence, and she didn't really care. They were free to miss out; all the more room for her and her team.

"Hexcellent, you've reached the rendezvous point."

Dispatch's voice brought her back to reality. She looked down and noticed a cluster of brightly-colored costumes dotting the ground. The Heroes that were waiting for them. For her. There was a moment as Hexcellent began to rise from Hopcules's shoulder that she genuinely thought it was her joy lifting her up. Then she felt the swirling wind and realized that it was Gale transporting her team to the ground.

Even as she was losing altitude, Hexcellent could see the mech, which was only a few blocks away. It was moving slowly and steadily as the other Heroes drove it toward her. She wasn't sure if it had noticed Hopcules or not, but as soon as she got the order, she'd make sure it couldn't pay attention to anything else.

"You know, I have seen some crazy shit in my days. Really, truly insane stuff. And this doesn't take the cake. . . but it's still pretty impressive."

The man speaking had his head tilted back as he took in Hopcules. Of all the people waiting for her, he looked the least like a Hero, wearing a simple outfit that was mostly notable for the large array of pockets. Eventually he turned from the bunny to the woman who summoned it, making his way over to Hexcellent and taking her hand.

"Pleasure to meet you, Hexcellent. I'm Jeremiah, and yes, that's my Hero name. You probably recognize most of the group from the news, but I keep a lower profile."

Jeremiah was right; as a Brewster resident, Hexcellent was quite familiar with Aether and Deadlift, to say nothing of Birdsman, Spring, Granite, and Misdirection, the rest of Elemental Fury. There were other Heroes as well, ones she'd seen on the news in other towns, Heroes who didn't call Brewster home. As she scanned them, another face caught her eye, one that lacked a mask yet was familiar all the same.

"Isn't that the fucking disintegration guy? Why isn't he in jail?"

"I have a name," the man muttered. He was wearing a white jumpsuit, standard issue to mark Supers in prison, and rubbing his wrists where handcuff marks could still be seen. "It's Eli, and I'm here for the same reason you are."

"You can summon a giant fire-breathing rabbit?" Hexcellent asked.

"He's here because he's got a talent we need," Titan explained, cutting off the conversation before it spiraled into a barrage of insults. "Jeremiah had him pulled out of jail to lend a hand in exchange for a reduced sentence. The armor on these mechs is tough, and Eli can get people in without having to punch through it."

"But you *can* punch through it," Hexcellent pointed out.

"Given the size of these things, having just one Hero search for the signal relay would take too long." As Jeremiah spoke, he began pulling what looked like cell phones with extra wires attached from his pockets and handing them to the various Heroes. "One of my teammates whipped these up in the last hour; *hopefully* they'll be able to find the device that's receiving the master signal. We're going to split up and cover as much ground inside the thing as possible. Aether and I will be paired up, so if anyone gets a hit on their detector, contact us and I'll head over to jam in the tracking device."

Jeremiah paused in front of Titan, only a few of the boxes left in his hands. "Since we don't want to do so much damage inside that the mech melts down, I'd prefer to have our more. . . destructive. . . members help the rabbit keep it busy. You okay with taking distraction duty?"

"I was going to demand it," Titan replied. "No way in hell I'm leaving Hexcellent on her own."

"This is pretty fucking far from being on my own," she said, jerking a thumb at the bunny whose shadow was looming over all of them.

"Still, these big ones are tough. I'm watching your back, so make peace with it."

"Titan really fits in better in the line of fire anyway," Jeremiah seconded. "And hey, at least it will make for good footage." He nodded to a nearby rooftop, where a news crew could just be made out pointing their cameras over the side. Now that she was looking, Hexcellent caught sight of another crew a block away, and a few more a street over from them.

"Wow, that is ballsy," Hexcellent said.

Jeremiah clucked his tongue. "Not every Super goes into our line of work. They've probably all got a way to protect themselves or vanish if the need arises. Even if they don't, I'm not turning them away. After all this destruction, we'll need some good footage of the Heroes fighting back the threat."

"And one corpie." Bubble Bubble's voice wasn't particularly loud, but it still managed to catch the attention of everyone nearby.

"The term is Privately Employed Emergency Response Super," Gale corrected.

"God damn right it is," Titan agreed.

"And we are thankful to have her, but time is running short."

Jeremiah finished doling out the boxes and turned to address everyone, effortlessly commanding their attention. Part of Hexcellent wondered how she'd never heard of him before; between the good looks and leadership skills, it seemed like Jeremiah would have a bit of notoriety.

"When the mech arrives, everyone is either on hunting or containment duty," he continued. "You know your team by whether or not there's a jerry-rigged phone in your hand. Gale, we need you to use Eli to erode the armor before coming in to join us so that there are plenty of easy entrances. Everyone else: get in, scan the equipment, and pray those damn things work. Those of you on the outside, contain the damage as much as possible, but try not to break the mech too bad. Remember, we're going to be inside the thing; not to mention that if you bust it beyond a certain point, everything useful inside will self-destruct, signal relay included. Also watch out for the smaller bots. They're sticking near it and we can't shut them down until we trace the signal. Other than that, have fun, and maybe try to put on a good show. The cameras are watching."

"Did he just actually tell us to have fun?" Hexcellent tried to keep her voice at a whisper only Titan and her team could hear, but from the snickers of a few nearby Heroes, it seemed to have carried farther than intended.

"Jeremiah is trying to keep the mood light. Going into battle tense doesn't help anyone," Titan told her. "Now, let's have Gale get you back on the bunny before the mech arrives. People are going to be counting on you to guide Hopcules and buy time for the Heroes to do their work."

"All while news cameras watch on, ready to judge every mistake I make. But no pressure, right?"

"Look at the upside," Titan said. "If we make it through this, that rabbit is marketable as hell. You'll have Hopcules plushies in stores by Christmas."

113.

As an agent and friend to a wide variety of Heroes, Lenny could have pulled any number of strings to be among the first people to be evacuated from Brewster. He hadn't bothered contacting any of his active Heroes, though, and instead called in a quick favor from a retired former client. The ones on duty had better things to do than worry about him. A quick teleport later and he was in his mountain home, a place he'd bought in hopes of spending time away from the job, focusing just on himself in the seclusion of nature.

The wide-screen television above the gas fireplace, wired up to a complete satellite package, betrayed his failure in disconnecting from the world. In fact, Lenny barely got any use from his cabin unless something threatened the town he was in and he needed a quick place to lie low. Sometimes he loaned it out to clients that needed to hide out from the press for a while as well. It was spacious enough to house four comfortably, or six in a pinch, and despite his intention of roughing it, Lenny had stocked the place with cushy furniture and high-end electronics, to say nothing of the booze. In a way, the cabin had served its purpose, though. He'd bought it for soul-searching, and what he'd uncovered was that he was not a man who wanted to disconnect from the job. He *was* the job, and he was happiest when he was knee-deep in it.

At the moment, he was juggling two phone calls, a half-dozen news streams on his laptop, and a live television feed of the fight in Brewster. The footage was grainy and far off, which was a damn shame; otherwise something like this would easily make the national reels for a week, minimum. Still, it was close enough that he could just make out the big robot being pushed through town, drawing nearer to another massive form with each step. The angle was shit; a skyscraper he didn't remember seeing before was blocking out everything save for the tips of a pair of ears. But Lenny was plugged in; he knew what was lurking behind the building, as well as how many of his clients were about to go take the last mech bastard on.

"Yeah, you heard me," Lenny snapped, his energy much higher than the weary clerk on the phone. "Ten thousand of the old Titan shirts. Well then, update the damn material, but keep the look as vintage as possible. Trust me, you're going to want to get ahead of this one."

A new figure appeared on screen just as the mech cleared the last row of buildings and approached the waiting ambush. It was huge by most scales, though compared to the robot it looked like a normal-sized bird. Lenny hadn't seen that one in quite a while. The screen shook as the news crew started moving, getting closer than was safe or prudent to the ensuing battle. Lenny hoped they stayed cautious, but he also hoped they didn't turn back. This was going to be solid gold.

"Go ahead and make sure all the Birdsman merch is stocked up as well, especially his bird plushies. Looks like he's going to be getting some screen time, too."

*   *   *

"Told you I had one more!" Birdsman yelled the barb at Titan from atop his final summon, a stone-colored bird with at least a twenty-five-foot wingspan. The creature looked like a statue come to life. With every flap, rubble flew from its wings. Despite appearing as though it weighed somewhere in the ton region, it effortlessly climbed higher into the sky, moving closer to the mech. The robot turned to face the bird, giving Gale and Eli the chance to start disintegrating holes in its hull.

"Ranged distraction team, we are go! Get in there and draw fire." Jeremiah's voice echoed through the area; he barely even needed the comms to give orders. "All of our melee people—and this includes Hexcellent and Hopcules—you hold back until we're inside. We don't need to dodge your bunny while trying to break in."

"Yeah, about that, why isn't it already attacking us?" Hexcellent asked, her voice nervous but determined. Seeing as she was currently standing on Hopcules's shoulder, braced for whatever attack the mech might throw, it was a fair and relevant question.

"This is Misdirection; I was told to keep you hidden until it was show time." The illusion-wielding Hero walked over from the group to stand near Titan and Hopcules. "We thought it might attack something as big as you, and like Jeremiah said, that could be problematic while the Heroes are breaking in. Plus, this gives you the element of surprise."

"How in the hell did you hide something this big?" Hexcellent asked, beating Titan to the question by only a few seconds.

"I'm not on a team like Elemental Fury for nothing," Misdirection replied. "I conjured a fake skyscraper around you. Around most of us, actually. As far as anyone more than fifty feet away can tell, this is just a building. Should let us keep the mech from knowing how much we're working with."

There was a crunch from behind, and Titan turned to find Granite standing nearby. Several feet farther away and he caught a glimpse of Galvanize, who was jogging over. "Our illusionist is top notch," Granite said. "With her, we never have to tip our hand on the battlefield."

"Mr. Granite," Galvanize said, breaking in. "Spring told me that you were looking-"

531

"Just Granite, and heck yeah I was looking for you. Heard you've been going around juicing everyone up, thought I might get in on that. I mean, I'm strong, but. . ." Granite nodded to the mech, which was currently being peppered with disintegration holes along with energy blasts from other Heroes while a dozen costumed figures raced to slip inside its torso. "That thing is probably stronger."

"I don't actually make you stronger, though," Galvanize explained. "I just bring you to the best you can possibly be."

"Still better than nothing," Granite said. "I have to be on top of my game, otherwise Birdsman and Roc-Steady are going to get all the attention."

"He named that thing Rocksteady?" Titan asked, momentarily dumbfounded.

"R-O-C, like the giant mythical bird. Also it's a pun since it's stone. And no, none of us has any idea how it can fly." Granite finished the explanation and looked at Galvanize, who simply took a step closer to the shifter currently composed of rocks and did what he'd been asked.

"Do your best."

Granite stiffened at the words then stretched his limbs carefully, testing their movements with the boost surging through him. "Not bad at all. I can tell I haven't broken any barriers, but I feel. . . good. Like I'm on top of my game. Titan, you getting in on this?"

"Eighty percent of the Heroes have infiltrated the mech's torso," Dispatch said, quietly speaking in their ears. "Melee distraction team, be ready. You'll be called as soon as the percentage passes ninety-five."

"Titan prefers to reach his pinnacle without help," Galvanize replied, unaware of the orders being issued across the comms.

"Well, in rescue work, suddenly using more strength than I'd planned could be dangerous," Titan replied. "I need near perfect control in those delicate situations." He looked at the stomping mech, and then at Hexcellent all the way up at the top of her rabbit's shoulder. As he turned, he also caught sight of a small group of reporters getting in for a closer view. Well, that would make Lenny happy, at least.

"But you know, seeing as I'm playing defense today anyway, a little extra pep in the step might not be such a bad idea."

"Really?" It was one of the few times Titan had seen Galvanize truly taken aback, even his composed smile faltering with uncertainty. "Are you sure? I mean, you don't actually need my boost. You're plenty strong enough as it is."

"No doubt about it." Titan took Galvanize by the shoulder and pointed to where the camera crew was setting up. They didn't know it, but when Misdirection's illusions dropped, those reporters would be in for a hell of a view. "However, there is one thing we can all agree on, be we Heroes or PEERS. Sometimes, you have to give the people what they want."

"Ninety-five percent mark cleared," Dispatch said. "Misdirection, drop the illusion; we now want all attention on the melee distraction team."

The air around the waiting Heroes shimmered like pavement on a summer afternoon. When the spectacle ended, the mech's eyes turned toward them. There were audible gasps from the nearby reporters as a giant armor-wearing rabbit suddenly came into view.

"That's our cue," Titan said.

"Then by all means, Titan. **Do your best**." Galvanize turned toward the giant rabbit as its legs tensed, ready to launch itself forward. "**You too, Hopcules**."

Titan's whole body tingled, like he'd gotten an unexpected rush of adrenaline. Carefully, he shifted his weight, noting the way the concrete cracked and splintered under him. In almost any other circumstance, this would be dangerous, but facing off against a giant metal monster was one of the few times he didn't mind having a little extra gas in the tank. If nothing else, it would be interesting to see just what his metaphorical top speed was nowadays. It had been a long time since he needed to find out.

"Thanks," Titan said, moving with extra caution as he stepped forward. "Now, stay by Topsy. This whole area is about to become a warzone." With that, Titan leapt forward, only to be passed by Hopcules a few seconds later.

114.

Whatever programming the mech had been built with, whatever counter-strategies designed around the data compiled from previous robot/Hero battles, it had most definitely not been given a ready response for being attacked by a twenty-story tall rabbit. Hopcules' first punch caught it completely by surprise, leaving a massive dent in its six-eyed head. The bunny followed up with a sucker punch to the torso. The echo from the second blow rang through the street. Hexcellent immediately heard Jeremiah's voice snap in her ear.

"Avoid the body blows, if possible. It's already tough enough to move around inside this thing without getting shaken like a martini."

"Don't mind Jeremiah, he's just mad because you made him fall and look undignified," Aether added, her tone much less annoyed. "But do please focus on the extremities. Those are going to do the most damage to the surrounding areas."

"Not a problem." Hexcellent tightened her grip on the bunny's fur and yelled up to its ear, "Grab an arm and snap that shit off!"

Luckily enough, an arm fitted with what looked like a half-dozen machine guns came toward them, no doubt intent on filling the attacking rabbit with countless holes. Before it could take aim, Hopcules grabbed the wrist area, just below the guns, and slammed another hand into the upper arm, straining the elbow joint. Since the damn mech didn't have a back there was nowhere to twist to, so Hopcules just kept piling on more pressure, trying to make the joint snap.

"I'm going to take a wild guess that Hopcules was formed during a time when you watched a lot of wrestling." Titan sounded surprisingly calm given that he was darting around on the other side of the mech, throwing punches into its legs as he tried to cripple the thing's mobility. Hexcellent could already see a tilt in the giant robot's stance, meaning at least one of its legs was now shorter than the others.

"I may or may not have enjoyed the occasional cage match in my childhood." Hexcellent heard the crunch and pop before she actually saw Hopcules pull away the front part of the arm. Her moment of triumph at seeing the threat neutralized was short-lived, however, as a blow from behind sent Hopcules stumbling forward. Only his gigantic feet saved him from losing his balance entirely.

Whirling around, Hexcellent quickly put together what had happened. While they were trying to take care of one arm, the bot had swung another around and fired a laser blast into Hopcules. Hexcellent scrambled across the shoulder to look down at her summon's back and assess the damage. A huge part of his armor was eroded, and there were singe marks along the skin with burned-off patches of fur. Hopcules didn't seem to have slowed down, but he had to be hurting.

"Don't worry, buddy. We'll pay him back for that." Even Hexcellent was surprised at the fury kindled inside her. Just the sight of her old friend in pain was enough to make her want to turn that fucking mech to bits so thin it could be mistaken for glitter. But she couldn't, because then it would win. So they'd just have to settle for taking away its limbs.

Hopcules swung back around to face its foe, and to Hexcellent's surprise, the mech stepped back slightly. It had seen that the bunny had the upper hand in a melee fight, so now it was trying to keep distance between them. The damned thing was learning, because of course it was: that was what these bastards did. Every time, every iteration, they just came back stronger and more organized, with no actual goal aside from collecting resources and-

"Titan. And Dispatch. And whoever else is listening. I figured it out." Hexcellent couldn't believe it had taken her this long to see what was happening. Though, to be fair, RTS had always been one of her least favorite genres to play. "I know what the robot's motives are."

"We're all ears." The voice was Jeremiah's; Hexcellent was relatively certain she also heard some explosions in the background.

"It's a video game." Hexcellent had to pause as Hopcules leapt out of the way to avoid another laser blast while working to close the gap. The mech kept sliding back, trying to line up its next shot while also dealing with smaller yet potent threats on the ground.

"Going to need some elaboration," Titan said.

"All of this: the mech, the robots, the motives, it's a real-time strategy game. You make troops then send them out to fight and get resources. You use the experience from those encounters to make more, bigger troops and repeat the process over and over until you can wipe out the enemy. That's why no one could figure out what the fuck these things wanted. *This* is what they want. These fights."

"Why in the hell would someone go to all this trouble just to play a game?" Gale snapped.

"No idea, but it's the first theory I've heard that actually fits the pattern," Jeremiah replied. "Though if anything, it drives home how much we need to make this work. An attack more powerful than this one and the city will be leveled. Distraction team, keep it up; we've got a potential match for the signal relay, I'm en route to confirm."

"Okay, no more slacking," Hexcellent yelled up to Hopcules. "We got one arm, three to go. You ready?"

In response, Hopcules leapt forward, barely avoiding the latest volley of laser blasts. Fire breath was out since it would melt the people inside the torso as much as the mech, but there was still good old-fashioned grappling. Hopcules slid its giant foot beneath the mech's legs, knocking three of the remaining four upward. At the same time, he grabbed onto the laser gun that had been taking shots at him with both hand-like paws and jerked upward, trying to use the weight of the falling mech to force a separation at the shoulder.

The idea was a good one, but if failed to account for one important element. After only a few feet, the mech's fall stopped cold. It righted itself, spinning another arm around to slam the back of Hopcules knees, this time successfully sending it to the ground. While Hexcellent couldn't understand how something that big could stop itself with one leg, Titan knew all too well what had happened as he watched the rabbit fall. Those damn gravity distorters, the ones that made the mechs viable in the first place. It had changed its weight to save itself.

Hopcules struggled to get up while Hexcellent did all she could to hang on, but they were no match for the mech's inhuman reaction time. The laser arm whipped around, pressing directly into Hopcules's head, between the ears and the eyes.

At this range, there was no chance the mech was going to miss.

115.

Instants. That was what it always seemed to come down to. All the planning, all the training, all the endless hours trying to imagine how one would deal with a situation, and the truth was that most fights and losses were determined in a span of less than a half-second. That was the hardest thing to try and teach potential Heroes, that in the dire moments they'd be leaning on their instincts. This was why the HCP was so tough on them: when those moments arrived, their reactions had damn sure better be the right ones or people would die.

Titan wasn't perfect. He had a list of names that proved that fact beyond all debate. But he'd been doing the job for a long time, and even if he'd been off for a while, some things never quite faded.

In that moment, as the mech swung its laser cannon towards Hopcules's head, with Hexcellent so close there was no way she wouldn't be caught in the blast, he moved without hesitation, because there was no time for such a luxury. He was betting everything, Hexcellent's everything, on the fact that the mech hadn't changed its weight back from when it stopped its fall. If it could stop itself on one leg, then maybe it could be moved by the same appendage. It was still a roll of the dice, one where snake eyes meant Hexcellent would die. If it came to that, she wouldn't go alone. The least Titan could, and would, do was make sure whoever made these mechanical monsters was sent to join her.

"Everybody hold on!" Titan roared into the comms as he wrapped his arms around the bottom of the mech's nearest leg. No time to try and drag; it could still get off a shot. He needed to completely disorient the damn thing. Slamming his legs through the concrete for stability, Titan's arms crushed into the metal of the leg, creating an unbreakable grip. With all he had, he jerked upwards and to the side, away from Hexcellent. It was ridiculous, it was a flea trying to move a rhino, but it was all he had. He was a strongman. This was the only thing he could do.

But by the gods, he could do it like no one else.

The robot rose from its position atop Hopcules, caught by surprise and unable to react to going suddenly airborne. In the span of seconds it realized what was happening, and Titan felt the metallic beast began to grow rapidly heavier in his arms. None of that mattered, though, because the real work was already done. Hopcules quickly rolled to the side and sprang back to its oversized feet. He looked unshaken, as near as Titan could tell by reading those glassy black eyes, and no worse for the wear.

"H-holy shit. Kind of thought we were goners there." Unlike her bunny, Hexcellent was clearly rattled, and Titan couldn't blame her for that. For someone with no real combat training, she was holding together better than a lot of others would.

"What kind of legendary Hero would I be if I let some asshole machine hurt my teammate?" Titan released his grip on the leg, which came crashing down a few feet away. He wondered if the mech was debating stomping on him, though it had to have realized what little good that would do.

"Clearly not the kind who can manage to keep things smooth for those inside," Jeremiah grumbled. "Mercifully, we think we've found the signal relay. If you can hold out for a few more minutes, I need to get the tracker inserted and let my team do their work."

"Put a little pep in your step, the bunny almost got taken out," Titan replied.

"Um. . . yeah. Birdsman, you're the veteran summoner here. Have any of yours ever. . . changed?"

Hexcellent's voice had gone from scared to confused, and it took only a quick glance at Hopcules for Titan to understand why. The giant rabbit was shifting before their very eyes, long serrated claws slipping out of his hands, and new spiky armor growing out of the old. From behind, a vast pair of bat-like wings sprouted. The wings flapped once, sending a breeze across the entire area.

"No. No, I cannot say I've ever seen anything quite like that before," Birdsman replied from atop his flying stone roc. "Trust me, that's the sort of thing that would stick in my memories. And my nightmares."

From above Titan, the mech took another shot with its lasers, and this time Hopcules didn't dodge. It took the blow right on its chest. The new armor burned but refused to give way. In one shift, the tables had turned and the weaker warrior had grown strong. For the first time, Titan had a feeling of what it must be like for others to fight him.

"I'm no expert, but I'm going to toss out a theory," Titan said, yanking his feet free from the concrete and making a run for the leg already dented with his handprints. Crippling mobility was the best way he could help now; the rest was going to be up to Jeremiah and Hexcellent. "Hopcules was supposed to keep you safe, right? You made him to fight your fears?"

"That's how I remember it, but I was a kid," Hexcellent replied.

"Like I said, this is just a guess. If we assume that's how it went down, though, then maybe Hopcules is still doing that. He came out so big because you were facing an overwhelming force. Then, when you almost died a few seconds ago, you got scared again, so he grew stronger."

"Can summons do that?" Hexcellent asked.

"Every Super is different, so it's possible," Titan reminded her.

"There have been cases of summons with alteration capabilities under certain situations." Dispatch was calm, which Titan imagined was only possible because she hadn't just watched a twenty-story rabbit shape shift. "However, none that we know of were on quite so *grand* a scale."

"As someone who has to listen to this without knowing what the hell is going on, may I just request that someone take pictures?" Jeremiah asked. "Because it sounds absolutely fascinating."

"Let's just say that after I lifted the whole mech, Hexcellent upstaged me." Titan grabbed the same leg once again, this time digging his hands in and climbing up toward the knee joint. The lasers from the mech's underside fired at him, but this did little more than singe his clothes. He really needed to ask for a raise; the suit costs were piling up.

"Oh, you want to complain? I just went from being a top-level summoner to some asshole on a bird," Birdsman added. "At least you got to do something cool. I'm flying around dodging shots."

"You know, this isn't quite what I pictured the conversations of Heroes to be like," Hexcellent admitted.

"We only sound like this when we're winning," Jeremiah assured her. "Which, by the way, we are. The tracker is implanted and my team is tracing the signal. Everyone inside the mech, evacuate. As soon as I get confirmation that we've found the location, Aether and I will be out of here too. Think you and your upgraded rabbit can handle things from there?"

Titan smashed his hand through the knee joint, causing the mech to wobble as it fired wave after wave of lasers and bullets at the Heroes keeping it distracted. When the machine tipped, he got a clear view to the other side, where Hopcules was flexing his claws and testing his wings. Hexcellent's words crackled over the comms a moment later, all traces of fear gone from her voice.

"You're damn right we can. Nobody puts my bunny back in the box."

116.

"Evacuation at eighty percent." Dispatch's reports were helpful, but it was visibly obvious that the mech wasn't clear yet. Colorful costumed forms could be seen leaping from the holes in its body, some breaking into flight while others vanished in midair or landed heavily on the ground.

Hexcellent stood on her rabbit's shoulder, waiting for the cue to strike as Hopcules dodged the occasional blast. The distraction team had done a great job: the damage to the surrounding area was almost minimal, and the smaller robots were being picked off or contained by the other Heroes. It was hard to call anything in a day like this a win, but knowing how much worse things could have been, Hexcellent felt proud about what they'd accomplished.

That pride was all the more magnified knowing that she'd been able to help. It was almost over; it had only been a taste of the life in the first place. Just one last course to go and she was determined to enjoy it. While Hexcellent didn't lick her lips in anticipation, it took effort. Part of her wanted to be sad at the ending in sight, at wondering when she would ever be able to summon her oldest friend again, but she pushed those thoughts away. There would be a lifetime of worry and mourning for lost chances when the day was won. Until then, she still had a job to do. For at least the next few minutes, she was a Hero. She was damn sure going to act like it.

"Evacuation at ninety-two percent," Dispatch said.

"The last of them should be out in the next thirty seconds," Jeremiah reported from within the beast. "As soon as they're clear, you need to take this thing apart. I'm not sure if the central system has a way to tell if it's being tracked, but at this point, we'd be idiots to assume otherwise. We have to scrap this tin can and then book it to the signal source before it has a chance to run."

"We've got teleporters on standby to get us close, and I'm ready to haul the team if it's a place they've never been," Gale told him.

"Evacuation complete, save for Aether and Jeremiah," Dispatch announced. "Also, Modus Operandi has confirmed that the signal has been traced to a location approximately thirty miles northeast of Brewster."

"Then that means we are out of here!" Jeremiah exclaimed. Seconds later, Hexcellent saw him and Aether drop from the middle of the mech's base, lasers passing through them ineffectually as they headed toward the ground.

"Hexcellent, you are clear for full engagement," Dispatch said. "There are zero known civilians in the area, so please emphasize expediency over caution."

"Dispatch, that was an order you really didn't have to bother giving her," Titan chuckled. "But good luck, Hexcellent. Everyone will be down here helping out, so tear it apart."

"We'll do our best." She stared at the mech, fending off so many other Heroes that it didn't even have time to worry about the giant rabbit standing on the sidelines. Maybe it thought they'd been scared away by almost getting shot in the head. Well, they had been scared, but it sure as shit wasn't away.

"Round two, mother fucker."

Hopcules barreled forward, and as it did, the costumed warriors parted to let it pass, already waiting for the impending charge. The newly-grown claws hit first, stabbing into the mech's armored torso with some difficulty. It was a sturdy bastard, Hexcellent had to admit that much, but the holes Eli disintegrated had weakened the structural integrity by a fair bit. Hopcules jerked upward and managed to shred through a chunk of the torso, exposing the gears and circuitry within.

An arm came whirling around, ready to try and put a hole in the mech's attacker, but this time she and Hopcules were ready for it. Twisting his head, Hopcules opened his mouth wide and bit down on the metal appendage with his mighty buck teeth. Before the mech could struggle free, the smell of melting metal lit the air as Hopcules finally was able to put his fire breath to use. Half of the arm clattered to the concrete, torn off by the combination of heat and strong jaws.

The mech tried to retreat, but Hopcules wasn't having any of that. Using the claws embedded in its torso, the giant rabbit lifted the mech upward until it was horizontal in the sky. Its arms whipped about, trying to line up a shot while the remaining legs kicked about futilely. Still, Hexcellent waited to give the order. If she wanted this to work, they had to wait for the perfect moment.

For a long, beautiful instant, the mech hung there, suspended by Hopcules's powerful arms. Then, at last, she saw it start to slide down the rabbit's claws at the same time she felt his shoulders begin to shake. The mech was turning up its weight again, trying to make them let go. She almost felt sorry for the mechanical monster; if only it had worked in a few wrestling games instead of all RTS, it might have seen what she was going for.

"Time for the Back-Breaker, bitch-bot!" Hexcellent yelled, and on cue, Hopcules slammed the mech downward. Not to the ground, where it would have cracked and dented but perhaps still survived, but directly on top of the rabbit's planted knee, where an armored spike happened to be pointing up to the sky. The mech came slamming down, one clawed paw on either side of the knee, pushing with all their might. If it had still been lighter, it might have endured; however, turning up the weight of its body cut both ways.

The mech cracked in half, its weakened torso unable to withstand the combination of weight and muscle that split it down the center of its chest. As soon as its pieces hit the ground, the other Heroes were ready, smashing through the remains or turning them to scraps from afar with ranged powers. No one was taking any chances of this thing getting back up. Hopcules even stomped on the remaining legs, turning them into little more than gleaming silver shards.

"You know, there are a lot of things I don't like about this job. Moments like this are not among them," Jeremiah commented.

"No shit. I need a cigarette after watching that," Aether added.

"You did good, Hexcellent," Titan told her. "A hell of a job. Now we've got to go make the most of what you did and finish things off. Are you going to be okay on your own from here?"

Hexcellent stood atop her giant rabbit summon and looked down of the smoldering wreckage of a monster that she'd bested, yet who hours ago had seemed completely unstoppable.

"I'll be fine, Titan. I just killed a giant robot; right now I am outright fan-fucking-tastic."

From her perch so high up, it was hard to make out Titan as he grouped up with the others, but Hexcellent was almost positive she caught sight of a smile on his face just before his voice came through the comms.

"You're damn right you are."

117.

Northeast of Brewster was a whole lot of nothing, at least as far as Titan was concerned. Some folks enjoyed the loping hills and quasi-mountains, good for hiking and camping and not much else. Despite his rough and tumble appearance, though, Owen Daniels had always preferred life in a city to the more outdoorsy world. Visiting his wife's family in the south had been his only real exposure to the country, and when he'd fled to start his bar, he'd at least picked a place somewhat near civilization. Their enemy's location didn't surprise him or any of the others. An operation of such vast size, the base had to be hidden out in nowhere; otherwise they'd have found it and put this whole thing to bed ages ago.

"This is the closest point I had," Relocate informed them. A teleporter who worked out of Port Valins, he had luckily done an internship in Brewster and had been able to see much of the town. There was no reason for him to have gone so far out in the boonies, though; even a teleporter's encouragement to travel had limits. A few freelance teleporters had been nearby, but they weren't likely to get the team any closer. Besides, Titan never liked taking those types to sensitive areas. DVA-certified transportation resources or not, he preferred to stick with Heroes when things were getting serious.

"We appreciate your help," Jeremiah told Relocate. "It's a few more miles from here, something Gale can easily handle. I'm sure you need to get back to the rescue efforts."

"The requests are already flooding in." Relocate tapped his right ear where Dispatch was no doubt alerting him to the dozens of civilians in need of saving. The robot threat might be suppressed, but the damage they had done had left countless people trapped or in danger. Every Hero that could be spared was pitching in to help, along with emergency services and dozens of PEERS teams. "If you need to make a quick getaway, I can meet you here. Otherwise, there might be a wait for me to get back."

"This isn't a team that plans on running," Gale told him.

"I didn't expect as much, but it seemed polite to offer." Relocate took one last look at his surroundings, refreshing his memory to make the trip back easier, and vanished in a shimmer of static.

"Gale, if you could follow my heading," Jeremiah said, stepping to the front. "There might be defenses out here: the nearer we get to the signal source the greater chance of that, so everyone be on guard. Aether, be ready to shift Gale and Deadlift if we come under fire."

"What about you?" Aether didn't bother asking about Titan, because the answer was obvious: he didn't need to be intangible. The very best those robots had thrown at him didn't leave as much as a mark on anything other than his suit. The bots were strong, but Titan had fought stronger.

"I'll be fine," Jeremiah assured her. "Worry about these two. Although, Gale, do your powers work when you're intangible?"

"Never had occasion to find out," Gale said. "Guess today's a good chance to learn."

Deadlift let out a soft groan. "Let's not tempt fate. Hopefully we'll make it to the signal without needing to take evasive actions."

"Hope in one hand, spit in the other. . ." Jeremiah didn't bother finishing the saying, instead listening attentively to a voice coming through his comm.

As he sat silent, Gale took the opportunity to whip up a whirlwind, raising them all from the ground. Jeremiah was in the front, since he'd be pointing the way, with Deadlift and Gale on either side of Aether so she could reach them. Titan was in the rear, a hardy shield in case something tried to come at them from behind.

"That way," Jeremiah said finally, gesturing out toward a hill overgrown with lush green trees. "Based on the topography my people are looking at, we'll pass over two hills and a small lake before we get to the right area."

With no more than the point of a finger they were off, tearing through the sky at breakneck speeds. Though she was doing a good job staying controlled, Titan could nearly feel the rage coming from Gale. He liked Brewster, but to him it was just a city. To her, however, it was a place of incredible importance. It was where her team had been based for decades, where the legacy of Elemental Fury took root. More than that, she'd lived there for years; she knew the city and the people in it intimately. This attack hadn't just been horrific for her on a human level, it had hit her personally. When they found whoever was responsible for it, Titan knew he was going to have to move fast. If the culprit wasn't captured quickly, Gale might do something she would ultimately live to regret. Killing was never easy, and if it was done without need she'd be weighed down by that sin for the rest of her life.

The ground below them flew by. In no time they were zipping past the lake Jeremiah had described. He motioned for Gale to begin their descent. Near as Titan could tell, there was nothing that marked the area they were heading for as noteworthy, just a small ravine and more hills full of trees. Of course, if the base could be seen from the sky, they wouldn't have needed to use such extreme tracking methods in the first place. Slowly, following Jeremiah's directions,

Gale brought them down, past the lip of the ravine, deeper into the crevice where the late-afternoon sun could scarcely reach. At last, Titan felt the familiar sensation of earth beneath his feet.

It turned out that the ravine was deeper than he'd perceived from the sky, a narrow slice in the land that felt like two walls looming over them. Thankfully, Hero gear didn't lose signal easily. Jeremiah began trekking across the rocky terrain, following the guidance of his unseen team. The more Titan watched Modus Operandi accomplish, the more curious he was about the other members. It wasn't unheard of for Subtlety Heroes to buck the spotlight, but a whole team represented by one Hero seemed peculiar. Then again, they were bound to be making all manner of enemies, given how efficient they were, and Subtlety Heroes often weren't known for their combat skills. Maybe putting up one lone giant target to go after made sense, assuming Jeremiah could handle the burden.

"We're getting close," Jeremiah called, waving for them to follow. "The signal is coming from nearby, and my team says this is the most likely point to have an entrance. If we don't find one, then I'm going to need Aether to do some intangible recon through the rock, and then Titan can bust open-"

Before Jeremiah could finish his plan, he took one step too far, and what seemed to be nothing more than a clump of rocks suddenly sprang to life. It whirred and clicked, whipping around and locking the barrel of its laser gun directly on Jeremiah. Titan started running as soon as he saw the motion, but he wasn't nearly fast enough. The sound of a high-pitched whine filled the air, then a flash of red shot from the barrel. After that, there was only Titan's thundering footsteps and the soft slump of a body hitting the ground.

The hole in Jeremiah's chest where his heart should be was still smoking, the horrid smell of roasting flesh wafting through the air.

118.

The gun was nothing more than scrap metal after two of Titan's blows, both of which were far stronger than were strictly necessary. Though he hadn't yet turned to make the confirmation, he knew what he'd witnessed while dashing over. Jeremiah was dead. Whatever enhanced endurance he might have had wasn't enough to withstand the laser blast. A hole in the chest was enough to kill pretty much anything, even a Super.

With the remains of the laser throwing off sparks, Titan turned to find the others clustered around Jeremiah, whose blood was soaking into the rocks. No doubt about it: he was dead, likely had been before he hit the ground. Aether's face was pale, and Deadlift seemed to be sniffling under his mask; the poor kid probably hadn't lost too many friends in the field yet. Much as Titan wanted to mourn the loss of a comrade—a loss hitting Titan harder than he'd expected—Jeremiah's death meant nothing if they didn't finished the job.

"We need to-" Titan's words died on his tongue as Jeremiah's pooling blood suddenly halted, then began to flow back into his blown apart torso. As it did, the burned out chunks of flesh lengthened and bones regrew. The whole process took perhaps five seconds, but when it was done, Jeremiah's body bore no sign of any injury whatsoever. If that alone wasn't disturbing enough, the sound of a rough cough escaped the fallen Hero's lips, and he shook his head as if coming out of a long nap.

"*What the fuck!*" Aether screeched, turning insubstantial and leaping backward. Even for people who dealt with superhuman abilities, someone coming back from the dead was a bit much. Gale and Deadlift both took defensive postures as well; bracing for attack was their default reaction in strange situations.

"Sorry about that," Jeremiah said, voice as calm as if he hadn't just had his heart hollowed out seconds earlier. "Little inconvenient, I know, but at least now we know to be on guard for traps."

"You were dead." Titan looked around for any proof of the injury, splatters of blood or flecks of bone, yet there was no sign of it aside from the hole in Jeremiah's shirt. Even the blood stains on the rocks were gone. "This. . . this is impossible. What you just did goes way beyond regeneration. This is time manipulation."

"Come on, if I was the first Super to travel through time, you don't think I'd work on a slightly grander scale than running a team of Subtlety Heroes?" Jeremiah slowly pulled himself to his feet and gestured over to the broken wreckage of the gun that had slain him. "Besides, if I never got shot, then you never would have beaten that device halfway to electronic hell. Appreciate that, by the way."

"Jeremiah, we all just watched you die. Regeneration can't fix death. Do you really expect us to just let this pass with no explanation?" Gale's eyes were narrowed, her emotions torn between relief and uncertainty of what to make of such a display.

"At the very least, we need to know how much damage you can come back from before we go any further." Deadlift thrust a thumb down the ravine, where logic said there were no doubt more traps lying in wait for them. "Not to be a dick about it, but knowing what actually kills you tells us who we should prioritize helping if things turn to shit without warning."

Jeremiah turned the argument around a few times before evidently landing on agreement with the point. "Very well, but I'm only giving you all the cursory overview. As a Subtlety Hero, I know far too well how important it is to have a few secrets kept close to the vest, especially about weaknesses. The long and short of it is that my body doesn't regenerate, technically. It's more apt to say that I lock my physical form in at a certain time, and my ability maintains that status quo no matter what happens."

"What the hell does that mean?" Aether had largely recovered from her outburst, though she was still giving Jeremiah a wary eye as he explained. No one, least of all Jeremiah, blamed her for the caution. Seeing a corpse pull itself back together was unsettling on a lot of levels.

"It means I pick a day when I'm exactly where I want to be. Fit, strong, energetic, and without any aches or pains. Then I activate my power. And until I turn it off, that's my body, regardless of outside forces like giant robots or laser cannons-"

"Or time?" It was Titan who interrupted, realizing exactly what Jeremiah was describing. Immortality. Maybe not perfect: if he was keeping secrets then there was bound to be a flaw or two in the ability. *No* power was unbeatable. Yet if he really did lock his body like he was describing, it meant aging wasn't something he had to fear.

The wide grin on Jeremiah's face answered before he formed the first syllable of his glib reply. "I haven't had enough years to say for certain yet, but by all accounts going forward, I'm going to look extremely good for my age, whatever that might be. Though at the rate I'm mowing through uniforms, I'll have a huge clothing bill and a lot of unpleasant death memories."

"Wait, do you remember dying from the laser?" Gale asked.

"I remember everything that happens to me before the power gets triggered," Jeremiah told her. "That's the drawback to my ability; I can recall every single time my life has ended, and let me tell you, those memories are not sunshine and rainbows. Still, it's the gift I have, so I make the most of it."

"And it sounds like a hell of a good one, but I think it's about time we started using *my* power." Titan turned toward the direction the laser gun had sprung up from. "Everyone, stay here. I'm going to see if there are any more traps waiting."

He began jogging forward, through the ravine's narrow walls. Within the first few steps, another gun burst forth from the rocks, firing directly at Titan's torso. The burning energy hit his already-exposed flesh. It fizzled uselessly just before Titan returned the blow, his force leaving only shattered scrap behind. A few more feet and another gun appeared, quickly meeting the same fate. Further in and an explosion from the ground tried to blow off his leg, succeeding only in tearing up his boot. Titan continued on, undeterred. Seeing a friend die, even if only for a few moments, had been just the kick in the ass he needed to remind him of his role in situations like this. It had been a long time since Titan was doing real Hero work, but with each step forward, it was coming back to him. His place was at the front, taking on every attack the enemy could throw, making sure his team stayed safe.

Titan would stand against the full assault, and only when it was spent would he call the others to follow. That was what it meant to be a team's shield.

119.

As it turned out, they didn't need Aether to search the walls for an entrance. The traps and devices Titan was charging through, while no doubt designed to keep unwanted guests from ever getting near the hidden base, served in this case as a trail of breadcrumbs leading the team of Heroes right to the door. True, it looked like nothing more than a ravine wall marking a natural end to their journey, but with one punch from Titan, before any of the others could arrive to suggest a more nuanced entrance, the reinforced door blew backward in shards, revealing a softly-lit, smooth metal hallway leading deeper underground.

"Well, there goes any element of surprise we might have had," Jeremiah noted as he, Gale, Aether, and Deadlift emerged from the wake of Titan's destruction.

"Between the cannons, mines, and laser grids, I have a feeling anyone in here already knew we were coming," Titan replied, words purposely absent anything resembling an apology. "If I can't surprise an enemy, I prefer to let them know I mean business, and nothing says I wipe my ass with your security quite like punching a door off its hinges."

"Actually, it looks like this didn't have hinges. It rose up to let people in, making it all the harder to knock down." Deadlift had walked to the doorway and was staring into the ruined mechanism of the entrance. "Quite a functional design. I mean, under different circumstances."

"Since time is now officially not on our side, how about we get going with this?" Gale suggested. "Jeremiah, do those voices in your head happen to have any insight on where the signal is coming from? Or are we flying blind from this point on?"

"Hey, they got us here, didn't they?" Jeremiah bristled a touch, more bothered by the barb than by his death only a few moments prior. "And no, I don't have direct lock on where we need to go. They can play hot and cold using my location and the signal strength, but this place is too deep and well-shielded to get the signal's exact coordinates. Besides, the machine sending the orders and the Super who built it aren't guaranteed to be in the same position, and we need to stop the latter more than the former."

"Then it looks like we're splitting up." Aether had gone intangible and walked down the hallway unbeknownst to the rest of them until she came sauntering back up. "Thought I'd do a bit of recon while you bickered about plans. The hallway splits off in three directions from here. If we're hunting two separate targets then it seems like we've got to cover all the branches to be safe."

"Safe would be moving as a team down each one until we'd searched them all," Titan pointed out.

"But that gives our Super better odds of escaping," Gale countered. "Aether is right: we need to scour the base as quickly as possible. Five doesn't split up evenly, so we'll pair off as needed. Deadlift, you're a rookie, no offense, which means I'll feel better seeing you with someone who knows what they're doing. Go with Titan. Since Jeremiah is apparently unkillable, but lacks much in terms of offense, he and Aether should be able to skirt past any obstacles they encounter. I'll take on my path solo."

"Shouldn't Titan go solo?" Deadlift suggested. "He's the one who would be in the least danger of getting hurt or captured."

"Gale can take care of herself just as well as I can," Titan said quickly, hoping to cut Gale off before she tore into the relatively new Hero. "She leads a team into dangerous situations all the time, and her power is suited to offense and defense. What she can't do is shield someone else as easily as I can. You're with me because if things go bad, I'll hopefully be able to take the brunt of whatever gets thrown at us."

"Make sure to stay behind him." Jeremiah patted Deadlift softly on the back. "Unlike me, your insides probably don't put themselves back together once they see daylight."

Titan didn't bother adding any agreement to Jeremiah's words. The image of his corpse splayed out on the ground was still fresh in all their minds, a perfect reminder of where one misstep in situations like these could lead. Instead, he headed down the hallway, once again taking his position ahead of the others. Unlike his trek through the ravine, Titan's heavy footsteps didn't trigger any cannons or traps; only echoes met him as he plunged deeper into the hidden base. Soon he arrived at the split Aether had described, three hallways branching off from the one he'd descended. Rather than waste more time debating, Titan merely looked back to make sure Deadlift was following and walked right up the one in the middle.

From behind, Titan heard Deadlift's hurried steps as he ran to catch up, while Gale, Jeremiah, and Aether all went to either side of them. Without knowing where any of this led, it was impossible to say who was on the fastest path, or the most dangerous. Though, Titan did have a hunch or two.

"Is there a reason you picked the middle hall?" Deadlift asked, speaking up to be heard from the several feet behind Titan where he was trailing. "It's fine if it's random, but since I've been so strongly reminded of my rookie status, I thought I might as well ask so I could learn something."

A few more heavy steps, and Titan caught sight of a bend in the hall. It might have been his imagination, but it seemed like a different source of light than the gently glowing bulbs along the wall was shining from around the corner.

"It wasn't random," Titan told Deadlift, even as he held up his hand for the other Hero to stop advancing. "You need to hang back here. There might be something ready to fire as soon as I turn the corner, and I'd rather not have you caught up in the blast if it's explosive."

"If we hadn't just walked through a valley of mechanical death, I might call you paranoid." Despite the sass, Deadlift came to an immediate stop, even going so far as to take a few steps backward. "What's my cue that it's safe to follow?"

"Depends. I might just yell for you, though there's always the chance that the room will be soundproofed, so I may come back this way or pass a message through Dispatch. Just be ready to move if I give an order. Especially if that order is to run."

"Consider me raring to go," Deadlift replied.

Titan started forward again, but Deadlift's voice caused him to stop as it yelled one last question from behind.

"If it's not random, then why did you pick the middle hall?"

"Just a hunch built on experience." Titan's mind swam back through the years of busting into bases, lairs, and dens of criminal activity. They didn't always have time to prepare defenses, but when they did, most followed a similar pattern.

"Everyone almost always puts the bulk of their defenses up the middle. And there was no way I was going to let someone else have all our fun."

120.

Though he was braced for attack, the light from around the corner wasn't coming from any sort of cannon, bomb, or even menacing robot. That would have made sense. No, what Titan found awaiting him as he headed down this new bend of the hall was far stranger than a mere defense mechanism. It was a catwalk, half-rusted steel stretched out over a deep hole before several elevators. He tested the metal carefully, expecting it to give way under his sizable weight, but found it didn't even wobble. Looking closer, Titan realized that while the initial structure had aged poorly, new parts had been rotated in to secure everything in place.

With each step, he waited, sure something from the dark chasm beneath his feet, where elevator rails went deeper than he could make out, would come leaping up to attack him. Yet his movement was greeted only by the barely-audible echoes of what sounded like some sort of distant activity.

"Dispatch, put me in everyone's ear," Titan said. Without bothering to wait for confirmation he continued, "Deadlift, you can go ahead and follow me in, just be careful. I could be wrong, but I'm pretty sure I walked into the top floor of a mining operation."

"Oh please don't tell me this whole thing was just Old Man Caruthers digging for diamonds and trying to throw people off the scent," Aether sighed. "If we unmask a *Scooby Doo* villain after all that destruction I'm going to be so pissed."

"Just throwing out a guess, but they might have been digging for ore," Jeremiah said. "They probably dug out as much as they could and bought up the rest on the down low. Robots take metal, and unless you've got access to a really gifted Super, metal doesn't make itself."

"That would have to be a lot of ore," Gale told them. From her side of the mic, Titan thought he could pick up the muffled sounds of wind and a small explosion. "Also, I met a welcoming committee. Not many of them yet, but stay on guard."

"Yeah, be glad you're not with us." Aether's voice was full of something that was not quite awe but certainly a sense of being impressed. "We found the factory section that's churning those bots out. Things are up and running, though most of them are incomplete. I think they sent every bot they had out after us today."

"Well, almost." Jeremiah's tone was about as close to worried as Titan had heard it since the giant mechs dropped from the sky. "I found what appear to be spare parts for a pretty sizable bot that doesn't look like anything we've fought so far. Smart money says this place has a watchdog that was left behind."

Titan heard the sound of footsteps on the catwalk and swung around, ready to beat back whatever mechanical guardian had been sent to stop him. Instead, he found Deadlift, who took a very healthy step back even though he was well out of punching range.

"Sorry," Titan mumbled, forcing himself to relax. "I'm a little on edge."

"And why wouldn't you be? We're just poking around a hidden, massive robot factory, standing atop a patchwork walkway over what sure looks like an infinite hole to nowhere." Deadlift took a careful peek over the side, then immediately pulled himself back to the center of the catwalk. "Okay, seriously, how in the hell did a place like this get built under our noses?"

"From the looks of most of the stuff here, I think it was made a long time ago," Jeremiah told them. "A lot of this equipment is crazy high-tech, but everything non-essential is still rusty and broken. This place might have been built back before Brewster was ever much of a metropolis. Old lair of a criminal who either went to jail or was buried is my guess, probably found by someone who didn't mind a fixer-upper."

"Not the first opportunistic squatter I've had to oust," Gale said. "When this is over, we probably need to catalogue this place and see what all is here. If it was a villain's lair, there might be useful files or documents."

"Hey, don't go stealing my lines. I don't run around kicking the shit out of bad guys from midair," Jeremiah replied.

Titan ignored them, not because he disagreed, but because his focus for the moment was on making it across the rest of the catwalk. Near the middle, things had gotten a bit shakier, and while the catwalk continued to hold his weight, Titan again found himself looking down to the empty gulf of darkness at his feet and wondering how long it would take him to climb back up. More importantly, he tried to figure out how he'd save Deadlift if the metal floor did give way.

Mercifully, he didn't need to think up an answer, as they both eventually made it all the way to the end of the catwalk and set foot back on the shiny silver ground. Titan continued forward until he reached a fork in the path. He began down the right side, holding up his hand so Deadlift would wait. Within a minute he could feel the heat coming from up ahead. If they were mining ore then they'd need a forge, and while it was possible his prey was hiding in there, Titan found it highly unlikely. This much heat from this far off meant the temperature in the forge was more than any human without enhanced endurance could comfortably withstand. It was possible, true, but his gut said to check the other branch first before going after long shots.

Backtracking to Deadlift, Titan headed down the left path, which after a minute proved to be absent of the wall of heat. He called for Deadlift to follow, who did so at a safe distance. They wound their way deeper into the hidden base, passing a few dusty workstations that had held up surprisingly well and one ancient computer that looked like it weighed more than the desk it was sitting on. Along the way they got progress reports from the others, who were encountering similar findings.

One thing worried Titan as they made their way farther through the halls: the others were dealing with patrols. Never too many and none so strong that they weren't easily handled, but still, the other Heroes were fighting robots. Meanwhile, he and Deadlift continued to encounter a whole lot of nothing. It was unnerving, all the more so because Titan had thought this would be the most perilous path. Why was this one seemingly undefended?

As it turned out, the answer to that question was waiting for him a few turns further down the hallway. In one angled step, Titan left the ubiquitous shiny hallway and entered a massive room with a dome-shaped ceiling. From the number of shattered chairs and retro couches, Titan guessed that once upon a time this had been some sort of break or social room. That was long since passed, though. Standing amidst the wreckage that it must have created while opening up the area was a nine-foot-tall robot unlike any that Titan had seen before. Thick limbs, glass eyes pulsing with green light, and all manner of small devices adorned the various nooks and crannies of its body.

Titan didn't even bother to turn; he trusted that Deadlift would take one look at the situation and know to stay back. This thing wasn't like the smaller robots. This was something special, maybe even a new model, a sneak preview at what would have come with the next encounter.

"Hey guys," Titan said, moving carefully into the large room. "Got a hunch that I found the watchdog."

As his foot crossed from the hallway over the room's threshold, the robot bolted forward. That, Titan had been expecting. What came next, however, took him by surprise. Its unwavering gaze stayed trained on him as its mouth parted and a thick, electronic voice echoed around them.

"*You!*"

121.

Of all the things Titan had seen the robots do since their arrival in Brewster, talking had never been among their bag of tricks. Hearing the robot angrily yell at him in recognition was enough to take even Titan by surprise, which was why he was a few seconds slow in raising his arm to stop the giant metal fist surging toward him. He managed a half-block, not that it made much difference. The blow sent him spiraling through the air until he crashed into a nearby wall, leaving a sizable dent in the dense material.

If its talking had been a surprise, then the robot moving him was an outright shocker. True, he hadn't been properly braced for the attack, but he still should have been able to compensate for such a strike. It hadn't even felt that strong, really, at least not compared to attacks from some of the more powerful Supers he'd brought down through the years. Yet he'd gone sailing like he was still fresh out of the HCP, and that was no small feat for anyone to accomplish.

"Do we know each other?" Titan asked, hurriedly rising to his feet and getting into a proper fighting stance. A surprise attack was one thing, but he'd be damned if he let this metal bastard toss him around so easily again.

"I know you. Ever since you appeared, the game has been tilted. You are an unbalanced resource and must be removed from the board. Father searched the enemy archives for every bit of data and video about you, Titan. Then he gave me strength and knowledge so that I could destroy you." Again, the robot charged, not even missing a syllable in its rant as it dashed across the floor. Another punch flew, this one on track for Titan's head, but the metal opponent no longer had the advantage of surprise.

Titan grabbed the fist as it drew near him, spinning the arm over his shoulder as he aimed to throw the robot into the wall. It tried to counter instantly, showing that perhaps the speech about knowing his moves hadn't been a bluff. Unfortunately for it, every counter it attempted relied on taking control of the movement or breaking Titan's grip, and the strength difference between them was just too much for it to overcome.

A loud cracking filled the air as the robot's torso smashed into the wall, eclipsing Titan's dent with one of its own. Rather than lie there or try and break the firm grip Titan still had on its arm, the robot kicked its legs against the wall. It was a small motion, and at its current angle leverage was almost impossible, which was why Titan was all the more shocked as they both went spinning through the air. In his moment of confusion, the arm in his clutches slipped away, and they both landed on the ground several feet apart.

"You've got one of those gravity distortion things," Titan said, understanding finally setting in. "That's how you sent me flying before."

"One of the many tools I was equipped with to bring you down." The robot couldn't smile; its facial features weren't constructed in such a way to accommodate expressions. All the same, Titan could swear there was something like a grin on its face as he watched the indentation of his handprint on its arm slowly undent. Great; this one had the self-repair capacity, too.

"You are an improper variable, Titan. The abilities you possess alone are imbalanced, but far worse is the effect you have on other enemy resources. Small threats became larger and non-threats became tremendously unbalanced assets in their own right. The common link at the scenes was you. You can sway the tide of engagements, and so I was made especially to counteract your presence."

"Yeah? They should have put more pistons in your arms then; I can barely even feel your attacks," Titan replied. Something wasn't sitting easy with him. This robot had to know that in terms of power, it was massively inferior to him. Yet it didn't seem rattled in the slightest. If anything, it was cocky. That was strange enough: who built dickishness into a simulated personality? But obviously there was some hidden card yet to be played, and the robot seemed to think it would turn things around.

"Not even with all the resources Father collected was he able to fashion a creature to match your strength," the robot agreed. "But not every engagement needs to be won by force. And not every punch is just a punch."

His feet were off the floor before he had a chance to so much as grab for the ground, not that it would have helped. As he rose rapidly into the air, Titan groped and spun, trying to wriggle free of whatever force was holding him captive. The trouble was that there didn't seem to be anything to fight against. It was like the strings keeping him anchored to the ground had been cut, and now he was just drifting in place with no method of moving forward.

"Though this last engagement was lost, Father gained a tremendous amount of data in the battles. I am the first of the next line. Rushed and imperfect though I may be, I was still gifted with the newest innovations Father could conceive of. He was inspired by the way you all crawled about in his mighty destroyer units, so he began producing insect-sized units that easily could be planted on an enemy. Normally, they would burrow into the skin, destroying the resource from the inside out. In your case, however, they serve as precise targeting locations, allowing the room's gravity distorter to manipulate your local field just perfectly enough to remove you from the battle."

Titan whipped his gaze around and caught sight of a small, ant-sized speck of metal as it moved between the burned away sections of his shirt. As he did, he took notice of the room again, this time with fresh eyes. He'd assumed the disarray of broken furniture had been cleared from the room's center for a slug-fest; now he understood the real purpose. The robot had taken away anything with which he might grab and use to navigate. This room, too, with its high domed ceiling had probably been selected for the task. Even the robot's appearance, bulky and muscular, had been meant to lure him in with melee expectations. The whole thing was a giant trap, and he'd stepped right into it like a damn rookie.

"So, what now?" Titan asked. His mind worked furiously as he tried to figure out what to do next. The projectiles he kept for such occasions were in a compartment on his belt, but with how resilient these robots were, there was no guarantee that even a perfect throw would take his opponent down. He needed to think of something, and soon. "You going to use me as a punching bag until you build up enough strength to do some damage? If you're supposed to destroy me, this is a pretty piss-poor job of it."

"Oh, have no fear; there are new weapons Father wants to test. You'll make an excellent guinea pig. But that comes later. And as for destroying you, a captured enemy asset is a neutralized asset. That will do until a permanent solution can be found. In the meantime, we both know you're not the only enemy who is attempting to assail Father's base." The robot turned, looking down the hallway where Deadlift would be, still waiting on a signal from Titan to move forward.

"I'll handle you after I'm done neutralizing the rest of your fellow assets."

122.

Despite his initial impulse, Titan forced himself to stay calm as he watched the robot head toward the hallway. Getting angry, while useful in the right moments of battle, did jackshit to aid clear thinking. Stepping into this trap was bad enough; he couldn't afford to stay snared while that bastard went after the other Supers. In terms of power alone, they were probably better than the bot, but the way it had been so perfectly equipped to deal with him left Titan fearful that he wasn't the only one it knew how to stop. Especially separated as they were, it might just manage to get the upper hand. Even if it succeeded once, that was too many times. He had to think of something, fast, to keep the damn robot's attention on him.

Yanking free one of his projectiles, Titan let the steel ball fly directly into the metal back. It pierced the surface cleanly—so cleanly that Titan realized he'd put more power into the throw than intended—before bursting out the other side and slamming into the ground. The robot, now with a small hole running through its body, turned to look at Titan yet remained silent.

"I didn't think we were done having our match," Titan said, another orb dancing along in the palm of his hand.

"A quaint notion. My brothers might have fallen for that, prioritizing the immediate threat over what seem to be secondary ones. But today you showed Father that we are weakened if we rely on his instructions alone. I was made greater, smarter, closer to his image. And I know a petty attempt at distraction when I see it. You are neutralized, Titan. Accept it gracefully, as a good resource should."

"For someone who's so smart, you don't seem to know shit about how comms work." That voice came from neither Titan nor the robot, but rather from Deadlift, who had darted around the corner. Over his head was a massive bucket, so large it must have been scraping the hallway's ceiling, securely nestled inside a dense section of metal at least three feet thick. Even a normal strongman would have struggled with the load, or at least been slowed by it, but Deadlift moved as if it weighed no more than a thought, which for him it likely didn't.

"The asset known as Deadlift. High strength capacity observed but minimal ability to withstand damage," the robot said. Its left hand began to glow with an ominous green light, one that Titan had no doubt would cut through the younger Hero just like Jeremiah in the ravine except, obviously, that Deadlift didn't have any healing powers. "Permanent neutralization will be-"

Whatever the robot's opinions on neutralization might have been, they went unheard as Deadlift swung his bucket forward. While the metal shit-talker was no doubt expecting some sort of solid mass, Titan's vantage point afforded him a peek inside the container to the red hot liquid bubbling within. Deadlift had raided the forge, which explained why there was a massive container between his hands and bucket. He swung his weapon and a golden-red liquid sprayed through the air in a wave of molten destruction.

Moving with appropriately inhuman speed, the robot darted to the side, getting clear of the fiery goop before it had entirely left the bucket. Their opponent came up with its arm raised, a muzzle sliding out from between its ring and middle finger as the whole hand restructured itself into a ranged weapon. Taking aim, it again almost looked like it was smiling just before it squeezed off the shot.

"You missed," it declared, and fired on Deadlift.

The beam of energy, no doubt meant to tear flesh and organs apart down to their very molecules, failed to pierce its target. This was not the fault of the robot's aim or the gun's firing. Rather, it was because a massive slab of muscular torso, still coated in burning hot metal, raced forward and put itself between the beam and Deadlift.

"No, he didn't." Titan could actually feel the heat from the molten liquid as it dripped down his skin, which spoke volumes to just how hot it really was. Deadlift hadn't managed to coat Titan completely in the stuff, but he'd gotten good coverage: enough to instantly kill a large number of those damn tiny robots crawling on Titan's skin while the residual heat cooked the rest. With no mini-bots to target, the gravity field couldn't lock on, and Titan was once again a free man.

"Thanks for the assist," he said, never daring to take his eyes off the robot, who still had a gun trained on him.

"I might be a rookie, but I still know enough to listen in for a teammate having a tough time," Deadlift replied.

"I can see that. Now why don't you slip back into the hallway real quick? This is about to get nasty, and I don't want any collateral damage."

Titan darted forward, well-aware that Deadlift would need a distraction to get clear. That was something he was happy to provide, as all the anger he'd been keeping at bay finally had an outlet, and it was the momentarily-befuddled mechanical bastard right in front of him.

The robot opened its mouth, probably to make a quip, but Titan didn't bother listening. It had been too long, he'd gotten used to working as a corpie, there were all manner of excuses he could make for himself about why he'd fallen into such a simple trap. None of them would have mattered, though. Not if he let his fellow Heroes pay the price for his mistake. Thanks to Deadlift, he'd gotten a second chance. As a man who knew how rare those were, Titan had no inclination to waste it.

His first punch shattered the bot's left arm, the one it had used to try and kill his friend. As he attacked, the robot tried to throw more of the mini-bots on him. The smelted liquid was still burning strong though, and they dissolved as soon as they made contact. The heat was adding something extra to his punches as well, flecks of molten metal spraying onto the robot and sizzling atop its exterior. The left arm was scrap in seconds, smashed apart with extra blows to ensure it couldn't be put back together.

"This is improper!" The robot was backpedaling, trying to put distance between itself and the rampaging Titan. "You are an imbalanced resource! That asset shouldn't have even been here, let alone been skilled enough to aid you. You shouldn't exist."

"There are plenty of people who agree with you, go ahead and get in line." Titan kept after it, refusing to allow any chance for new plans to spring into the damn thing's head. This was how he should have attacked from the start. It wasn't his job to play with these things, taking his time and enjoying the fights. He was supposed to clear the path, no matter what lay ahead of him. Another strike, and this time the robot's right leg broke away, turned to shards under Titan's stomping feet.

A flash of red light filled the air as the robot fired from a gun on its right hand. The laser hit well, right in Titan's torso, but only succeeded in leaving a small red dot on his chest. That alone was pretty impressive, by Titan's standards, anyway.

Seeing its attack fail, his opponent attempted to flee, crawling away slowly with its remaining limbs.

"Why?" The cocky tone had faded; what remained was pleading, so close to human it nearly made Titan hesitate. Then he remembered the attempt to kill his teammate seconds ago, and he continued his pursuit. "Why do you exist?" the thing asked. "Why do you continue breaking the parameters?"

Another audible crunch as Titan wrecked the last leg. The right arm half-heartedly swung around to clock him, and he caught it effortlessly. The robot stared up at him, its last limb captured. Small compartments on its chest opened, deploying miniature bombs and laser blasts that bounced uselessly off Titan's looming body.

"Why won't you quit? Why won't you just *die*?"

"That's easy," Titan said, ripping the last arm free from the robot's body and wrapping his mighty hand around its dense head. "Because I haven't earned the right yet."

One tug and the head was clear of the torso. Less than a minute later, the body was reduced to scrap. Titan stood over it, waiting to see if enough remained to try and repair. Only when it remained still did he relax, turning the robot's head around in his hands as he looked at the destruction scattered throughout the room.

"When you die, it's over," Titan said, all too aware he was talking to a lifeless hunk of metal. "No more work or fear or responsibility. I don't deserve that kind of peace. Not until I make amends for all the things I've fucked up."

123.

It took some time for Deadlift and Titan to continue on, mostly because the latter paused to try and get as much molten liquid off his body as possible. As the material cooled it became easier—a few flexed muscles could shatter the hardened metal—but it still required a solid five minutes before Titan felt he'd wiped away enough to continue.

During that time, Deadlift said nothing, merely watching in amusement as the older Hero was annoyed by a substance that would have killed most people outright, Supers included.

"You really are indestructible, aren't you?" Deadlift noted as Titan finally stopped trying to clean himself off. "I had a hunch that stuff wasn't going to kill you. . . I mean, I've seen you take a lot of damage. . . but you didn't even lose a step. It could have just as easily been room-temperature water for how much it bothered you."

"No one is invincible, or indestructible, or unkillable," Titan replied automatically. "Not me, not people like Jeremiah, no one. Always keep that in mind. When Supers forget that, bad things happen. Sometimes they go out of control with power and need to be brought down. Sometimes they lose their nerve during a tough fight and innocent people die. No power is perfect. As someone who has spent a big chunk of his life training and fighting other Supers, I should know."

Titan looked around the room, noting that there was only one exit out aside from the hallway they'd entered through. With nowhere else to go, their path forward was obvious. As they began to leave, however, he noticed that Deadlift was keeping closer than before. It was tempting to chastise the rookie, but given that Deadlift had just saved him and possibly the rest of the team, Titan held his tongue. The kid had shown good judgment so far; if he wanted to stay closer then that was his call. For now.

"You know, I've gotten that speech from a lot of people, Dean Bishop key among them. Yet every time I see more of what you can do, I find myself wondering just how true it is. Maybe someone could have killed you when you were young and inexperienced, but now. . . I watched you lift a mech today, Titan. And shrug off who knows how many attacks. You're really going to stand there and tell me you've never once considered the possibility that you might be the exception to the rule?"

Without warning, Titan stopped walking. He turned to face Deadlift, all too aware that their comms were still on. That was fine, though. This was something the others should hear, just in case they ever needed the information.

"Strong as I am, Deadlift, I'm still vulnerable to things I haven't faced before. True, after years of Hero work that's a small category, but it's a big world with new Supers appearing all the time. And to answer your question, no, I've never thought myself invincible. Because I know how the DVA plans to kill me if I ever go out of control."

Lifting his hand, Titan delicately tapped the side of his temple three times. "There's a Super out in Kentucky with the power to manifest brain aneurisms. Never went Hero, since he didn't think his power was suited to protecting people, but sometimes the DVA taps him to bring down especially dangerous or troublesome criminals. Temporarily Authorized Hero Asset, same exception they used for Hexcellent and Eli. I've got no resistance to that ability, and I've never been called on a case to fight anyone with similar powers. That's how they'll kill me, if I ever go rogue."

"Holy Hell," Aether whispered over the comms. "They told you about this? Just gave you the name of your executioner in case ever you stepped foot out of line?"

"Actually, Titan was the one who suggested we keep the aforementioned Super on retainer, just in case." Dispatch was as calm as ever, slipping in only to correct a misassumption in the conversation and then going silent.

"Why would you do that?" Deadlift asked.

"Jeremiah, Gale, either of you want to field this one for me?" Titan asked.

"Because Heroes need to be aware of their mortality," Gale replied. "For those of us like me and Deadlift, because it keeps us smart and safe in dangerous situations. For those like Titan and Jeremiah, it keeps them grounded, reminds them that even *their* actions have consequences."

Deadlift stared at Titan with new eyes, though whether they were filled with respect or incredulity Titan didn't have time to puzzle out. He merely turned back around and continued walking down the mysterious hallway, idly wondering if he'd have to fight another of those talking robots. He hoped not; there was something about destroying an opponent who could have conversations that left a bad taste in Titan's mouth. AI was impossible, as far as the official records went, but that didn't mean it would stay that way forever.

"As an aside, the DVA probably has assets that Titan isn't aware of to tap, backups in case he decides to snuff out his failsafe in advance," Jeremiah added. "I've poked around enough to know they've got contingency plans for me, and I'm nowhere near as dangerous as he is. Well, not as immediately dangerous, anyway. Given a little time and research, I can be a real bastard in my own right."

"Yeah? Well, you need to get your bastard ass over to me," Gale said. "I could be wrong, but I think I just found what we're looking for."

Before he'd even realized he was moving, Titan's hands had already formed fists. All that destruction. All those people hurt or worse. If he was mad, then Gale must be outright murderous. They had to pray she'd found the computer rather than the Super, otherwise no one would be able to stop her if she decided to take revenge.

"Did you find the computer or the guy who built it?" Titan asked, unclenching his fists so that he could cross his fingers.

"Both, I think. It's. . . well, it's pretty damn weird if you want the truth." The anger Titan had noticed in her earlier seemed to be ebbing, replaced with confusion. "I'd love some second opinions, especially from those of you who actually know something about tech."

"Great idea, but how do we get to you?" Deadlift asked.

"Using the communicators for coordinates, I believe I can offer rudimentary directions to Gale's location," Dispatch offered. "I have been mapping the facility as your teams progressed, and there are several areas where I suspect paths intersect. In the event I am incorrect, the barriers between hallways would be easily overcome, be it by strength or intangibility."

"Oh good, so I might have to punch through walls in an underground lair with who knows how much rock overhead. Nothing to worry about there." Despite his grumbling, Titan trusted Dispatch's judgment; there was really no other option as a Hero. And if Gale really had found something interesting, he wanted to get there as soon as possible.

"All right, Dispatch, tell us where to go."

124.

"I'll be honest; I don't have the damnedest idea what I'm looking at here." Titan didn't particularly feel ashamed admitting that, both because he knew no one would be looking to him for technical expertise and because he had a solid hunch that he wasn't the only baffled one in the group.

Getting to Gale had been relatively painless. Dispatch's guesses were largely correct and Titan only had to punch carefully through one wall in order to keep him and Deadlift on the right path. Once they arrived, however, both strongmen immediately realized just how out of their depth they really were.

The contraption before them was massive, so tall it went halfway up the twenty-foot wall of this odd cavern, a mishmash of various electronics, lights, and devices that seemed to come from a half-dozen different technological periods. In the center was a modest-sized terminal with a dark screen directly adjacent to a large metal sphere with wires running all over the rest of the setup. It was the most striking point of the area in the first place, even without the corpse sitting in the chair.

"This is just a guess, mind you, but I'm going to say he's been dead for at least months, probably years," Aether announced. While Jeremiah was combing the wall of electronics, asking questions and getting unheard replies from the rest of his team, Aether had taken it upon herself to inspect the corpse hunched over in the chair. No one asked why she felt familiar enough with decomposing remains to inspect them, though most just chose to assume she had some medical background and leave it at that.

"No immediate wounds that I can see, which points toward natural causes, an internal attack like poison, or another Super. This place doesn't have any signs of a struggle, but with how much work has been done, that doesn't tell us anything for sure. We'll need an autopsy to get solid information, but based on pure speculation, my guess would be that this guy sat down to do some work and then fell over dead midway through. Could be the ticker, or the noggin, or any other number of things, but something gave out on him."

"You can tell that's a guy?" Deadlift asked; the parts of his face that were visible under his mask had paled noticeably as Aether looked over the corpse.

"Geez, it's like none of you bothered to take a biology class. Yeah, I can tell it's a guy. You want me to go into how?" Aether replied.

Deadlift shook his head adamantly to the negative. Aether didn't push the issue, which Titan appreciated. There was already so little of his costume left, the last thing he wanted was to get the remainder sprayed with vomit if Deadlift lost his stomach.

Fortunately, the line of discussion quickly fell through as Jeremiah clapped his hands from over by the console.

"All right, people, based on what my team can tell me through the comms, though we absolutely need to have a tech-Super come check this out, all accounts point to us having found the heart of the operation. This is the thing that's sending the signals, and most likely remotely handling all the mining and robot construction."

"Then let's tear it apart." Gale summoned the beginnings of a tornado so quickly that the end of her sentence was muffled.

Jeremiah repositioned himself quickly between the terminal and Gale, a move Titan would have deemed brave if he didn't know Jeremiah could heal from whatever wounds she inflicted.

"Yes, yes we could do that. Or we could just work on disconnecting it from all the remote operations until someone with tech-based abilities can come study it," Jeremiah suggested. "As horrible as the robot attacks were, this still represents a marvel of technology. Look at the things it's been creating, adapting, and improving, all without human interference. Hell, not half an hour ago it made a talking robot designed specifically to neutralize Titan, just based on the battles we had today. That is some astounding work, even more so now that we know there was no human behind the wheel."

"All the better reason to destroy it now before it builds a threat we can't handle." Gale hadn't dismissed her wind, a fact that escaped none of their attention. "Smart or not, this thing has been trying to wipe out us, and Brewster as a whole, for months."

Titan was moving before he'd even realized it, Gale's words stirring the memory of Hexcellent's theory. The truth of the matter was, he agreed with Gale. Maybe this thing was a technological marvel unlike anything the world had ever seen, but it was also dangerous. He'd been forced to bring down fellow humans who'd managed far less damage; a machine didn't get a pass for the carnage in its wake. Unless. . . it didn't know any better.

Before anyone could object, which they certainly would have, Titan moved the corpse away from the terminal, leaned over the ergonomic keyboard, and punched the space bar. For a long moment, nothing happened. Then, slowly, the dark screen began to flicker to life. At first, Titan didn't know what he was looking at; he'd never had much interest in the digital realm. Bit by bit, though, he puzzled together what he was seeing, and as it all clicked he shook his head in disbelief.

"I'll be damned. Hexcellent was right." Looking over his shoulder, he motioned for the others to come see the screen for themselves. "It's a game. A timed strategy or whatever. The map looks like Brewster, too. I think our dead programmer was playing it when he died, maybe trying to train the computer to do exactly what it did. Probably part one in a nefarious scheme where the rest was never hatched."

The rest of the group approached, taking in the display for themselves. It was all there, measured in bars and numbers that meant nothing to Titan. But some things were unmistakable: the map of Brewster, the six locations where the mechs had been deployed, even the little dots tracking the remaining Heroes that were helping secure damaged areas.

"Weird as this is, and I am definitely not saying it isn't strange, I don't see how it changes things," Gale told them. "This computer is still bent on wiping out our town. I say we carve it up now before it has a chance."

"Gale, with all respect, do you have any idea what we're looking at here?" Jeremiah asked. "This thing created its own troops, researched classified technology and stole it to improve them, adapted its designs and strategies based on how we reacted. . . it *learned*. I'm not the guy to say if something is or isn't artificial intelligence, but this has got to be the closest we've ever come as a species to creating it. You're talking about destroying one of the most incredible scientific achievements in history because some asshole left his game running."

"We've seen what it can do on accident. You really want to give someone the chance to use this thing on purpose?" Gale countered. "It's too strong, too dangerous. We have to destroy it now."

"You know, that's what a lot of humans said about Supers when they first learned about us." Aether's voice was quiet, yet strong enough to carry through the whole cavern. "Something having the potential to be dangerous isn't a good reason to kill it."

"It's not alive," Gale shot back.

"Are you sure? I mean, really sure? I heard the robot Titan fought, and it sounded pretty aware of what was going on. Misinformed, yes, but aware," Deadlift told her. "I'm not saying you're wrong. In fact, I'm on your side, Gale. This thing nearly murdered me and my team with its robots, and it wrecked my town. It deserves to be killed. I'm just making sure we all acknowledge that that's what we're talking about. Killing."

"Machines aren't alive." Gale didn't sound as sure as she had moments prior, but she still refused to back down from her point.

"Two in favor of wrecking it here and now, two against," Jeremiah summarized. "Titan, it looks like you're the deciding vote."

Slowly, Titan walked from the terminal over to the dense metal sphere. Even if he knew almost nothing about high-tech electronics, he'd set up enough lights and media centers in his day to understand that the device all the wires ran to was the most important part. It was the heart, or maybe the brain. Regardless, he was pretty sure that if he smashed it to pieces, that would be the end of their problems. Titan raised his hand over the device, only a few inches from the dark polished surface. It wouldn't take much, one good blow and it would all be over.

"I think," Titan said, slowly lowering his arm until his fingers rested against the smooth metal. "That everyone deserves a second chance. Potential artificial life included."

Epilogue

The restoration of Brewster would not be a quick process. Though the Heroes had performed admirably, containing the robotic threats and responding to unexpected challenges with speed and efficiency, the fact still remained that entire city blocks were rendered unlivable amidst the destruction. Within days, the DVA had set up temporary housing areas for those thrust from their homes. In a week, they'd brokered a deal between insurance companies and local hotels to get those impacted somewhere more stable. The first time a city was partially destroyed was a complete clusterfuck as everyone ran around, trying to figure out what to do. Nowadays, however, the DVA had the process down pat.

Not that their sole concern was taking care of the humans impacted by the disaster. One by one, every Hero in a command position at the scene was brought in for debriefing. While things could have been worse, it didn't change the fact that people had still died and millions of dollars in property damage had occurred. That was the sort of aftermath the DVA couldn't afford to shrug off and accept, meaning they went through the scenario with a fine-toothed comb, making certain that no Hero had acted rashly or used excessive force that might have exacerbated an already bad situation.

For his part, Owen's interview was mercifully brief. Though he had brought in a Temporarily Authorized Hero Asset and destroyed a mech with only one other Hero as backup, he'd also been careful to run things through Dispatch every chance he had. No one knew better than he that what the DVA wanted the most out of this was a scapegoat, someone or thing to point to as having failed. Their other option was telling the public that even with every Hero doing their job well, incidents like this could still happen. Although it was true, that wasn't the sort of truth that made for a happy populace. They needed their Heroes to be flawless, or to have the imperfect ones cast aside. But the DVA would have to search elsewhere for its sacrificial Super. Titan had played things careful and by the book, which Dispatch would back him up on.

Lenny was waiting for him as Owen left the meeting and immediately yanked off the blue tie that was too small for his thick, muscular neck. It looked all the more ridiculous atop his Titan costume, and Owen was glad to be rid of the idiotic formality. The short agent fell into line next to him as they walked over the polished stone floor of Brewster City Hall. The DVA had set up temporary offices during the research and recovery efforts, partially to be seen around town doing their duty, and partially because it wasn't cost-effective to fly or teleport every Hero they wanted to interview off to D.C.

Neither said a word until they were clear of the building, at which point Lenny lifted his bushy eyebrows upward and cast a scrutinizing glance at his client.

"Well?"

"I'm clear," Owen replied, what should have been cheer in his voice soured by the experience of telling his tale while a panel sifted through every detail, searching for fault. "Unless they find something way out of left field that I'm not even aware of, nothing will blow back on me."

"That is quite the relief." Lenny dug about in his pockets until he found a pair of sunglasses that were comfortable, if not terribly up-to-date with the newest fashions. Overhead, the afternoon Brewster sun beat down on them, warming the prominent bald spot on Lenny's exposed head. "Let me tell you, with all the orders we've got coming in for Titan merchandise, the last thing I needed is you to be under investigation."

"I can't imagine that much is really moving," Owen said.

"Are you kidding me? Between the classic Titan gear, the new stylized versions, and that little photo of you going on everything from shirts to mugs, we've got suppliers dealing with serious backorders, and that's *after* I told them to stock up."

Owen suppressed a groan at Lenny's mention of the picture, but only barely. Evidently, amidst the brave reporters who'd ventured near the chaos of the battle was one especially intrepid photographer. That young woman was likely now a superstar at her paper, as she'd captured dozens of incredible images of the action in progress. One had especially caught on with the public, though. It was a picture of Titan as he'd lifted the mech overhead to save Hexcellent, though neither she nor Hopcules were easily visible in the shot. Instead, it just looked like he was hauling the thing up from the ground because he could, and while he wasn't especially fond of the attention the picture was garnering, he did have to admit it was a pretty incredible image. If nothing else, the world seemed to have suddenly remembered that on top of every scandal and rumor surrounding him, Titan was one thing above all else: powerful.

"At least that will give me some spare cash while I get things up and running. Any word yet on Hexcellent's negotiations?" Owen asked.

Lenny nodded, yanking out the keys to his car and pressing a button to unlock the doors. "Word came down while you were inside. She's going to have to buy out Mordent's contract with her for the name and advertising rights to the Hexcellent brand and her original summons."

"Those mother fuckers." Owen spat the words, although he'd known going in that she was facing a tough battle.

"Hey, let me finish, all right?" Lenny and Owen both slipped into Lenny's car. The passenger seat was already moved all the way back to somewhat accommodate Owen's mighty frame. "She has to buy out the contract on all that, but the good news is she should have plenty of cash to do it with. Mordent only locked down the summons she had when she signed on, since no one expected her to be pulling out any new ones. They tried to pull some crap about Hopcules being preexisting, but in this case the contract fucked 'em, since it outlined exactly what summons she had and their characteristics. Probably thought they were being slick by pinning her property down. Anyway, I tore that to shreds, and the arbiter agreed. Hexcellent has complete ownership of the Hopcules property and merchandising rights associated with it. Which, let me tell you, just from pre-orders looks like it will be more than enough to handle the Mordent contract."

"Good." Owen watched as Brewster City Hall faded into the distance and they began their trek to the next destination. "And I know I've said it before, but thanks for handling that."

"Consider it a personal pleasure," Lenny replied. "That Greene prick was fun to beat. Plus, it seems like I built up a little goodwill in the PEERS community. Already had three of the bigger names approach me about representation after they heard I'd taken on Bubble Bubble as a client."

"The legendary Lenny, working with someone other than Heroes? Turn the car around, we need to go find some reporters and alert them to the news," Owen said.

"There is always room at my table for anyone who earns," Lenny replied, not a trace of shame in his voice. "So, where can I drop you?"

"Mordent Holdings' central office," Owen replied. "While I was in there, I got some news of my own, and I shouldn't wait to share it with my team."

"Well well well, look who it is: the conquering Hero, come to pay us little people a visit?"

Despite the seemingly harsh words, Hexcellent barreled through the room and wrapped Owen in a giant hug as he entered the penthouse. In the chaos and fallout of the last week, he and the PEERS team had barely gotten to see one another. Except, of course, for when he stopped by to make the big announcement. They'd taken it well, all things considered. Deep down, he had a feeling they knew as much as he did that it was inevitable.

"I'll have to speak to Greene about updating security. We can't have any Tom, Dick, and Harry just wandering in here when they please." Topsy hauled himself up from a chair in the kitchen and walked over, giving Owen's hand a good shake. "It's only been three days; did you need to check up on me already?"

"Maybe I came by to see if you needed advice," Owen replied. "Hero Liaison isn't the world's easiest job."

"Oh, I'm aware of that. We've been working nonstop with cleanup and rescue efforts. It's enough to have an old Hero feel like he's making a difference again." Topsy released his grip as Galvanize, Zone, and Bubble Bubble all made their way over to greet and talk with their former Hero Liaison. There was no ill-will in the separation; they'd understood that he needed to be in a place where he could do the most with his abilities. Plus, Owen had left them in the most capable hands he knew of.

"What brings you by?" Galvanize asked, getting to the root of the visit as only a team leader could. "Don't get me wrong, I'm glad to see you, but I assumed you'd be crazy busy getting everything up and running."

"You're not wrong," Owen agreed. "But in the rush of handing things over to Topsy, there were a few items I left unfinished. Can't very well go starting a new chapter in my life without wrapping up the old, now can I?"

"Uh oh, is this where you demand a match against all of us to see how much we've grown or something?" Bubble Bubble asked.

"No," Owen replied. "This is where I give you each a proper goodbye. And I think you're the best one to start with." Owen scooped the pale, copper-haired woman up in a big bear hug, eliciting a squeal of surprised joy from the once-always-stoic Super. "I'm going to miss you, kid. Don't go back into that shell of yours 'cause I'm not on the team anymore, either. I'll be just down the road, and I can stop by anytime I want if needed. Also, try and keep away from dating directors."

"See, now where was that advice when I needed it?" Bubble Bubble asked, still grinning as Owen set her on the floor. Her expression grew confused as he produced a white card from his pocket and held it out to her, however. "What's this?"

"Parting gift, albeit a joint one. Lenny and I pulled some strings to set you up with a new image consultant. Given the ground work you laid during the director fiasco, and the eyes on the team after the attack, we thought it was time get you set up with someone who could help you sell the real you, not just whatever image some brand was pitching. Ludwig is among the best in the business."

Tentatively, she reached forward and plucked the card from his hand. "You're sure I can trust him?"

"Lenny says the guy is solid, and I trust Lenny with my life. More than that, I'd trust him with my family's lives. Nothing is guaranteed, but if it goes south then just let him or me know and we'll handle it," Owen assured her.

That done, he turned to Zone, who was actually looking at him rather than glaring, which was a marked improvement from when he'd first arrived.

"You still don't really like me, do you?"

"I'm not a fan of a lot of the choices you've made," Zone replied, his tone honest yet lacking any venom. "But it seems like you're trying to do your best to make amends. I can respect that much, at least. Just don't slack off. People are looking at you again. I hope you show them something worth seeing." Slowly, Zone extended his hand, and Owen accepted it. They were never going to be as close as he was with the others and both knew that. They'd reached a place of peace and mutual respect, though, and that counted for quite a bit in Owen's book.

"Thank you, Zone. I genuinely appreciate that. And I have something for you, though it won't arrive until later this week. I called in some old favors and there's going to be a healer dropping by. I think you've got a few good years left in you, so I want to get those knees taken care of," Owen said.

"That's a nice gesture, but healers can't fix the accumulated wear and tear I put on my body; they just treat immediate injuries. Trust me, I looked into it."

"Actually, that's only true of *most* healers," Topsy interjected. "If Titan is talking about the man I'm guessing, then he'll have no trouble patching you up. Your knees— all of you, really—will be good as new."

591

"And I want to give you this," Owen added, pulling another card from his pocket before Zone could really wrap his head around what Topsy had said. When the reality of what Owen had given him truly sank in, it would likely be an emotional moment. Zone deserved the right to have that in private, if he so chose. "It's a phone number where I can be reached, set to route through the DVA to reach me wherever I am. But it isn't actually for you. It's for your brother. Anytime he wants to talk, get some perspective, or even ask questions about what it takes to get into the Hero game, he can call me. If I can jump in this late in life, maybe he can too."

Wordlessly, still reeling from the implication that his knees would be fixed, Zone accepted the card and held it between his fingers like it was made of glass. Owen turned away, letting Zone have space to process everything, and moving on to the leader of a team Owen had grown to respect immeasurably over the last few months.

"I really hope you didn't get me anything," Galvanize said, speaking before Owen had a chance. "It was gift enough having you on my team. Titan, you being around brought us all closer together, not to mention put us in the national spotlight more than once. You made my team better, and that's all any PEERS leader could ask for."

"Shit, kid, you really know how to steal someone's thunder," Owen told him. "As it happens, I don't have a parting gift for you, but the DVA does. After seeing how much you helped during the attack, they want to put you on retainer for work as a Temporarily Authorized Hero Asset when the occasion is needed. The pay rate is decent, but more importantly, it should make sure you and your team keep getting the media exposure, even after the shitshow known as Titan is gone."

Owen paused, taking in the younger man who'd shown such cool, smart judgment every step of the way in their time working together. Had he come onto another team with a different leader, this journey could have taken some very different turns. In a lot of ways, Owen owed more to Galvanize than anyone else, perhaps even Lenny. It was a debt he'd never really be able to clear, not that he wouldn't try. Working toward the impossible was becoming an oddly-familiar goal in his new life.

"I also want to say thanks. You made room for an out-of-practice Hero that was a media pariah and walked in thinking he was better than the job. In my years, I worked with a lot of folks who do incredible things. Still, you may be one of the most impressive people I've ever known, and being a Super has nothing to do with it."

Owen and Galvanize shook hands one last time before Owen turned again. Though Hexcellent was next in line, he moved past her, meeting eyes with Topsy and pulling a folded set of pages from his back pocket.

"Parting gift for you, something to help round out the team," Owen told his old friend.

Topsy accepted the pages and flipped through them, a look of cautious skepticism slowly appearing on his face. "You want me to recruit a criminal?"

"Eli's a decent kid with a very useful power," Owen replied. "Given his willingness to help me on the bridge the night he was arrested, and his cooperation during the robot attack, the DVA is considering letting him do community service as a PEERS to pay his debt to society. He'd need a Hero to take custody of him, though. Talk it over with Galvanize; see if you think he's a good fit. I've got faith that whatever you two land on, it will be the right choice."

That done, Owen finally faced Hexcellent once more. Though he'd bonded with the whole team to one extent or another, there was no denying that he and the tattooed young Super with dyed black hair had forged an especially close connection. Looking at her now, Owen found himself a bit regretful that his life had fallen apart before he managed to bring a daughter into the world. Of all the things he regretted from his years living a lie, his children were absolutely not among them.

"I know I already got my present," Hexcellent said, preempting the announcement. "Lenny helping me negotiate ownership of my own image and summons was more than enough."

"Well, you're right and you're wrong," Owen told her. "That was the goodbye present, but there's also something else for you. If you're willing, why don't you and I go for a ride?"

*   *   *

From their vantage point, Hexcellent could just make out several people floating in the air, some in costumes and others wearing practical outfits designed for work. She and Owen were a ways off from the ravine with its secret base, which was the talk of Brewster as countless brave reporters tried to sneak close enough for a scoop only to be found and turned away. The official story on what had been found there was minimal, though that didn't stop all manner of rumor from swirling about.

"Show me what you've got." Owen stood near her, eyes never wavering as he waited for the demonstration to begin.

"Can I have a minute? My stomach is still fucking churning from that trip." Hexcellent had been surprised to discover that Owen's version of a 'ride' was running through town at top speed while she clung to his back for dear life.

Though he'd kept a careful grip on her legs at all times, it hadn't made the journey any less terrifying. Or nauseating, for that matter.

"No one gives you time in the field. You have to be able to work under all sorts of conditions," Owen told her.

Hexcellent let out a few choice swears under her breath, but she also closed her eyes to focus. This was harder than her usual summons, the ones that sat so close to the top of her mind, bound to the milestones in her life that had shaped who she was. For this one, she had to go deeper, past the woman she'd become to the child she'd started out as. In a lot of ways, it was like distilling everything about her down to the purest, most innocent form. That was where her true guardian dwelled.

A pop filled the air, and next to Hexcellent stood a three-foot-tall rabbit on its hind legs, wearing a colorful suit of armor. It looked from her to Owen several times, then leaned its head against the summoner's leg in a nuzzling motion.

"Damn, that is beyond adorable." Owen shook his head; he couldn't even imagine how many of these things would be on the shelves come next Christmas, to say nothing of the more intimidating versions still showing up on news reports. "Not quite as potent, though."

"Yeah, well, I'm not really all that scared right now, am I?" Hexcellent countered. "I talked to some of those DVA guys and the Heroes who debriefed me: the running theory is that he came out so strong because I was fuckall terrified. No threat means he's the old-fashioned fluffy version."

"That's what I'd heard too," Owen said. Determining a Super's abilities was often a game of elimination, creating and discarding theories until one finally seemed to fit. In Hexcellent's case, they'd had very little to go on and an inversely large motivation to understand what made her summon tick. An adaptive rabbit that could grow twenty-stories-tall when the need arose wasn't the sort of power they'd want to let run loose without knowing how it worked.

"Kind of too bad, when you think about it." Owen sat down in the grass, watching the floating Supers in the distance as they ensured none of the workers in the ravine were disturbed. "With the PEERS gig, the fluffy guy won't have too many chances to really flex his stuff. Only so much call for an unstoppable bunny in rescue work."

"Never know, the little bastard might find his time to shine." Hexcellent rubbed Hopcules between the ears as she also took a seat on the ground. It was nice: out here away from the city's center, she could almost forget about all the destruction and work that awaited them back in Brewster. "And even if he doesn't, at least we got one hell of a chance to live the dream. Thanks for that, by the way. I never thought I'd actually get to play Hero, but because of you, I did. Even if it was just for an hour, that time meant more to me than I ever realized it would."

"Glad to hear that," Owen said. "Because if you're up to the challenge, you might be able to have that experience again." Reaching into his back pocket, he pulled forth the last of his documents and handed it to Hexcellent, who unfolded the page and began slowly reading.

Owen was silent as she absorbed the words; something like this might take a few minutes to wrap her head around. That was why he'd taken her out here, where the world was more peaceful. That, and in case Hopcules had come out in his big form once more.

"I don't understand," Hexcellent finally said. "I mean, I know this is an acceptance letter, but. . . I didn't even apply."

"The dean of Sizemore and I are on good terms," Owen explained. "We sat down and had a long talk about you. About your past, about you cleaning yourself up and giving back to the community, about who you were under the makeup. Dean Jackson is a hard man with some patience issues, but he's also the type who believes people can change. With my recommendation, he agreed to accept you into next year's freshman HCP class. That's why I gave Topsy the folder on Eli, so he can serve as a potential replacement. The spot in Sizemore is yours, if you want it."

The paper in her hands was shaking, and wordlessly Hopcules wrapped his furry arms around Hexcellent's torso. "You're serious? This. . . this is real? I can be a Hero?"

"That's up to you," Owen said. "Getting in the HCP is a lot easier than staying there, and few Supers ever reach graduation. Make no mistake, you'll have to prove that you belong there every day, or you'll be cast out like so many before you. But if you can do the near-impossible, then yes, Hexcellent. You can be a Hero one day. This time, for real."

She was hugging him before he even noticed her move, tears running across his shirt where Hexcellent's face was pressed into his shoulder. For once, this was a costume cleaning that he wouldn't complain about.

"Titan. . . thank you so much. There's no way I can really do this though, is there? I'm already past college age, and my face is all over the place in advertisements. Even I know Heroes have to keep their identity secret."

Gently, noting the wary eyes of Hopcules, Owen rested his hand on top of her ink-black hair. "You only have to keep it secret as a student; after that it's a choice. Don't worry about your age either; lots of people do college later in life. Hell, if anything it makes you less likely to be suspected of being in the

HCP. As for the face, as long as you cut back on the makeup, switch hair-dyes, and cover the tattoos, I think you'll be unrecognizable. No one is going to hunt that hard for a corpie that left her team."

"Except that I summoned a giant rabbit that half the town is talking about," Hexcellent reminded him.

"About that: you may have noticed that the rabbit is all they're talking about. No one got a good picture of the woman riding its shoulder, and the DVA is holding back that information pending your acceptance. So far as the world is concerned, Hexcellent was just the goth PEERS that summoned demons. The only people who know the truth are Mordent, who are too smart to break a DVA gag order, other Heroes, and your teammates. If you want, we can let the news out. You'll probably be the most popular PEERS in the country overnight. Or the DVA can designate the situation as classified, and you become a nobody freshman in the HCP next fall and tackle the PEERS past if you make graduation. It's all up to you, Hexcellent."

"Hannah." Slowly, she lifted her head from his shoulder, though the tears were still falling freely. Her dark makeup was streaked and smudged, already fading to show the woman who dwelled underneath. "Can't very well go by my old corpie name at school, now can I?"

"No, I suppose not." Owen leaned forward a bit, meeting the glassy-eyed stare of her guardian rabbit. "You and the others are going to need to take care of her from this point on. She'll be plenty scared more than once working through the Hero Certification Program."

Hopcules nodded, and though it might have been Owen's imagination, he thought he saw the barest traces of claws peeking out from Hopcules's fuzzy fingers.

"Good rabbit."

*　　*　　*

Once she'd regained her composure, Owen dropped Hexcellent, Hannah, off at the hotel lobby where an older, seemingly-innocuous man was waiting to discuss the details of her enrollment. Dean Jackson would bring her the rest of the way up to speed, making sure she truly understood what she was facing if she chose to attend Sizemore. He'd probably try to scare her off, at least a bit, as the program had little time to waste with those that couldn't handle the harsh reality of what they were undertaking. The effort would fail, though, of that Owen had zero doubt. He'd seen the bravery and determination in that girl's soul. Now that she had a real shot at her dream, nothing would make her turn away.

With his former team seen to, the time had come for Owen to look ahead.

Bounding through town, he ran to the abandoned district where the team once known as the Wild Bucks made their home. Juiced and Kaiju were both in the gym area, working hard just as they had been when he last saw them. Neither had been seriously injured in the battle with the robots, though both had seen the limits of their abilities more than once. For some Supers, not being powerful enough when it counted destroyed them, shook their confidence and drove them away from future confrontations. Heroes, however, were made of sterner stuff. At least, the ones Owen respected were. When they failed, it lit a fire under them to become better, stronger, more capable for the next time around. And it reminded them that no Super was unstoppable alone. Trusting their team was more important than any individual ability.

Sometimes, even Owen needed to be reminded of that.

Deadlift was in the makeshift office, reviewing documents. He glanced up at the massive form of Owen as it entered, shaking his head in annoyance. "You sure you don't want to take over the leadership position here? I figured when you asked to join I'd at least be free of the paperwork. I mean, you are the most experienced Hero on the team."

"And with experience comes wisdom, such as knowing that being a leader means having to deal with the boring crap like paperwork," Owen countered. "Besides, I think you've got this well in hand. I'm good at hitting stuff; you handle things like tactics and planning."

Although there had been no shortage of teams offering Titan spots when the robot battle dust settled, Owen had decided to throw in with Deadlift and his crew. In part it was because he needed someone he trusted looking after the PEERS, and Topsy wouldn't budge until his people were taken care of. But more than that, Owen wanted to be there because he knew how precarious their position still was. This was a team that deserved to exist, and if his presence could help them stay afloat, then it was a worthwhile endeavor. Besides, there was something he just liked about being back in these barebones quarters; it reminded him of his early days, before the press and the merchandising and the attention. Back when it was all about the job and the people in the trenches with him.

"Well, the good news is that we just got word from the DVA, and the name change is officially approved," Deadlift told him, setting down a crisp page atop his desk. "All it needs is your signature. But I do have to ask, for the umpteenth time, are you really okay with letting us have this? It's a strong legacy, and I hate the idea that we might tarnish it."

Owen leaned forward, grabbing the paper and a pen that that seemed downright dainty in his oversized hand and scrawling "Titan" across the blanks

Deadlift had marked. "Maybe we'll drag the name down; maybe we'll raise it to new heights. Doesn't matter either way. It wasn't doing anyone any good just sitting there in the history books. But you all had to chuck the Wild Bucks; that was a reputation that needed to be abandoned. If your lot wants to resurrect this antique, I'm not going to be the one to stop you."

With a final signature, Owen pushed the page back over to Deadlift, who examined it carefully. He doubled-checked each line to be sure everything was in order, just like a good leader should. Owen had high hopes for this kid, as well as for Juiced and Kaiju. That was why he'd refused to take over as head of the team. One day, Deadlift was going to an incredible Hero and a respected leader, but he needed experience to get there. Owen's job was to guide the next generation, not take over for them.

"As far as I can tell, this is all in order," Deadlift said. "Once I send a copy to the DVA, the Gentle Hammers will officially live again. I still can't believe you got all of the old team to sign off on letting us use the name, though."

"You do Hero work with someone long enough, there's not much you won't trust each other with," Owen replied. "And truth be told, I don't think any of them were happy with how that legacy ended, a bunch of people just drifting apart. Win, lose, or draw, at least this gives the Gentle Hammers a chance for a new ending."

"On that note, we're being tapped for patrol duty tonight," Deadlift told him. "There's been some increased crime and looting in the wrecked sections of town, so Heroes are being rotated around to keep the peace. So try to hurry back."

"Who said I was going anywhere?" Owen asked.

To that, Deadlift replied with a sarcastic laugh. "Come on, we both know you're only here checking in. In an hour you'll be out the door again, going to the same place you've spent every spare moment you could for the last week. Just be back by eight, our patrol run starts at nine."

"Yes, sir." Owen rose from his chair and snapped off a crisp salute. They both knew he'd be back by the deadline. This was his team, and when they went out, they'd do so with Titan to watch over them.

"Oh, and give Jeremiah my best," Deadlift called after him as Owen left the office.

*   *   *

Moving the massive device had been no small task, although having several Supers with tech-based abilities made it far easier. The biggest concern, of course, was that unplugging the wrong wire might do irreparable damage to a wholly unique piece of technology. Thanks to a lot of effort, portable generators, and more than one teleporter working in tandem, they'd managed to get the wall-sized computer out from the hidden lair and in to a privately-owned storage building, one carefully cut off from all wireless signals the computer might use to begin causing trouble again.

Owen had to surrender his cell phone as he entered the building, handing it off to a squad of DVA agents carefully guarding the door. They were there to handle the mundane stuff, ensuring that no one accidently brought high-tech devices inside. So far as anyone knew, the computer had to be hardwired to connect to other systems, but no one was willing to take a chance on being wrong. Especially not at the rate at which it seemed to be learning.

Several Heroes were present inside the central area, along with a few Supers and tech-savvy people brought in as DVA contractors. Most of them

Owen didn't recognize, though given how far apart their fields of specialty were from his own, that wasn't too surprising. Allegedly, Modus Operandi was heading up the investigation and assessment, though Jeremiah seemed to be the only one who was on site. Even Gale stopped by more often than they did, in what she called 'due diligence' to ensure nothing got out of hand. Perhaps to make up for his team, Jeremiah was always there, and as Owen stepped through the entry station, today proved no different. The Subtlety Hero was watching over a crew of workers while they catalogued every bit of the device down to the screws.

"Has anyone figured out for sure if this thing is alive or not yet?" Owen asked. It was the burning question on everyone's minds, and while some had made declarations already, no one had conclusively proved their point one way or the other.

"You don't really need me to tell you that determining sentience is a long, inexact art again, do you?" Jeremiah replied. He didn't seem tired in the slightest, despite having been awake since they'd infiltrated the base. Owen wasn't even sure Jeremiah needed to sleep, given the way his power worked. It was an ability that seemed exceedingly simple, yet upon inspection was complex and multi-faceted. Not unlike its owner, actually.

"I keep hoping one of these smart people will figure it out." Owen nodded to the array of techs combing through the device, paying special attention to the one sitting at the terminal. "How about the guy typing? He made any headway?"

"Loads," Jeremiah said. "This thing can learn at a remarkable rate and adapt on the fly. We've already gotten it to understand that the game it thought it was playing was real, and that the deaths it caused were not digital."

"Was it remorseful?"

"It assimilated the information and then spat out an apology." Jeremiah slowly rubbed his temples, as though a headache were coming on. "Some wanted to use that as proof of intelligence, while others thought it was just a very sophisticated program replying the way it was designed to when an error was pointed out. Hand to god, every hour I spend watching these people bicker makes me wish a little more that I'd had you smash the thing."

"Something tells me that tune will change if they officially declare it to be AI," Owen countered.

"A big if, at least from where we are now." Jeremiah let his hands fall away and looked at Owen with a long gaze. "Hey, you want to go get something to eat? I've been on duty here for days; it's time for someone else to pick up the slack."

"I've got a few hours until I'm on patrol, getting some food might not be the worst idea." Owen checked his watch, a battered old analog model that still barely passed the entrance tech-inspection. "Food truck?"

"Quaint as that is, I was thinking something a little nicer. I could pull some strings and get us a table at a lovely little bistro downtown," Jeremiah offered.

Owen slowly lowered his hand, noticing for the first time the mischievous glint in Jeremiah's eyes. "Sounds pretty fancy for just grabbing a meal."

"If one must eat, one should do it well," Jeremiah said. "And besides, I did say that I'd ask you on a proper date eventually. Things are calm for now, so it seems like as good a chance as any."

Although he'd known in the back of his head this was coming, Owen was still taken by surprise at the declaration. The way Jeremiah could be so cavalier and open about these things was still foreign to Owen, and in truth, it was something he admired about his fellow Hero. In spite of how he'd seemed in their first impression, Jeremiah did have some worthwhile traits, not the least of which was the fact that he was one of the few other Supers that had an unnatural relationship with the aging process. He was someone who didn't need protecting, someone who had a set of skills entirely apart from what Owen could do, and that was intriguing.

Besides, it was just dinner. Maybe it would be wonderful. Maybe it would be a disaster. But things would happen, and Owen would move forward. He'd put himself on ice over a decade ago when a choice of passion had brought the world he'd so carefully constructed crumbling down around him. Ten years plus was long enough. It was time to get the rest of his life moving again, and Jeremiah was at least a first step with whom he had the job in common.

"Get us a reservation for tomorrow," Owen told him. "If we're going out, then we'll do it right, not with a quick meal before I have to run off for patrol."

It was Jeremiah's turn to be surprised, arching a single eyebrow upward. "I'm glad to have you accept, though I must say I thought it would be more difficult. Finally giving in to my irresistible charm?"

"Don't push your luck," Owen advised him. "I just decided to try something new. We can always call it off if you get too annoying."

Jeremiah held up his right hand with the palm facing Owen. "I shall be on my best behavior. Scout's honor. Well, Hero's honor; I didn't fare so well in the scouts. Guess this means I don't have to use the gift I had planned to soften you up with. It can just be a token of my esteem." From one of the many pockets on his costume, Jeremiah produced a small card with a phone number penned across the clean white surface. "Friend of mine who graduated from Lander a few years back. I know you've been angling to get a seat at their end-of-year exams; she's someone who can get things moving."

Owen accepted the card, turning it over once and committing the number to memory, just in case. "How many favors you think she'll pull out of me?"

"It won't be cheap, but shouldn't cost you an inordinate amount of your time, either," Jeremiah replied. "Though I am curious why you're keen on peeking in on an HCP class."

"Maybe I'm looking to take an intern." While that was a ruse to keep Jeremiah's curiosity at bay, the idea actually didn't seem intolerable as Owen considered it. He was already taking younger Supers under his wing; perhaps he'd try the role in an official capacity. Roy and Hershel would almost certainly refuse, but there were rumors that Lander's juniors had more than a few heavy-hitters. Owen might see for himself, assuming he could pull enough strings to get in the door for their end-of-year exam. That would be a vacation to look forward to, one he'd earn after several more months of hard work.

"About dinner," Owen said, tucking the card into his pocket. "Nowhere too fancy. I'm not a tablecloth and place setting kind of guy. Since you asked, you can pick, but my rules are that it has to have good food, good beer, and not ask for anything fancier than blue jeans."

"You are really putting me to the test, aren't you?" Jeremiah let out a heavy sigh, though he didn't look quite as downtrodden as the tone made him out to be. "I'll rise to the challenge and find a suitable establishment, though, of that have no doubt. I suppose it's a good thing you're giving me the extra day, all things considered. Pity nonetheless; I was hoping to start the date as soon as possible."

"Good thing you're such a resilient guy. Something tells me you'll live with the disappointment," Owen said. "Now if you'll excuse me, I need to go get a briefing from these eggheads and then head back out to downtown. There's a lot of work to do, and I'll be damned if Titan is going to miss any more of it."

About the Author

.

Drew Hayes is an author from Texas who has now found time and gumption to publish a few books. He graduated from Texas Tech with a B.A. in English, because evidently he's not familiar with what the term "employable" means. Drew has been called one of the most profound, prolific, and talented authors of his generation, but a table full of drunks will say almost anything when offered a round of free shots. Drew feels kind of like a D-bag writing about himself in the third person like this. He does appreciate that you're still reading, though.

Drew would like to sit down and have a beer with you. Or a cocktail. He's not here to judge your preferences. Drew is terrible at being serious, and has no real idea what a snippet biography is meant to convey anyway. Drew thinks you are awesome just the way you are. That part, he meant. You can reach Drew with questions or movie offers at NovelistDrew@gmail.com Drew is off to go high-five random people, because who doesn't love a good high-five? No one, that's who.

Read or purchase more of his work at his site: DrewHayesNovels.com